THE GOD PROOF

The God Proof

Jeffrey Kegler

CreateSpace Publishing

ISBN: 978-1-4348-0735-9

Front cover: Bouchard's Beach in Pacific Grove CA, with Excelsior, the rock climbing sea lion. Back cover: Cabrillo Point, in Pacific Grove. Photographs and cover design (be kind) by the author.

795812$1_0$

To my mother

To the Reader

This is a novel, but it is about a real proof claimed by Kurt Gödel, Einstein's closest friend. Many people have tried to prove God's existence. You can certainly doubt that it's possible. What you can't question is that if anyone could do it, Gödel could. *Time* called Gödel the greatest mathematician of the last century.

Gödel was younger than Einstein and far less famous, but those in the know considered him Princeton's second greatest genius. Johnny von Neumann, inventor of the computer, called Gödel's work "singular and monumental." Oppenheimer, scientific director of the project that built the atomic bomb, called Gödel "the greatest logician since Aristotle." Gödel earned his reputation with airtight proofs of unexpected results. There has never been another mathematician like him before or since.

The shy Gödel feared ridicule. He probably told Einstein about his God Proof, but he told nobody else until 1970, and he never went public. After Gödel's death, his papers were found in careful order. We know what is missing and what is not. Everything was there, with two exceptions: the notebooks with his work on the God Proof.

1 Armenta's Rock

Pacific Grove, California, Monday, January 7, 2002

Armenta saw my visitor arrive with the notebooks before I did. Armenta's rock is seven hundred feet out to sea. She can see things that I can't see from my balcony. Armenta is dappled, five feet long, shaped like a football, and eccentric in her choice of a haul-out rock. She's a harbor seal.

Watching Armenta from a sea kayak was a girl in a chestnut ponytail. Armenta is used to attention, but that morning she seemed skittish. Another kayaker was riding the swell beside the ponytail. The ponytail's companion kept her hair in a dark pageboy and her eyes inshore.

My eyes were on the ponytail when she almost capsized. She was pointing something in Armenta's direction out to the pageboy. The ponytail tried to paddle and talk while she pointed, so she wasn't watching the surf when a big three-wave set came in. The first one pushed her off balance and the second listed her kayak hard. I thought for sure that the third would roll her into the drink, but somehow she torqued herself upright and rode it out with nothing worse than a lost paddle. While she looked around for it, I turned my binoculars to Armenta.

The ponytail must have thought Armenta was having a seizure. When I brought Armenta into focus she was pulling her nose and tail flippers into her body. She scrunched up as much as she could, then began to writhe. Her contortions stretched her back out. Full length again, Armenta started all over with another scrunch.

Each scrunch and writhe cycle turned Armenta's nose a few degrees toward me. A seal who wants to swivel around in its haulout has to do that — its flippers are useless out of the water. It's very awkward and I've seen tourists break out laughing at the sight. Seals don't move around a lot in their haulouts, even the ones who haul out on flat rocks. Which is every harbor seal I've ever seen except for Armenta.

For reasons I can't imagine, Armenta hauls out on a rock shaped like the nose cone of a missile. She rests her belly on the blunt tip, extends both head and tail out and up so she's in a kind of banana shape, and balances

1

like that for hours. You rarely see normal seals turning on their flat haulouts. I never expected to see Armenta do it on her nose cone.

I heard heels click on the bricks below just as Armenta faced into my binoculars. I lowered them and leaned out. Nobody on the bricks. The footfalls were now inside the covered staircase leading up to my apartment. Was it Lorraine?

I dismissed the idea. Not that there were a lot of other possibilities. I'd just moved to Pacific Grove and I didn't have friends of the kind who just pop by. Ditto for clients.

Heading in from the balcony, I caught my binocular strap on the card table. Up and over and down it went with a crash. My coffee mug landed on the floor, spilled, started to roll, went under the railing, disappeared over the edge, and smashed on a rock.

Out at sea, the ponytail heard the noise and looked in. She'd found her paddle. The pageboy pretended she didn't hear anything. The footsteps in the staircase stopped. I leaned against the balcony door and listened.

Armenta snorted, dove from her rock, and was gone. I looked across the bay to the dark mass of Loma Prieta. The view was why I'd gotten this apartment, but now looking at the mountains reminded me of the life I'd had behind them in Silicon Valley with Lorraine.

Footsteps resumed inside the staircase. I crossed my combined office and living room, let my visitor knock a couple times while I composed myself, then opened the door.

She was about fifty, olive-skinned and attractive. I felt I'd seen her before. But she was not Lorraine. Lorraine would not knock and wait to be let in. Something I might have remembered.

"I hope you are open for business," she said. Even in Paris she'd have looked smart. Parisians would have admired the way her dress set off her complexion, too dark for a Frenchwoman. The one false note was her briefcase. Not her color and too large. "I tried to call, but couldn't get an answer," she added, as if sharing a confidence.

"Oh. Yeah. Come in," I said.

She made straight for the chair in front of my desk and sat down. Some freak circumstance had left the corner of the desk nearest her free of clutter. The briefcase glided down onto it. I cleared more space. She fiddled with the latch. The briefcase looked new.

"Would you like some water?" I asked. I needed some desperately.

"Yes, thank you."

I went around to the kitchen and grabbed two bottles of designer water and glasses. When I returned, she had solved the mystery of the latch. I sat behind the desk. She raised the lid. I saw fifties, twenties and tens. Stacks of them.

Tentatively, she counted out fifties, then met my eye. "Could you work from the other side? I think it's best to count in tens." She had not introduced herself. Given her reception, that was hardly her fault.

I cleared more desk space and joined in the counting. Waves crashed. The kayak girls circled. The gentlest of warm, sweet-smelling salt breezes blew in from the balcony. Distant gull cries punctuated the steady rustle of bills. When I reached for the last stack, my fingers brushed the back of her hand. I think it was twenties. She laughed, took the stack, split it, and tossed me half.

"There should be $20,000," she said. There was. In the portfolio of the briefcase she pointed out an envelope. The receipt inside said the money was a retainer for my services at the rate of $80 an hour. My rate had been $80 an hour once. It was now $95, if I ever found work.

I decided that Bouchard Beach Software and Investigations had a special rate for large amounts of business prepaid in cash by beautiful women. It was $80. I signed the receipt.

She put the receipt back into the envelope and the envelope into her bag. "I need your help with something. It's inside." A cardboard box was all that was left in the briefcase. She pointed at it.

I took the top off the box. Two old manila envelopes were on a stack of several hundred fresh, loose, eight-and-a-half-by-eleven pages. It looked like a manuscript. It might tell me who she was. I was still flustered and felt awkward asking her name.

I pulled a paper grocery bag from a shelf, swept the cash into it, and put the cardboard box on the desk. Then I shut the briefcase and put it behind me.

Both envelopes had German handwriting in the corner, which I didn't make out right away. Someone else had written "God books" on the top one, more recently and in English. I felt a tingle. I decided it was the cash.

I eased the notebook from the top envelope. It was about six inches by nine, with a marbled dark brown cover. The only thing written on the cover was the Roman numeral "XIII".

It was the sort of notebook you might use to take notes in class, if you throw your notes away right after the final. It had a spiral binding, the kind with the wires that destroy the pages almost from the moment you get it out of the store. The notebook was decades old. I opened it carefully.

At the top of the first page was

Phil. XIII
VI.45 – IV.46

"Philosophy Notebook Thirteen, July 1945 to April 1946." I had a feeling that was familiar, though I couldn't imagine why. I leafed forward, going easy on the pages. The first few had started to tear loose at the top.

The paper had grayed, but wasn't brittle. The notes were in light pencil. Most were in a shorthand, but there was some plaintext German and many equations.

I looked back at the German handwriting on the envelope. It said "Notebooks from Kurt Gödel".

I looked up at my visitor, worried I might be staring, and forced my gaze back down. How had my visitor found me? My business is helping clients secure their computer systems. Gödel was a hobby of mine, but how could she know that? Mathematicians who work with computers know about Gödel as matter of course. But when I started very few computer specialists were mathematicians and now almost none are. Did my visitor make a lucky guess? That didn't seem likely.

That these were really Gödel's notebooks seemed even less likely. Those were in Princeton. I looked back up at my visitor. She seemed pleased with my interest.

I turned to the other notebook. It had a sewn binding and a title on the cover:

Theo. 2
Ontol. Bew.

The first line was easy enough. "Theology Notebook Two". The second line took me a second, but when it hit me my breath stopped. *Ontol. Bew.* stood for *Ontologisher Beweis*: Ontological Proof. That was the name Gödel used for his God Proof.

I walked over to a bookcase, pulled down volume 3 of Gödel's *Collected Works*, and checked the numbers and dates on the notebooks against the ones given in *Collected Works*. They matched. I was looking at the lost notebooks of Kurt Gödel.

2 The Lost Notebooks

Four days after Christmas 1977, the greatest logician since Ancient Greece entered Princeton Hospital. His problems were familiar. Gödel's wife had returned from a hospital stay of her own to find him seriously underweight. Kurt Gödel had waited too long this time. Fourteen days into the new year, he was dead. Five feet six inches, sixty-five pounds, said the death certificate.

Gödel had long held a delusion that he was being poisoned. When it was at its worst, Kurt would eat only if Adele fed him. With her away, paranoia had won out. Gödel had starved himself to death.

For better and for worse, Gödel was not like ordinary human beings. He lacked many human failings. As the logician Takeuti said, there was no one else "so considerate, fair, deep and broad-minded." Another noted that Gödel was "above competition." But Gödel's behavior often bewildered his friends.

Long before his death, word had gone around that Gödel was working on a proof of God's existence. There was no enthusiasm. Back then, God was a forbidden topic. Even today, scientists are expected to write about things that keep God at a safe distance. Gödel did not like controversy.

Gödel's will left his literary estate to Adele. Gödel had saved and filed nearly every scrap of paper that crossed his desk. He'd kept academic notebooks going back to primary school. Letters, even the ones cranks wrote him. All his library checkout slips. Financial records starting from his student days.

Adele immediately threw the letters from Kurt's mother into the trash. The future will never know what her mother-in-law thought of her. Lots of the criticism seems to have been about Adele's spending. She tossed all the financial records for their married years. Everything else Adele left intact.

Adele died in 1981. Gödel's papers went to the Institute for Advanced Studies in Princeton. That's the place where Gödel worked.

The archivists in Princeton found a lot of their work had been done for them. Gödel had grouped his research notebooks by subject and he often

5

numbered them, dated them, or both. Gaps stand out. Only two items appeared to be missing from Gödel's research papers.

The philosophy notebooks in Princeton begin with a notebook numbered zero, a convention whose benefits were rediscovered by computer designers decades later. From zero, the sequence runs unbroken up to twelve. There is also a notebook fourteen and a notebook number fifteen. The archivists did not find a "Philosophy Notebook Thirteen".

The first page of notebook fourteen contains an explanation. There, Gödel wrote that thirteen was *verloren*: lost. Based on the dates from the other notebooks, "Philosophy Notebook Thirteen" was written between June 1945 and July 1946. This was the time when Gödel was focused on the God Proof.

Gödel left no explanation for the other gap. The archivists found only two theology notebooks: "Theology Notebook One" and "Theology Notebook Three". If this was anyone else, you'd think there must have been a "Theology Notebook Two". With Gödel, it's pretty much a sure thing. I believed both notebooks shared the same fate, because both shared the same content.

I had never for a moment believed Gödel lost either notebook. There's no record of him ever losing anything else. Anything. Before my visitor arrived, my theory of what happened to the two missing God Notebooks was simple. Gödel was timid about debates, even academic ones. The idea of a public debate on God with him at the center would have frightened Gödel. One day Gödel felt so frightened that he burned the God Notebooks. That had been my theory.

3 Case 2007 Opened

I ruled out forgery. Forgers prefer art. Forging two entire notebooks by Gödel would take a lot of time and effort and not even bring pennies on the dollar compared to knocking off a Van Gogh or a Modigliani.

I lifted the blank pink sheet that protected the manuscript. I'd lucked out. My visitor's name was on the title sheet. Sue Shrift. No wonder she looked familiar. Her photo was on the jackets of a complete set of her books, shelved a few feet away. Gifts from Lorraine.

The projected volume 5 of the *Pranashtan Records* was very much in the news at the moment. Sue's most recent postponement of the publication date had been announced in late December. That morning her publisher's stock had opened in the 60s. The day she visited me it was struggling at 37.

There was lots of talk about Sue's next book, both on Wall Street and off in the la-la-land where I figure her fans have to be living. Nobody in the press had seen a draft. They didn't even know what to call it. I was looking at the title page. Volume 5 was going to be *Hypatia's Quest*.

"How did you hear about me?" I always ask this, but this time the question was not routine.

"I was guided to you." This was Sue Shrift, so I almost believed her until she added, "And you have a good reputation."

I let it ride. Sue didn't have to answer my questions. If I forced the issue she could just take the notebooks back. I very much wanted to look at them. And I'm just not inclined to pester twenty G's with a lot of questions. "Have you read them?" I asked.

"Oh, no. I'm not the math type. And I don't read German. Anyway, they're in code."

"Not really code," I said. "A shorthand called Gabelsberger."

"I knew coming here was the right thing. I knew you would be the right person."

Gödel's hundred or so surviving notebooks are almost all in Gabelsberger. So it was like we were in Mexico City and I'd predicted the next guy we'd meet would speak Spanish. But I took the praise.

"Frankly, I'll have to brush up on Gabelsberger." The truth was that I would have to learn it from scratch. "Do you know what the notebooks contain?"

Sue's smile was like being caught in the lantern room when the lighthouse keeper hits the juice. "Something wonderful," she said. "This is going to be my best book. One I'd trade all the others for a chance to write.

"Once we saw God everywhere, in sunrises, in the trees, in the design of our own eyes and brains. Science has explained them all away. Science has disenchanted our world. We call the Middle Ages of Europe, the Dark Age. That's wrong. The Dark Age is now.

"On Sunday, people get a little religion. The rest of the week it's science, Darwin and Freud. Darwin tells them they are the product of eons of selection, eliminating anything except the raw will to survive. Freud tells them their inner self is irrational, dangerous, perverted and infantile.

"It's no wonder there is so much unhappiness. Our religion is so outdated even the worshipers don't believe it. They just hope out of desperation there's something behind it. It's a wonder people aren't more miserable then they are.

"Science does not give people a reason to live. It does not feed their souls. I want to bring God back. I hope the notebooks will do that."

I didn't feel like asking the next question, but I needed to. "You own these, then?"

Sue made the transition easily. "Mom left them to me."

Sometimes a client thinks things in my possession are safe from the law. It's a hope I need to kill. Gödel was supposed to have left everything to his wife, who in turn left it all to the Institute for Advanced Studies. Some New Jersey lawyer was not going to believe Sue, at least not before demanding solid answers to a number of questions with insulting implications.

I made my standard speech, painstakingly worded to sound unrehearsed. "Now, you understand. If someone gets a subpoena, court order, whatever, affecting these, I have to obey it."

"There's no problem. They are mine."

That took care of that. The grocery bag full of cash answered all the other questions I ask new clients, except one.

"What should I do as a first deliverable?"

"I need the notebooks translated if I'm going to use them."

"Is this for your book?"

"For one of them," Sue said. "Volume 5 may be too far along for me to do much with it, but I want to center my next book around what's in these notebooks."

"If you're going to use them in one of your books, you'll need more than a literal translation. It won't be clear what Gödel is up to without some explanations and background."

"Marvelous. Yes. You seem to know what I am going to ask before I ask it."

"How about this? To determine what I have, develop a detailed schedule, and give you a level of effort is probably going to take me a full week. Would getting back with a schedule and level of effort by the start of business Tuesday of next week ..." Here I made a show of turning to the calendar. It's good to emphasize the deadline, even to the point of a little playacting. "Yes, eight days from now." I turned back. "Does that work?"

"Yes. I am not reachable directly. The briefcase has a business card for my lawyer."

I picked the briefcase back up. Its portfolio had the usual business-card sized pocket with the clear plastic window. The lawyer's card was there. I put it in my wallet.

Sue's reticence about her home address didn't offend me. Many famous people live around the Monterey Peninsula. It's a local tradition to respect their privacy. And a client who doesn't give me her home address won't demand I pop by for daily breakfast meetings.

Sue pursed her lips. "I thought that if you were current on my work, it would help you understand what I'm looking for. That's why I've given you the latest draft of *Hypatia's Quest*. You'll keep it in the strictest confidence, I hope?"

"Nobody sees it but me, it won't leave this office, and no copies will be made."

"Perfect."

I slid the briefcase across the desk.

"No," she said. "You keep it with the notebooks."

Sue's exit was cordial but quick. She may have sensed my eagerness to start in.

I forced myself to go slowly. The text was mostly in Gabelsberger, but the equations were not. Equations are a shorthand in themselves. It makes no sense to write them in another shorthand. The philosophy notebook had three or four equations per page. The theology notebook was all Gabelsberger, except for one page where there were four equations that I recognized.

I put the theology notebook aside and went back to "Philosophy Notebook Thirteen", copying the equations out onto a yellow legal pad. I didn't want to flip through the actual notebooks more than I had to. Until I had a Gabelsberger book, the equations were all I could read.

The layout was careful and the handwriting was steady. I saw some relativity theory and what looked like quantum mechanics. I began to wonder if if this wasn't some of Gödel's other research, not his God Proof work.

I ended up filling fifteen pages. Toward the end of the philosophy notebook were the four equations that I'd just seen in the theology notebook. They were the assumptions from the 1970 version of Gödel's God Proof. So this definitely was the God Proof.

4 1970

We don't know how long Gödel kept his God Proof secret. Decades, at least. An early version is dated "around 1941." Gödel probably would have kept silent even longer, but in 1970 he thought he was dying.

Gödel might have had a real medical issue. If so, it quickly became the least of his problems. Gödel's hypochondria was his worst enemy. He decided his doctors were plotting to kill him, fired them, began to starve himself, and took up smoking.

Gödel didn't want the God Proof to die with him. He showed it to Dana Scott, a top logician, then at nearby Princeton University. If Scott had reservations about the God Proof, he had lots of company. But when Kurt Gödel tells you he has an important result and it will die with him unless you help, you don't just walk away.

Kurt Gödel is often called the greatest logician of the last two thousand years. That probably understates it. Kurt Gödel is most likely the greatest logician who has ever lived. Only two logicians compare, Aristotle and Euclid. We know nothing about Euclid. The books with his name on them are compilations — a lot of the work is not Euclid's. Assuming there even was a Euclid. Euclid might be the pseudonym of a committee. If Euclid was a real person, he probably died around 270 BC.

Euclid may never have existed, but his claim to beat Gödel is better than Aristotle's. Aristotle, who died in 322 BC, was real enough, and he is often called the founder of logic. Frankly, that's a crock. His system of logic is almost useless.

Aristotle's logic did dominate the Middle Ages. And because of that, those one thousand years yielded exactly one logical argument that's of interest today, an argument produced by someone who broke ranks and didn't use Aristotelian logic.

It's said the logicians of the Middle ages counted angels on the heads of pins. In fact they did nothing even that interesting. When the modern era began, a real logic was needed. Aristotle got the toss. Modern logic takes the Euclid compilation as its starting point.

That one interesting result from the Middle Ages is important. The guy who broke ranks was Anselm of Canterbury, and what he came up with was an outline for a God Proof. That was in 1078 AD. Gödel's 1970 God Proof followed the Anselm approach.

Dying or not, Gödel didn't seem ready to have his name attached to the God Proof. All that came out in 1970 were handwritten notes and the handwriting is not Gödel's. It's Dana Scott's.

The notes contain around three dozen formulas. The symbols have labels like "God", "positive", and "essence". The math is explained, but not why the symbols have the names they do. Even with the math there's plenty of room for guessing. One thing is clear. Gödel thought he could take Anselm's Argument and turn it into a rigorous proof.

Gödel narrowly survived his 1970 illness. His friend Oskar Morgenstern, desperate, called Gödel's brother back in Austria. Rudolf and Kurt had always been close and Rudolf Gödel was a doctor. Rudolf immediately flew out to Princeton. We don't know what he did, but it saved Gödel's life.

Over the next decade, Scott's handwritten notes from 1970 circulated quietly. Gödel never showed his God Proof to anyone again.

5 Meep-meep

When I looked up from my desk, there was no sign of the two girls in the kayaks or Armenta. I remembered the broken coffee mug. I took a plastic bag downstairs, cleaned up, and took the pieces around back to the trash.

I felt an urge to go straight upstairs. But the haze of the morning had finally burned off. It seemed best to force myself to take a break. I set out on the Recreation Trail.

Making an effort to admire the arc of the bay swelling under a clear sky, I walked the five blocks to Lover's Point Park. At the park, I had genuinely begun to relax when I remembered the twenty G's sitting in a grocery bag next to my desk. There wasn't enough time left in the day to go to the bank and deal with the formalities for depositing that kind of cash. I wasn't dressed for the evening chill. I headed home.

There was nothing I could do about the money until morning. Back in the office, I decided to give the theology notebook one more look. It was all Gabelsberger except for the four 1970 equations, just as I remembered.

I went out to the balcony with the notes I'd made earlier. Red sparks flashed at me from windows in the small city of Seaside, reflections of the setting sun. Even across five miles of bay, they were blinding. I set my table back up, picked up the things which had spilled, and sat down. The light faded quickly. When it was too dim to read, I folded the notes into a pocket and looked out to sea.

In my youth, a popular cartoon featured Wile E. Coyote, a would-be predator. Wile E. was eager to make a meal of a roadrunner named Road Runner. Road Runner's habits were as predictable as his name — he always ran on one of the few roads in their native desert, announcing himself with a loud "meep-meep". Coyote does his homework and lays a well-planned trap. The outcome seems sure to be nutritious.

Suddenly, in the distance, a meep-meep is heard. Moments later, Coyote's trap is destroyed. Road Runner disappears, unharmed, into the distance. Coyote's plan was doomed from the start, a victim of the laws of cartoon physics, although even with hindsight it is not easy to say what those laws are.

Gödel's proofs are like that. Each of his two biggest papers centers around a long series of formulas which are expected to obey a rule. Gödel shows the simplest of these formulas obeys the rule. He shows the rule holds for the next, then the next. Gödel tackles more and more complex cases. Again and again the rule holds.

Each case is slightly different. Sometimes Gödel produces a new insight and the result comes off elegantly. Sometimes earlier results are used to make the current case look easy. Each new result is another tool in his bag of tricks. Expectation builds. Nothing seems out of reach.

Then comes the meep-meep. Gödel presents an equation that does **not** follow the rule. He proves that it doesn't. With the last trick, the spell is broken. The rest of the proof is about why the rule did not hold, and what this unexpected state of affairs means.

A long series of equations in the lost philosophy notebook followed a pattern. I had a guess what it was. A book I'd stored near the Monterey Airport could tell me if my guess was right. If it was right, and Gödel's flair for the dramatic held, that pattern would be the key to the whole proof. I decided to go out to the Airport tomorrow, after the bank.

When I could see nothing out in the bay except the red light atop Loma Prieta and whitecaps caught in the headlamps of passing cars, I went back inside. I put the notebooks back in their envelopes. I considered slipping them into the portfolio of the briefcase, but even with their envelopes for protection, I worried this might damage the bindings. I took Sue's manuscript out of its cardboard box, put the notebooks into the box, and slid it onto a nearby shelf.

The briefcase looked handy for my trip to the bank. I upturned the grocery bag over it and poured in the cash. I wasn't sure why I bothered taking the briefcase back and sliding it under the bed. My apartment has one entrance and it's very visible on a well-patrolled avenue in a safe neighborhood of a very quiet town. About the notebooks I worried even less. They're not exactly the sort of thing that appeals on sight to the average thief. I assumed that nobody knew they existed. Twenty-four hours earlier I hadn't.

Bedtime seemed the perfect time to take on Sue's manuscript. Flipping through, I had to admit she was getting better. In her first book, settings and props were conjured out of nowhere, used to lurch the plot forward one step, then forgotten. Following the action was like watching the traffic go by in the minimum security ward of a mental institution.

A mental institution is exactly where the nation's editors thought they would wind up if they accepted Sue's first manuscript. Most of them had gotten a chance at it before Sue self-published.

That's all it took. One reader told another, who told another. The first printing sold out in three months. The next dozen sold out even faster. It was all word of mouth. They're out there.

A major publisher smelled cash, advanced Sue her first million, and started printing her book by the hundreds of thousands. Sue had mixed feelings. She was happy to see copies available in the stores. But the contract with the publisher made her feel obligated to quit her job teaching school in King City, and she's always regretted that.

Lorraine's fondness for Sue's books was hard for me to figure. I pictured Sue's readers as naive, the one thing Lorraine is not.

6 A Thing about Locks

I'd spoken to Lorraine perhaps twice before Kamamaya Accounting exiled us from its Silicon Valley office to that endless gig in St. Louis. I knew she worked hard, was well-liked, and that management expected wonders of her. She was closemouthed about her past which, since Lorraine was attractive enough to be interesting, started some of our coworkers talking. Lorraine fought back with charm and petty bribery. I wondered why she didn't just answer a question or two, lying if that's what she preferred, and save herself some trouble.

One reason, I was to find out, was her resume. Lorraine had the kind of experience Kamamaya was looking for, but if she told them where she'd gotten it, they wouldn't have touched her. The alternate reality described on her resume easily got her hired, but it was so far from the truth that almost anything Lorraine let slip about her real past could cost her the job.

I didn't know about Lorraine's resume when I went to St. Louis. If I had, it would only have increased my confidence in her as the right kind for a Project Manager. Matsya, Inc. was the client and we were to set up a web store. I was slotted to be her tech lead.

Lorraine is not a techie, and not even her resume tried to claim that she was. People often assume that project managers know something about the technology they manage. We don't tell the clients they do, but we don't go out of our way to discourage misimpressions either. Some rare PM's are lapsed techies, and perhaps remember a thing or two, but that's beside the point. They are there to deal with budget and management issues. The relationship between a PM and their tech lead is like that between a lieutenant and his platoon sergeant. The lieutenant is in charge and what he says goes, but life can be short for green lieutenants who don't listen to sergeants.

Kamamaya's Silicon Valley office had already put a crew of a hundred or so consultants in place. At times I felt as if they were hand-picked losers, but I knew that management wouldn't put in that much effort. They were a quick, random selection from low bidding body shops with high markups.

16

Our crew did know that the longer the work took, the more money they made. Lorraine and I had our hands full trying to keep things moving.

The crew wasn't lazy. They were avid snoops and gossips. Lorraine and I often needed to be out of earshot. We started doing a planning session every evening, usually in Lorraine's room. Rank hath its privileges and Lorraine had a suite with a separate working area and a view. More often than not she was late, delayed with meetings or calls. She gave me a key. Her room was a better work space than mine and I could be productive while I waited.

Ten weeks into the gig, another Kamamaya manager asked me to talk to a job candidate in the evening. The manager had given his prospective hire the number for the phone in my room, so Lorraine and I agreed to meet there. She didn't ask for a key and I forgot to offer her one. I was always first anyway.

When I returned to my room, I collapsed toward my usual chair. Halfway down I realized she was already sitting in it. A last minute maneuver avoided a collision, but her laptop, full of precious data, leaned precariously from the arm of the chair. I rescued the computer with a diving grab. Flat at her feet, I cradled it and gasped in relief.

Lorraine laughed. "With all that tech stuff you must get pretty distracted."

"Long day," I said. I rolled over. "I guess the maid let you in."

"No. I let myself in."

"It was unlocked?"

Lorraine, who usually handled everything with aplomb, suddenly seemed at a loss. "Actually, it must be me who's getting distracted with all this Matsya crap," she said.

I wondered how distraction gets you past a locked door, but I kept my mouth shut while I picked myself up from the floor.

Lorraine's face settled into a decision. "Please keep this quiet back in the office. I don't usually carry keys."

That explained exactly nothing. "Yeah?" I asked.

Lorraine reached into her pocket and pulled out some metal strips, variously tapered and hanging from a strip of leather. "I use these," she said.

"Lockpicks?" I'd never seen a set before, for good reason. In some states, being caught with a set at a place and time that show 'intent' sends you to jail. Other states say carry a lockpick set, go to jail, period. I'd never read the Missouri statute. "Why do you carry those?" I asked.

My naivety seemed to amuse Lorraine. "I just told you. Instead of keys."

"Why not just carry keys? They're easier."

"These are light and open everything," she said. "With practice, they're just as fast as a big chain of keys."

"Practice?"

"I use these for my room here instead of that big clunky hotel key. When I got to your door, I just let myself in without thinking," she said. Dropping her amused tone, she added, "I'm really sorry."

"Don't be sorry. What were you supposed to do? Stand in the hall? But if you'll forgive my curiosity, I'm thinking of the learning curve."

"Learning curve?" Lorraine glanced at her laptop, still on the floor.

I bent down to pick it up. "To get that good with lockpicks, you had to have learned somewhere," I said.

Lorraine settled back into the chair. "That's the thing about answering questions about the past. Every answer just makes people more bewildered. Don't you find that?"

I handed her the laptop. "I never get questions about my past. When I bring it up, folks walk away or go to sleep."

Lorraine took the computer and smiled. "I learned to pick locks in the circus," she said.

"Circus?"

Lorraine looked up at the ceiling. "The trouble with these small rooms they give you tech leads is they're echoey." She looked back down. "They are cosy, though."

"You were in a circus?"

"My first job was in a circus. It's probably all changed now but traditionally in a circus nothing is ever locked. You can't really lock a tent and carrying a lot of keys was a good sign that you weren't circus people. Of course, lockpicking is a traditional part of circuses, going back to Houdini and probably before."

"Can you pick locks while tied up six feet deep in shark infested water?"

Lorraine shook her head. "I haven't tried."

"You'd have been better prepared for project management. It sounds as if you liked the circus."

"I loved the circus. I felt more at home there than anywhere before or since." It was a good way to drop the subject. Lorraine indicated a book on the table next to her chair. "I didn't know Ocean had a book."

She was talking about *The Life of Ocean of Awareness*, my reading in the evenings. I was surprised that Lorraine was interested. The month before we'd left Silicon Valley, the Dalai Lama had come to Stanford, and almost half of our office had gone to see him. Lorraine was not one of them.

Then again, I hadn't gone either. I read Tibetan stories mainly for enjoyment, having been turned on to them when I was assigned the *Life of Milarepa* in college. Tibetans share our love of freedom, have an optimism about it we've lost, and refuse to take seriously any book not full of fantasy and enchantment. Sadly, we seem to insist that a serious story must be sterilized of both. It's hard to picture anyone a century from now wanting to read the literature we think of as important today.

"Ocean has a bunch of books," I said. "How else does anyone hear of a Tibetan saint from a thousand years ago, except from a book?"

Lorraine laughed. "It's an oral tradition, silly. It's not a book thing." She chanted some foreign-sounding verses.

"What was that?"

"It's where you had your bookmark. *Ocean's Song of Instruction for Entering the Action.*"

"Huh?" It didn't sound familiar.

Lorraine smiled. "The name is translated wrong. That's why you don't recognize it."

I was still getting over the shock from the lockpicks. All I could do was splutter. "Translated wrong?"

"You really ought to change rooms. The echo is going to get to you sooner or later."

The phone rang and I reached for it like a life buoy. I wondered who it could be from, then realized this was the job candidate I was supposed to interview. Lorraine waved goodbye and let herself out.

○ ○ ○ ○ ○

When Lorraine and I let the crew know we'd become lovers, they responded with the kind of ho-hum reserved for the stalest news. They probably knew what was coming before I did. Lorraine took care of letting management back at Kamamaya know. They decided not to have a problem with us until after the St. Louis gig.

By then Lorraine and I expected to see the second coming of Christ before we delivered on the web store. We were also realizing that that bothered nobody but us. To our management back at Kamamaya Accounting the gig was a revenue stream. Finishing it was throwing away money. To our crew, finishing the job meant unemployment. And Matsya was just using the gig as a way of bribing Kamamaya to go easy when it audited Matsya's books.

It seemed like a great time for Lorraine and I to move on, and our problem with Kamamaya's guidelines on manager–report relationships was a face-saving excuse to find a fresh start elsewhere. I begged Lorraine to start her next job with a resume something like the truth.

By then I'd learned her reason for lying. It was about as good as they come. Lorraine had proved her management skills by building a good-sized nonprofit from nothing. Unfortunately the nonprofit she'd built was the Bhadrachakra. When she and I were back in Silicon Valley, Bhadra and his Bhadrachakra were the kind of story that sold newspapers.

Bhadra first got himself noticed with a pamphlet explaining Buddhism to Westerners. Buried deep in it was a two-paragraph footnote on a practice well-attested in the history of Tibetan Buddhism — karmamudra. Sacred sex. Members and contributions began to trickle in. Bad publicity followed and the trickle became a flood.

The reporters didn't have the hard facts to come out and say it, but they clearly believed that at the Bhadrachakra, karmamudra was a lot more than a historical footnote. The stories often mentioned the Bhadrachakra's cofounder, a woman who went by the Buddhist name of Ocean. Prior to the Bhadrachakra, she'd been a minor act in a small circus under the name of Lorraine Dark. Bhadra's second-in-command for a decade, she had left suddenly and without explanation. Nobody had heard from her since.

Lorraine was nervous about letting me know that she and an ex-boyfriend had founded what was probably not one of the country's ten most notorious cults, but definitely made everybody's top twenty. I will admit it wasn't my ideal. But I think that the rare man who needs more to worry about than he can find in the present, should look to the future. The future he might be able to do something about. Nobody ever made a dime worrying about the past.

Not that the past can't change. While Lorraine was still running things for Bhadra, she used some of the money that poured in to fund fellowships to bring outside scholars and artists to the Bhadrachakra. Their campus was located on California's Lost Coast — a stretch so rugged that the builders of California's Route 1 simply gave up on it and routed the coast highway inland. A tiny fishing community with a harbor and an unattended airstrip was nearby. The only other way in was a one-lane dirt road which wound for twenty miles up and down uninhabited mountains.

The Bhadra Fellowships continued after Lorraine left, although Bhadra's reputation tended to scare away all but adventurous or impoverished intellectuals. The year before Lorraine and I met, Bhadra's fast living caught up with him. With his death, the fellowships to study in isolation among the redwoods looked more enticing. Talent attracted talent and acceptance as a Bhadra Scholar became prestigious. The Bhadrachakra plunged headlong into respectability.

In Northern California, a year out of the papers and you're a pillar of society again. Lorraine emphasized her Kamamaya experience, but her new resume came clean about the Bhadrachakra years. We both landed jobs at

Heavensent Computers, back in Silicon Valley. Kamamaya accepted our resignations with a regret that seemed genuine and dropped big bucks on our send off.

○ ○ ○ ○ ○

Lorraine and I were long gone when the roof fell in. Matsya, one of the nation's wealthiest corporations according to Kamamaya's audits, was discovered to be less than worthless. The numbers had been fake for at least a decade. As a result of that lapse and others, the regulators forced Kamamaya Accounting out of business.

I read about this in the papers, sitting across the breakfast table from Lorraine in a San Jose apartment where I was living the happiest years of my life. A lot of the folks from Matsya still don't know what the problem was and why one day it all ended, suddenly and forever. They saw the name on the building. They thought that meant there was something there. They still look up now and then, thinking the big letters might be back up on the top floor, silver against the black wall.

I'd rented this small apartment on a rock out in the ocean as a new start for Lorraine and me. In October, she had told me she was not coming. In the weeks that followed, every time the phone rang I knew it was not her. Every time it rang, I thought of her anyway. I got tired of it. I unhooked it.

7 Tuesday was a Bad Day, Part 1

PG, January 8

The knocking seemed like part of my dream at first. In the dream, I was in the Tibetan heaven where the sky dancers, or dakinis, keep mind treasures — the lost books that we in the human realm are not yet ready for. The queen of the sky dancers looked a lot like Sue. She was offering me two mind treasures that looked a lot like the Gödel notebooks, when another dakini waved four of her six arms in protest. Six Arms demanded proof that I met the five traditional requirements for a treasure finder: wondrous signs at my birth, miracles once I was grown, instant and full comprehension of the scriptures, visions, and a consort.

In the dream world, as in waking life, I was in big trouble on all five. But lack of a body consort was killing me with the sky dancers. "No consort, no mind treasure," insisted Six Arms. A third dakini fluffed her wings and pointed out that she was between treasure finders, and that no tradition required a body consort to be a mortal woman. Six Arms made a crack about the difference between mind treasure dakinis and cut-rate love goddesses. Fluffy Wings started to cry. Six Arms said a few more un-dakini-like things, grabbed the notebooks and ran into a cloud. The other dakinis ran after her. From inside the cloud, I heard pounding.

I woke up and realized someone was pounding on my door. I had one leg into my sweatpants when noise stopped. I worried I'd miss my visitors. I needn't have. They were preparing to break the door down.

I had a dozen visitors, divided into three teams: Talkers, Lookers, and Muscle. The Talkers had done the knocking. When they decided my dream was running too long, they called in the Muscle.

Entry to my apartment is from a small landing at the top of a steep staircase. It's perfect, if you're expecting a siege. People can sidle past each other on the narrow staircase, but it's just as fast to wait. The Muscle had waited for all the Talkers to get downstairs before they started upstairs.

This gave me me just enough time to save my door. I opened it and looked out at four big guys squeezed into fourteen square feet. They looked confused. I had left them nothing to break down. Talk was called for, but the Talkers were downstairs.

"We're coming in," growled the youngest of the Muscle. He may have felt a hankering for the glamour and high pay of the Talkers. The leader of the Muscle silenced him with a glare.

My visitors were not criminals, at least not of the blue collar kind. Home invasions are committed by people who set their own hours. They don't start at eight thirty in the morning.

"We have a warrant," said Alpha Muscle.

"I need to see it."

He yelled down the stairs. "Who's got the warrant? We need it up here." A piece of paper was run up the stairs to Alpha Muscle, who relayed it to me.

I glanced at it. It said "WARRANT" in large caps. It was not in crayon. It was not in Urdu. It was not on scented paper. It was not in any other way obviously bogus. I waved them in.

The leader of the Muscle stepped in far enough to stop me from changing my mind. He sent the rest of his team downstairs. I read the warrant while we waited for the Talkers and Lookers. He gave me a friendly look to show that he in no way thought this reflected on my hospitality.

When the Talkers and Lookers were inside, Muscle leader nodded good-bye and went downstairs. I saw him join the his team and two Pacific Grove police officers on the other side of Ocean View Boulevard. If I was thinking about jumping off the balcony, running through traffic, crossing the Recreation Trail, throwing myself over the thirty foot bluff, and drowning myself in the ocean, I could just forget it. I'd never get past them.

My office is not big. Seven was a crowd. A Federal Marshal who looked five years overdue for retirement took the warrant from me, announced he had it, then handed it back to me again. Feeling relieved, he introduced the women who were leading the raid: Priscilla Wolf and Carrie Beedis from the Center for Total Surrender of Louisville, California. I thought the CTS rang a bell, but I wasn't sure. If this was the outfit I was thinking of, it was not known for this sort of thing.

What was happening to me is called a copyright raid. Remember Civics class, where the teacher told you that your home could not be searched except by law enforcement? How a judge couldn't just license a private party to burst into your home and look around?

Well, that's changed. Movies, video games, software, etc., have been getting ripped off. The companies that sell them convinced Congress that they need to charge into people's homes to protect their investments. Not get law enforcement to do it, mind you, but do it themselves. They still do need a warrant from a judge. And they have to bring along one law officer.

The intent was to make the world safe for this year's Hollywood blockbuster. You know, the one just like last year's, only with better special effects. But the new law soon was perverted to less noble ends.

If you want to really scare the bejesus out of someone, charging into their home without notice is a great way to do it. All they had to do was find a judge who would buy a story. It took all sorts of organizations just a few nanoseconds to figure that out and some became notorious for this kind of legal strong-arming. But I didn't remember the CTS as one of them.

Priscilla let it be known she preferred to be called Cilla. Later I learned she thought Priscilla sounded "prissy". She had the kind of classic features that look good even tense, lucky for her, and was dressed the way the sensible girl dresses when ransacking apartments. Gray sweatshirt, jeans, athletic shoes.

Carrie looked like she was on her way to a job in a beauty parlor and had stepped in the wrong door. Tight red top, knee-length black leather skirt slitted to the thigh, clear high heels, makeup done by someone who wrongly thought she was plain looking. Carrie kept giving Priscilla the kind of glances you give a stranger you hope will be sympathetic. Priscilla didn't return them.

The Federal Marshal does not lead a copyright raid. He's there to see that the two sides behave themselves. I assumed this meant that Priscilla was leading the raid, but keeping my mouth shut saved a miscue. Officially, Carrie was the leader.

After polite hellos, the Lookers went to work. I wasn't sure what to expect. In theory, a copyright raid is not as much trouble as a real police search for evidence of a crime. On the other hand, when it comes to situations with a potential for violence, you like to deal with professionals. Folks for whom it's a regular job like to keep things under control. Put amateurs in charge and any crazy shit can happen.

Except for Harry, Priscilla and Carrie, all my visitors were ops with Banana Slug Investigations, a local PI firm which the CTS had hired for the occasion. The Banana Slug guys seemed to know what they were doing, which was reassuring. In theory, it was up to the Marshal, Harry, to keep everybody in line. He seemed like a fine fellow, but probably would have been the first to admit that he was getting a little old for the rough stuff.

Priscilla and Carrie helped search. Watching Carrie examine shelves in that outfit was entertaining, but I recalled my manners. I invited Harry, also at loose ends, to join me in brewing a fresh pot of coffee. We had to work around the Looker who was searching my kitchen shelves, but soon we were watching the impatience-resistant Pyrex carafe fill. It was becoming like any other cozy domestic morning at Josh Bryant's when I heard a dull crash from the office.

Three or four books had fallen to the floor. Priscilla had started through one shelf a bit too aggressively. It was no big deal, and my strategy was to keep it low-key. But it couldn't look as if I didn't care. I crouched down next to Priscilla, and made a show of examining the spine on one of the books.

Two of the Lookers flashed glances at Priscilla. She looked defensive. Mission accomplished. "Harry," I shouted back toward the kitchen, "we've got to have enough for two cups by now."

We did. Harry and I retreated to the balcony. The Muscle and the officers were still waiting in case I was seized by the delusion I was a lemming and headed straight for the ocean. In the water behind them, an otter had a pup. Harry and I passed the binoculars back and forth. Sea otters are really cute. The tide was going out, but Armenta's rock was still underwater.

My place is not big. Time for the final "show and tell" soon arrived. One of the Lookers got a camera and started systematically taking shots of my office. The main purpose of this is to prevent the raidee from trashing his own things after the search, and blaming the raiders. But it's been known for these photos to be put on the Internet without the raidee's permission. Once the photographer had finished with my office, he moved on to other rooms. The rest of us crowded around my desk.

I wondered how I'd been so dim. Priscilla was the girl with the pageboy. Carrie's hair was out of the ponytail, but she was clearly the other kayak girl. The kayak did more for her than her current outfit.

Carrie spread out the booty. The haul was Sue's manuscript, the copies of Sue's books which Lorraine had given me and, in clear evidence bags, the Lost God Notebooks.

My heart sank but I didn't see a lot I could do. If I made trouble I'd be restrained, handcuffed, and handed over to the two police officers, waiting outside in the hope I would not start their morning with a lot of trouble.

I doubted their grab was legal, but I wasn't going to tell the raiders squat about who gave me the notebooks or why. That kind of information might have been exactly what they were after. Anything Sue wanted the CTS to know, her lawyer could tell them.

Priscilla looked over the take and sneered. She darted back into the bedroom. When she returned she had the briefcase with the cash. "This too," she said.

Harry spoke tentatively. "I don't think the warrant covers cash."

"These are ill-gotten gains, the direct product of theft." Priscilla's tone was shrill. Her team looked worried.

I chimed in. "If you wanted to seize cash you could have asked the judge. You didn't. It's not in the warrant because you didn't ask and you didn't ask because the judge would not have allowed it."

"It's covered and we're taking it," Priscilla said.

I looked around the desk. I actually had no idea what they told the judge or what he would have done. Carrie was perplexed and would just as soon leave the money. Harry was on my side, though hardly to the last bullet. The Lookers were hired by the CTS. Their faces did not conceal their worry, but the CTS was their client. I formed a mental picture of Sue's lawyer. It told me to shut the hell up.

I never got the chance to say anything stupid. Priscilla snarled disgust with the lot of us, turned, stamped down the stairs, jumped into one of the cars, and drove off, never having taken her mitts off the case with the money.

Her departure bewildered the Muscle downstairs, who looked up wondering if this was their cue to stomp on somebody, and if so, who. As the default stompee, I was worried. But Harry stepped out on the balcony and waved them off, like a victorious general sending his veterans back to the plow. They gathered together to pass cigarettes, giving me my best chance of the morning to toss myself into the ocean.

It would have been an anticlimax. Priscilla had left us like actors in a theater whose stagehands have forgotten to bring down the curtain after the play. One of the PI's picked up Sue's books and the manuscript. Another cradled the Lost God Notebooks. My eyes followed them out the door.

Harry was last to leave. I locked up behind him. Vehicles started on the street below. I heard Carrie asking around for a ride.

I walked back into the apartment and checked the closets for leftover PI's. My books were disarranged, but nothing was damaged. My computers hadn't been touched.

I went out to the balcony. My visitors were gone. The tide had exposed Armenta's rock, but she wasn't there.

Safe and alone, I looked for the equations I'd copied from Gödel's Notebooks. After a few minutes of rising panic, I thought to look in the laundry hamper. The notes were in the pocket of yesterday's shirt.

8 California's Home Village

PG, Tuesday

I pulled the card for Sue's lawyer from my wallet. Mike Rawls. The name sounded familiar and a quick check on the Internet told me why. Rawls was local, based in Monterey, but he had handled big technology cases. Genuinely dangerous in the courtroom, he was even better at settling in time to leave lots of money for everybody. His biggest settlement was literally for billions. Monterey address or no, Rawls asked downtown SF fees and got them.

I wondered if I had given Rawls any reason to land on me. If so, I was about to find out what it is to be landed on by the best in the business. I decided to collect my thoughts before I called him. I looked at my book-shelves, and corrected a couple of the more irritating rearrangements. My eye landed on a book with a section on the Center for Total Surrender.

The CTS was started quietly by three MD's on the faculty of a medical school in Southern California. They'd developed an interest that would probably have hurt their careers had it become widely known. It was in a book called *The Days of Zurvan*.

Even after the last of the doctors retired and they went public, they wouldn't reveal who wrote *The Days of Zurvan*. The Zurvan who speaks in the book says he is a spirit personality who last took human form in the sixth century BC. Rumor has it that the channel for Zurvan's words was a patient of one of the doctors, permanently confined to a psychiatric hospital. The doctors said only that Zurvan's book has to stand on its own, and that drawing public attention to the channel would accomplish nothing.

Zurvan says he was born in Babylon. His mother was Jewish, exiled there with the rest of her people, and his father was a Zoroastrian priest — a Magi. As a young man Zurvan traveled to India, where he studied with the Buddha and Lao Tzu, the founder of Taoism. According to Chinese legend, Lao Tzu was last seen at one of their frontier posts, disgusted with society and headed west. Zurvan says that Buddha's sangha is where he wound up.

When Zurvan finished his studies in India, he returned to Babylon and took up his father's trade as a Magi. The Jews were in the midst of shaping what eventually become the Old Testament, and Zurvan followed developments among his mother's people closely. As an assistant, Zurvan purchased Pythagoras, the guy after whom the theorem about triangles is named.

Pythagoras had been studying in Egypt when the Persians invaded and took him prisoner. Zurvan learned that a very bright young Greek was part of the booty from the Egyptian campaign and persuaded King Cambyses to sell Pythagoras at a price that fit a Magi's budget. After ten years of service, Zurvan freed Pythagoras to return to Greece.

Zurvan lived through the greatest religious revolution of all time. Pythagoras, Lao Tzu and Buddha, if they didn't change who are as human beings, certainly changed who think we are, and for most purposes that's the same thing. Religions before 600 BC had little patience with people searching for meaning in their lives. The gods of Homer's Iliad batted mortals about the way we do tennis balls, except modern tennis players give more reasons for what they do. Today we simply won't put up with the gods of the Bronze Age.

With Pythagoras, Lao Tzu and Buddha, religion becomes something that a modern human can find acceptable. Lao Tzu and Buddha have hundreds of millions of followers. True, hardly anybody anywhere claims to be a Pythagorean, but in his effect on the material world, Pythagoras is far more important than the other two. Pythagoras is the man who taught the world to do science. It was his idea that mathematics should be based on proof, and that science should based on mathematics and observation.

o o o o o

None of this explained why the CTS had decided to toss my crib. It was time to call Mike. I stood for a few seconds waiting for the dial tone. Then I remembered the phone wasn't hooked up. Thank God I'd never gotten around to canceling the phone service. For now, one live phone was enough. After crawling under a table to find a phone jack, I tried again.

I was quickly on the line with Mike Rawls himself. I tried not to act surprised and gave Mike a short account of my morning's entertainment.

He didn't sound bothered. "The court will make them give us back the retainer. In the meantime I'm sure you need the money. I'll replace it today and ask the court to give the funds they seized directly back to Sue."

"Thanks, that really would help."

"I don't know what those CTS folks can be thinking. They give me the creeps, frankly. When people are chasing dreams instead of living life, bad shit happens."

I started to ask Mike what the problem was between Sue and the CTS, but he had paused to exchange a word with somebody. "If you're available," Mike said when he came back on the line, "why don't you come into the office? If we're going to be a team we should get to know each other. I can write you a check for the retainer while you're here."

Sounded great. I'd ask Mike my questions face to face when I got the check.

The address on Mike's business card was just outside the boundaries of Monterey's old Spanish fort. The fort is gone except for some wall and its chapel, which is now called the San Carlos Basilica. It's big for a chapel, but tiny for a basilica.

The fort, perhaps five hundred feet square, was the capital of California for eighty years. After the Anglos came, it crumbled and a mixed use neighborhood crept toward the church like crabgrass. This carelessness for the past could have had worse effects. The neighborhood still feels like a village. A state park with exhibits and guides would be more informative, but less homey.

Mike's office is a faux adobe of two stories with a wooden balcony that runs the length of the second story. The style is called Monterey Colonial although it's not truly pre-Anglo. There's more than a hint of New England in it. But it pays an affectionate tribute to the Californio heritage and makes for an attractive and usable building.

Inside, a cordial receptionist waved me to a chair. I started to choose my magazines with the care appropriate for a long campout. Mike had a nice selection of periodicals, and I experienced a tinge of disappointment when he greeted me before I could so much as glance into the stack.

We shook hands. "Didn't Sue warn you about your guests?" he asked.

"No. You mean she knew?"

Mike turned toward his office, beckoning me to follow. "Sue certainly knew that the CTS folks have been restless lately. They've been threatening litigation. I am a bit surprised she didn't mention it."

I was tempted to tell Mike he'd have felt even more surprised if his own place had been turned upside down. Mike waved me to a chair inside his office, sat behind his desk, gave some of the papers on it a very dirty look and picked one of them up. "Could you help me with a few points?"

"Sure." I braced.

"Sometimes the guy's name is spelled G-o-e-d-e-l, with two *e*'s, and sometimes it's spelled G-ö-d-e-l with just one. Which is right? Both?"

"Notice that when it's *Gödel*, the *ö* has two little ears over it. At least it should. The ears are called an umlaut and that's important in German. The *oe* is another way of indicating the *o* is umlauted. So it's *Goedel* or *Gödel*, but never *Godel*." At the moment I was a bit more interested in why I had been raided than I was in German spelling, but a fellow who won't let out some line is not going to take home any fish.

Mike smirked. "The *e* after the *o* is in case they're in Stalingrad and have fired off their last umlaut."

"Kind of. Just remember, there's no *god* in *Gödel*."

"That's good. Now at least the stuff coming out of this office will be spelled right. What about these notebooks? Will they convert me from atheism?"

"It sounds impossible," I said, "but Kurt Gödel was known for coming up with proofs that everyone else thought were impossible. He might have done it."

Mike leaned back. "I guess we'll know once you have the notebooks again."

"Basically. A few notes slipped out about this proof in Gödel's lifetime. People also published a few things after Gödel's death, trying to figure out what he was getting at."

"But how is a proof going to convince anyone that God exists? A proof can't bring something into existence. I mean, something exists or it doesn't."

"Bringing things into existence by proof is easy," I said. "It's done all the time."

"Really?"

"We know there's a number two that way. We know every number has a number after it, and we know there's a number one. So we prove the number two into existence. And that's how we get three, and four, and so on. And we care about numbers unless we don't care about the difference between one BMW and two of them."

"Which I do," Mike said.

"You also do something like it in court."

"How's that?"

"Say you show one guy relied on another's word. That reliance proves a contract exists between them. The contract that you proved into existence can get a court order issued, which can have big effects in the real, material world."

Mike shook his head. "Yeah, well, I'm good, but I don't know how I can get the court to order God to exist."

The receptionist appeared at the door. "Here's the check, Mike. You said to bring it in the moment it was ready."

"Absolutely," Mike said. "Give it to Josh here. It may take his mind off all this stuff about God."

"Twenty-five thousand?" I said. I looked up at Veronica. She was the most beautiful woman I'd ever seen.

"I talked with Sue," Mike said. "The raid has clearly made things more complicated. There may be expenses. There will definitely be additional demands on your time."

"Paying two retainers must be kind of tough."

"Thanks," Mike said to Veronica as she closed the door. Then to me: "The court will give us the cash back. The CTS had no right to take that."

"Their team was openly split on the question."

"They made the wrong choice. I expect the judge to be furious at the way they exceeded the warrant, in part because they conned him into going way out on a limb even with what he did put into it."

"What the CTS's problem? Why the raid?" I asked.

"They say they own the ideas in Sue's books. They've been sending me letters to that effect for some time. I answered the first couple saying 'see you in court', and the last few I've just ignored and waited for the other shoe to drop."

"You and Sue expected a raid?"

"We certainly expected some sort of next step, a lawsuit, maybe even a subpoena. The raid was a surprise," Mike said.

"I've never heard of the CTS conducting a copyright raid."

"So you have heard of the CTS before?"

"Barely," I said. "As far as I knew they were a few research MD's who once they retired came out of the closet with this weird book. People gave the doctors a lot of crap about it, but they took it quietly and didn't go around bothering folks."

"The original doctors are all dead now. The CTS now includes a couple of A-list actresses, a Nobel laureate, a rock band and an assortment of millionaires."

"It's hard to picture their board meetings. I didn't know they were that big a deal."

"They still don't look for attention. They were an entirely live-and-let-live crowd until someone gave them this copyright idea. Suddenly they've got it in for my client." Something about my face made Mike add, "With a lot of legal battles, there's a long history behind it. But some of the nastiest start from just about nothing."

"What's with this copyright claim?"

"It's bullshit," Mike said, "as anyone awake in the first week of the Intellectual Property course in law school would know. Apparently this judge either didn't take an IP course, or nodded off. The CTS claims *The*

Days of Zurvan is the first scientific presentation of theology, and all others are their property under the copyright."

"Scientific?"

"I know. If all the science in both of them were combined and turned into gunpowder, it wouldn't blow your nose. Don't tell our client I said so," Mike added, with a grin that indicated he'd enjoy nothing better than me doing exactly that. "Anyway, it's just nonsense. Copyright covers the way you express an idea, not the idea."

"So if that's not the copyright law, where did this warrant come from?"

"Judge Gaunilo does insurance cases. He obviously has no clue about copyright."

"Don't they keep judges from ruling in fields they don't understand?" I asked.

"They try to. They do specialize. But the copyright judge was on vacation and Gaunilo was filling in. When push comes to shove the system is run for the convenience of the judges. If that conflicts with quality justice, justice can be the loser. The way the judges figure it, hell, dockets are getting cleared, and there is always the appeals court."

"So this stuff does get straightened out on appeal?"

"In theory," Mike said. "In practice, appeals cost a lot, even by business standards. Substantial companies have been forced out of business by silly legal rulings. Stupid decisions almost always do eventually get thrown out on an appeal by somebody. The principle of law wins, but it's often too late for a lot of the parties."

"You're not encouraging me."

"This won't be one of those cases. Gaunilo is an idiot as far as copyright law goes, but an adequate judge in the areas where he knows the law. And he does know what you do with a party who pulls fast ones on the court. You can't copyright cash. That much even Gaunilo can figure out. It is seldom a good thing to piss off the judge."

"What about Gödel's notebooks?" I asked. "How did the CTS even find out they existed? They were the real target of the raid, weren't they?"

Mike rolled his eyes. "Christ, you and Sue are a pair. It's like $20K in cash walking out the door is a minor incident. But, yes, the timing makes it look like these CTS wackos were after the notebooks. They probably learned about them from this loony assistant Sue had to fire. The assistant now is with the CTS and that's probably how they got this bug in their ear."

"How can they claim Gödel's notebooks? They were written before the Zurvan book, so there can't be a copyright issue."

"They had no more right to the notebooks than to the cash, and Gaunilo will see he's been scammed and that they just used his warrant as an excuse to put their mitts on anything they felt like taking."

"Do you know why they left my computers untouched?"

"Did they?" Mike looked surprised.

"Yeah. Never went near them."

"I don't, all I can do is guess. The computers would not have been their primary objective, and they really flimflammed Gaunilo. Maybe they didn't want to press their luck. That's one possibility."

"And the others?" I asked.

"When you search computers these days, you've got to have an expert on computer forensics along on the search team. The CTS probably put the raid together in a hurry, and they may not have been able to find a computer guy in time. Or maybe they just didn't want to spend the money."

"Mike." Veronica leaned back in. With no check to accessorize her outfit, she was merely attractive. "Sue on the line. Will you take it?"

He would. After a bit he handed me the phone. I agreed to meet Sue downtown at an office for an outfit called the Pecunia Society. No, she had nothing further for Mike.

I hung up and Mike resumed. "Suppose people just refuse to accept the proof."

"You can reject a proof the same as any other belief, but the proof tries to make it cost you."

"Cost me?"

"You can reject a proof because all proofs are based on assumptions," I said. "So just find an assumption you don't like and scratch it out."

"Sounds pretty cheap."

"Not necessarily. Suppose the assumptions are all facts about arithmetic, so if you don't believe in God, you don't get good change for a fifty either."

"That would convert me and most atheists," Mike agreed. "So the idea is 'one plus one equals two, therefore God exists'?"

"Probably not even Gödel could deliver on that. But there are other assumptions crucial to ordinary life that Gödel may be using."

Veronica knocked. "Mike, your lunch appointment."

"This is one I can't miss," Mike said. "Do you think Gödel succeeded?"

"Get the notebooks back and you'll be the first to know," I said over the handshake.

There was almost an hour before I was to meet Sue. I decided to go to the bank. I half expected Priscilla and Carrie to pop in with automatic rifles. But I was still clutching the check when I reached the teller.

9 The Pecunia Institute

Monterey, California, Tuesday

The address that Sue had given me did not ring a bell, but I recognized the building. The Albatross was built in the 1920s by a developer who believed that Monterey needed an office building with a real downtown look to it. Nobody had ever felt the need before. Nobody has felt it since.

The five stories of art deco stand in the only neighborhood where they might belong. They don't. Perhaps a few tourists nostalgic for the closed-in griminess of Manhattan find the Albatross a relief from the sun and openness of Monterey.

The Pecunia Society was on the third floor. A soft chime announced my entry. The Society's office had its own hallway, wider and with a higher finish than the halls in the building. This space must have been remodeled for the tenant. There were four doors, two on the left, two on my right, and chairs. I sat down.

A woman in an expensive black business suit darted from the far right door. Her eyes found me, pierced, then flipped away in disappointment. Sue emerged from the door opposite. The woman turned to Sue, chirped with relief, and poured out tears and words.

I studied the walls. They were covered with pictures. A female figure, drawn, painted or engraved, was in most of them. Pecunia? She was the voluptuous type, whoever she was. She stuck to two styles, both of which suited her. Less often, she wore a simple blue robe belted with a rope. Sue's tunic dress echoed that look. Pecunia herself favored lush red gowns lined in gold.

The most spectacular piece was a mural filling the wall opposite the entrance. In it, Pecunia, calm and dry, stood in a storm-whipped ocean. Her right hand dropped gold pieces into the waves. Her left, palm up, signaled stop. Behind Pecunia the sun rose as the typhoon raged. If that happened in real life, you'd expect stunning light effects. They were there. Rainbows whirled inside rainbows. Rays turned new, sharp colors with every sparkle. Pecunia's skin and clothing glowed softly amid the brilliance. It was hard to believe it was a mural. I would have looked closer, but I worried about disturbing the conversation.

"I've been just mouthing the words and thinking about other things," the woman in black was saying to Sue.

"Heather, Heather. Did something happen?" Sue cooed back.

"Well, all of sudden the words hit. It was like I was speaking to a best friend, not reciting."

"All the times before were important. A part of you really did the devotion, even when you thought you held back. You can never hold back from God with all your heart. We never deceive God, just ourselves."

"Oh. Thank you."

"You don't have to believe God will give you what you need. You just have to doubt that He won't. Doubting is easy enough. And the doubt gives God the space he needs to act inside us."

Heather wept quietly. Sue put a little firmness in her voice. "The money we gave you to do the earlier devotions, you have to repay that."

Heather stopped crying and looked at Sue intently.

"Each time you come in, bring a five and we'll exchange it. That will repay. And for that day's devotion we'll give you a new one."

Heather started to reach for her wallet. "I'm not sure I have a five."

"No," Sue said. "Not today. I thought today might be special. I got this." Sue produced a ten dollar bill in a clear plastic display case. Heather gave Sue the look a child gives his parents the first time he figures out what Christmas is.

"When the repayment is done, Monica will schedule us together again. Now Mr. Bryant has come here because I need his help. It's been very rude for me to leave him sitting here. You'll be OK?"

Heather had been giving me all the regard you'd give a wallpaper stain. She now looked at me as if I were a radiant six-armed god sprung to life from one of the paintings. She wondered at a creature so powerful even Sue might seek its aid. I found myself wondering.

With more cooing, Sue shepherded Heather to the door. Another soft chime deep inside the suite. Sue smiled and sighed.

"Thank you for the patience. She was scheduled to be gone half an hour ago. But it would have been wrong to hurry her. You must wonder what was going on."

"Since you mention it, my curiosity has gotten the best of me. Was ten dollars all that important to her? Her clothes looked expensive. That's easily a $1,000 outfit she was wearing."

"Just her shoes were $300. Follow me. I wanted to show you through anyway." Sue steered me into the room Heather had burst out of. The chairs, the two side tables and the wall paneling were a sumptuous oak. Three of the walls were crowded with Pecunia images. A projection screen filled the far wall.

"This is one of the devotion rooms." Sue flipped a switch. The screen lit up with a Pecunia image, a simple, colored line drawing without perspective. "Heather was doing a visualization."

"Why this one for the visualization?" I asked. "Pecunia looks almost alive in some of the others."

"When an architect does a blueprint, the house does not look as natural as it does in a sketch. But a blueprint is the best aid to someone building a house. Our participants visualize Pecunia. This is their blueprint. Images which look good to modern eyes show irrelevant detail. They make it hard to focus on the essentials to visualization."

Sue turned the projection off. "In your business you keep secrets. I hope you'll keep this one. Actually, Heather's case made the papers nationwide, so it's not really a secret. But the less said the faster it dies down.

"Heather is a VP at a consulting firm. She's happily married, makes a fortune and is very successful. Her boss does not know what he'd do without her. Some years ago everyone was stunned to discover her embezzling. The DA was brought in, prosecution started and it looked like her career was over."

"It wasn't?"

"Heather's lawyer took the tack of leveling with the prosecution, giving them full details of where the money had gone, and complete freedom to talk to his client. Everyone took a deep breath and rethought the matter." Sue paused. "Heather has a shopping compulsion. She went on sprees. It was purely irrational, because she could never wear the clothes or jewels."

"Why not?" I asked.

"Her husband knew, and was on the lookout. So she hid the things, then sold them without ever wearing them."

"Meanwhile embezzling?"

"Yes. In this life, we all cause ourselves needless agony. Heather's way of doing it is just more obvious than yours or mine. Heather lived a miserable existence. She knew she eventually would be caught. She risked jail, almost lost her career and spent a fortune, and all for things she knew in advance she would never use or keep."

"Obviously she is not in jail. What happened?"

"Her department was doing much worse financially without her, even taking into account losses due to her embezzlement. She pled guilty, paid the money back and received a suspended sentence, a promotion and a raise. And she's desperate to get whatever sends her on these shopping sprees out of her life."

"You do therapy here?"

"This is a spiritual practice, not therapy."

"How did you get into this?"

"Many people with problems come to me because of my books. I think a lot about them."

Sue ushered me back through the hall and into the second devotion room. The same beautiful oak, the same layout, but larger. There were chairs and tables enough for a small meeting. A text was on the projection screen:

> Pecunia, devoted one, loving Companion of God,
> I cannot remember you, and forget God.
> When I see you in Plenty, I see the Perfect Thought.
> When I see you in Simplicity, I see the Pure Thought.
> Whenever I touch Money, I will remember
> Who it is,
> What it is for.
> Pecunia, devoted one, loving Companion of God,
> I cannot remember you, and forget God.

Sue frowned, perhaps at the waste of electricity. She opened up another panel hidden in the oak and flipped a switch. The screen went black.

"What was going on with the five dollar bills?"

Sue laughed quietly. "That must have seemed strange. To help people get past money fears, we pay them to do their devotions."

"Five dollars can't be a lot to her. She must come here from Silicon Valley."

"SF, actually."

"So it doesn't even pay gas."

Sue shrugged. "The amount doesn't matter when it comes to our feelings about money."

10 Walking with Einstein

In his last years, Einstein told Oskar Morgenstern the only reason he showed up at his office was to have the pleasure of walking home with Kurt Gödel. The Einstein–Gödel friendship may be unique in history. In no other age has its greatest scientist and its greatest mathematician been such close friends.

Those walks must have been quite the experience for the shy Gödel. By now, every child recognized Einstein, and autograph seekers routinely ambushed them. Probably none of them recognized the neatly dressed younger man who Einstein was speaking to in German.

Einstein probably had his doubts about Gödel's God and his proof. Einstein was a pantheist. In Einstein's case, pantheism meant that God was all of existence and all of existence was God. God did not create the world, He was the world. It was nonsense to talk about God judging the world or intervening in it. For God to perform miracles made no sense — the laws of nature were God and that was all the miracle one could want. Why should God change water into wine, when God was the water and the water was already perfect?

Gödel's God was not like that taught in churches, but it was lot closer than Einstein's. Gödel's God was separate enough from the laws of nature to be able and willing to break them. God knows the world could use some miracles.

Gödel might have questioned how Einstein's God could be not just indifferent to all the evil in the world, but directly present in every cruel, vicious and senseless act. If God is not moral, how can any of us be? In return, Einstein could ask why Gödel's God created the world if he wasn't going to be responsible for it. It must have been quite the discussion.

11 The Bouncing of Priscilla

"I'm surprised I've never heard about this place," I said. The Monterey Peninsula can be like a small town, and Sue gets press.

"Publicity hasn't served our purposes," Sue said. "And frankly, I worry about the reaction."

"You mean to mixing money and religion?"

"That's the least of it. There are deeper prejudices than that. Like against questioning reality."

"Questioning reality?"

Sue's gaze was friendly, but unwavering. "Let me put it another way. Do you think for yourself?"

I fought an urge to step back. "I like to think so."

Sue turned back to the hall. "We're taught in this culture to consider ourselves individuals, people who think everything out for ourselves. We don't accept authority without any explanation. But that's how we accept our idea of reality. Most people accept the world of traffic and shopping centers without any explanation."

"What explanation do they need?"

Sue chuckled. "In our society, shopping centers tend to be matters of faith."

"What else can people do, but believe what they see?" I asked.

"The problem is that people believe what they see without really looking. People go through life in a daze. I want to wake them up."

"Can I play devil's advocate?"

Sue chuckled. "Speak right up. You don't have to raise a cloven hoof for permission."

"Why wake people up? What's the issue?"

"The issue is happiness versus misery. There's no room for God or a soul in a world of material things. Material things are facts. They don't depend on us. We depend on them. As supposedly hard facts, they don't even depend on God."

Sue went over to a door in the hall. A plaque on it said 'Workroom'. "The reality of hard, material facts is supposed to be beyond question. I don't know if you've noticed, but it can make people nervous even to talk about it."

Sue jiggled the doorknob. "Locked," she said. "I'll get the key." She motioned toward the office, and I stepped aside for her. "Questioning reality is very close to admitting you don't know what it is," she said. "And what happens to people who don't know what reality is?"

"They'd have trouble holding a job."

At the office door, I hung behind. Sue saw me hesitate and waved me in. "That's right. People who don't know what reality is, can't cope. They're locked up for their own good and everybody else's. That's why people put up a block against thinking about reality."

The office was a complete contrast to the expensive furnishings I'd seen in the hall and the devotion rooms. The two metal desks looked like rescues from a landfill. Sue talked while poking through the drawers in one. "People hate their shopping mall reality. They're miserable. They want out."

Sue gave up on one desk and shifted her search to the next. "They are miserable enough to talk about God, to want to find Him." She raised her voice to carry over the rattling in the drawers. "But they still can't bring themselves to believe anything outside the shopping mall reality is truly real. God's not there, so if he exists, it's in Heaven. And Heaven is a different place, very, very far away."

"Can a visualization fix that?" I asked.

Sue held up the key in triumph. "The shopping mall reality has total power over people's minds. To defeat it, I need to create a power that can compete. But it's so powerful that I can't explode it from outside."

"So a Goddess of Money works from the inside?" I asked.

"Money is what the mall is all about. Nobody can question Pecunia's right to be there. But Pecunia is subversive. You can't believe in the reality of money, and still think that we live in a world of purely material things."

"Why not?"

"Follow me." We went back to the workroom door. "Money is just an idea," Sue said as she fiddled the key. "A dollar bill is just a picture illustrating an idea, the same as our Pecunia images. It proves that at least one major part of the material world relies on the power of ideas."

"I think I'm getting this," I said. "The more someone is obsessed with money and shopping, the more this gets through to them. So it's perfect for someone like Heather."

"Yes. Her obsession had been her personal highway to hell. Pecunia shows her it is really the fast path to God. A path which she has been given a special talent for traveling."

The door yielded and Sue motioned me in. The room was perhaps twenty feet by forty, but so full there was little room to stand. There was a framing table, easels, drawing and drafting tables, steel flat files, multimedia cabinets, light boxes, viewers for sorting slides. Pictures covered the wall. More leaned in deep ranks against just about every vertical surface. I could see not just Pecunia pictures, but diagrams, pictures of banks, and larger than life pictures of banknotes.

"Pecunia is the image of God." Sue swept her arms out. "Pecunia is the material world. The material world is really, when correctly seen, the image of God." Her face lit up. This laboratory of imagery, incubator and graveyard, excited her more than the finished products in the devotion rooms. "Ideas form our material reality, not vice versa. As long as you accept the material, shopping world as more real than ideas, rejecting its values does no good. All it does is makes you crazy, the way it did Cilla."

I stopped scanning the room and looked at Sue. "Priscilla Wolf?"

"Yes."

"You know her?"

"Oh, yes. I've known her for some time." Sue put her arms down, and sat on a stool. Some of the brightness left her eyes. "Cilla contacted me years ago, and was very helpful. But she wanted to start a Pranashtan Church. I just kept saying no. We don't need another church. Then, two years ago, Cilla started to organize a Church of Pranashta without telling me. She told people I'd appointed her to do it. People were used to Cilla doing things for me. She's great as an organizer."

"At the raid, it seemed she wanted to be in charge."

Sue nodded. "By the time I found out, Cilla projected that in another twelve months there would be thousands of members and a budget of millions. I think she was right. But I had to destroy the whole thing. I felt like a vandal doing it, but it was just another church. Probably even more a product of ego than most of them. It had to go. It was all a terrible waste, a big mess."

"Had money been collected?"

"Thank the Goddess, not much. But it was all spent. Some of the donors refused my offer to repay them. But repaying the others made it an expensive mistake. The Goddess is kind to me, but so many better things could have been done with the money."

"Mike told me that a former assistant of yours started the trouble between you and the CTS. Was that Priscilla?"

"Yes. Cilla blamed me for everything. I had to go to court, get an injunction, a restraining order, the works."

"I didn't see it in the press," I said.

"There wasn't much. Cilla felt humiliated and didn't want press. And I put everything out into the open, but in ways that made it look boring. I sent out press releases, full of all the organizational and legal particulars. Most news rooms threw them away without reading them."

I needed to ask another question about Priscilla, but decided to sit on it for a bit. "Was there something in here you wanted to show me?"

Sue's eyes lit back up.

12 Follow the Money

"Do you know where money comes from?" Sue had pulled a diagram from a drawer. It showed arrows emerging from some boxes and going into others. The arrows were broad and thick, the boxes had impressive names, and the arrows had some pretty fancy labels of their own.

"Do you mean printed bills?" I asked. "Or how money is really created?"

"Good for you," Sue beamed. "Most people think money is created when it's printed."

I was glad I was doing well. "No, the Bureau of Engraving and Printing only exchanges printed bills for money that already exists. Money is created by the Federal Reserve."

"Yes! You see how this connects to Pecunia ..."

"Actually, I don't," I said.

"I have trouble sometimes convincing people that money is not a material thing, that it's an idea one hundred percent. They initially think it's the idea connected up to the printed bills. But most money is an entry in a bank's computer. The part in printed bills is small change."

I looked back at the diagram for an arrow with a friendly label. "I guess this shows the Fed creates money in something called 'Open Market Operations'."

"What that means is they buy things. And they use a check to do it. The money backing the check is just a computer entry they make when they write the check. The Federal Reserve literally wishes money into existence. They record it in their computer, and, poof, it's there. They don't do anything even as physical as printing cash."

"I didn't notice this diagram outside."

"We're not sure how to work it up as a visualization. For Pecunia we have centuries of religious practice to go by. A visualization has to reach people in their souls. We can explain it to the mind, or even show it in a picture that catches the eye, but it's harder to catch the soul."

Sue motioned to the walls. "You see many different attempts at drawing Pecunia in here. Outside, we currently use just two. Pecunia in the blue

43

robe is the Goddess of Simplicity. We might call it poverty, but Pecunia enjoys simplicity. The gold lined red gown is Pecunia as the Goddess of Wealth."

We started out of the workroom. "Did you say you think Priscilla is crazy?"

"Priscilla has crazy doubt."

"Huh?"

"When you're trapped in the shopping mall and doubt God, that's just doubt. When you refuse to admit you are trapped, you drive yourself crazy. Crazy doubt. People like Cilla pretend the problem is disbelief by other people."

Sue sat in one of the chairs. I sat next to her. "Doubt or crazy doubt. The choices aren't good."

Another of Sue's smiles. "There's a middle way. You can get beyond shopping. If you do, the fact that others are still in the mall does not bother you. You ask them what they bought. If you think it is nice, you say so. If you really like it, you go out and buy one yourself."

"You're the same as everyone else?"

"Pretty much. The difference is that you do not hate the mall. Because if the mall is real to you, on some level you feel trapped. A trapped soul hates."

"That whole Church of Pranashta business must have been painful."

"It was. Cilla created new Pranashta materials without my knowledge. I was just horrified. She doesn't understand. It's sounds egotistical, but Pranashta is my baby. When I see it turned into something I don't believe in, it hurts."

Sue shifted to face me. "But I'm glad you brought it up. The blowup with Priscilla connects with Pecunia. I realized I need to do something beyond the books. A lot of good things happen here. But I worry about expanding. Right now it's just people we know, or referrals from them. Maybe that's how it will always be."

"Have you been trying to expand?"

"I don't know if I'm being a coward, Josh, but no. I worry about how this will be represented once it's out in the public. The conventional churches pretend they are indifferent to money."

"Yeah, but they can be greedy enough."

"That's not the main problem," Sue said. "In pretending not to care about money, conventional churches are refusing to deal with the issues which obsess people most of their waking and dreaming hours. When you counsel people, you find that money is the number one trouble spot. Sex is second. And it's not even a close second."

Sue motioned at the mural of Pecunia Churning the Ocean on the far wall. "Here we look at money closely to see what it is. If it's an idea we can deal with it the way we deal with an idea. We can rethink it. We worry that God is just an idea. Well, all our problems are just an idea. If we look at which ideas are true, and which false, good things will happen."

"That mural is stunning. How is it done?"

"It's a holograph. One of our members did it. The technology is new and the materials were expensive, so the artist needed a donor to help with the cost. It's their joint gift to us. We had to widen the hallway and do a lot with the lighting to get it to work, but it was worth it."

Sue looked at the clock. "I'll have to go in a few minutes. What with the raid, you can't have learned much about the proof."

"I think I know some things. It's the kind of proof called 'ontological'. Gödel has a new approach."

"Ontological?"

"An 'ontological proof' is where you try to show God exists because our idea of God requires it."

"God comes into existence just because of His idea?"

"If the Chairman of the Federal Reserve can do it, why not God?"

"This is wonderful! But, one question, if you can answer it yet."

"Fire away."

"Suppose I'm an atheist. And I just say I have no idea who God is. Then there's no proof, is there?

"Actually, there is. If you're an atheist, you say God does not exist. You therefore have a definition of God. You can't say there is no Bigfoot, unless you have some idea about who Bigfoot is."

Sue jumped up and clapped her hands. "Despite everything, this is working! I'm so happy. I was guided to bring the notebooks to you, but I was not sure why until now. You're a gift."

13 The Prior Loses Sleep

Bec Monastery, Normandy, France, 1078 AD

God is a lot older than the idea of proof. Humans worshiped gods and goddesses for centuries unnumbered without having any idea of what a proof is, much less any desire for one.

In fact, nobody seems to have wanted proofs of anything until the Greeks. Apparently it started in their courts. Before the Greeks, there were legal proceedings. But the idea was that every party should be acting as part of a social order which was also divine. These courts had no place for individuals with rights.

In Greek courts, individuals had rights and competed to assert them. To win their cases, they looked for proofs to present in court. The Greeks started to look for proofs outside the courts as well, and that changed geometry. Babylonians and Egyptians knew lots of facts about triangles. But they didn't prove them. They used facts and formulas that were known to work, and left it at that.

The Greeks rewrote geometry. Suddenly it was all about proving things. Thanks to the Greeks, high school geometry teachers today labor to prove things about triangles and quadrilaterals to dazed students who would be quite willing to take the teacher's word for it.

It took a while for the proof game to get around to God. Some things we never demand any proof for. We don't demand a proof when we're unhappy. We accept misery on faith.

God had the same privilege for a long time. That He was out there, few doubted and fewer cared to prove. But around 1078 AD, in the Norman French monastery of Bec, its Prior began missing meals and losing sleep. This kind of self-denial was typical of saintly men like Anselm. It alone would not have worried his monks. But Anselm of Bec, of all men, was not paying attention at mass. Some monks saw the Devil at work.

14 Tuesday was a Bad Day, Part 2

PG

From the bottom of my stairs, I looked out at Armenta's rock. She wasn't back. Up in my office, I noticed a light flashing. My mind went back to a time before I unplugged my phone. I used to get things called messages. I'd forgotten how to retrieve them, but I looked it up.

A cordial female voice told me she represented the State of California. Banana Slug Investigations had filed a complaint against Bouchard Beach Software and Investigations, my company. The complaint was also against me personally. BBSI and I were alleged to be doing private investigations without the required license. The voice in the message could not have been chirpier if I'd won the California Lottery. She gave me a name and callback number, but added I needn't bother. Full particulars would arrive shortly, by certified mail.

I wasn't sure what Banana Slug's beef was. Maybe this was additional harassment on behalf of their client, the CTS. Maybe Banana Slug figured I was competition, and wanted to drive me out of business. They had a good chance of doing that. The way California licenses PI's, I'd have to show three years of relevant investigative experience. "Relevant investigative experience" usually means either being a cop or becoming an indentured servant to an ex-cop.

It seemed that Bouchard Beach Software and Investigations might have come out of its cocoon only to die inside twenty-four hours, like some species of butterfly I've heard about. Of course, the butterflies do nothing but have sex in those twenty-four hours. I hadn't planned that well.

I didn't have to do anything before I got the certified letter. This butterfly still had time on the clock.

Then the phone rang.

15 Tuesday was a Bad Day, Part 3

PG

The room was very quiet. I watched myself pick up the phone and heard my voice say "Hello".

"Josh, this is Walter Hazlitt from Heavensent." Walter had been my last boss at Heavensent. "I don't know how to ask this, but I have to. Is Lorraine there?"

"I have not heard from Lorraine since October. I can understand why you might think otherwise." I remembered Walter as a decent guy, so I resisted the temptation to tell him to mind his own business.

"OK … Look, the reason I am asking is nobody has seen her for over two weeks."

"You mean nobody at Heavensent?" I asked.

"Nobody at all as far as we can find out. Three Sundays ago she got on a plane at LAX bound for San Jose. That's the last we know."

"Just ran off? That's hard to believe. Heavensent was important to her."

"We've called everybody we can think of," Walter said. "Believe me, asking you is a last resort. She's not been seen at the office, and has blown off a long list of appointments. Customer meetings, even two big TV interviews. This could hit the papers."

"Did you report her missing to the police?" Listening to my own voice, I sounded strangely matter-of-fact.

"Yes. Frankly, we've had some people stake out the apartment and talk to the neighbors. If Lorraine wants us out of her life, wants to get away, that's fine, but we are starting to worry."

"What do the police say?"

"They took the report, but there is no evidence of a crime," Walter said. "And a missing persons report really should be made by a relative. You don't know of any family, do you?"

"I don't. She was on her own very young. She did not talk a lot about how that happened or why."

"In our files, she put you down as her contact in case of emergency."

"To be honest, it's been a while since she and I have talked," I said. "Someone else in her life is a possibility."

"I know this has gotta be damn hard."

"Who saw her last?"

"A guy sat across from her in the Canadair Jet," Walter said. "He and the stewardess remember her boarding and sitting down. They do not remember her getting off. She is shown in the boarding records. They do not remember seeing her for the last half of the flight. But they are sure the plane took off with her on it."

"She might have changed seats."

"The stewardess thinks she'd have noticed. Though she's not completely sure. Nobody saw her in San Jose, nobody has seen her since."

"Maybe she camped out in the lavatory," I said.

"That is something the stewardess does keep an eye out for. She swears that could not have happened."

"Well, noticed or not, she didn't dematerialize. So she landed in San Jose."

"The airplane is the last place she is known to have been," Walter said. "Anyway, it's our security guys who are working this. Do you remember Oka Ohoma?"

"Sure do. What's he up to?"

"He'll be retiring soon, but he is handling this investigation."

"Oka is leaving?" I said.

"Yes. It's quite the story. If you are all right with it, we'd like you and Oka to talk. He knows more details and has some questions."

"Great."

"I'm going to talk to Oka now." Walter said. "Expect to hear from him soon. He's doesn't stay late, so he may call you from home."

"I'll be in all evening."

"Good, Josh. It's nice to talk to you. Take care of yourself."

I'd kept a couple of things back from Walter, which was no big deal. Oka was in charge of the investigation and I could tell him if I decided to come clean.

Lorraine wouldn't have wanted me telling anyone at Heavensent about her family. She never knew her birth parents. She'd been put up for adoption as an infant, and ended up in a series of foster homes.

None of the foster homes were really bad, Lorraine had said, in fact most of her foster parents were nice. But she decided to have a grudge against the world, and her way of expressing it was petty theft. Lorraine was headed for juvenile hall just when a circus came through town. When the circus left, she went with it.

Lorraine thought joining that circus was the best decision she'd ever made, but she did have one regret. The couple at her last foster home had been especially nice, and she'd left without a word.

The next of kin issue was a technicality about how to fill out a form. To deal with that, Oka did not need to know the details of Lorraine's childhood. The other thing I'd kept back was more likely to be relevant.

At the Bhadrachakra they maintained that Lorraine was a reincarnation of Ocean of Awareness, the great eighth century Tibetan saint. They took that seriously. So did Lorraine, though in the years after Bhadra she'd had to focus on other things.

When I moved to PG, Lorraine began to read about Ocean. Ocean was a frequent topic in our phone conversations. Lorraine's interest exceeded mine, and after a while I was just letting her talk to be polite. By October, something about Lorraine's fascination with the teachings of Ocean of Awareness was making me uneasy. In our last conversation, Lorraine talked about little else.

Oka took his time. I gathered my books on the God Proof. They made a small pile. There are many books about Gödel and his work. Almost all of them ignore the God Proof totally. Most of the others say nothing useful — a sentence or two, sometimes just a sneer. In a few places, the notes from 1970 are reprinted. A handful of books and articles actually discuss them.

I was still reading at nine. By then, I knew Oka would not call until morning.

16 Scattered Wax

Bec Monastery, 1078 AD

Anselm's God Argument is a few paragraphs of medieval Latin with an unusually precise feel. It reads like the abstract of a modern proof.

In the last decades, logicians discovered Anselm's Argument has more than just the right feel. Logicians formulated a new branch of logic that allowed them to reason not just about things which are strictly true or false, but also about the slippery, maybe-true-or-maybe-false things which are closer to what we find in the real world. They call the slipperier truths, modals, and their logic, modal logic. With modal logic they could check some of Anselm's key ideas. A thousand years before their work, Anselm had gotten it right. The first half of his God Argument is rock solid.

How Anselm did it, I do not know. He did not have access to the good logic texts of his own time, never mind ours. The library at Bec was a few dozen books, almost all of them theology or canon law.

Any library was an oddity in the Norman France of 1078 AD. The rulers of this corner of France were descended from Vikings, pirates who looted and burned monasteries for a living. Just over a century earlier these Vikings had changed from raiders to rulers. The King of France acknowledged their right to the land in return for their promise not to sack Paris. The Norman's promise was not watertight, but it was given in return for lands they had already taken. Seemed fair.

At this point Bec was not likely to be sacked and burned. The Normans had become Christians, and allies of the Pope against other Catholics. The Prior of Bec played a major role in maintaining the important relationship between the Normans and the Pope.

As Prior, Anselm was technically just second in command. But the Abbot, Herluin, was old. For at least a decade the priors had run Bec Monastery for him. Bec needed a Prior with his mind on the job. The Normans continued to have a well-deserved reputation for violence and local warlords were not above trying to strong-arm Bec out of its land rights.

So it worried Anselm's monks when he became absorbed with a God Proof to the extent that he neglected food and sleep. If this was saintly

51

distraction, it would have been bad enough. But during services, Anselm's mind was elsewhere. Could the Devil be at work in their beloved Prior?

Anselm himself wondered. He tried to put the God Proof out of his mind, but whenever he did, it tormented him all the more. He had no choice but to let it work itself out.

The God Proof came to Anselm at a midnight service. He wrote it out on wax tablets. Writing it out on parchment would have made the proof a matter of permanent record, but that was expensive and Anselm held off. The monks breathed easily. Talk about the Devil began to die down. Anselm became himself again.

But things at the monastery did not go straight back to normal. The wax tablets disappeared and were never seen again. Anselm rewrote them from scratch and assigned one of the brothers to watch them.

The next night, that brother put the tablets beside his bed before he lay down to sleep. Nothing disturbed his slumber, but he woke in the morning to find the wooden frames of the tablets scattered around the room. The wax had been shaken out of them and broken to bits.

Anselm reassembled the wax pieces like a puzzle. Once again he copied out his proof. But this time he wrote the God Proof on parchment, for posterity. And only then did normal life return to the monastery of Bec.

17 The Thousand Year Hmmm

"Does Ultimate Reality exist?" That's Anselm's Argument in four words. Say yes to that and you've said God exists. And, Heaven's sake, how do you say the Ultimate Reality is not real?

Pose this question to your friends and most of them, even those who believe in God, will say "Hmmm". The argument just seems too pat. Something has to be wrong with it, but they're not sure what.

We now have a thousand years of discussion on the Anselm Argument. Most of the great names in philosophy have stuck an oar in. "Hmmm" is a fair summary of what they've said. By itself, Anselm's argument is not a coercive proof, the kind of proof that forces people to change their minds. It has its fans, but even a lot of people who believe in God don't buy Anselm's Argument. As far as convincing atheists, forget it.

But while you're perfectly free to not buy Anselm's Argument, a "hmmm" is a long way from a proof that Anselm is wrong. There's no accepted counterargument to Anselm. His critics agree that he's wrong, but they don't agree why.

Gödel set out to translate Anselm's Argument from Latin into math, and show that it was right. It doesn't sound easy, but it's exactly the sort of thing Gödel had done before.

He'd done it in the Freedom Proof. There Gödel had proved something most mathematicians thought was not just wrong, but plain daffy. With Anselm's Argument, Gödel would seem to have a lot more going for him. It probably either works or it doesn't. Whichever way it goes, somebody is likely to put it in the bag someday. Why not the greatest logician in history?

18 Person of Interest

PG, Wednesday, January 9

I was up early. Armenta hadn't returned. Oka called just after eight.

Oka first made sure that Walter had broken the news. Then he told me something Walter hadn't. "The police want to speak with you."

"About Lorraine?"

"Right. We pushed the police, so they are checking out suspects."

I closed my eyes and let that sink in. "Shit," I said. I should have already known what Oka was telling me. The boyfriend has to be on the suspect list. Statistically, he's behind it more than thirty percent of the time.

"I guess if they're not looking at me they're not doing their job," I said. "No other leads?"

"You are it, my friend."

Oka waited for me to fill the silence. "This is just sinking in, so forgive me if I seem shaken."

"Quite all right. Remember, you didn't hear that from me."

"Sure."

"Legally, you are not forced to talk to them," Oka said. "But if you don't, or they think you are stonewalling or just a suspicious, nasty guy, they'll make it difficult for us to involve you in our investigation."

"Involve me how?"

"We want to hire you to help look at her home directory here, to go into her apartment with us and look around, and to check out her computer there. Maybe something else, but that's all I can think of now."

"How do we get permission to go into Lorraine's apartment?" I asked.

"From you, Mr. Josh. She never took your name off the lease."

"Is that legal?"

"If nobody is going to make an issue of it, then for all practical purposes it's legal." That made sense. If Lorraine showed up while I was tossing her place with Oka and the boys, she wouldn't sue. Hunt us down and kill us one by one, maybe. Sue us, no.

We settled a few details: the officer to call to arrange the interview, my rate, and so on. Oka told me the police were saying they couldn't get a search warrant to enter Lorraine's apartment, but might be willing to go in with my permission. I promised they'd get it.

I had intended to tell Oka about my last phone conversation with Lorraine. But now that I knew I was suspected of her murder, I couldn't. If I started to spin stories about strange and forbidden spiritual practices from Tibet, it would look like I was trying to divert suspicion, and had chosen a particularly warped way to do it.

I did not want it to look like I was avoiding the police, so I called them straight away. The officer sounded very professional, but he was obviously eager to talk to me. We set the appointment for Thursday morning at my place.

I'd forgotten to ask Oka where he was going to after Heavensent. I'd been rude. And I was curious. What the hell. He'd tell me when I got up there.

I tried to resume work on my notes, but just stared at the equations, unable to concentrate. The notes reminded me of the book I had wanted from my storage space on the highway to Salinas. I had been planning to get it on Tuesday, before all hell broke loose. Just as well. Today I could use a drive.

19 Shudda Wudda Cudda

You run a red light but get through safe. Do you try it again? You see someone take a turn at Russian roulette and the gun doesn't go off. Do you take a turn? Why not?

Modal thinking is the reason you don't. Thinking about possibilities. Bad things that could have happened, even if they didn't. It's pretty basic stuff. But philosophy didn't begin to get a clue about it until the 1960s.

Possibility, stuff that "could have" happened, is one of the modals. "Should", "would", "might" and "must" are others. Modals are things which we think about even though they aren't always actual facts. Things that should have happened, things that could have happened, things that might have happened.

You think in modal terms all day long. You might not get your money back. You could win the lottery. You should have known there might be a lot of traffic. If you had known, you would have taken a back road. Then you would have made it on time.

Scientists do as much modal thinking as any of us. When they test a medicine, they leave a control group. The control group gets a placebo, not the real medicine. What would have happened if they did get it? That's what the test is to find out. Things that might have happened. Modalities.

The first half of Anselm's Argument asks you to assume that God might exist. Not that he does, just that he might. OK, Anselm says, if God might exist, then you can prove that he does. Nine hundred years later, after C. I. Lewis's work of 1918 and Saul Kripke's in 1963, we know that's right. One half down, one half to go.

Because you've still got to show God might exist. That half they didn't prove solid. That was the half Gödel needed to show.

20 Empyrean Storage

East of Monterey, Wednesday

Empyrean Storage is on a hilltop overlooking Monterey Bay. Sun pours in. Low sage brush hills to the east and south don't block a single photon. The runways of Monterey Airport to the north radiate heat. To the west, all of Monterey Bay from Pacific Grove to Santa Cruz glistens under a huge sky. It all looks white and indistinct, like one of those movie scenes where they overexpose the film to show that the hero is dead and in Heaven.

The storage is in corrugated metal sheds on concrete foundations. Asphalt lanes run between the sheds and along the chain link perimeter fence. I watched a half dozen private planes take off and two more land before I went to sort through my stuff.

I nodded hellos to other tenants and snuck glances. Like me, they were better off putting it in the dumpster, saving the rent, and getting on with life. But I kept quiet. Those are dangerous thoughts. A few months prior, in these very corridors, Willie Post had spoken out, and paid the price.

Willie was a quiet, empathetic young man with a clipboard and a survey form. He asked customers questions. What did they keep here? Why? Willie was gentle. Unhurried. Nonjudgmental. Surrounded by half-forgotten mementos from the lost corners of their lives, people opened up. They spoke and thought about themselves in ways they never had before. Some cried. A few felt a deep personal liberation. Lots of them rethought their need for all that stuff.

Canceled leases and overflowing dumpsters brought attention. The owners were surprised to learn about Willie. They had not hired him.

Willie was arrested. The District Attorney's office struggled to think of things to charge him with. Trespass was about it. But one of the tenants whose life Willie had changed was a lawyer. He took the case pro bono and handled it like the whole Bill of Rights depended on it. The main defense theory was that Willie had permission to be there from some of the tenants. It looked good. Remember, the defense only has to create doubt.

The prosecution had budgeted for a minor case. They cut a deal. Willie pled to something the *Monterey Eagle* reporter had forgotten by deadline time. Willie was looking at thirty days suspended, until his sister popped up from Minnesota. She told the court she'd drive Willie straight back to their family in Mankato. After a short recess, the DA told the court he liked the idea. In fact, the DA chipped in for gas, though that wasn't in the paper. I heard it from the *Eagle* reporter when I ran into him in a fern bar on Cannery Row.

21 Stuff Rules

My stack of boxes was three deep, four wide and in places four boxes high. I prayed my book was not in the box at the bottom in the inside corner. Not all prayers are answered. By the time I found the book, I'd taken nearly everything else in the storage space out into the hallway. Of course, it was at the bottom of the box.

The pattern I'd seen in the equations from the philosophy notebook made them look like comprehension principles. A "comprehension principle" is a rule which a mathematical system uses to accumulate stuff — a stuff rule.

Stuff rules always make the same kind of statement. They say "Suppose you have something, well, in that case you have something else." This gives them a certain look.

A stuff rule needs something to start with, but not much. For the numbers, zero is plenty. You then say, "If I have a number, there is a number after it." That's a stuff rule, one that will take you to the billions and beyond. If you want negative numbers, just use another comprehension principle that says, "Every number has a negative." A few more comprehension principles, and you get fractions and points and lines and dimensions and shapes and surfaces and a lot more than that. From very few stuff rules, you can wind up with lots of stuff.

So perhaps I should have known. The logic books I found in storage told me that, of the couple hundred equations I'd thought were "stuff rules", most probably were not. A few might be. Summing up, I still didn't have a clue what these equations were.

I had hauled enough books into the hallway to start a small town library. I figured I might as well poke through them. I grabbed a few books on modal logic. I threw away some wires I didn't need, put my stuff away, closed up the space, bought a large bottle of diet cola and took a stroll. I was admiring the hills when Mike called on my cellphone. Sue was with him in his office. He asked me to meet them.

22 The Institute for Advanced Studies

Veronica waved me in. Mike told me that Judge Gaunilo had scheduled a hearing on the notebooks. "It's on Wednesday a week from today," he said. "There's a new wrinkle. A place called the Institute for Advanced Studies has claimed the notebooks. I have no idea who they are. When I was served the papers I thought they were another bunch of New Age fanatics, but Sue has never heard of them."

"There are lots of groups who can be called New Age," Sue said genially. "Particularly back East there are many I've never heard of."

"Actually, I know who they are," I said. "Not a New Age outfit, not by a long shot. It's the Institute where Gödel worked."

Mike furled his forehead. "Are they part of Princeton? Princeton is joining as an amicus, like they were a separate party. I thought Gödel had been at Princeton."

I shook my head. "No. There's a lot of confusion about that. There's a town called Princeton. Princeton University is in it. So is the Institute for Advanced Studies. But the IAS is a completely separate outfit. There's even been bad blood about the IAS stealing Princeton University faculty. IAS faculty don't have to teach and can spend full time on research of their choice."

"So Gödel didn't teach at Princeton."

"Right. He was at the IAS. Einstein was also at the IAS, not Princeton."

Mike's brow unreefed a furl. "So that's why these IAS people say they are Gödel's heirs. But why do the papers filed with the court say the stuff is in Princeton University's Library?"

"The IAS does not have an archive library and doesn't want to start one. Princeton University has a very good one, right nearby. The Firestone Library of Princeton University keeps Gödel's papers, but the IAS owns them."

"So their claim to be Gödel's heir has a foundation."

"What everybody has believed up to now is that Adele, Gödel's wife, inherited all his papers, then left them to the IAS." I turned to Sue. "You may remember I asked about ownership."

"I wondered about that," she said. "And then you said something about court orders and all that."

Mike snickered. "Our friend, Josh here, thinks he's protecting himself with that double-talk."

"And making sure the client is not hiring me when they should be going to an attorney," I said. "Right. If you've got a better idea you won't charge me for, I'd love to hear it."

"Sue's ownership is solid," Mike said. "The letter from Einstein should carry the day."

"Letter from Einstein?" I was not clear how Einstein's old correspondence was supposed to help us.

Mike turned to Sue and said "You didn't tell him about this?"

"Just that the notebooks were from Mom. That's all he asked."

I didn't suspect Sue of stealing. She probably did inherit the notebooks like she said. But someone along the line had gotten these things out of New Jersey, and I didn't see how that could have happened legally.

Mike smiled and pressed the intercom. "Zoe, you there?"

"Yes," answered the intercom.

"Josh Bryant, here in my office, needs a copy of the Shrift Notebook Provenance File."

"Certainly. Should I do that now?"

"If you can. I'd like it ready so he can take it with him when he leaves. Sue," Mike said, "since Josh knows so much about these notebooks, why don't we invite him in on our Friday meeting?"

23 The Letter from Einstein

Iwas back in my office by late afternoon. I didn't see Armenta and hadn't since Monday. I'd gone a few days without any glimpse of Armenta before, but that was always during periods of high waves or high daytime tides. At night, I can't see out there, but marine biologists say that's foraging time for harbor seals. I had never seen Armenta's haulout bare, dry and above tide in daylight as much as I had in the last three days.

I flipped through the "Shrift Provenance File". It had wills, notes, receipts, letters and so on. I turned to the Einstein letter first. Like the rest of the file, it was a copy. Mike had the original in a safe somewhere. It's worth a few K at auction.

○ ○ ○ ○ ○

Albert Einstein
Institute for Advanced Studies
Princeton, New Jersey
May 13, 1947
To Whom it May Concern:
I write this to record my pleasure at meeting today, Frau Eva Garten, the good friend of my most dear and esteemed friend, Kurt Gödel. Kurt's descriptions of this most charming lady made me eagerly anticipate this day. Meeting her, however, I must accuse my good friend of having fallen well short of the facts.

As a memento of our wonderful days in Vienna, Kurt gave our lovely friend two notebooks, items of the greatest importance. I confess that before meeting Frau Garten, I did wonder if these items were not better off going with Kurt's other papers. Few people could have eased my misgivings more than Frau Garten has.

Kurt wishes, and Frau Garten graciously agrees, that in the lifetime of himself and his wife Adele, these notebooks will be kept secret; and that they will pass to Katrina, Frau Garten's daughter, and from Katrina on to her children. Kurt also requested, which again was most kindly granted by Frau Garten, that these notes should in any case be kept secret so long as this unhappy century may last.

Fraulein Katrina, when you see this letter, let it convey my special greetings. It is my profound regret that it was not possible to meet you in person. Kurt believes that you or your children will know what to do with these notes. My valued friend is continually telling me that there are ways of knowing things beyond those I recognize. Certainly there are many things I don't know. If these notes do anything to ensure the next century is not like this one, God will be in them indeed.

Very truly yours,
[signed] A. Einstein
(Albert Einstein)

24 The Letter from Eva Garten

Most of the "Shrift Provenance File" was documentation, useful in court, but adding nothing. The gist was in two of the letters. One was Einstein's. The other was written the day after the meeting by Eva Garten for her daughter Katrina, then seventeen. Apparently this was intended not to be mailed, but to be shown to Katrina at some later date.

○ ○ ○ ○ ○

May 14, 1947
Beloved Katrina,
Now I must write the whole thing down. I wish you could have gone with me. I asked to bring you but it could not be, so forgive me. Instead I am writing you this letter. Professor Einstein said I should, for you, and in case people ask about the notebooks later. But none of this can make any sense to you, so let me explain.

Yesterday I met Albert Einstein. Some day you'll remember this trip of mine to New Jersey. I told you it was to pick up some money I was owed. Well, it was not a debt but a gift from my beloved Kurtele whom I knew from Vienna. But I've never told you of Kurtele.

Remember the Berkeley Professor who visited on his way to LA? Well, he was not really there to talk about a translation job, but instead to deliver a message that after all these years Kurtele had something he wanted me to have. I already planned, you know, to visit my sister in New York in May, so it was arranged. Of all things, Kurtele has become good friends with the famous Einstein! Kurtele was always so smart I knew, but friends with Einstein! Dear one, I can hardly believe it.

Because of Adele, everything was arranged through Einstein's office. Adele is such a dear and was such a friend and has had to do so much for Kurtele I know. But Adele gets so jealous, and they begged that she learn nothing of this, the meeting and the gift and everything. They assured me that all was going to be very proper, and if Adele knew, it would be a huge upset and over nothing. Adele was such a dear one but I remember how she got angry, especially about Kurtele.

Katrina, it really was too cute. To see Kurtele after all these years and Professor Einstein the chaperone!

So I arrive and there they are, Kurtele almost like before his illness which is so very sad, and Einstein just like in the newsreels. You would not believe Professor Einstein! For a start he would not hear of being called anything but Albert and he acted to me like a uncle. He had lived in Vienna and in Berlin and he talked and talked about the old days. Oh, Katrina, what it was like before the Nazis! Sometimes it seems all of us are here in America but it is not like Vienna was.

Kurtele was happy I could tell. Even before the illness, he was no blabbermouth, but he enjoyed Einstein's stories as much as I did. Katrina, you have no idea! If Einstein were not the smartest man in the world, he would be the kindest and the funniest. His stories! I was there all morning, and never stopped laughing. Einstein knew all the places and it was so wonderful to think of those times again. It was like I'd known him all my life.

Kurtele had two notebooks for me, and some money. These notebooks are special, they both say. Poor Kurtele has been trying to prove that God exists! Kurtele is such a smart man, and knows so many things, but one wonders and Kurtele has his illness and says the strangest things sometimes. So your poor simple mother blurts out, in front of not just Kurtele, but Einstein, "Proving God? Is such a thing right to do?"

Oh, how they both laughed! Of course I realized what I had said and was so relieved they weren't mad at me at all. Oh, I can be such a silly goose. But they laughed as if I had said the cleverest thing.

Einstein says, "You see, my friend, God must exist because He hates your proof!"

Kurtele tells him, "But would someone that hates a proof of His own existence be God?"

Einstein still was laughing. "It depends how bad the proof is! I like Frau Garten's proof much better than yours."

Kurtele's eyes were bright, so bright I remembered Vienna. "Of course, I see," he said, "and the fact that hers relies on mine does not make mine correct."

"Precisely!" Einstein said, "your proof does not have to be any good to validate hers, it just has to exist! And we know yours exists, because now all three of us have seen it!"

When the laughing was done, Professor Einstein and Kurtele talked about the notebooks, and showed them to me. They were in a shorthand that is not the one they teach now. I must teach you German. I was going to when you're older and how the time is going by! But the truth is, these notebooks are all some kind of mathematics and for all I could make of them they might as well have been in Egyptian hieroglyphs.

They've made arrangements with the bank near us for their safe keeping. I promised they would be kept secret, certainly for as long as I hope to live. In 2001 the secrecy can end unless, God bless them, Kurtele or Adele are alive, because Kurtele was quite specific that publicity is something he wants neither for himself or Adele. Professor Einstein seemed quite in agreement. "Imagine living the way I have to," was what he said to Kurtele.

They also said I must leave them to you, as if, dearest, I would do anything else. Also, they should go on to your children. They gave me some money, for expenses they said, but actually an amount which will be quite helpful.

It was then afternoon, we had chatted for the whole morning, and they walked me out to a cab. For Einstein, this was quite the effort because no less than three people jumped out at him for autographs and then the cabbie wanted one, too! I wanted one for you, but after all this I was afraid to ask. But Professor Einstein was carrying a large envelope and at the last moment he opens it and inside are signed pictures for the two of us. This he gives to me apologetically, saying, "I get so used to signing things I am like a circus exhibit. I hope you will humor this old trained monkey and accept these for your daughter and yourself." I do not know what kept me from weeping.

I did cry in the cab seeing Kurtele and Einstein together waving at me. Kurtele of course is still so smart. He and Einstein are just the dearest of friends.

Katrina, Kurtele's illness was the saddest thing of my life. How wonderful things were before. I think it was because of the Nazis. He didn't talk badly about them. I could not imagine how he could seem so indifferent to those awful people. But he certainly did not support them or like what they did to his friends. I think he kept it inside and it made him crazy. If not for Adele he would have died.

Adele can be a hard woman. She has been hard about so many things. But Kurtele would have died without her and she needed to be hard. We must not hate Adele for being hard.

Now the Salinas Valley is my home, not Vienna. I am an American and you were raised one. The Nazis are gone but Kurtele and I and the kind Professor Einstein, we are all now here to stay. So many sad things happened but, Katrina, you must live a life with no time for regrets.

Fondly, Your loving mother,

Eva

25 If Possible, Then Real

Princeton, 1947

Anselm had shown that if God could exist, he does. The idea is that God has to be an all or nothing thing, or He's not God. A God who only exists at certain times of day is not really what we'd call God. A God who only exists depending on whether your team wins the Superbowl is not really God. If God exists for Jane, he's got to exist in Tarzan's world.

In other words, if there is any circumstance under which God could have existed at any time, then He exists everywhere, all the time and regardless. It works the opposite way as well. If there is any circumstance where God might not exist, even for a moment, then there is no God. All or nothing.

It sounds convincing. And now that they've invented the math to check it, we know it works.

But that's just half the job. You've still got to show that God is possible. It's not clear how Anselm was trying to do that. Anselm points out that someone might say God does not exist. Anselm calls him the Fool. But the Fool has an idea of God. He couldn't say God does not exist unless he has an idea of who God is.

One way of reading Anselm is to say the Fool's idea of God amounts to a possibility of God. Since a possible God is a real God, that's enough to prove God exists as a fact.

But a lot of people have trouble taking a Fool's idea as a real possibility. After all, we have a lot of ideas about things which not only don't exist, they're just not possible. Circles with sharp corners. A highway that goes on forever and never circles back. Geese that lay golden eggs. It's not clear that Anselm didn't have something else in mind. Is he saying that the Fool's idea is a reflection of something deeper?

Gödel wasn't buying that God is possible just because a Fool can think about Him. He would have just said so. He wouldn't have filled one notebook with equations and another with shorthand.

26 The Alibi Question

PG, Thursday, January 10

I'd set my alarm for six. The police were coming at nine, and I'm a slow starter. I drank coffee on the balcony while I waited. The tide was above Armenta's rock.

The two San Jose officers were on time, soft spoken, polite and unfriendly. They spoke carefully and listened with determination. Detective Edward Pauls seemed to be senior. He asked permission to search Lorraine's apartment. He wanted it in writing, and he got it.

For the questioning, Detective Jean Woods took over. All went smoothly until they asked about my move to Pacific Grove in July 2001.

"When did you next see her?" Detective Weeks had asked.

"I didn't see her again," I said. "San Jose was the last time." The officers glanced at each other.

"Did you quarrel?" Detective Woods did not vary her tone of voice during the entire interview.

"No."

"You did not quarrel, but you never saw her again?"

"We spoke over the phone," I said quickly. "I tried to talk to her weekly for a while."

"Tried?"

"Lorraine was very busy, and traveled a lot. It was hard." Don't get defensive, I reminded myself. Don't joke. Don't wisecrack. Keep explanations short.

"Did you contact her at all after July 2001?"

"Yes. We talked on the phone."

"Did you talk to her weekly or not?"

"At least that much at first. Then less and less." I didn't add that I'd unplugged the phone in late November. I told myself it wasn't relevant.

"When was the last conversation?"

"In October."

"Did you quarrel then?"

"No. Oh, no."

"But you didn't talk after that?"

"No."

"What did you talk about then?"

"I congratulated her on her birthday. I can't specifically remember it all, but a lot about how things were going at Heavensent. The strategy which she was promoting to customers, the media, TV appearances, her travel, the latest reorg." The truth was that Lorraine had talked about her Tibetan obsession almost the entire time, but no way I was going there with the police.

"And you never talked after that?"

"No."

"Why did you break up?"

"We didn't break up."

"You hadn't seen her since July, she told you she wasn't moving here, you didn't talk after that, but there was no break up?"

"No."

Detective Woods consulted her notes, then repeated her questions about my last conversations with Lorraine, changing the wording slightly. This time, as I listened to myself tell Detective Woods that Lorraine and I had not broken up, it sank in. Lorraine and I had broken up whether I wanted to call it that or not, and the detectives knew it.

Detective Woods turned to another page of notes and asked me the alibi question. "Can you tell us where you were on the Sunday Lorraine was last seen, December twenty-third, between seven fifteen and eight forty-five PM?"

I sat back, thinking that my ordeal was coming to an end. "Here, in the apartment," I said.

"Can anyone confirm that you were here?"

"The neighbors might remember seeing lights, or seeing that my car was in. Most of the places nearby are second homes. A lot of the owners aren't around this time of year."

"You realize this could be important."

"Yes. Very much so."

"What if we were to tell you that we have proof you were called that evening during that period of time and there was no answer?"

And now I had to tell them. "I had the phone unplugged from late November on."

"Unplugged?"

"I wanted to be alone and think. In late November I unclipped my phones from the jacks. I only hooked them back up Tuesday." This sounded dumb even to me.

"But you kept paying for the service without using it?"

"I didn't think I would disconnect permanently. Reconnecting is a hassle."

Detective Woods was now outside her script, but undismayed. She made some notes.

Her partner filled the pause. "Which is your business phone and which your personal line?"

"I didn't have a separate personal line. I took business calls at all hours. I just gave out the same number to all callers."

"So the line you unplugged was your only line for both personal and business?"

"My only voice line, yes. I kept a line plugged in for the computer."

I give my tormentors points on professionalism. How they kept from snickering at my story, I don't know. "So business calls to you could not get through?" Detective Pauls asked.

"Yes."

"Clients would not be able to reach you?"

"I had closed all my cases at that point."

"New clients would not be able to reach you?"

"Correct."

"Former clients with an issue could not reach you."

"Not by telephone. No."

"People selling you services, with questions, having problems with your tax returns or not getting your bill payments, none of these could reach you?"

"No."

"Is the business your only source of income?"

"I get some interest from savings."

"Does your business need to be built up over time?"

I considered protesting this line of questioning. But I couldn't deny he had a point. Unless I wanted to throw up my hands and ask for a lawyer, a teddy bear, or a vodka martini, I was in for the ride. "It does, yes. Unclipping the phone did my practice no good I am sure. I just wanted to think for a while."

"What about?"

"About where my life is going."

"Is your phone connected now?"

"Yes."

"It will help us if we can reach you by phone. Will it stay connected?" This question may have been intended to be intimidating, but I heard it with relief. It told me that they did not plan on arresting me then and there. Maybe they planned to stop at the outlet mall and needed the back seat empty. Maybe listening to me repeat this stupid story all the way back to San Jose was more than they could stand.

"Yes," I said. "I will leave it connected. There's an answering machine, too."

"Why did you reconnect the phone?"

"I have a new client."

"Who is that?"

"Matters concerning my clients I prefer not to talk about. In terms of finding Lorraine, I don't think that raises an obstacle."

They glanced at each other. Detective Woods resumed. "Can you think of any reason Lorraine would have called you that Sunday?"

"Are you saying she called me?"

"Let us ask the questions," Detective Woods said. I started to form an insincere apology, then thought better of it. I waited. She repeated the question.

"No. I'd have no idea why."

"Did you plan to see her that day?"

"No."

"Did you plan to pick her up at the airport?"

"No." My answers were implied by answers I had already given. Answers they did not believe.

"She would have had no reason to contact you?"

"That I don't know."

"Would you know of any reason she might call you?"

"Just to chat. Perhaps some news. I would have welcomed the call."

"But didn't you say your phone was not hooked up?"

"Right," I said, flustered. "If I'd thought there was any chance she'd call I would have had it hooked up."

"So this means you had decided by late November she was unlikely to call?"

"Yes. You're right. I must have."

"Are you concluding that from my questions? Or do you remember it?"

"I would not have unhooked the phone if I thought Lorraine would call."

"If you had not argued with Ms. Clausewitz, had not broken up, and if your last conversation was all about work, why did you conclude she would not call?"

"She hadn't called me for a while."

"And that made you think she wouldn't?"

"She'd been leaving it up to me to call."

"So, to be sure, you did not hear the phone ring around 7:18 PM that Sunday?"

"No."

"You did not hear the phone ring around 7:43 PM that Sunday."

"No."

"And you did not hear the phone ring around 8:27 PM that Sunday."

"No."

"You did not talk to Ms. Clausewitz that Sunday?"

"No, not after October."

"You have not talked to her since December twenty-third?"

"No."

"You did not see Ms. Clausewitz that Sunday?"

"Certainly not."

"You have not seen her since?"

"No."

"Are you sure?"

"Yes."

"Would it surprise you if we had cell phone records showing Ms. Clausewitz called at those times?"

"It does." I added weakly, "I wish I had talked to her."

"Do you have any idea what she might have wanted to talk about?"

"No."

"Did she have any enemies?"

"Who might have considered foul play? Certainly none I knew of."

"Do you know of any reason she might want to disappear?"

"No."

"Do you know of anything else that might help us find her?"

"No."

○ ○ ○ ○ ○

The two officers left as politely as they arrived. Detectives Wood and Pauls had zeroed in on the weak spot I didn't know I had. Stupid and innocent, I looked clever and guilty.

I don't know what else I could have done. Details of Lorraine's past lives wouldn't have made the police happy. And I was not going to give the officers a tutorial on Tibetan mind travel. Not with them already thinking

I was a sick puppy. Lorraine's talk about mental projection gave me the willies, and God knows what the police would have made of it.

My story might have been more believable if I'd pretended that last phone call was very short. Hell, I could have claimed it never happened. But the percentages aren't good when you hide an evasion with a lie.

I suppose once I'd realized that breakup was the word for Lorraine and I, I could have reversed myself. But it would have hurt more than helped. The police would have taken a change in my story as confirmation that I was playing games with them.

In this long book I read once, a guy named Dostoevsky makes the point that a good cop is a good psychoanalyst. Of course, if the cop is trying to make a homicide rap, you are better off crazy. Dostoevsky missed that angle.

27 The Gödel Effect

Our last phone call frustrated Lorraine. She felt she wasn't getting through to me. Gödel would have sympathized. Einstein talked with him as an intellectual equal, but everyone else had trouble with Gödel.

Noam Chomsky one day asked his fellow genius what he was up to. Gödel told him that he was trying to show the laws of nature aren't based on observation. Chomsky, seldom at a loss for words, didn't know what to say to that.

An astrophysicist confirms the Gödel Effect. His conversation with Gödel stopped dead when the topic of the natural sciences came up. Gödel told him he didn't believe in them.

A philosopher was more persistent. He was astounded to discover a man of Gödel's intelligence didn't believe in evolution, and he told Gödel so. Gödel, trying to be helpful, replied that Joseph Stalin was quite intelligent and didn't believe in evolution either. The philosopher just couldn't go on.

When Gödel applied for U.S. citizenship, Einstein realized that if Gödel pulled a conversation-stopper at the hearing it could cost him. Einstein and Oskar Morgenstern decided they'd better tag along. Sure enough, as they set out, Gödel told Einstein and Morgenstern he'd discovered a contradiction in the Constitution. The United States could be turned into a dictatorship, a discovery Gödel felt he needed to share.

The greatest logician of the last two thousand years was not easily diverted from a line of reasoning, but this was Einstein. Einstein began with a few small jokes, then took some of his funniest stories out of mothballs. But even an Einstein can only do so much. They needed a lucky break.

At the courthouse, they got it. They ran into Judge Forman, a friend of Einstein's. Forman plucked the three out of line, and ushered them into his chambers.

Einstein and Morgenstern had barely finished sighs of relief when something inspired Forman to observe that it was fortunate that the United States wasn't a dictatorship. It was the opening Gödel was looking for. Words sprang out like tigers from a cage. Judge Forman staggered. Einstein made eye contact. Forman recovered, nodded, cut Gödel short and force-marched him through the rest of the questions and answers.

The shock from the Gödel Effect could be remembered long after the idea that caused it. Apparently that's what happened this time. Nobody seems to know what Gödel's insight into the U.S. Constitution was. Too bad. It might be useful.

Brilliant innovators say baffling things. So do madmen. Gödel was both. Unless you were brighter than Gödel you couldn't know whether the madman or the genius was speaking. Even Einstein never thought he was that bright.

Except for Einstein, nobody was better at talking to Gödel than the young logician Hao Wang. Wang was urged to study philosophy with the reclusive genius, but Wang wanted to pursue his own work and talked to Gödel only off and on over the years. Gödel did not push his ideas, so the conversations followed Wang's interests. Time, for example, is a central concept in Gödel's philosophy, but Wang changed the subject whenever Gödel brought it up.

Wang had even less interest in the God Proof. He published a version in one of his books "for completeness," but he didn't claim to understand what he published. Afterward he discovered he'd copied it wrong.

In his later years, Wang realized he'd lost a priceless opportunity. Despite that, we owe Wang a lot. We know little of Gödel's philosophy. Without Hao Wang, we'd know almost nothing.

The philosophy is important. Gödel didn't do math for its own sake. Every proof had a point. Gödel was a philosopher who was too shy to publish philosophy. He spoke through proofs of beauty and power, or not at all.

From Wang's account of Gödel's philosophy, it's easy to see why he kept it to himself. It was like nothing taught in the philosophy departments. Gödel believed that knowledge does not come from observing the material world, that there's a meaning behind history, that intuition is essential and can be developed to be highly accurate, that's there's an afterlife, and that there are demons and other higher beings.

Every one of Gödel's major proofs is an attack on the "hard facts" world-view. To show that cause and effect do not take place in the physical world, his Time Travel Proof makes time run in circles. Gödel's Doubt Proof shows that we are correct in our beliefs only if we are unsure that we are correct. His Infinity Proof shows that even as mathematical an idea as the infinite is beyond the understanding of formal mathematics.

Gödel proofs all have the same "feel". They're like jokes just a little too clever to be funny. They're unexpected. They stay unexpected. They're hard to keep in your head. They don't sit easily next to the materialist beliefs we've come to accept as common sense. If they weren't proved beyond doubt, we would not believe them.

His greatest is the Freedom Proof. It's sometimes just called "Gödel's Theorem". Gödel was just twenty-four when he found it. Logicians agree that the Freedom Proof is the greatest logic proof of all time. But it's an argument for intuition, and against logic.

28 Liar Sentences

How do you prove God is possible? How do you even say "God is possible" in mathematical terms? If there was a way, Gödel could find it. Translating ordinary ideas into mathematics was his talent. That was how Gödel scored the Freedom Proof. He took a sentence that says "I am a lie" and translated it into math.

The Freedom Proof was the biggest surprise in the history of mathematics. Proofs are usually of things believed to be true. Rarely does a mathematician prove something generally believed to be false. Gödel's achievement is one of a kind. The Freedom Proof was something nobody had even suspected was possible.

Gödel showed that there were things that are true but can't be proved. In fact, he **proved** that there are true things that can't be proved. To mathematicians, it would have made more sense if Gödel had produced a talking cat. They might not have believed that cats can talk, but at least they could form a mental picture of a cat giving a math lecture. What a proof of unprovability might look like, nobody had any idea.

Nobody but Johnny von Neumann. Johnny von Neumann was a fast thinker, something not all geniuses are. He was stunned, but he saw Gödel was right.

Johnny later invented the first modern computer, and his architecture is still the basis of every computer made. Johnny also invented game theory, along with Oskar Morgenstern. I've mentioned Morgenstern as Gödel's friend.

Von Neumann explained the Freedom Proof to other mathematicians. Then they too were stunned. But they accepted it. A few checked. Most took Johnny's word.

For the Freedom Proof, Gödel took a liar sentence and rewrote it as a statement about numbers. A liar sentence is any sentence which says it is a lie. "This is a lie" is a liar sentence. Is a liar sentence true or false?

If a liar sentence is true, what it says is true. Well, what it says is "I'm a lie", so it's a lie. Which means it's false. So if it's true, then it's false. That's a contradiction, so a liar sentence can't be true.

Since a liar sentence can't be true, let's say it's false. That doesn't work either. If what it says is false, and what it says is "I'm a lie", then it's not a lie after all. Which means it's true. So if it's false, it's true. So a liar sentence can't be false either.

Liar sentences are contradictions. For sentences, that's not a problem. Sentences don't have to be either true or false. The sentence "A red dream gently scratches its back" is not particularly true or false. It's just nonsense.

But you can't say that well-formed statements about numbers are nonsense. "Two plus two equals three" is false. "Two plus two equals four" is true. All well-formed statements about numbers have to be true or false.

Proofs are like apples. One bad one and the whole barrel is gone. In math, from one contradiction, you can deduce every false thing. So if you could encode "this is a lie" into a statement about numbers and prove it either true or false, it would make doing mathematics the same as telling fishing stories. You might as well make up good stuff, because you'll be believed equally well no matter what you say.

People were sure math made sense, and did not have any contradictions. The numbers we use to count things are part of math, and we use them a lot. If there was a problem, we think we'd know by now. So nobody thought liar sentences were a problem for math. Because nobody thought you could turn a liar sentence into a well-formed sentence about numbers.

Until Gödel did it.

29 Case 2008 Opened

PG, Thursday

The tide had exposed Armenta's rock, but she was a no show. I wondered if I'd take the rap on Armenta, too. What is the penalty for killing a harbor seal? I pictured the police arriving. I would deny everything. I was imagining the police confronting me with a phone message full of incriminating snorts and barks, when the phone rang. It was Oka Ohoma.

"Josh. I'm surprised you're answering the phone, and not somewhere committing heinous crimes. Did I catch you on the way out?"

"Very funny. You know I always have time for your harassment. You've talked to the police, I take it?"

"Yes. They called. They didn't exactly give you a glowing character reference."

"Right. It looks like I'm the number one suspect, though they didn't say so."

"They didn't tell me that either. They did say if I have the choice of hanging out with you or Hannibal Lector, to play it safe and stick near Hannibal."

"So I guess our gig is off."

"Wrong as usual, my dim-witted friend. I have a soft spot for desperate, evil men, and anyway we were looking for a heinous evildoer to round out the team. Can you be here in the office, nine thirty, Monday morning?"

Oka and I worked out details. The police interview had been a disaster, but Oka needed me to search Lorraine's files, and to provide legal cover for entering her apartment. The only way the police could prevent Heavensent Security from hiring me was to arrest me. Oka was not going to tick the police off any more than he had to. He had promised them I would be heavily watched.

Between looking through Lorraine's computer accounts at Heavensent and searching her apartment, Oka figured I would be up there all day. I usually calculate case numbers based on the date, so they don't reveal how much business I'm getting. This time I didn't bother. The last case number

I'd issued was still fresh in my mind. I gave this case the next number: 2008.

30 No Proof, So It's True

The liar sentences Gödel discovered are questions about real problems in the daily life of ordinary people. Have you ever dealt with a software bug? A network outage? A computer virus? A system that was broken because of any of these? Then the Freedom Proof has been an issue in your life. Computer failures can kill people, and sometimes do. We may be talking theory here, but we're certainly not talking just theory. Even without getting to the issue of freedom.

Now, OK, you say, let's be real. You and I know one plus one is going to be two whether you can deduce it or not. We don't need proofs to know things about numbers. The Babylonians knew one plus one is two, and they never proved anything. They did math by trial and error.

But there's a difference between math by trial and error and math by proof and deduction. Trial and error is the way they figured out how to build fighter planes back in the 1950s, before they worked out the math for aerodynamics. Trial and error did the job, but they lost a lot of planes and a lot of the young men who were flying them.

At first glance, it seemed that math was back to the Babylonians and trial and error. Math by proof and deduction looked like a total loss.

The problem is this: if there is any contradiction in arithmetic, you can prove anything, whether it's true or false. If even one liar sentence is provable, you can prove that three ten-dollar bills are change for a twenty. You can prove that one ten-dollar bill is just as good. So are three one-dollar bills. And your geometry will prove that triangles and circles have four corners, just like squares.

Since a contradiction makes everything provable, all the true things would stay provable. Squares would still have four corners, and two ten-dollar bills would be correct change for a twenty. But even so, it was just no good. A math where false things are just as provable as true things might as well not bother with proofs.

Everybody agreed they needed a way of proving things that left some things true and others false. They had to find a way around the Freedom Proof. And they did. The top mathematician of the time, David Hilbert, got angry just hearing it. He could get as angry as he liked, for all the good it would do him. He didn't have a lot of choice.

Here's the way around: We know that a liar sentence must be true or false, but we don't prove it either way. We separate the idea of "truth" and "proof", so that the Liar Sentence which read "I am a lie" now reads "You can't prove I am a lie". If we don't prove the liar sentence is a lie, then it's true. That's how Gödel showed that something can **be true**, but be impossible to **prove true**.

The details of the proof were clever enough. Whole fields have grown out of them. But what's uncanny about Gödel is that before he put all those clever details together, he had to see the end result, an end result nobody else imagined.

As long as we don't prove that a liar sentence is true or false, it can't conflict with itself. It's not a contradiction until we prove that it is true or prove that it is false. The liar sentence is harmless as long as we stay wishy-washy.

Liar sentences are OK in math, **so long as there are no proofs for them**. It's safe for them to be true, just so long as you don't prove that they're true.

Which is why David Hilbert got mad. Ever since the Greeks, proving things was what mathematics was all about. Proving you couldn't prove things was turning things upside down.

31 The Freedom Proof

Especially irritating to folks like Hilbert was that liar sentences are not just things you can ignore. They are not all theoretical questions. Not by a long shot.

Why does software have to have bugs? Why can't you just check it completely? It turns out that "I am a bug-free computer program" is a liar sentence. It is one of things you can't prove. It's true or false, but you can't know which.

Why do you have to keep updating your virus checker when new viruses come out? Why can't your computer just check itself for viruses? The Freedom Proof strikes again. "I am virus free" is a liar sentence. You know every program either contains a virus or it doesn't. Which one of these is true, you can't always know. You're forever at the mercy of punks writing new viruses.

Liar sentences are things we want answers to every day. Answers we will never find. A computer cannot prove itself bug-free, which is a shame because bugs cost us a lot of money and trouble every year. Life support equipment runs on computer programs. Computers fly planes, and they have flown one full of tourists straight into a mountain.

○ ○ ○ ○ ○

None of this sounds very liberating. What makes Gödel's translation of the liar sentence into math a Freedom Proof?

Imagine the Freedom Proof was false, so that everything which was true, you could prove to be true. In that case, computers could self-test for bugs, and viruses could be reliably eliminated for all time. Complete, perfect, self-contained computers and networks of computers could be built. Dictatorships and bureaucracies would have no need for thinking individuals. One big, networked computer system could run our lives without outside input.

The Big Brother Network, powerful, complete, self-proving, flawless. Ultimate weapon of the bureaucracy. Big Brother could be sure his network was following his orders. His network could check itself. Nothing could stop the Big Brother Network.

If it is possible to build a Big Brother Network, we know eventually somebody will. We'd live in the knowledge that freedom was doomed.

But freedom is not doomed. Networks will always have problems they can't solve for themselves. They will always have a need for creative individuals, no matter how much the owners of the network wished individuals did not think for themselves.

The same freedom which means you can never snuff out the virus writer, means you can never stop the power of intuition. That's why it's a Freedom Proof.

Nobody expected there was a God Proof out there. Nobody thought there was a Freedom Proof until Gödel found one.

32 Poof!

By pinching the notebooks, Priscilla and Carrie had saved me embarrassment. I'd stretched the truth with Sue, letting her believe I knew a little of the Gabelsberger shorthand that Gödel has used in the notebooks. I expected to just grab a book about Gabelsberger and pick it up on the fly. It didn't work that way.

What I told Sue turned out not to be any ordinary, everyday lie, but a certified Grade A howler. In Gödel's German language schools, shorthand was a standard part of the curriculum. Everyone learned a shorthand. But it wasn't always Gabelsberger. A little civil war of the shorthands raged until 1926. In that year they made peace. Peace is more efficient than war, but the road to peace is not always the most efficient one. They settled the issue of who would have to change by forcing everyone to change. A third shorthand, equally unfamiliar to both sides, replaced them both.

After 1926, Gödel continued to use Gabelsberger. Of course. He'd been taught it in school. But there'd been no classes in Gabelsberger for twenty years when he wrote the God Proof notebooks.

I expected textbooks for a shorthand which has been obsolete for three or four generations might be hard to obtain. It was worse than that. I could discover only three texts on Gabelsberger anywhere in the U.S. All in the non-lending collections of research libraries on the East Coast. If I could talk the libraries into letting me near the books at all, I'd have to read them there. Maybe I could piece Gabelsberger together from books about the history of shorthand. I was glad I had a little while.

The meeting to prepare for the hearing before Judge Gaunilo was in the afternoon. I brought along some of my books that talked about what happened to Gödel's effects. They were a big hit. Mike copied pages from them. He'd know opposing counsel's story better than they did, and have the Einstein letter to spring on them. My upcoming trip to San Jose weighed on my spirits, but Sue and Mike were dancing on air.

"Damn if you haven't got me looking forward to these stupid notebooks," Mike said.

◇

"Once Josh gets a look inside them, you might have to become a believer," Sue chirped back.

Mike leaned back and waved his arms expansively. "Sue, you remind me of one of my professors in college. The man was a philosopher and for years he'd been trying to prove to his classes that he didn't exist. You know what happened to him."

"I think I'm about to hear," Sue said.

"Over the decades, his arguments got better and better. One day, there was a poof of smoke behind the lectern. Then silence. When the smoke cleared, he was gone."

"Were you in class that day?" Sue asked.

"I may have heard about it afterwards." Mike smiled. "But, seriously, reality is reality, and a proof won't change it. Those two notebooks won't make commerce come to a halt, buildings fall down, or airplanes plummet from the sky."

I wanted to jump in, but Sue spoke first. "A proof can't change physical reality. But it can change everything you believe about it. One hundred eighty or so disunited Spanish bandits conquered an empire of millions in Peru, because their arrival demolished the way the Incas looked at the world. The way of life of the Plains Indians ended when the buffalo was killed, not because they couldn't find another source of food, but because their view of the world was based on the buffalo as Master of the Hunt."

"Those were primal cultures," Mike said. "Advanced material culture, for all its defects and hypocrisy, does do things for people's understanding."

"Material facts don't change who we are. In this society, if everyone believes you are rich, you might as well be rich. In fact, you probably soon will be rich. And we know people for whom belief, or love, has ended. Their world ends with it."

Sue turned at me. "You've been very quiet," she said. "You must have something to say about this."

Something about Sue's look pushed what I had to say out of my mind. After a moment, it came back. "Mike, your examples were all physical things. They only apply if you insist God is a physical reality. That He's got to have a street address, or live on a mountain or in the sky. If you insist that anything real has to be physically real, you've defined God out of existence."

"Like the philosophy professor!" Sue said. She did a magician gesture with her hands. "Poof!"

"But reality is physical," Mike said.

"Then there's no justice or love?" I said.

"Constructs in the mind," Mike said. "At best. Spend a day in court."

I tried again. "And the court? It's just a pile of stone where guys with fictitious tags like judge and lawyer talk about things in their imagination, like law, precedent, etc."

Mike's eyes gleamed. "I take it back, maybe you have spent a day in court. Because that's not a bad description of it."

"And money is just an imaginary construct?" beamed Sue.

"Oh, Christ," Mike said. "Pecunia again."

33 The End of the Thousand Year Hmmm

Monterey, Friday

"Mike kids you a lot." The meeting had broken up and Sue and I were out on the sidewalk.

"Mike's a good friend. He's also gotten me out of more than one jam over the years. I'm glad to let him believe whatever he likes. Although his arguments against ..." Sue looked up Abrego Street.

"Arguments against?"

"Arguments against God. Mike's ideas are something I need to address for my readers." Sue's eyes were on a blue minivan coming down the street.

"Mike didn't make any arguments."

"You heard him." The minivan slowed, vainly looking for a parking space. "All the talk about God being a delusion."

"Yes, but I didn't hear any arguments."

"Well, OK, but he obviously meant science." The minivan passed us and double-parked.

"Sue, there aren't any scientific arguments against religion."

"Well, then why do ..." Sue stopped and looked me in the eye. Two cars maneuvered around the minivan. "Will you be in tomorrow afternoon?" Sue asked.

"Yes," I said. The woman driving the minivan tapped the horn.

Sue waved at her and stepped out into the street. "I'll call," she said over her shoulder.

I was back at my apartment before dark. No Armenta. In my neighborhood of summer residents and second homes, Armenta was the character everybody recognizes. She didn't do her marathon balancing act every day. Sometimes she got lazy and flopped herself over her haulout like a sack of grain hung over a fence.

But most days, there she was, perched on her highly visible rock like a cigar on a finger tip. When the Olympic torch went under my balcony, the announcer in the car behind the torchbearer noticed Armenta and commented on how well she exemplified the Olympic spirit. If Armenta was really gone for good, a lot of people would miss her.

I looked over the published sources for the proof again. The more familiar I was with these, the faster I'd make progress once I had the notebooks back. Reading them through doesn't take long. If you count every last scrap, the 1970 Scott version of the proof, the three versions Gödel kept in Princeton on loose sheets of paper, and the notebook entries from 1944 and 1954, we're talking maybe eight printed pages.

One of Gödel's loose sheet versions is very like the 1970 notes and may have been the one Scott copied. The other two are early drafts of the 1970 version, one dated "around 1941" and the other undated. It struck me as significant that all the copies of the proof that Gödel kept after his meeting with Eva Garten were on loose sheets. From 1947 on, Gödel could quickly destroy every trace of the God Proof in his possession without losing any of his other work.

Although the notebooks Gödel left in Princeton don't have any copies of the proof, there are helpful comments in two of them. A 1944 notebook has two pages with a few lines about God proofs in general. And while Gödel let Eva Garten take "Philosophy Notebook Thirteen" back to California with her, the next notebook in the philosophy series, number fourteen, was still in Princeton. Seven of its pages contained ideas related to the God Proof. Those pages were written in 1954.

This time through, I realized that these scraps of paper had already done something major. They didn't settle the issue of Anselm's Argument, but they nailed down what you had to believe if you were going to buy into it. Everyone seemed to have missed it, but the thousand year hmmm was over.

34 If Consistent, Then Possible

1078 to 1970

Not everybody who didn't like Anselm's Argument had been content to say "hmmm". Anselm, recall, had argued like this: "God is the Ultimate Reality. Can you imagine the Ultimate Reality not existing? Of course not. Therefore God exists."

Anselm himself was and is in high regard in the Church. In his lifetime, he was Archbishop of Canterbury. In 1494 they made him a Saint, and in 1720 they named him a "Doctor of the Church." That means he's one of thirty-three saints whose teachings are regarded as especially important. For all the respect Anselm gets, his Argument has always been regarded with a little suspicion. After all, if someone can prove God exists for himself, does he really need the Church?

The first real shot at a counterargument was the "Blessed Isle Argument". It makes fun of Anselm, but with very serious intent. "Imagine the best possible island, the Blessed Isle," is how it goes. "Surely existence is part of an island being the very best it can be. Therefore the Blessed Isle exists."

We've explored the world's oceans at this point and found no perfect islands yet. But even in the eleventh century, it was clear to the biggest landlubber in the monastery that you can't reason a Blessed Island into existence.

One thing to notice here. Like many criticisms of Anselm, the Blessed Island Counterargument sheds no light on what is wrong with Anselm's Argument. It just tries to show that something, somewhere doesn't work.

Math has developed a lot since the eleventh century and it has yet to find a problem in Anselm's Argument. In fact, the more we learn about logic, the better Anselm looks. It may be too early to declare Anselm's Argument an established fact, but for a thousand years gunslingers have been rolling into town and calling it out and it's still drinking at the saloon.

It's not clear when exactly, but sometime during or after 1944 Gödel found the secret of the Anselm quick draw. The Anselm Argument depends on a small set of assumptions. These were the four equations that I had recognized in both of the God Notebooks. The ones from the 1970 proof.

These four assumptions, or axioms as they call them, all boil down to one thing. For the Anselm Argument to work, the idea of God has to be consistent. God can't be required to be both beautiful and ugly at the same time. God can't be an oxymoron, like an "authentic replica", a "live recording" or a "new tradition".

With the discovery of the four axioms, Gödel showed why the Anselm Argument can work for God, without reasoning a Blessed Island into existence. The idea of a Blessed Island contains a contradiction, one which it doesn't share with the idea of God.

What if the idea of God contains no contradictions? Then a thousand years of wondering are over. The Anselm Argument is a win.

35 The Bad Way

I was worried about Lorraine, but worry was all I could do until Monday. I was glad to have the Gödel stuff to take my mind elsewhere. Friday night I worked on the proof into the early hours, and I set an alarm to wake me Saturday morning. With sleep to catch up on from Friday night, I hoped I'd be able to sleep Saturday night as well.

The alarm did get me out of bed, though my brain was slow to get going. While I waited, I rearranged my shelves. Every book or article that makes any kind of comment on the proof went onto a shelf near my desk. I had no trouble fitting them all. There are lots of books about Gödel but most ignore his God Proof. Even the ones on my shelf usually had only a page or two. All the relevant material would have fit into one slim volume.

It was strange that nobody, at least nobody I remembered reading, had remarked on the big step forward Gödel had taken with the Anselm argument. Even atheists should celebrate what Gödel did, if they really care to get to the bottom of the matter. If and when atheism refutes the Anselm Argument, it'll be because Gödel teased out Anselm's hidden assumptions. But ours is not an age that wants to prove God or disprove Him. We are uncomfortable with God and would like just to forget about Him.

The tide was falling, but Armenta's rock was still somewhere below the waves. I settled in for another look at the "Lost Notebook" equations. I spread them out to either side on the desk, laid volume 3 of Gödel's *Collected Works* in front of me, opened to the 1954 notes, and let my eyes and thoughts wander.

The few scholars who wrote about these notes hadn't made much of them. Toward the end, in four numbered paragraphs, Gödel talks about potential proof strategies. One of them is the one he uses in the 1970 notes. Which makes what he says about it, very strange. He calls it *der schlecte Weg*: "the bad way".

I went back to the lists of equations, trying again to make sense of the pattern. There definitely was one. My guess they were comprehension principles had proved wrong, but I still felt sure I knew that pattern from somewhere.

The phone rang. I tried to hold on to my thought. No use.

"This is Sue. Good time?" I'd forgotten. Sue had said she would call.

"Sure," I lied. "What's up?"

"Remember outside Mike's office? Scientific arguments against God? You said they're weren't any."

"Right."

"Why do so many people say there are? Why do so many people think belief in God is irrational and a weakness?"

"Emotional weakness, you mean? It's really the opposite. Science isn't equipped to be a religion. People turn it into one anyway out of insecurity. There are good arguments against God," I said, "but science has nothing to do with them."

"So what are you telling me? I should just say in my book that scientists are completely wrong about their own field?"

That was when I gave Sue the Self-verification Argument. It surprised her the way it surprises most people brought up on self-assured pronouncements from the "hard facts" crowd. The "hard facts" philosophy of life was dead on arrival and the specialists and any scientists who bother to study the philosophy of their own field have known that for a long time.

Sue wasn't buying. She wanted references. I remembered there's one article on the Self-verification Argument that's considered definitive. I promised Sue I'd find it. I asked her if I could have until Tuesday. I really wanted to get back to Gödel. Tuesday was fine with Sue. While I was on the phone pacing the room, I looked out the window. Armenta's rock was above tide now, but Armenta wasn't on it.

The Self-verification Argument demolishes a building that was ready to fall down on its own. The hard fact is that the "hard facts" viewpoint never was very good at describing what scientists do and think, never mind the rest of us. Science is mostly theory, held together by a very few observations of fact, and those usually made under a narrow range of conditions. No physicist has ever measured a measurable percentage of an electromagnetic field. Evolution has lots of fossil evidence, but even more missing links.

For a lot of scientific "facts", observation is not even possible. There weren't any instruments at the Big Bang, no cameras saw life emerge from the oceans, and thermometers at the Heat Death of the Universe ain't gonna happen. Life and the universe are born as pure theory and will die as pure theory. Facts are scattered exceptions along the way.

I went back to the pattern in the equations that was nagging me. On a hunch, I skimmed Gödel's *Collected Works*. That did the trick. I found the equations, exactly as I'd remembered them. They were in an 1958 article.

One big problem. The equations were game theory. You know. Games with moves, players, winning strategies, those kinds of game. The pattern might be the same, but it was coincidence. I'd hit another dead end.

At least my plan for a good night's sleep worked. I went to bed early and slept well. Her rock stayed above water until sunset, but I never saw Armenta.

36 The Valley of Heavenly Delight

PG, Sunday, January 13

Armenta's rock was underwater when I set out in the morning. Behind it forty miles of coast arced north to the city of Santa Cruz. After an hour of driving I was in Santa Cruz and exiting the coast highway to climb into the mountains on Route 17.

Officially, 17 is not a highway. The turns are tighter than the rules allow and the road is banked to dump you off as often as to keep you on. On the uphill side there's no shoulder, just a wall of rock. The other side has a narrow shoulder between the road and a reliably fatal drop, unobstructed by guard rails.

That makes Route 17 like a lot of other roads in the Western U.S., but it has something most of the others don't. A world class rush hour. Living in the Santa Cruz Mountains is an alternative for Silicon Valley workers. In California alternative living is not enforced, but it is expected. Frequent power interruptions, tree falls, landslides, and narrow roads halfway up cliffsides are things Californians will pay extra for. Real estate in the near wilderness of the Santa Cruz Mountains sells for big city prices. It's a land of expensive off road vehicles that spend most of the time stopped in traffic.

There's no rush hour Sunday and I was soon over the summit. The descent into Silicon Valley often stuns drivers hitting it for the first time. It's the scarp for the San Andreas Fault, and it is steep. The valley looks like a forest from above, if you dare take your eyes off the road to look at it.

Before World War II, it was called the Valley of Heavenly Delight. The mountains I was driving over block most of the rain. Then the main product was oranges.

After the war, the sunny climate attracted the defense industry. Technology followed. By 1961 Jack Kerouac, combining an alcohol binge with a return visit, could lament urbanization as an accomplished fact. "Citycitycity," he said. The liquor brought Kerouac the right word for everything before it killed him.

In 1971, the Valley of Heavenly Delight was renicknamed Silicon Valley. Twenty years later, I arrived. By then, imagining Silicon Valley as orange groves was like imagining Manhattan during the Ice Age.

I'd picked a hotel I knew, so it surprised me when I couldn't find it. I saw nothing but semidetached homes in close formation. I looked for the hotel, its berm, its lawn just wide enough for a couple of trees and a pylon sign. No sign of any of them. Did I take the wrong exit?

The third time around I spotted the temporary sign. It was in a thicket of others all pointing into the development of semidetacheds. Straight off the sidewalk, the driveway became an alley through fourplex canyons. If the front doors opened out they'd block traffic. Another temporary sign directed me into a side alley that snaked off to the left. At the end of it was my hotel. The hotel grounds were gone, every last blade of grass.

I could see nothing from the balcony of my room except freshly painted wood frame and windows with the sticker still on them. It wouldn't bother the developer to hear I didn't like his new places. I couldn't afford them. I closed the curtain and hauled out my laptop and some printouts.

I was pretty sure what I was going to send Sue, but I wanted to read it first. It was the 1950 article by Carl Hempel, twenty-two pages long. The Self-verification Argument is basically a one-liner. I was curious how Hempel was going to stretch it out.

Common sense is just philosophy that doesn't know where it came from. The Hard Facts Philosophy that many think is their own personal gem of innate wisdom has founders and started in a specific time and place: the meetings of the Vienna Circle in the 1920s and 1930s. Shelves groan under the books written about the philosophy of the Vienna Circle. Those books call it by several fancy names. "Logical Positivism" is the commonest.

The Hard Facts Philosophy maintains there are only two ways to determine truth. One is observation of the material world, and the other is logical deduction. The idea behind it was to take scientific methods and apply them to the rest of life.

Every philosophy responds to an emotional need. The Hard Facts Philosophy claims to be an exception, which makes it a good example. No scientist has ever worked or could ever work using the Hard Facts method, much less live their life by it, though many have claimed to do both.

The Hard Facts Philosophy has a basic, glaring flaw, one big enough to make it stand out as the big loser in any lineup of history's flimsiest philosophies. The Self-verification Argument. The Hard Facts method is not a hard fact. It does not verify itself. In fact, according to its own rules, it is wrong.

Look at its two rules for truth. Is the Hard Facts method an observed fact of the material world? It's a theory, and you can't see, hear, smell, taste or touch a theory, so clearly no. And you can't logically deduce it from material observations, either.

Carl Hempel had attended meetings of the Vienna Circle. I'd heard a lot about his 1950 article, but I'd never actually read it, and I didn't want to pass it on to Sue until I did. As it turned out, Hempel couldn't make the Self-verification Argument fill even four pages, so the rest of the article dealt with other problems with the Hard Facts Philosophy. Hempel certainly could pick and choose. For one, Gödel's Freedom Theorem demolishes the Hard Facts Philosophy. Math can't explain itself, and since science requires math as an explanation, science can't explain itself either.

But to refute the Hard Facts Philosophy, you don't need to get even that complicated. Why do science? There are reasons, but none of them are scientific. Science requires you to believe the world is comprehensible. Why believe that? There are reasons to, but not scientific ones. Why expect the laws of nature will hold five minutes from now? After all, we know what's true of the past is not always true of the future, and science doesn't tell you that it is. Science can't explain, justify or motivate itself. It certainly can never explain, justify or motivate us.

Science has no reason to pick a fight with God. If explaining science also gives people a reason to wake up in the morning, just what is wrong with that? Science never made us push God aside. Blaming science for our issues with God is like blaming the gloomy fourplex canyons that surrounded me on the guy who invented the hammer.

37 The Chickens of Pianosa

Sunnyvale, California, Monday, January 14

I sent my email to Sue in the morning, while waiting for room service. The hotel was four blocks from Heavensent. I walked.

In the lobby I told them I was expected. The guard called Oka's admin, gave me a temporary badge, and buzzed me in. At Oka's office door, I paused. A meeting was underway. But before I could sneak away to the break station to kill time, Oka spotted me. "Just our man! We're waiting for you. Come in, come in."

"I hope I'm not late. I had nine thirty. Is that right?"

"Yes, yes, my friend, but when you're expecting a desperado, people get overeager. This is Ross, he's been with me some time." Ross shook hands and smiled.

Oka pointed out a heavyset man in his fifties. "This is Gil, our most recent hire." Recent was the last thing Gil looked. He easily had ten years on Ross. Gil was angled into the far corner of the cramped room and didn't try to get up to shake hands. He didn't smile, either.

"So you guys remember what I told you," Oka said. "Watch Josh here close. Even check out the bathroom before you let him use it. I saw this movie once where the guy arranges to have a gun in the bathroom. Then he comes out and blows away everybody in the room."

Ross and Gil laughed. But later, in my old apartment, they checked in and behind the toilet tank exactly the way Oka suggested.

"You guys go and tell Krishna that our desperado will be over in a few minutes. I want to talk to him alone. I'm a super bad macho cowboy." Oka waved a large black garbage bag, one of the heavy ones with a yellow draw string. "If Josh tries just one thing funny, I'll bring you his pieces in this garbage bag."

Ross and Gil smirked and were off.

Oka changed tone once we were alone. "Josh," he said.

"Yo."

"Josh, I remember you and Lorraine together. If you were to confess now to murdering her, I still would not believe it. The police never knew you two, and are just trying to do their job. And we need the police if we are going to find Lorraine."

"I didn't do a very good job in talking to them," I said.

"I don't know what you could have said. But they have not settled on you as a murderer, and I keep telling them, they should look somewhere else. Be patient."

"Rely on it. I have no choice."

"You knew her best," Oka asked. "What do you think happened to her?"

"I think she decided to disappear. In San Jose women are not often snatched off the street without a trace, and Lorraine was smart and streetwise. Someone could kill her maybe, but with no noise, no witnesses, no physical traces, no known motive, nothing? Lorraine? Not likely."

"Too," Oka added, "she left only about $20K in cash."

"That's a lot of money on the side of the tracks I grew up on."

"It's enough to buy half of the island I grew up on. But Lorraine, you, and I are all a long way from where we grew up. Lorraine had exercised options worth over a million dollars. She was not a big spender and I don't think she lost it all in the market."

"So she threw away $20K to misdirect us?"

"Not even threw away. You are her heir. She might not mind giving you a gift. Unless she is pronounced dead, she can always come back for it. And even if she were pronounced dead, then popped up again, wouldn't you be good for the money?"

Time for a change of subject. "What's this about you retiring?" I asked.

"Yes. I'm retiring. You remember I have this name that even most people in Indonesia can't pronounce."

"Right." Certainly most Americans couldn't pronounce it. 'Oka Ohoma' was as close as they got, and being a practical guy, Oka went with it. These days he claimed not to remember what his name was originally.

"And because of it folks were always kidding me about Oklahoma. So maybe three years ago I took the wife and kids on vacation. Oklahoma turns out to be a wonderful place and the kids loved it."

"What's to do there?"

"Lots. You have to promise me you'll come visit."

"Come visit?"

"Yessiree, Josh. We've bought a big ranch just outside Sallisaw. The wife is visiting there now, doing stuff with the house. As soon as the kids are out of school, the whole family is moving."

"What are you going to do there? Just take it easy?"

"I've got a partner there and I'm going into the poultry business. You remember me talking about the Pianosa Bantam? The taste is quite different and my brothers and I have been trying to get it accepted in the premium chicken market. We have a plan, and now we need to raise enough poultry to supply our test markets."

Pianosa, somewhere in the Java Sea, was Oka's home island. It had been a sort of cruel paradise. Since prehistoric times two tribes shared this small island. "Sharing" meant the men taking every opportunity to kill each other and steal their women and chickens. The result over the generations was intelligent men of a cheerful fatalism, women who can make a man's blood boil in his veins with a giggle, and poultry whose genes are a valued part of every modern breed.

The finest fowl bred along the Java Sea was the Pianosan Bantam. The Pianosans had ranged up and down the islands, purchasing breeding stock from reasonable owners and taking stronger measures with the others. Pianosans refused to sell their own birds into flocks off their island well into Dutch times. Men were expected to earn their living through fishing or piracy. The literal translation of the Pianosan word for coward is "chicken seller".

"Evildoers all over the Internet will cheer when they hear you are leaving the business," I told Oka.

"Thank you, my friend. Now we should join Krishna, Gil and Ross. But first, this is a very big deal." Oka held up a two page document. "Legal insists you copy it out word for word and sign it. Lorraine was handling very sensitive stuff. You don't trade our stock, do you?"

"No. It's all gone."

"Great. Well, I don't mean great you sold, but it does make things easier. The guy in the office next door is in New Orleans. You can sit in his office while you copy this over."

I executed a signed holograph copy. In addition to the confidentiality language, it warned me that anything I said to Oka's crew could wind up used in court against me. All of it went without saying and I had no problem with the agreement. I returned and Oka checked my copy carefully against the original.

When he finished, Oka smiled. "If you promise to behave, I'll leave the bag here." He held the garbage bag up by the drawstring. I threw up my hands in submission. He stuffed the bag into a bookshelf and we were off.

Krishna's setup for going through Lorraine's files was convenient. I had worried it would be one of those awkward arrangements where I gave instructions and another guy typed on the keyboard. Instead, Krishna had arranged for me to have my keystrokes captured, leaving a record of everything I typed. I was working with copies. Any alteration or destruction I made would have no effect, except to show what I was trying to hide.

I could guess why the big deal about the nondisclosure. Not a day went by when Lorraine did not get an email from several of Heavensent's CXO's. Every week she would have at least one exchange with everyone above the VP level. Before I left, Lorraine was busy. After, she must have done meetings all day and email all night.

A lot of the traffic would be quite useful in making money on stocks. In particular, there was extensive discussion of companies that Heavensent might buy. As far as anything explaining Lorraine's disappearance, I came up blank. The CFO was strident in his objections to some of her sales projections. But I didn't think that would drive him to murder.

We had lunch in the Heavensent Cafeteria. I tried to participate in the conversation, but my thoughts were elsewhere. I ate in silence while the others talked.

38 Logic in the Way

Vienna, Austria, 1926–1930

As a student, Gödel was almost normal. True, he was the life of no parties, but he had friends, went to coffee houses, attended lectures and meetings, and was popular enough with women to attract some catty remarks.

He was quiet. When he did speak, it was concise, incisive and usually about mathematics. Those who asked him for advice found him willing to help and knowledgeable. That he was very bright was obvious.

While Gödel was a student, the Vienna Circle was in its full glory, hammering out the Hard Facts Philosophy at a gathering every Thursday evening. Gödel attended many of them. In later years, Gödel was often said to be a founding member of the Hard Facts Philosophy, much to his chagrin. He held many of the people in the Circle in high regard, but he had no use at all for their philosophy.

Vienna had a lot of intellectual gatherings, but the Vienna Circle was the most prestigious. It was not easy to join. Karl Popper, later to be a famous philosopher, tried to get invited but could not. The philosopher Wittgenstein disliked Popper. Moritz Schlick worshiped Wittgenstein and Schlick was the leader of the Vienna Circle. Wittgenstein was able to keep anyone he didn't like out of it. Wittgenstein himself never bothered to show up.

Gödel thought Wittgenstein was arrogant and ignorant, but he kept quiet about it. Gödel had been introduced by his advisor, Hans Hahn, a Circle member in high standing. The Circle considered Gödel an asset. Even while a student, he was clearly their best logician.

The Hard Facts Philosophy recognized both mathematics and experience as sources of knowledge, but it by no means held them in equal affection. Logic was suspect, tolerated only because there was no way to eliminate it from science. Logic dealt in assumptions, and "assumption" is just a fancy word for something taken on faith. Worse, with logic and math, you could sneak an argument for God back into science. Why is it all these beautiful equations work out so well?

Come down to it, logic was the wooden horse left at the door and the

Trojans of the Vienna Circle knew it. As Hans Hahn put it, logic seemed "to stand in the way." But there's no science without math, and the Hard Facts Philosophy aspired to be the philosophy of science. They had no choice but to wheel the horse inside.

The Vienna Circle had a plan to deal with logic, a plan blessed by their high priest Wittgenstein. Wittgenstein pointed out that it is an observed fact that people use language, and that languages have rules, syntax, grammar, all that. Well, the Hard Facts Philosophy said, math was just one set of rules for language. Just that and nothing more. Concepts in math had no reality of their own. The Vienna Circle assumed Gödel was working out the details to show this.

But by 1929 Gödel knew the details didn't work out the way Wittgenstein or the Circle thought. Quite the opposite. The Freedom Proof would show Wittgenstein's explanation was totally wrong. Math's own rules don't describe all its truths. Truth, even in mathematics, doesn't follow rules. True concepts are their own reality.

Gödel doesn't seem to have explained any of this to Hans Hahn. The conference where Hahn had complained that logic "stood in the way" was the one where Gödel announced the Freedom Proof.

39 Fare Well Arms

Fare Well Arms was as I remembered it. What little personality it had was pleasant. Similar apartment complexes ran for miles on both sides of the avenue. Three stories. Stucco painted a light pastel. Balconies outside sliding glass doors. The better managed were able to keep tenants from using the balconies for storage. The more pretentious had a fountain. At Fare Well Arms, palm trees partially hid the exterior.

I still had two sets of keys. Outside the landlord's office, after we signed the rental papers, Lorraine had laughed and tossed hers to me. Just in case, Oka had arranged for a locksmith to meet us there. Until he knew more, Oka preferred not to involve the apartment management.

We had no trouble finding the locksmith. He was parked right in front of the glass doors to the main lobby. His skill and speed at changing locks were trumpeted by large red letters on his side panel. We killed some time while Oka persuaded him to give up this prime spot for one out of sight. Then I led the group down a palm-lined walk toward the glass doors of the front entrance.

Halfway there, I saw Mrs. O'Brien on her cane. A little slowing of our pace allowed us to take the door and hold it for her just as she was opening it.

"Hi, Josh. Forget your key?" Mrs. O'Brien was one of those retirees who are mixed blessings as neighbors. I prefer them. My doings tend to bore the daylights out of even the Mrs. O'Brien's of the world. If I were ever robbed I'd expect her to have full descriptions of the burglars. But our proceedings today were a little too dubious for me to feel glad about running into her.

"No, I have it." I flashed the key I had intended to try.

"You're that boy who was living with Lorraine, aren't you?"

"Yes, ma'am. I'm Josh Bryant."

"Haven't seen you around much. What are you doing with all these folks?" Had she caught the Keystone Cops routine with the locksmith truck?

"Please keep this quiet, but we are starting a software company."

Her eyes narrowed. "I lost a bundle on one of those."

105

"Really? Which one?"

"Vaportouch. My broker gave me this glowing story, and they were gone within the year."

"You don't say. Mr. Ohoma, wasn't that one of yours?"

Oka walked in and started to explain to Mrs. O'Brien how he had Exercised Due Diligence, Conformed to Generally Recognized Accounting Standards, and Fulfilled his Fiduciary Responsibility while throwing her money away. The rest of us followed. In the lobby we split into the lazy and the claustrophobic. The lazy took the elevator. The others followed me up the stairs.

We reunited in front of the apartment. The clean off-white walls still had the same engravings. Big tropical flowers very much preoccupied with their sex lives. I fumbled with my key and my memories. My betrayal of Oka into Mrs. O'Brien's hands was a quiet satisfaction, but it left me reentering the scene of my happiest hours in front of a crowd of strangers, bored and waiting on me to get started with their jobs.

I looked in. A fine dew had condensed out of the chill air. Lorraine had left the heat off, and the police had not put it back on when they did their search. I stepped back and let the photographer by. The rest of us remained in the hall. Oka had set a strict procedure. The place would be entered in stages. The photographer was first. Gil, Ross and I were last. Me because I wasn't trusted. Gil and Ross because they had to watch me.

We kept silent in the hall. I had warned them that the soundproofing in these apartments had skimped on the halls. Any conversation there would be heard behind the neighbor's closed doors as if we were in their living rooms.

Oka's team was fast. We were soon cleared to enter the living room. I stepped into the entry. To the right, a hinged passage door led to the two bedrooms Lorraine and I had used as offices. Ahead of me, through the sliding doorway, I saw two of Oka's people searching the kitchen. Behind them was the dining area. I went through an archway to the left.

Against the far wall of the living room was one of Lorraine's wing chairs. Its arms were covered with yellow fingerprint dust, but I resigned myself. Gil and Ross watched me sit down, and moved into the dining area. It opened off of the living room and they could keep an eye on me from there.

There was lots of light. Oka's ops had opened the sliding glass doors to get to the balcony. There was no dirt, and no dust except the stuff laid down when they were looking for fingerprints. It was like a well-staged model apartment. It suggested possibilities, but didn't give you the feeling there was anyone to mind if you moved right in.

I didn't see a tree or presents. Not even a red ribbon. Lorraine was supposed to have landed the night before Christmas Eve. My eyes felt moist. I turned so Gil and Ross couldn't see and ended up facing into the built-in bookshelves.

My shelf was still empty. I'd taken my books when I moved out. Three books lay flat on the other one. I got up to look. On top was Ocean's *Journeys of Marpa*. The book Lorraine had mentioned in that last, strange conversation. I flipped through, then put it back. The next one down was a book on "sex magic" that I remembered Lorraine reading.

I didn't recognize the third book. It was small and thin and had a title on the cover in German which I found hard to make out. I opened to the title page and nearly dropped the thing. Gabelsberger. A textbook on it. Berlin, 1920. The book I'd been trying to get and couldn't find.

Why was it here? Lorraine spoke Spanish like a native and Tibetan pretty well, but I don't think she could read either one, and I was pretty sure that she didn't know a word of German. Whoever this book came from, they at least knew something about the notebooks and their history. The CTS? With the original MD's gone, the CTS wasn't all that scholarly.

The folks at Bhadrachakra, now they were scholarly. And they might have a grudge.

40 Ocean of Awareness

The Bhadrachakra, 1975–1985

In the early days at the Bhadrachakra, there were power struggles. At this point being a Bhadra Scholar is more than respectable, it's positively prestigious. Most of the academics accepting Bhadra Fellowships wouldn't have a clue who Lorraine was, even though she started the program, but those in the leadership at the Bhadrachakra should remember her. She hired most of them.

Bhadra and Lorraine had met in the circus. Lorraine was proud of her circus past and didn't hide the fact the current incarnation of Ocean of Awareness once performed under the name Lorraine Dark. But Bhadra didn't want his followers knowing about the days when he went around the country faking levitation.

Bhadra was Tibetan, but he was not a lama, and nobody had ever empowered him to teach. He'd been a hanger on at an ashram in the States until he found himself unwelcome. After a series of odd jobs, he landed in the circus.

Why they had booted Bhadra out of the ashram, even Lorraine didn't know, but subsequent history provides plenty of good guesses. "I see now that there was a lot to criticize in Bhadra," Lorraine told me once. "I became his lover very young. But he only did with me what others did, and lots more wanted to. With important differences. He regarded sex as sacred. He taught me to think of myself as a goddess. He was a scoundrel, and he took from me. But he gave back to me, like nobody else did. I owe that scoundrel so much."

Lorraine pushed Bhadra to give his first public talks. When these were a big hit, she helped him write pamphlets, including the one with the footnote on karmamudra that started it all. In the footnote, Bhadra mentions that a secret tradition of sacred sex once played a major role in the history of his lineage. He doesn't actually say he had been taught that tradition or even that it continues down to the present day. This gentlest of hints wafted into our sex-crazed society like a fresh breeze hitting liquid hydrogen.

Remembering back, Lorraine gave things a positive spin. "Suppose all the time men spent thinking about sex were turned into prayer. The world would turn into heaven on a dime. Harnessing even a tiny fraction of this energy would improve the world so much we wouldn't recognize it."

As a theory that's solid. Execution is another thing. "We drew a lot of strange energy," Lorraine admitted. "And a lot of strange people."

Bhadra didn't name the Tibetan Buddhist lineage he was speaking for. He didn't belong any of them. That aside, what he claimed was generally true. Tantra is pretty much a synonym for sex in the Western world, so most people here don't realize Tibetan Buddhism is Tantric Buddhism. A lot of Tantrics are celibate. The Dalai Lama is a Tantric.

If you go back to the founders of Tibetan Buddhism, karmamudra played a big role. The histories make it clear that they are not talking about symbolic acts, either. Almost all of the early leaders of Tibetan Buddhism practiced karmamudra. One text goes so far as to say you can't gain liberation without it. Another claims that the founder, Lotus Born, had karmamudra on an industrial scale. Seventy thousand consorts. Whew.

No female saint went for this record. But Ocean of Awareness and Machik Lapdron, two of the most important, yielded to no man in the importance they placed on karmamudra.

"Ocean and Machik became Sky Dancers in one lifetime," Lorraine told me. "To a Sky Dancer, the true self of all men is her lover. This is a matter of identification with the goddess. It was not having sex with every man they saw. Though they certainly did have lots of sex."

What about all the celibate Tantrics? That's perfectly consistent with tantra. Tantra is about bringing spirituality into all of life. The way the Western mind works, we hear that and ask "Does all of life include sex?" Well, yes, they say. "Aha!" we respond. "So Tantra is all about sex!"

Saying Tantra is all about sex is like saying the Catholic Church is all about music. It's not. That's just false. That said, you can hear a lot of really fine music in Catholic churches.

Lorraine certainly heard sweet sounds still. "Karmamudra is the easy way. With a consort, you don't have to visualize the ultimate bliss. You open yourself up to her and she creates the experience for you." Orchestrating all the karmamudra in the Bhadrachakra took quite a conductor. Bhadra was exposed to a lot of temptations. He succumbed to as many of them as he could.

"I didn't think Bhadra was deceiving me at the time," Lorraine told me. "I know that sounds impossibly stupid. But I loved Bhadra, and believed in what we were doing and in what we taught."

Women in the Bhadrachakra envied Lorraine's place as Bhadra's consort.

With hindsight, Lorraine realized Bhadra played many of them along. A few of the women made an open play to supplant Lorraine. They wound up out the door. Others cultivated Bhadra more discretely and awaited their day.

That day came when the other women were willing to do something for Bhadra that Lorraine couldn't. Rumors about Bhadra's sex life weren't his biggest problem. His biggest problem was his drinking. Even in the circus, that was often out of control, but the success of the Bhadrachakra made it worse. Bhadra's other followers helped Bhadra hide his frequent binges. They wanted to have others think that they were close to a great teacher of the Diamond Vehicle. They wanted to believe it themselves.

After a decade, Lorraine saw that the man she loved was killing himself and that if she stayed all she could do was watch. She left in 1985. Several years followed during which the Bhadrachakra became known for its wild parties. These ended when Bhadra's health collapsed. The Bhadrachakra was secretive about exactly when that happened, but certainly by 1990 Bhadra's partying days were over. He died in 1992.

The evil Bhadra did seems to have died with him. It turned out that the Bhadrachakra's leadership, although it had a blind spot about Bhadra, was capable and dedicated. While he was alive, Bhadra's shenanigans had drawn attention away from the Bhadrachakra's steady output of monographs, fellowships and critical editions. After his death, the work went on and the quieter pursuits moved to center stage.

Lorraine never considered going back. The senior leadership at the Bhadrachakra were people who'd been Lorraine's rivals for Bhadra's attention, and most of them had been happy to see her go. Later recruits were drawn by its academic respectability and would be turned off by reminders of the scandalous early days.

Lorraine continued to carry the torch for karmamudra. "I don't understand people's problem with sacred sex," she told me. "To say you are against sacred sex is to say you want empty physical coupling. What's so moral about that? All of our lives should be devoted to God. God didn't create sex to be an exception to that.

"Every society that decides that it's too morally pure for sex is violent. And societies that decide women need to be protected from sex usually decide they don't need protection from much of anything else, unless it's something that would give them a voice in their lives. Societies that don't revere sex, don't respect women. Societies that don't respect women are violent. The choice is tantra or violence.

"Tantra is about the goddess in every woman. She has the ability and desire to bring joy and peace to every man she sees. But men cherish their misery and anger. They take pride in it. In their foolishness, they see the openness of the goddess, and they call it promiscuity, and her a slut.

"The Goddess is eager to unite with all men. Accepting that all-embracing love is the only way to end suffering. Men who speak of 'whores' or 'sluts' are hiding, keeping alive their own suffering by holding love in contempt."

I once suggested to Lorraine the problem might be taking karmamudra into a society which is not ready for it. "What do you think I did when I was Ocean?" she answered. "Tibet was a lot less safe for women than the modern United States. Ocean traveled alone a lot, and on one occasion was caught by bandits who intended to rape her. She turned this into their empowerment. They turned their lives around, gave up banditry. Eventually the bandits became teachers, beloved by their students.

"This is not something an ordinary woman could do. Ocean was one of the great karmamudras of all time. She was fully in control in any situation. I couldn't do that in this life. My purposes in this incarnation are not served by that kind of power.

"You have no choice but to mix sex and religion, if you want real religion. The draw sex has is not just physical. It's not even mainly physical. Suppress it and it comes back stronger than ever. Religions which reject sex promise to provide a meaning to replace it. But people don't want meaning. They want experience."

○ ○ ○ ○ ○

Once Lorraine and I moved on to Heavensent, some of her organizational smarts rubbed off on me. I got kicked up a rank. With her resume problems behind her, Lorraine was able to move out of project management and into publicity, the job she really wanted. Heavensent put her in front of the camera for the first time and a discovery was made.

Stick Lorraine between the weather blonde and a commercial, and deft, on-message sentences flowed in perfect sync with the allotted time. Give her three minutes and she'd have everyone who'd wandered near a television at the time wondering how they managed to live without Heavensent Systems. Lorraine started to be visible. She became visible enough that some people back at Bhadrachakra might have noticed her.

Lorraine and I had assumed that folks at the Bhadrachakra had no interest in old grudges. Had we thought too soon? Did they think her TV appearances made her a threat to their jobs or their newly august image?

And then there were the women who'd had a moment in Bhadra's arms where they thought they'd found it all, spiritually and emotionally, and then had it yanked away. Did a few years erase the betrayal they'd felt?

41 Gabelsberger

Whoever had put the Gabelsberger book on my bookshelf, I needed it. I didn't expect a problem from Oka and his crew.

I heard a knock at the door. We'd closed it. You never value your privacy more than when you're invading someone else's. Nearest the door, I went to check the peephole. It was Oka, somehow released by Mrs. O'Brien.

I let Oka in and held the book up in front of him. "I'm going to take this with me, unless there's a problem."

Oka's reaction was not what I expected. "I am not sure," he said, then called Gil and Ross over. Maybe he was peeved at me because I sicced Mrs. O'Brien on him.

Gil, the new guy, was sure. "He shouldn't take anything", he said to Oka.

"I'd be glad to let you look at it first." I didn't see why I needed to allow them to do anything, but it pays to be agreeable.

My gesture did not impress Gil. "It stays here." He spoke like he was giving an order, an order to Oka and Ross as much as to me.

This was getting ridiculous. Oka was a paying client and deference was appropriate, especially in front of Gil and Ross. But a one day gig requiring 150 miles of unpaid travel was more trouble than it was worth. I was here because of Lorraine. Oka knew it and it didn't matter whether Gil ever figured it out. If this crew had any legal right to be here, it was as my guests. If Gil was insubordinate, I sympathized with Oka's situation, but I wanted the book.

I stared at Oka. If Oka could not settle the matter, I could call the police and throw them out. Once alone in the apartment, I could take the book or anything else I liked. But anything I said would narrow Oka's options. I kept my mouth shut.

"Come, let's talk." Oka waved Ross and Gil into a far corner. I settled back with my book into the wing chair, like a child eager to show good behavior. Oka had not been this big on consensus before. He relied more on management techniques found tried and true on the pirate ships of the Java Sea. Perhaps impending retirement was making him soft.

They kept their voices down. I did not make out the words, but I could hear Gil growl. If this was what he was like as a rookie, imagine him with some experience under his belt. They conferred so long I had time to skim the book and get a feel for Gabelsberger.

When Oka came back, he had one of the techs with him. "Give Ethan the book," Oka said. "You'll have it again before you leave." Throwing the bunch of them out would have been more entertaining, but Oka was a pal, and a good contact.

As far as I know, Ethan didn't even look at the title. He waited until Gil seemed distracted and quietly handed it back to me. Ethan had put it in an evidence bag, which was useful. I smiled a quiet thanks, just as another growl came from Gil.

Gil stalked across the room without looking at us. Ethan and I exchanged a worried glance. Gil button-holed Oka in the dining area. Oka's face showed that whatever Gil had to say was finding a ready ear this time.

Ethan slipped back to Lorraine's office. Ben Franklin warned his country-men that those who don't hang together, hang separately. What Ben ignored, and Ethan knew, is that hangmen are as fallible and lazy as the rest of us. In the process of gathering people, they often miss a few of the minor players.

Gil and Oka drew team members aside, and conferred with them one at a time. Krishna and Ross returned to their tasks, but Ethan and the others went out the door without looking at me. If this was still about the shorthand book, the going was getting really strange.

Then Gil and Oka went out of apartment together, also without a glance at me. Ross was with me in the living room. Krishna was busy in Lorraine's office.

Ross looked around furtively. He walked over. "I know this sounds weird," he said, "but just look over into the entry." I clutched the Gabelsberger book tight inside its bag. "Humor me, just for a second," Ross said.

I did as directed. "Keep looking there," Ross said. "I'm going to walk over to that hall. When I get there, you come over and then I'll explain."

He crossed the entry, glanced back, and waved me in. Maybe it was some-thing about the apartment. First Lorraine goes wacko, next Gil, now Ross. I did as I was told. When I was around the hall corner, Ross said, "Don't look out any window. Gil spotted someone watching us with binoculars from the Spencer House. If I told you that in the living room, your automatic reaction is what?"

"Look out the window."

"Right, and our spy knows we are on to them. Oka and most of the guys are trying to catch him. We're bringing in the police."

"Is there a crime?"

"We're calling it trespass until we know who he is and how he reacts to a few questions," Ross said. "Look, the place is pretty much checked out, except Krishna is finishing up in the computer room. Just stay away from the windows until I get the clearance from Oka. They should drop the hammer on our spy in a bit, and then you can do anything you want. Except don't mug Krishna."

My old office was a good start. It had no windows at all. Lorraine and I had worked at home a lot. When we had to choose offices, she offered me the larger room, with the windows. But Lorraine's job was as important as mine. Her title outranked mine, not that that means much in Silicon Valley, especially when comparing techie to non-techie.

I had counteroffered. It was a serious corporate matter. We should do it in a typically screwed-up corporate way. Whoever was paid more got the big corner office with the windows. Lorraine and I put pay stubs on the kitchen table face down, faced each other like gunfighters, and flipped them over. She won, narrowly. And fortunately. Her title, duties and pay shot through the roof almost immediately thereafter. Practical considerations would have forced an embarrassing switch back if I had won.

My old office was almost as empty as I'd left it. A cardboard box had papers belonging to a project Lorraine either finished or never got to. Another box looked destined for charity, as did the few clothes in the closet. Some birthday wrapping paper leaned in the corner. Gift for a coworker, probably.

I was not doing a real search. The police and Oka's team had already done professional searches. Oka had asked me to wander through. Since I had lived there with Lorraine, something might strike me.

Keeping away from the window, I went back to the kitchen. Cooking had never been a big part of our lives. The kitchen things were clean and put away. There wasn't much inside the refrigerator. I made a big show of opening cabinets and checking inside them. I didn't want to rush Ross.

My office and bookshelves gaped like open wounds. But in the master bedroom, my side of the walk-in closet had filled in with Lorraine's clothes as if I'd never existed. The healing was just as complete in both bathroom cabinets. I asked Ross if I could go near the windows.

"Check out the computer room," he said. "Tell Krishna I said it's alright. I'll check out what's going on with our spy."

Ross whipped out a cellphone. I joined Krishna. I'd been, in effect, Lorraine's on-site technical support. Her office was very familiar ground for me. Rather than check stuff in the apartment, Krishna was copying disks for detailed inspection back at Heavensent's offices. He asked me to double check a box of CD's and floppies he felt he could safely skip. He was right, he could.

In the dining area, Ross had finished up. "I talked with Oka. He said five minutes and you can go out on the balcony with semaphore flags if you want."

Checking in with Ross had already shown me most of what there was to see in the front of the living/dining area. I counted down the time in the wing chair. Then I entered the master bedroom, crossed it to the glass doors, slid them open, and walked out onto the balcony.

I went back in to open bedroom drawers. I had not asked about another boyfriend. I certainly had to believe that possible. The police seemed to focus on me. Maybe the other guy had a solid alibi.

I soon finished and plopped into a folding chair on the balcony. It faced the Spencer House, a big tourist attraction. I watched visitors wander its eastern grounds.

If there was another guy, he left no trace. Maybe they spent their time at his place. The bed had been stripped, probably by the police, and the sheets taken away. I would expect Lorraine put laundered sheets on the bed before leaving on a week-long trip, but you never knew.

Across the street at the Spencer House, a small figure in a hooded sweatshirt and jeans opened a door on the wall of seventh floor of Fortitude Tower. Was it a woman?

The door was off limits. I knew that from having lived across the street. It wouldn't have been hard to guess. That door opened onto thin air. Beyond the threshold, there's no balcony, no landing, nothing. A step forward means a fall of seventy feet.

The figure leaned out and grabbed a drainpipe. Without testing, she put her weight on it. One of the brackets holding it to the wall pulled loose and fell. The pipe leaned her back to look up at the sky.

Of the views available to her, the Hooded Marvel might prefer the one of the clouds. The drop behind her was nasty. She looped her arms and thighs around the pipe and shimmied back toward the wall. The pipe bowed under her weight until her knees were higher than her head.

Wood snapped, loud enough to hear across the six lanes of traffic. A second bracket bent out the board it was attached to. It must have been well nailed. Had this bracket pulled loose like the first, Hooded Marvel would have been dumped head first, most likely to her death.

She was in no comfortable position as it was. Upside-down, she started to slip. She clenched legs and arms and stopped sliding. She tried to shimmy, fighting gravity.

I ran across and called to Ross. He joined me on the balcony. Hooded Marvel had barely moved. A small crowd assembled below her. Ross punched at his cellphone.

Hooded Marvel's legs let go. "Oh, my God," I said. Ross stopped dialing and looked up. Hooded Marvel flipped herself around. The pipe swayed. Something creaked. She kept her grip.

Hooded Marvel reclasped the pipe between her thighs. Ross started dialing again. Turning around had taken her almost to the end of the pipe, but she was now right side up. Seven pulls of her arms brought her to the high point of the arched pipe. Ahead of her, it curved back down to the building.

Hooded Marvel repeated the flip she'd just performed, this time with a half turn. This move was tricky, but again it paid off. When she wrapped her thighs back around the pipe she was right side up and in excellent position to descend.

Nearing the wall, Hooded Marvel got overeager. An especially violent jerk of her legs jarred the third bracket completely out, nails and all. It fell to the ground. The pipe swayed. She stopped. With the third bracket gone, the second couldn't hold. It broke off and fell. She held tight. Beside me, Ross had connected on the cellphone. He tried to describe events to Mr. OK.

The pipe leaned Hooded Marvel back another twenty degrees. The fourth bracket groaned, but held. Very slowly, Hooded Marvel started to inch down. Nothing broke. She didn't speed up again until she reached a section of pipe still firmly bracketed to the wall.

Four seconds later she was on the ground and headed for the wall. Avoiding the crowd forced her to duck under the drainpipe, which was bobbing over the lawn like a giraffe looking for low forage. So far, no autograph seekers and no security. I wondered which would be first.

At the ten foot high brick wall, Hooded Marvel paused. Covered with ivy but topped with barbed wire, it was conflicted about its role. Hooded Marvel ran along it, then went out of view for several seconds. "Where is she?" Ross asked.

"Dunno." Not having to deal with the cellphone, I could track her through crowd reaction, but her last move was making them drop their arms and gape.

Hooded Marvel shouldered herself to the top of the wall. "There!" I said. Careful moves took her to the other side of the barbed wire. She poised to jump, then paused. Below her was a San Jose police officer talking to someone in plain clothes.

Ross yelled "Hey" and pointed. I didn't think his voice could carry across the traffic. But the plainclothes guy noticed Ross. One of the Spencer House staff, he knew that all the fuss somehow related to our apartment across the street. He and the officer turned and looked toward us.

The Hooded Marvel did not wait for a second break. She landed behind them, darted around the corner, and was gone.

42 Karmamudra

"Aren't you ever going to ask me about karmamudra?" Lorraine said.

This was several months after we'd become lovers. No, I wasn't going to ask. Not that I didn't wonder. When, back in St. Louis, Lorraine had told me that she was the Lorraine Dark aka Ocean who'd cofounded the notorious Bhadrachakra, the news came as quite a surprise. Lorraine had been concerned about how I'd take it.

Bottom line for me was that it didn't change anything and I liked it best when Lorraine was happy. Questions were not going to make her happy, or for that matter get me much in the way of answers either. What Lorraine wanted to tell me, she would, when she was ready.

I said "When do we start?"

She laughed. "Let me tell you a story."

"A story."

"Yes," she said. "The Story of Ocean of Awareness."

Once upon a time Tibet had many kingdoms. One day in the kingdom of Karchen, the king was making love with his queen. As she closed her eyes to receive him, she saw a golden bee come from the west. The hum of its flight was like music. On top of the king's head was a wheel of light. The bee flew into it.

"You're whispering," I told her.

"Then come closer."

On the forehead of the beauty below him, above her two passion closed eyes, the king saw a third, open and unblinking. Outside the castle, people swore they heard thunder, felt the earth move, and saw lightning. The spring at the foot of the castle wall gushed, and spread into a lake.

"Quite a start."

"The real fireworks are coming."

Nine months later, I was born.

"You?"

"Me. Ocean."

Because a lake had formed at my conception, they named me Ocean. Even very young, I was beautiful. So beautiful my father thought that, whoever he gave me to in marriage, others would make war. Father hid me away, but word of my beauty leaked out. The kings of two nearby kingdoms learned of me. When I was thirteen, both insisted on having me. And, as my father had feared, both were willing to go to war.

"Meanwhile you'd fallen in love with a poor potter?" I suggested.

"No. To marry me he would have to be an excellent potter, and a Buddhist as well. Don't let your mind wander," Lorraine said. "Yes. Here we go. Will that keep your attention?"

I felt air come out of my throat, but I don't know what sound it made.

"Much better," Lorraine said.

To prevent war, my father told me to choose one of the kings. I refused. Both of those kings hated Buddhism. I had a well-favored human body. A body like that is a precious opportunity.

"I'll say."

"Spiritual opportunity, twit."

I was going to achieve full liberation in a single lifetime. I would not give that up. Not to be a barbarian's queen.

Father was furious. He gave me an ultimatum. If I did not choose one of my suitors, I would be put out of the palace, the prize of whoever took me first. To join the chase, each king had only to promise to accept its outcome. I still refused. I was pushed outside the walls, alone and hunted. I fled, not knowing where.

King Zhonnu's men found me first. But I had already begun to develop magic powers. I sank myself into a boulder up to the waist, and denied him his trophy.

"Faced with magic, he had to give up, right?"

"No."

Men in those days were familiar with sorcery. From a desperate young girl of remarkable beauty, it was almost expected. King Zhonnu took up a branch, pulled off my clothes, and whipped me. I gave into the pain. I came out of the rock and he carried me off.

But that night in his camp, before he could take me to his tent, I prayed to the Buddhas of the ten directions. They fogged the senses of my captors and I fled to the mountains. I was near territory belonging to King Wongchuk, who had lost the hunt. Wongchuk sent men to scour the mountains for me.

King Zhonnu heard of this. He accused Wongchuk and my father of conspiring to cheat him. He prepared his kingdom for war. My father had done nothing to help me or Wongchuk. He told Zhonnu this and sent messengers to appeal to the Emperor.

Wongchuk's men soon captured me. They tied me over a horse and led it to his castle. But the Emperor's messengers got there first. The Emperor said that he would remove any king who broke the peace. And he ended the quarrels by taking me as one of his concubines.

The Emperor was old, and devoted to his first wife, who shared my love of Buddhism. I was able to study the scriptures and remained a virgin.

Even in the history of Tibet, that was a dark time. Bandits made human sacrifices of the people they robbed. In the capital, the temples were drenched in animal blood. The more the animal suffered while dying, the priests believed, the more it pleased the gods. People tried to forget their own pain by inflicting pain. The two kingdoms that had fought over me called this religion, and that was why I had no desire to be queen in either of them.

The great Buddhist teacher, Lotus Born, was the hope of this time. The Empress adored him. He was a favorite adviser of the Emperor, who offered him one of his kingdoms. Lotus Born wanted to do much in Tibet, but he would not accept a kingdom. He said that would not help. He asked the Emperor for a greater treasure, one of greater spiritual potential than any throne. One whose power would last longer and extend wider. One which had taken many lives to create. A treasure that could bring Buddhism to Tibet. A woman. Me.

"You?"

"Me. Ocean. We can stop if you're having trouble following."

"No, no, I get it."

"Really?"

"Really, I do."

"Good. I knew you would. You're as wise as my great Lotus Born."

The Emperor gave me to him as a gift. I was so happy. I was his kingdom. These feet and these hands were four continents. From my central mountain his castle would rise. I was still so young when I came to him, just sixteen. I felt very ready, but he made me wait. I needed to prepare for my empowerment.

"Empowerment?"

"The empowerment which would allow the energy inside me to unfold. And, yes, that on the physical level would make me a woman. Lotus Born had me do regular meditation, breathing exercises, yoga. Coincidentally, these are the same exercises I've been teaching you."

"Are there coincidences?"

"Yes, when there are meant to be. The exercises were to prepare my body for the energies that Lotus Born would release in my mandala."

"Mandala?"

"A Mandala is a circle. Within my circle are drawn gods, goddesses and all the energies of all the worlds. A well drawn mandala enfolds the cosmos tight."

"Careful or the world will end."

"You're my Precious Guru. You not only have control, you are control. You'll manage. I just know you will."

I grimaced. Lorraine-Ocean flowed on.

I was young. Through the good karma of many lives, I had earned birth in a well-favored body. The yoga had rapid effect on it. But even the few weeks needed for my training seemed forever. I thought I would die from longing. Lotus Born said not to fight the longing, but to take it as the object of meditation. Feel its intensity. Harness its energy.

Lorraine jumped up.

Two days before my empowerment, he didn't appear for my lessons.

Stunned with Lorraine's removal, I threw myself on my back and sucked in air. She spoke rapidly.

I went to his rooms. They were empty.

Lorraine threw on a light robe. I didn't try to catch her. Parts of the robe clung to her and soaked a deeper blue.

The ministers had heard that a virgin from the Imperial harem had been given to a common scholar. They said it broke tradition. They said it was a disgrace. They made a scandal. They forced the Emperor to exile Lotus Born to India. And I was told to pack for exile in the Lhotrak Valley. We would be several years journey apart.

Lorraine turned to me and smiled. She slowly settled back astride me. Her voice was soft.

Only a few days away from the palace, Lotus Born met my guards. It had all been just a show for those ministerial fatheads. He led me to the Cave called Sky Dancer Theater. Lotus Born told me that my empowerment would begin the moment I stepped inside. And it did. Soon he was showing me the first of the Four Joys.

"Four?"

"Four. Now, my love, it's important to remember these are inner, spiritual experiences. The physical is just a metaphor, a comparison with something we can understand to help us picture something we don't yet understand. You won't get attached to the physical sensations, will you?"

"Perish the thought."

"Good."

Lotus Born showed me the First Joy, Pristine Awareness. It is simple and direct. Its metaphor is the initial touching in love making. Kissing. Embracing. It's varied. In Pristine Awareness you experience the play of the six attractions.

"Only six. You've got more than that."

"We've talked about the traditional six attractions. Do you remember them?"

"Your face, your shape, your skin."

"Features, form and color. That's three. Do you remember the others?" She guided my hand.

"The way you feel."

"Smoothness. Four." Again, Lorraine cued me.

"The way you move."

"Right. Carriage." Lorraine planted her hands on my chest and pushed herself back a bit. "Wait."

"Wait?"

"You can't do that because you're not done. There were six, remember."

"I give up, tell me."

"No, you're supposed to know."

"Umm, her skill at flower arrangement."

"No."

"Whether she can bake or not?"

"No."

"I give up," I said.

"Her voice, imbecile, the sound of my voice."

"I'm a beast. How could I forget the music of your voice."

"Now, my handsome beast, ... "

The Joy of Pristine Awareness is the value of the empowerment. It had to be strong and stable in me, and it was. The girl, Ocean, was ready for the next Joy to unfold in a woman. Lotus Born took his vajra in hand.

"Vajra?"

"Yes, my ignorant lover, vajra. An object which is both diamond and lightning bolt, and much more. It's an unstoppable force and an immovable object. Tantra is Vajrayana, the Vehicle of the Vajra."

"It's a mystical thing," I teased.

"Nothing is more real than an a full, flaming, vajra, fierce and strong in its glory."

"He took it in hand?"

He shook it at me like a spear! Then he roared with a laugh and spoke mystical syllables which resounded in the three worlds.

"Am I up to this?"

"You are, because I am. In Ocean's arms all her lovers become spiritual masters. Woman is the sacred ingredient. That's why Lotus Born needed me, even though in that incarnation she seemed an inexperienced girl."

She checked. "Your vajra certainly seems to be up for it. For the rest, I'll just have to carry you. I'm good with virgins."

"Virgins?"

"It's your first karmamudra. Don't worry, I'll be gentle."

"Like Lotus Born was with you."

"Lotus Born came at me like a wrathful demon and I loved it. Anyway, I have a lot of practice with virgins."

"You do?"

"Ocean, remember?"

"Huh?"

"The story."

"Oh, yeah. Right. The story."

I, the woman Ocean, was to go on to teach karmamudra to many a body consort. I became a great saint. Just as any saint would want to feed a hungry child, so I feel compassion for men trapped in misery by their lusts.

I serve beings both as a goddess, and by reincarnating as a woman. To the angry, I am completely receptive and open. My serenity turns anger into joy. My peace turns aggression into love.

In the Sky Dancer Theater that day, Lotus Born's face sent out rays of light of every hue in the rainbow. They illuminated every corner of the universe and returned. His face absorbed them and became wrathful.

"Wrathful?"

"It's Buddhist wrath, the good kind."

"Eh?"

∞

"Buddhist wrath is your own fears and resistances reflected back at you. If you hide negative emotions away from love, it cannot reach them to liberate you. Wrathful Buddhas show you what you are hiding. They show you what holds you back. Lotus Born was showing me the hidden barriers that I needed torn open.

"If you want the empowerment" he told me, "you must offer up your mandala." His wrath cut through me. Without hesitation, I dropped all resistance. I put shame and lust aside. In the nakedness of Pristine Joy, I hit the surface of everyday appearance without a ripple and sank like a stone. I lubricated my mandala with five sacred substances, and spoke these words: "Do your will with me, hero of bliss! Eager and happy, I beg you to fill the innermost mandala with bliss." I stirred the mandala with three fingers until I moved on the floor of the cave like a snake. His vajra uncreased.

"A vajra has creases?"

"Not then, it didn't."

It readied for the place of honor at the center of my mandala. It was smooth and firm, fierce and strong, innocent of every wrinkle. With a movement like a hook, it gathered my emptiness . . .

Her voice trailed out, half squeal, half sigh. I felt Lorraine's shudder run through me.

The vajra had seated itself fully on the throne of the lotus that is the womb of the Consort. All appearance flooded with glory. In the rainbow light, pure reality showed . . .

The interruption was longer this time. Lorraine's arms and legs clamped around me. Her lungs emptied on a single mezzo-soprano note, long and resonant. It held steady, then softened. Then disappeared.

With the entry . . .

Lorraine coughed. Not enough air had returned to her lungs. I stroked her back. She began again.

With the entry of the vajra jewel into the lotus mandala, we entered into the Second Joy, Self-increasing Joy. Joy had awakened and now grew by feeding on itself.

"Are you sure you're not a joy or two ahead of me?"

"It's not a physical thing. You keep forgetting that." Lorraine laughed softly. "But that's OK."

I, Ocean, Sky Dancer, turn the man who lusts for me into a God. Bring everything to me. Aggression, hatred, fear, stupidity, vulgarity, brutality. My power makes you the man of my desire, a teacher, a God.

125

Let your lust carry you into the dance with me. As God and God-dess our dance is the magic that creates the universe. What you felt as need is really power. What you took for lust is beauty. Everything is new. Joy increases out of its own energy.

Now that you see your lust as pure, you can accept yourself, the joy increasing, the vajra hardening, the energy flowing down your spine. Inside you Gods and Goddesses dance in wheels of light. Joy builds until Joy . . .

○ ○ ○ ○ ○

Lorraine kissed my cheek. I didn't know if she had finished that sentence or not. I was on my back. She lay at my side, nipples hot against my skin. "They call that Third Joy, the No-Joy," she told me. "It fills your entire mind, so you can't think of how it could ever end. But in our ordinary lives, everything comes with its end and its opposite.

"Without discipline, we feel the Third Joy coming and try to be present when it comes, but we're not there when it fully arrives. We only remember going into it. Coming out of it, we feel that a release occurred.

"But we don't yet know how to bring something that has no end or opposite into our world, where everything is limited, partial and opposed. The Third Joy can't be remembered or understood. It's Joy beyond what we can know. And so we call it the No Joy.

"The orgasm is as close as most come to the No Joy. It's as close as most want to come. But you can live a life in the No Joy, and leave behind all the joys that bring anxiety with them. The No Joy contains nothing but itself.

She rolled on top of me. Our bellies were so wet she almost slipped across and down the other side. She caught herself and belly surfed up my torso to look down at me. "And the No Joy is not the last one. In physical sex we also sense the final Joy, the Innate Joy, but very, very dimly. The afterglow is a faint image of it.

"In the afterglow, the No Joy has come and gone. We don't remember Joy in its fullness, but within our body and soul are its effects. The Innate Joy is not an experience. It is inescapable, a part of all experience. It is something that is so much a part of us that we cannot lose it, even by dying. In fact, death can bring us closer to the Innate Joy. Death eliminates distractions."

○ ○ ○ ○ ○

"Many of the people attracted to Bhadra forgot the significance of a rela-tionship," Lorraine told me later. "Bhadra himself forgot it once he got recognized. Karmamudra is not about the sex act, it's about relating to

Ω

a consort, the mudra, a specific woman. Coupling with various different bodies, even when it's highly pleasurable, is not karmamudra. It might be good sex, but it's not karmamudra.

Karmamudra is about the exchange of energy between you and your mudra. The energy it releases is calm and powerful and changes your life. If you get attached to the sex outside the relationship, you lose that energy, and you lose yourself. That's what happened to Bhadra."

43 Spirits and Spies

Ross didn't say anything when he finished his phone call. It seemed obvious that the Hooded Marvel had been our spy slipping the net. Krishna had a half hour's worth of Lorraine's disks left to copy. Ross and I talked about everything else but the spy while Krishna finished. I grabbed the Marpa book and the sex magic book on the way out. The Marpa book had stayed on my mind and I had plans for the other one. If Ross noticed, he didn't care.

Distracted with thoughts about Lorraine and the books I had looted, I was easy prey for Mrs. O'Brien's ambush in the hall. "I want to thank you for introducing me to Mr. Ohoma," she said sternly. "He's a life saver. Until I met him I didn't know what I would do. You must thank him for me when you see him."

"Really? That's nice. We're on our way to see him now."

"Well, then, you'd better get going. Someone so much on the ball is not a man you should keep waiting." She rapped her cane and turned her back. I wondered if she really needed that cane. Without it, she was my prime suspect for the Spencer House spy.

I planned to go back to Pacific Grove that night. Krishna would stay into the evening to help me look over what he had copied. Oka usually left at five, so I went straight to his office.

"Here's the keys to that apartment." I told him. "You may want to get in again. I don't see any reason why I would."

"Thank you, my friend. Her rent is due soon, so Heavensent will try to pay it for a while."

"You made a big hit with Mrs. O'Brien."

Oka nodded. "Yes. Yes. Marvelous lady. You, my good but dim-witted friend, should listen more to your elders. Of course, she confirms you are a desperate man, definitely number one suspect."

"Of course. Speaking of suspects, I'm dying to know. What happened with our spy?"

Oka motioned me to a chair.

○ ○ ○ ○ ○

The Spencer House is a huge four story Victorian. A historic monument in private hands, it supports itself by charging a stiff admission. The house has around two hundred and fifty rooms, depending on how you count them. The main levels contain dozens of fireplaces, bedrooms, skylights, trap doors, and staircases. There are hundreds of window frames, doorways and stairs, and thousands of window panes. Garrets, cupolas, attics, and gables rise above the main levels. Towers go up to seven stories.

"Victorian" means the whole thing is wood frame with fancy ornamentation. Maintenance is almost comically expensive. It takes a full time staff of six, starting over whenever they finish, just to keep up with the painting. If this cash sink were donated to the State, the Parks Department would demolish it. They've done that to many a lesser upkeep nightmare. The owners of the Spencer House flog their money pit as a haunted house, and enough cash rolls in every twelve months to keep it standing another year.

Indra Spencer started construction on the house when she moved to California in the 1880s and continued it until her death four decades later. In that time the house certainly grew, but construction never had a final goal and completed portions were often torn down.

There are two explanations. The one that the owner peddles is the better yarn. In it, Indra, the most intelligent, charming, and attractive debutante of her day in Boston, marries Alden Spencer, owner of the Spencer Rifle Factory. The happy couple soon have a child, but in its first year the baby wastes away with marasmus. Almost immediately thereafter, Alden dies of tuberculosis. Inconsolable, Indra now has sole possession of a fortune which means nothing to her. She turns to a prominent spiritualist for answers.

Spencer was a trusted name in rifles among those who cleared the West. The spiritualist looks into the ether and sees the vengeful spirits of the many Indians killed by the reliable and effective weapons manufactured by the Spencer factory. These spirits killed her baby. They caused the painful death of her husband. They do not rest. They do not allow her husband and son to rest. Indra herself will not escape their rage. Unless.

The spiritualist advised Indra to move out West and build a large, beautiful house to welcome the spirits. Work on this house must continue every hour of the day, every day of the week, all the weeks of her life. Her generous offering would bring the nobler spirits to forgive. Spirits still confused by thoughts of revenge would become disoriented in its layout. These malicious spirits would be lost and harmless, and their hatreds would fade. With Indra's passing, they would find peace. The house could remain behind.

Others would see it as a needless extravagance. But a physical embodiment always is. Don't we know we are spirit beings?

All this talk of spirits upset many former employees of Indra's. Over the years, they came forward to say that Indra was a fine person with an interest in invention and home construction. All the construction was part of this hobby. Her ex-employees described Indra as a private person deeply saddened by the early loss of her family. When she became the subject of wild rumors about dealings with the spirit world, she chose to ignore them.

The loyalists have less of an axe to grind than anyone. They were there. They knew Indra. The spirit story sounds like commercial puffery. But it's the one I believe.

The proof is the Spencer House itself. It's big on sevens. There are seven kitchens, seven towers and seven elevators.

Thirteens are even more common. There are thirteen bathrooms, thirteen gables, thirteen cupolas and thirteen chimneys. Staircases usually have thirteen steps. Windows usually have thirteen panes. Floor sections thirteen rooms. Walls thirteen panels.

A lot of the "features" Indra designed can have no human purpose. Like the staircases that hang from the ceilings. These have railings, though I'm not sure why someone who can walk upside down needs them. Other staircases at first look normal, but the risers and treads are reversed. They're designed for someone who can hover horizontally.

Some sideways, upside-down, and normal staircases connect, corkscrewing their way through the house. Others dead-end in a floor, a wall, or a ceiling.

Some hallways dead-end in walls. Some ceilings have doors and windows. There are doors and windows in the floors. Skylights that look up to other skylights. And doors that open to walls or, as in Fortitude tower, a fatal drop.

And in the whole huge house, there is no mirror anywhere. Not one. This was not an experiment in home construction.

The Spencer House management did not want its facilities used as a lookout. But they also had limited patience for games of cops and robbers. Paying clients were circulating through the building in three tour groups. More were waiting in line at the front gate.

Oka did some speed diplomacy. In a few minutes, they put together teams to cover the end of the house near the spy nest. They thought it likely the spy would hide or run for it.

Indeed, the spy nest was empty when Oka arrived with Officer Squalls of the San Jose police and Todd, the Spencer security chief. It was one of many rooms Indra had never finished. There was no furniture or clutter, just dust. The walls and ceiling were bare, unpainted wood frame.

Ghosts may be allowed to wander Spencer House unescorted, but paying visitors are not. Rooms rotate in and out of the tours, but many have never been on a tour route. This was one. Oka silently pointed out places which might yield fingerprints or shoeprints.

They were looking into the adjacent rooms when Todd's radio squawked. Two floors below, a woman had bolted straight into a team of Spencer House people and stopped. She wore a paisley dress, a floral scarf, and sunglasses. The team asked her if she was lost. She looked back, saw another team of two behind her, and moved to slip past them.

The second team was Bernard and Marcella. Marcella was a Spencer tour guide. Alone, she probably could have slowed the spy long enough to let the other team catch up. Bernard, one of Oka's guys, was twice the spy's weight and wide enough to fill the hall. He'd made a lot of stops, first in high school football and later with the Cupertino Police.

Bernard was barely able to step out of the way in time. He had to, because both teams were bluffs. Todd had insisted that all the physical stuff be done by his own security staff or the police, and that every San Jose officer have one of his security staff with him. If the chase had taken place on Heavensent's campus, Oka would have said the same thing. There was no way he'd give strangers a license to get rough on his turf.

Marcella, Bernard and the others pursued, reporting to Todd as they ran. Todd put the other teams on the chase. "Remember, we don't want injuries," he cautioned.

Todd also called down to the gate and had them hold up the tours. This meant lost revenue for Spencer House, but Todd was worried. When he put the walkie-talkie down, he asked Oka and Officer Squalls, "Do either of you have a set on our frequency?"

Oka was ashamed of having missed the echo. In an adjacent room they spotted the walkie-talkie behind one of the bare studs. The spy had been organized enough to monitor Todd's frequency. Near the walkie-talkie were the binoculars.

The spy had a good lead, but she made a mistake. She climbed a floor and turned around. Perhaps slipping by Bernard so easily had fooled her. She might have decided the opposition was just two teams, both so drag ass that a simple double back would be more than enough to shake them.

The spy entered a hall just as Gil and one of Todd's people came in the other end. Gil caught the spy's eye. She did not try running past him. When she finished her 180 degree turn, Gil's team was at a dead run close behind.

On the third and fifth floors, teams heard the commotion and followed it. Boards behind, above, and below the spy thundered with feet. She ran into a room with an open trap door and sat down at the edge, legs dangling. Gil came in in time to watch her drop.

Todd saw a chance to herd the spy into Faith Balcony. "I'm headed to the one-way door," he radioed after giving orders to the teams. "If she winds up in Faith, I don't want an arrest before I get there. Let me hear everybody roger that."

Todd's sense of the layout was perfect. The spy ran a few steps, met a pursuit team, turned, and saw Marcella and Bernard coming the other way. The spy's only unblocked route was a short hallway to the side.

Both teams were bluffs, but the spy didn't know that and in the heat of the chase, the teams might have forgotten it themselves. In particular, Marcella had made it clear to Bernard she took their earlier brush-by as a humiliation.

The spy did not make a fresh attempt on Bernard's honor. She turned fast, stumbled, headed toward Faith Balcony before she was fully upright, bumped into a corner, and fell out of sight with a wounded cry that the unsympathetic Marcella later described as "like an animal." The door to Faith slammed shut.

Marcella radioed Todd with the news.

"Good work," Todd answered. "To repeat, do not enter the balcony. We will be at the one-way door shortly. We'll make the stop."

Todd issued some orders to the other teams, then Marcella came back on. "Todd, we have blood here. There's a protruding nail that apparently caught her on the side. I have a piece of her dress."

"Roger. Remember, it's evidence." Marcella's tone may have suggested to Todd that she wanted the rag for her trophy case.

In the two minutes it took the lead team to reach Faith Balcony, Todd was busy on the radio. He summoned First Aid and called an ambulance.

It's called Faith Balcony because it overlooks Faith Kitchen, the main kitchen in Indra's day. Even for the Spencer House, Faith Balcony is an unusual room. There are four doors. Two open to solid wall. The one-way door Todd had mentioned only opens going into Faith Balcony. There's no doorknob on the balcony side. The only convenient way out is the door the spy had slammed behind her. She might also leap the balcony railing, but the kitchen was ground floor, two stories down.

As they approached, Todd radioed his people in the kitchen. "Talk to me. What's going on up on the balcony?"

"Nothing, Chief. She ran around, slammed doors for a while. But it's been quiet up there for a full minute."

"Roger." The lead team was now at the one-way door. "I'm going in."

But it was their day for empty rooms. Faith Balcony was deserted. A torn and bloody paisley dress lay on the floor. Todd stepped around it to the door across the balcony and opened it. Marcella and Bernard sat together at the end of the hall. Absorbed in conversation, they didn't look back. Another team was behind them. Todd looked down. The teams in the kitchen were bored and killing time.

Back on the balcony, Oka had opened the two doors that led into solid wall. He met Todd's eye and sheepishly closed them. Todd went on the radio. "Her dress is here, but she's gone. Look around folks, just in case we missed something. We'll check here."

Todd restarted the tours and called off the ambulance. Faith Balcony and Kitchen were off limits for the rest of the day so the police could gather evidence. The Spencer guides can handle this. They enjoy the chance to show the parts of Spencer House usually skipped due to time. At least this is what Marcella said to me when I met her at her wedding to Bernard.

44 The Bigfoot Proof

Can we prove Bigfoot into existence? Dubious. The big guy is out there or he's not. Proof didn't seem to have anything to do with the existence of the Blessed Island, either. And if the Bigfoot Proof is a lose, why should a God Proof work?

But there are things for which existence in theory does mean existence in fact. Money is one. As Sue told me at the Pecunia Institute, money is purely an idea, and everybody thinks and acts like money is real. Of those who genuinely don't believe in money and act accordingly, most are in institutions or other situations where they can be taken care of by people who treat money as if it were a hard fact. The number ten is real, unless you don't care how many fingers you have, and a number is an idea.

With his 1970 axioms, Gödel nailed down what's needed for the Anselm Argument to work. It seems Bigfoot is out of luck. The hairy fella's problem is consistency.

Bigfoot is a spacetime object. For objects which need space and time to exist in, the only way to prove they are consistent with what's out there is to go out and look for them. Theory by itself doesn't make a spacetime object into a fact. That's also the problem with the Blessed Island. It would have to go somewhere, and less than perfect islands, continents and oceans have prior claim on every last bit of real estate.

Many objects don't need a home of their own in spacetime. For these, it's not necessary to go out and look. Ideas definitely can and do bring them into existence.

Truth is a example of something that exists because of its idea. If you believe anything is true, then Truth itself must be real. Suppose you say "Nothing is true". If this is a true statement, there must be such a thing as Truth. If it's false, there also must be such a thing as Truth. Truth exists because the idea of truth is consistent.

If the idea of God is consistent, then God exists. If.

45 The Ghosts of Pianosa

"Any ideas who our spy was?" I asked Oka.

"I was going to ask you for your guesses."

"I don't like to say this, and you've thought of it anyway, but if someone was tossing her crib, Lorraine might get curious."

I didn't mention Priscilla or Carrie. Dearly as I wanted to light a fire under the two girls, I could not mention them without ratting Sue out as well and that's not what my clients pay me for. I doubted Sue would wear a floral accessory with paisley. Except for that she was my prime suspect.

"We found a hairbrush in the apartment," Oka said. "It will probably yield DNA. And we've got a ton of DNA from the woman we chased."

"So we'll know."

"Not so fast, eager friend. The spy and the woman we chased might not be the same person."

"But the identical dress?"

"Gil has a good eye, but he saw the spy at over a thousand feet. That's a long way to make out a dress, especially if you only see the arms and shoulders. I also saw the spy, and I am not so sure as Gil. Really what we are going on is that the spy was well organized and the fugitive in paisley was quite clever, agile and determined. Both had very unusual MO's for Spencer House trespassers. They are there on the same day and their vague descriptions match. But while the MO's are not inconsistent, there is no real matchup. Probably the same person, but by no means beyond doubt."

"Does Todd think we chased the wrong woman?"

"He considered the possibility. Particularly if she has a ticket, she might have quite the lawsuit. Todd afterward was just as glad we didn't catch her and I might add, none too happy with me for dragging him into this."

"Really?"

"Indeed. I made promises about his prospects for employment here. When I come in tomorrow, I will have to check with my management about whether I can deliver on half of them. On top of that, he's getting a caseful of the world's finest chickens, plucked and ready to barbecue."

"If you think the spy and the fugitive might be two different women, what about the Hooded Marvel?"

"That one is very hard," Oka acknowledged. "And it connects with the difficult question of where our fugitive went. She didn't have a change of clothes with her when she ran into Bernard and Marcella. Did she hide a change of clothes somewhere, like near that last trap door or on Faith Balcony? That seems unbelievable foresight."

Oka leaned his fingers together to make a tent. He was enjoying himself. "Or did she escape in her underwear unnoticed? Hard to do, but in that case she might find a change of clothes left somewhere. None are reported missing so far."

"How could she have escaped?"

"It's possible she found the one-way door open, and closed it behind her. Or figured out a way to jimmy it without leaving damage. She also could have leaped the railing to the kitchen before our Teams arrived and somehow slipped past. But there really does not seem like there was time for this. And, remember, she was hurt."

"Was there blood in the kitchen?"

"None in the kitchen and none past the one-way door."

"How wounded was she?"

"We don't know. A superficial wound can bleed like mad. But she was not bleeding enough to seriously weaken her. That takes a lot of blood and the hall would have been slippery with it. Based on the location of the tear, the nail probably caught her in the left side, above the waist and below the ribs. A puncture there could even be fatal, but the tissue on the nail suggests more of a long, very nasty scratch than a puncture."

I said, "It's difficult to think she went on to be the Hooded Marvel."

"Yes, and your Hooded Marvel left no blood anywhere. Not the tower. Not the drainpipe. Not the lawn. Not on the wall. Not on the sidewalk. Very possibly, the Hooded Marvel was a young person doing a crazy stunt. Only the timing connects her."

"So who was the woman who ran into Faith Balcony? A ghost?"

Oka caught my sarcasm. "Josh, you've been to my house and seen the family shrine. What you call ghosts are my religion."

I began to splutter out an apology, but Oka laughed and waved it aside. "You are a good friend and I hope I may speak frankly. Your Caucasian civilization has achieved so much because it emphasizes experience common to all cultures. So anyone from any culture can learn your Western science of physics from a book and win a Nobel Prize.

"But this common experience is a lowest common denominator. What humans experience, different cultures experience in different ways and under different names. You Westerners say that means they do not exist. But of course they do.

"They say there are ghosts in that house. Shakespeare has ghosts. My family pays respect to the spirits of those gone and that is part of what we believe. Why won't you believe that we affronted a restless spirit and she left this world, leaving only her dress?"

I considered asking why the spirit would spy on us with binoculars. Or why spirits wear dresses but not underwear. "It's five thirty," I said. "You want to be out of here."

"Yes, soon. When the wife is out of town I stay later. But I do have to make some phone calls. I'll let you know what we find, amigo."

46 The Part of "No" That We Didn't Understand

Austria, 1930

There's a story of a philosopher who was well known as an atheist. It may have been Bertrand Russell. Someone asked him, what if he died and he met God face to face? Wouldn't he feel quite the fool? "Not really," said Russell or whoever. "Rather I should ask God why he'd kept such a low profile all these years."

Why do we need a God Proof? Why doesn't God make his existence so clear that there's no debate? Why let people doubt? Why let them worry? Why give them a chance to be wrong?

Why doesn't God announce Himself, clearly root our existence in His and be done with it? Why isn't it evident why we are here in this world? If God exists, would he allow decent, intelligent people to wonder what their purpose is in life? Why does God hide from us? Isn't that all the proof anyone could need that God doesn't exist?

The answer to this comes from Gödel's Doubt Proof. The answer Gödel gives is not new. There's been a lot of talk by theologians over the centuries about freedom and doubt, belief and faith. For many, that has sounded like excuse-making, a sad, desperate attempt to keep up belief in the face of the obvious. In Gödel's hands, this answer became as sure and as solid as two plus two equals four.

○ ○ ○ ○ ○

When Gödel found the Doubt Proof he was actually looking at the Consistency Question. Is the world consistent? Circles are round. Are they also square? Two and two is four. Is it also five? Consistency allows some things to be true and others false. Inconsistency makes everything and its opposite true. You really have to expect the answer to the consistency question to be "yes". The alternative seems just too bizarre.

It wasn't like Gödel to come up with the answer everyone expected, but with consistency it looked like he'd have no choice. In an inconsistent world, you can answer the Consistency Question and any other question "yes". In a consistent world, "yes" is the obvious answer to the Consistency Question. So that's two choices. One is "yes" and the other is "yes". You wouldn't think even Kurt Gödel could pull a surprise out of that one.

But he did. The Doubt Proof showed the answer to the Consistency Question was "no". There was a part of "no" that we didn't understand. A part that meant "yes".

○　○　○　○　○

The Doubt Proof started out as a quick consequence from the Freedom Proof, so quick Johnny von Neumann nearly poached it. It would have been almost fair if he had. Without Johnny there at the conference in Königsberg, the Freedom Proof might have gone unnoticed for some time, what with Gödel keeping its real meaning secret from his own thesis adviser and all.

Not that Johnny needed to justify poaching. If you publish and you miss an easy consequence of your own work, somebody else beats you to it. That's just tough. Part of being a mathematician is knowing when it pays to let the Johnny von Neumann's of the world in on your secrets and when to stonewall them.

The Doubt Proof would have been well worth poaching. David Hilbert, the one who had gotten so mad at the Freedom Theorem, was the leading mathematician of the time. As the century changed in the year 1900, Hilbert challenged his colleagues to solve a list of twenty-three problems. Number two on the list was the Consistency Question.

Hilbert didn't seriously expect that circles were square or that two plus two is five. He was sure that math was consistent. What Hilbert was asking for with the Consistency Question was proof.

The Consistency Question is different from any other in mathematics. Consistency is basic to mathematics. If you don't have some things that are true and some that are false, the mathematical game, and all the real life that is built on it, cease to make sense. Consistency had forced Hilbert to accept the Freedom Proof, much as he hated it. Hilbert either had to accept that there were true things that could not be proved, or else that math was inconsistent.

Consistency is so basic and so important, you're allowed to use circular reasoning. A proof with circular reasoning is like this one that I'm the Dalai Lama.

Assume I'm the Dalai Lama.
Therefore, I'm the Dalai Lama.

This concludes my proof that I'm the Dalai Lama.

This sort of argument is not convincing. In math, assuming what you want to prove is cheating. It is not allowed, except for proving consistency.

Consistency has to be the exception. If you're inconsistent you can prove anything, including that you are consistent. So if you believe your proof of consistency really means anything, you're assuming consistency. You're forced to cheat. A consistency proof is not much more than a double check, like when you count your chickens from one end of the yard first, then count them again starting at the other, just to make sure both counts are the same. You could have missed the same chicken both times, but it's better than nothing.

Von Neumann saw what Gödel had missed at first. A liar sentence is true, Gödel had showed, but it can't be proved. That's assuming consistency, which you have to do because an inconsistent system can prove anything. So Gödel was saying "If the world is consistent, then a liar sentence is true."

Von Neumann saw this could be turned into the second step of a proof:

One: The world is consistent.
Two: If the world is consistent, then a liar sentence is true.
Three: A liar sentence is true.

Step Three was exactly what the Freedom Theorem had proved you can't prove. You can't prove "A liar sentence is true" unless you're inconsistent. Proving Step Three is not acceptable. Something has to give.

To avoid getting to Step Three, either Step One or Step Two has to be thrown overboard. Step Two is not going. Its proof is as solid as they come.

The only thing left to eliminate is Step One: "the world is consistent." That's the Consistency Question. You can't prove consistency.

There's an exception. There's one way you can prove consistency. If you're inconsistent, you can prove anything, including consistency. The logic of Steps One, Two and Three doesn't have to bother you if you're inconsistent, because everything is both true and false at the same time.

The answer to Hilbert's challenge is "No, you can't prove consistency, unless it's false." Meep-meep.

Bottom line, it turns out the Consistency Question is another liar sentence, one of those things that are true, but which we can't prove. It says "no" but it means "yes". There is a part of "no" we don't understand.

○ ○ ○ ○ ○

There are rules about poaching in math. Johnny wrote to Gödel. Partly because it was polite to let Gödel know. Mainly because it put Johnny's Consistency Proof on the record, with a date.

But Johnny von Neumann had a surprise coming. Gödel had already gotten the Doubt Proof on his own and sent it off to a math journal. Math journals carefully date stamp everything that comes in. Gödel's earlier date was on record. Johnny von Neumann had been beaten to the punch. That didn't happen very often.

Johnny never ventured into logic again, but he and Gödel kept crossing paths. Gödel continued to share his work with Johnny, and Johnny was a good friend to Gödel when they worked together at the IAS. It was the computer which Johnny pioneered that made Gödel's work important in daily life. Today they are buried in Princeton Cemetery, a few steps apart.

47 Why Does God Hide?

Austria, 1931

In 1931 Gödel published the Doubt Proof and the Freedom Proof together. No mathematical paper before or since has had as much impact. Until Sue walked in the door with the Lost God notebooks, I was sure that record would stand forever.

At first, it is unsettling not to know we're consistent. If we're inconsistent, we will believe the false along with the true. Our beliefs will be totally incoherent. We'll be insane. The Doubt Proof forces us to doubt our own sanity.

I don't want to make it sound too dire. The Doubt Proof does not say we're incoherent or insane. Indirectly, it says exactly the opposite. If the Doubt Proof is correct, and it is, there is something we don't know. If there's something we don't know, we are safe from inconsistency.

There are lots of things the Doubt Proof does not prevent us from knowing. Knowledge of things that don't involve our own beliefs is safe. We can know lots of things about the material world, about our bodies, about other people. It's only when we have beliefs about our own beliefs that things become Gödelized.

But while we can know a lot of things, we can't be sure of anything that we know. Being sure is a belief about beliefs. When we say that we're sure, we're saying that we believe that our own beliefs are correct. It seems safe enough, but that's Step One toward proving the liar sentence, and the moment we do that we're wrong. Whenever we're sure we know, we're fooling ourselves very, very badly.

Looking at the coherence and sanity of our own beliefs is like testing a stick of dynamite. The only way to be totally sure is to set it off, but then it's gone. It's like pumping the air out of a box, then sealing it. If we open the box to check that the vacuum is still there, we've lost it.

We have to live with doubt, and we can. We use vacuums in engines and dynamite in construction. It is even possible to be completely right, as long as we don't know it. It is certainly possible to be consistent, as long as we

142

don't know that. In fact, if we don't know that we're consistent, then we must be.

○ ○ ○ ○ ○

It's typical of Gödel's ideas that they don't look like good news at first. The Freedom Proof limits what we can know, and freedom is often annoying and sometimes deadly. The Doubt Proof is a follow-on from the Freedom Proof. Because we are free, sane and self-aware, we will live in doubt. We will not know that our beliefs are coherent, or in fact, that the world itself is coherent. We can be certain that, if the world is coherent, we'll never know it. We have to either take it on faith, or allow ourselves to wonder.

If the world is not coherent, it and we have no purpose and no meaning. God exists in an inconsistent world, of course, because everything both exists and does not. But what can God mean in such a meaningless world?

If we know our purpose in the world, we don't have one. Our doubts allow the world to have meaning. A God who makes life coherent and gives it purpose is possible only if we are not sure He exists.

Life has to be a Mystery. If God appeared directly to us, told us what He was, and what we meant to Him, we'd either have to stop thinking, dumb ourselves down so that we don't understand Him, or go insane. Realizing what God is and what that means would destroy us. God hides because He loves us.

○ ○ ○ ○ ○

Nobody suspected there was anything deep hidden in the Consistency Question until Gödel answered it. Nobody thought there was a Freedom Theorem until Gödel found it. Nobody thought there was a real physics of time travel, until Gödel produced the equations. A God Proof may sound unlikely, but if Gödel said that he had one, I was inclined to take notice.

48 The Island of Monterey

Krishna and I found nothing in the files from Lorraine's apartment. I was out of there just after ten PM and considered going back on Route 17. Late hours usually mean no traffic. But I was tired and took the inland route, Highway 101.

To get from 101 back to the coast you go through Castroville, the scene of Marilyn Monroe's first break. In 1947, the town decided to crown an Artichoke Queen. Marilyn was their first. Castroville didn't go on to stardom, but it's had no crisis of values. Every year another young girl puts on the crown that Marilyn Monroe once dreamed of, steps into an open car, and is driven down Merritt Street, waving to the crowd and smiling.

A mile west of Castroville, I picked up the lights of Pacific Grove across the Bay and turned south onto the coast highway. The Salinas River is five minutes down the road. I pulled over and walked out onto the newly rebuilt bridge. The previous winter had set records for rain and this span had collapsed. From the middle of it, I thanked the river for the damage it had done, and tossed the sex magic book into the water.

Lorraine's focus that January had been a bid for Sauftmarlowe, a smoke-stack company based in the Midwest. At first, I didn't think her concern unhealthy. It was the sex magic book that had me worried. I hoped work would take her mind off of it. I had no clue they were connected until she told me. "Tonight I want to do something special."

"It's special every night," I said.

She brushed that aside. "No, really," she said. "Do it for me. Our union brings together the energies of the universe. We can use these for good. When you peak, think of the contract coming in. I will, too."

Few people in our society make more money than they know how to spend. Lorraine and I had been two of them. Big incomes, simple wants, no children, lots of vested stock options. But when we're obsessing about money, it's really something inside us that's missing.

I promised yes. I couldn't believe I was doing a good enough job of lying

∞

to fool her. But Lorraine needed to believe this would work. Over the next nights a thing of joy became a part of the commercial scramble.

I started to sleep on the couch. Lorraine had other exercises for harnessing the universe's power. This was just one. If she noticed it fade from her life, she didn't tell me. I noticed, the way you notice an eighteen wheeler coming head on when you're in the passenger seat.

The conference in Monterey was like a gift. We drove down the coast highway together. While there, I got her to sightsee. I didn't ask her to take the time. I knew better. I found the clients she was chasing and talked them into it. She followed the clients.

Then came the rain. It rains on the Peninsula most winters, but not like it did that winter. The skies opened up and sheets of water came down for hours. The airport closed. Power failed. The Pajaro and Salinas rivers flooded. The Carmel River flooded the road to the east in ten places. Praise its name, it took out the bridge going south to LA. You couldn't even get out the long way. Monterey was an island.

We were trapped by the sea, alone, and without the juice to recharge our laptops. Unable to work, Lorraine was the woman I'd fallen in love with. Wouldn't it be wonderful to live here, I asked her. And Lorraine said yes.

We both felt some loyalty to Heavensent. Lorraine was on a project that would fall apart without her. My own project was almost finished. We agreed that I would go down first and get settled.

Lorraine and I had planned a vacation for my last week in Silicon Valley, but an emergency arose in Boise. She had to cancel and I was alone when I locked the door on our apartment for the last time.

○ ○ ○ ○ ○

I was home just before one AM. The postman had left a notice. He'd tried to deliver some certified mail while I was gone. I had no phone messages, praise be.

I looked back toward Fare Well Arms. The purple mass of Loma Prieta was hidden in the moonless night, but I could see the flashing red light on top. I set the alarm for eight. I expected an early call about Sue's hearing and the notebooks.

To wind down for sleep, I took the Marpa book to bed. I skimmed to jog my memory of that last telephone conversation with Lorraine. She'd been very excited about this book.

Marpa had married an incarnation of Ocean of Awareness, so that Lorraine, in all seriousness, spoke of him as an ex-husband. Once, when all this past lives stuff was getting a little much for me, I asked Lorraine why she didn't remember any of this before she met Bhadra. Lorraine's answer was that forgetting was a gift to her from the Sky Dancers, a gift she had earned when she was Marpa's wife.

49 The Gift of Forgetting

The Lhotrak Valley, Tibet, March 2, 1063 AD

Ocean had promised Marpa's disciples that she would stay in the castle, watching from the window. No matter what. She kept her promise as Marpa chased the disciples and kicked the animals who got in the way. She'd seen many a rage from this man, but this exceeded any of them. Young Teacher was the only child old enough to be suspected in their scheme. He was safe, sent into town. They thought the disciples would be young enough to run, but it was becoming obvious they'd underestimated the old man.

Marpa taught that you should live in the moment. That he certainly was doing. He was absorbed in his tantrum like a child. Marpa did a lot of the farm work, but everyone thought it was his frequent rages that kept him young.

In the yard below Ocean's window, Marpa caught up with Lucky Owl and landed a solid blow. Lucky Owl clutched at his arm. Great Magician pulled Marpa away. Marpa turned after Great Magician. To give Lucky Owl more time, Great Magician pretended to fall. Still holding the arm, Lucky Owl made good his escape.

But Great Magician had misjudged. Marpa did not go straight after him. He went into the shed. When he reemerged with the ax handle, Great Magician was back on his feet, but cornered between the stables and a ledge.

Ocean screamed and ran out of the castle across the yard. Marpa swung. Great Magician broke his vow to give up sorcery, or perhaps was lucky. But in dodging the first blow, Great Magician lost his balance. He fell, this time for real. Marpa would not miss the next blow.

Marpa had the ax handle fully raised when Ocean put herself in front of him. When she saw the look in his eyes she was more scared than she had been in lives. He didn't seem to recognize her.

"Is this still for the children?" she said.

Marpa stopped. The awkward forward angle of his arms forced Marpa to lower them. Ocean knew it was best to let Marpa think that nobody noticed he was backing off. She turned and kicked Great Magician, pretending to punish him. "Go, get out!" she said, trying to sound angry instead of afraid.

Great Magician was reluctant to leave her with Marpa, but skirted the yard and ran into a door.

Marpa stabbed the handle into the ground. "You're all in on it. You've hidden my gold and my baggage."

"Look at you. This is madness. You don't need another yoga. Tibet has all the teachings it needs."

"With Naropa's last teaching, our son could be Tibet's greatest teacher, even greater than Lotus Born. I'm leaving to find Naropa. If my baggage doesn't follow me, then I'll die on the trail. Good bye."

He turned and headed up the trail to the pass. Exhausted, Ocean closed her eyes and dropped to the ground.

Two long lives ago, Lotus Born had released Ocean, and told her to pass the teachings on. She traveled widely and taught many. When Lotus Born left, she was Tibet's most prominent teacher. In that first life, Ocean stayed on until she was very old. Even so, her students were devastated when she insisted it was time for her to join the Sky Dancers. Ocean promised to watch over them and all of Tibet, and to return when needed.

Never had she been needed as much in this life. Tibet had fallen back into superstition. Once again, human sacrifice and the torture of innocent animals were called religion. Only pockets of Buddhism remained, in remote corners like the Lhotrak Valley. This was the same Lhotrak to which Ocean was headed as an imperial exile when Lotus Born rescued her. It was a karma she had cheated in that life, but was more than making up for in this one.

Marpa had been born in the Lhotrak. As he grew up, nobody thought he would be much of an asset to the world. Certainly not to religion. For valleys to either side, he was known for his hot temper. In Tibet it is easier to get known as a saint than a hothead. The competition among the hotheads is stiff.

Marpa's temper was so bad that his family wanted him gone. They couldn't understand where the young madman got the idea that he wanted to study Buddhism in India, but they gladly financed it. He might come back with profound teachings for the benefit of titans, gods, the two kinds of hell beings, humans, and animals. He might fall off a cliff. Either way, big win.

In the Sky Dancer Realm, they had seen that this was the man Buddhism needed in those dismal times. Ocean reincarnated to be his wife. She was beautiful and of age when Marpa stunned everyone by returning with highest recommendations from the famed Naropa.

Great Magician poked his head out of the door. "Ocean, Mother, are you alright."

"I am fine. And you?"

"Good. Lucky Owl's arm should mend."

"Get the Teacher's things. Hurry. Try to reach him before sunset. I will tend to Lucky Owl."

Naropa had held one of the top posts at Nalanda, Buddhism's most prestigious university. He gave that comfortable post up to live a life of poverty, chasing after the teachings of secluded holy men.

This turned Naropa from a successful academic into a popular hero. In every age, men who prefer real spiritual growth to its official trappings and material rewards are rare. The people called Naropa a yogi of great accomplishment, a mahasiddha.

Something possessed the mahasiddha Naropa to empower the young pepperpot from Tibet to teach. Naropa's say-so was enough to get even Marpa regarded as a saint.

Great Magician came back into the barn where Ocean was treating Lucky Owl. "I came to ask if there is anything you need before I depart," he said.

"Yes," Ocean said. "Break off one of the boards as a splint. But quickly. Marpa's supplies must get to him."

"They are already on their way. I sent the others ahead of me with them. I can help you set Lucky Owl's arm and still catch up."

Ocean knew Marpa needed to be the man he was. Great Magician was an example of why. This gentle young man, the same one who'd been ready to meekly take the blow from Marpa's ax handle, was the most feared man in Tibet. Just Great Magician's terrible presence made Marpa's farm immune from bandits.

Relatives had cheated Great Magician's mother of their inheritance. In return the mother had pushed Great Magician to learn black magic. He could and did kill in many ways, but hailstorms were his specialty. Great Magician's mother had died in the resulting duel, but not before hundreds of her enemies perished.

His mother's death ended whatever interest Great Magician had in the feud. The price the relatives had paid for their victory made Great Magician the most feared man in Tibet. But Great Magician cared nothing for his new fame. He felt only guilt. He had heard of Marpa, and went to offer himself as his student and servant.

The day Great Magician arrived, the farmhands and even some of the more cowardly students had fled. Marpa treated it like just another visit from a student without money or recommendations. He accepted Great Magician as a student and mistreated him worse than any of them.

Ocean saw the patience and power of a great saint and artist growing within Great Magician. He had something of the spiritual power of her own son, Young Teacher. Ocean knew that Great Magician's crimes and sufferings would enable his message to reach people that her own son, whose life was much happier, would have trouble understanding.

The Sky Dancers had told Ocean that this would be her best life. She had doubted that, but accepted the need to reincarnate. The Sky Dancers also told her that it would be best if she reincarnated without the ability to remember her past lives. Ocean drew the line there. She had refused to give up her memories of that first great life with Lotus Born.

Both in her life with Lotus Born and in this one with Marpa, her lover was not just the greatest teacher of the time, but Buddhism's hope for the future. But Buddhism was in worse condition than it had been in Lotus Born's day. As Lotus Born's consort, Ocean's wide travels centered on the capital, and her lover was renowned there. Even his enemies admired Lotus Born for his learning and wisdom. As Marpa's wife, she had never been outside the Lhotrak, and her husband was regarded as half-mad even by his disciples.

Marpa's faults made him all the easier to love. Children were a new and wonderful experience for Ocean. She knew she would be totally happy if she could only put Lotus Born's gentle touch out of her memory and immerse herself in this life. Ocean asked the Sky Dancers to let her change her mind. She prayed for the gift of forgetting.

50 Tuesday After was Also Bad

PG, January 15

Mike called around eight thirty in the morning. "Where were you yesterday?" he said. He wasn't being pleasant.

"On business for another client," I said.

"You have an exclusive obligation to us."

"I do?"

"Do you claim not to know that?"

"Yes. I don't remember Sue making the request and I certainly did not hear it from you."

"Don't you think a $25K advance means an exclusive?"

"It means I have very little time for other work, yes. I'd bc happy to make this an exclusive."

"We already have an exclusive arrangement, which you have not lived up to."

I took my time answering. Mike did not jump in to fill the silence. "Perhaps we should talk face to face," I said. "Is it OK if I come over to your office?"

Mike didn't offer me an appointment, but he didn't forbid me to go there either. When I blow a big account, I like to do it in person. It's just good business.

51 Of the Schuar, and of Their Gold

In Mike's office, Veronica beamed. But I was not ushered right in. I had time to bask in Veronica's smile and to get a really good look at some of Mike's magazines. I read an interesting study on the archaeological evidence for Kings David and Solomon of the Bible. According to the article, it is pretty sketchy. A single inscription does name Solomon, but digging for anything more is likely to start another Mideast War.

Next I devoured an account of the Schuar people, an Amazon tribe best known for shrinking the heads of their enemies. Their first Western contact was with the Spaniards. The Schuar gave their guests gold in friendly fashion only to find that, rather than creating warm feelings, it made the Spaniards pushy.

So they killed all the Spaniards except the governor and a priest. The governor was tortured until he revealed the location of his hoard. The Schuar brought out his gold, built a great fire and melted it down. Forcing the priest to watch, they poured the gold down the governor's throat. Then all eyes turned to the priest. "Go," their chief told him, "and tell all who will listen, of the Schuar, and of their gold." The Schuar were not visited again until well into modern times.

I had just started a piece on what the crews who flew the B17s had to put up with in the way of cramped space and high altitude conditions without the proper equipment, when Mike startled me.

"Come on in."

I could have started by pointing out that since Mike hadn't seen me right away that he too must have other clients. But it was no time to be a wise guy. There hardly ever seems to be an right time to let our inner wise guy express himself, and this may be a source of many of the world's ills.

Mike led off. "You have to drop your other client immediately."

"I expect no further work from that client."

"Can you guarantee me you'll have no further contact with them?"

"No contact? I haven't billed them. I can't refuse to take their calls."

"That makes it easy. No bill, no obligation. Just return their retainer."

I wasn't about to tell Mike that I took a retainer from Sue but didn't ask for one from Heavensent. "I can't simply drop a client without a word," I said.

An unseen seagull complained outside. The gull had a long time to lay out his case before Mike spoke. "My client is extremely serious about this. Enough so to pursue extensive litigation."

"I recognize that. If I had realized your concern I would certainly not have accepted that other small amount of business." This was a lie. If Lorraine was dead or in trouble, I would not for the world have stayed out of it. Mike might even know it was a lie, which was fine. He could not prove it false and as a lawyer he should admire a well-crafted lie.

I poured it on. "What if another client asked about my progress in your interests? I can't be fully forthcoming with you on details of that other client's business without betraying them. Because someone apparently is interested. I was followed yesterday. The police got involved."

"Who was it?" Mike's tone showed interest, whether genuine or not.

"There was a chase and he escaped." The "he" was deliberate misdirection. If Mike knew nothing, it made no difference. If he did know something, my chances of catching one of California's best lawyers in a slip were tiny. But you try.

"So we'll never know," Mike said.

"Not necessarily. He left a ton of DNA." I watched Mike's face. It revealed nothing and I continued. "I am fully aware that full scale litigation over this would ruin me financially, even if I won ..."

"Which you would not."

"But if potential litigation was the main thing keeping me discreet, whoever presented the greatest legal threat could dictate how I deal with my other clients. I'd just be bounced every which way by legal threats."

"Which is a good reason why you should not have accepted other business."

"I will end the other relationship, and do only what is absolutely essential not to leave them hanging."

"For all our sakes that absolute essential had better be nothing or damn close to it. Sue is furious over this. If you think I am giving you a hard time over this, wait until you talk to her. Because frankly, she had me squirming over this matter. I don't mind saying that when she decides she wants to be intimidating, she can make me wish I was dealing with other lawyers. I don't know how she does it, but if I were you I'd want to make her happy. Sue wants to meet you in the Presidio Chapel. You know where that is?"

I did. On my way out, I wondered why Mike had not demanded the retainer back. He wouldn't get it and we both knew that, but I had expected some arm twisting.

52 Tuesday After was Also Bad, Part 2

The Presidio Chapel, now San Carlos Basilica, was the church in California's home village. It's only 30 feet wide and 120 feet long. Monterey was not a big place then. Today it's the home church of the bishop of Monterey, which means it's a cathedral, the smallest Roman Catholic cathedral in the U.S.

Trying to spot Sue, I walked down the nave and looked into each arm of the transept. I was not sure if she was there yet. Several women who might have been Sue sat in the dimly lit pews.

I decided to go back into the nave, sit in a conspicuous place, and wait. I'd just started down the aisle when a woman in a pew near the door gave me a discreet wave. She wore a hooded cloak over a dress the same deep black. She rose and headed out the door. I followed. When she reached the light, she looked back. It was Sue.

"Did Mike tell you that the CTS will have to give up the notebooks?" she asked. Sue seemed genuinely glad to see me. She turned to cross the street.

"No. In fact we didn't talk about the hearing at all."

Sue headed into a playing field. Following her was like a journey back into the old Presidio. The neighborhood that grew up in front of the old fort hid the ocean from us, just as the original front wall would have hidden it then. In the old Presidio, its wall, lined with homes, offices and storerooms, would have surrounded us. Near where the wall once stood, a chain link fence enclosed the one-story buildings of a school.

On the other side of the field, Sue sat down on a bench and waved me to join her. We faced back to the 1794 church, its original sandstone facade overwhelmed by a later bell tower under a towering redwood. I wondered what had happened to all the anger Mike has warned me about.

"A lawyer showed up representing the Princeton folks," Sue said. "He claimed the notebooks belonged to them. I don't think the lawyer himself was quite sure of who exactly in Princeton he was representing, except that they believed they were Gödel's heirs and they wanted the notebooks."

"Obviously he got nowhere if you are getting the notebooks."

"I am not getting the notebooks. Not right away. The court will be."

"Huh?"

"Judge Gaunilo realized the CTS had tricked him and scolded them from the bench. Mike might have gotten a contempt hearing, but knowing how confused Gaunilo gets when more than one thing is before him, he decided against pushing our luck."

Sue pushed her hood back. Did it remind me of one of her characters? "Mike turned out to be exactly right," she said. "When the Princeton lawyer popped up, Gaunilo got very distracted. He wanted to delay to another hearing date. Mike pointed out that we had evidence, that the Princeton lawyer did not, and that any delay would leave the notebooks with the CTS."

"Precisely the one party who even Judge Gaunilo knew they did not belong to."

"Right. I wanted Mike to make more of the fact that our Princeton fellow didn't seem able to figure out who he represented. He seemed sure he was representing Princeton University, but the paperwork said his client was the Institute for Advanced Studies."

"Mike didn't bring that up?"

"Not really. He told me it would only confuse Judge Gaunilo further. I swear everything seems to confuse that man."

"Mike's got a rep as a courtroom tactician. If that's what he thought, I'd hate to bet against it."

"Oh, I know. It is just this judge. He's not an evil man, he is actually almost too kind. But he seems bound and determined to give my mother's notebooks to anyone else but me. I believe that if no one showed up to try to take away my notebooks, Judge Gaunilo would go looking for people."

"But the CTS did not get to keep them, so Mike must have come up with something."

"Mike got a recess and convinced the Princeton attorney that if the notebooks stayed with the CTS, bad things could happen. The Princeton attorney took the point, and when court reconvened he motioned to have the court take possession. We joined in the motion and the CTS attorney did not object. You could hear Judge Gaunilo sigh with relief."

"So in effect this guy shows up, is not clear who his client is, does not have any evidence, and whatever he says is golden."

"Mike tells me this is typical of the way Gaunilo works. He quickly gets lost in anything but the simplest case. So he tries to split the difference, figuring that way he's safest. He figures he is sure to be half right, even where one of the parties is completely in the wrong. And if the truth does lie half way in-between, then he has gotten it perfect."

Sue sighed, then continued. "The gentleman from Princeton looked to Judge Gaunilo like a neutral, third party. He even comes from a prestigious East Coast educational institution, even if nobody is sure which one."

"Gaunilo has gotten the law down to a science," I said. "When does the court get the notebooks?"

"Today at five PM is the deadline. There'll be another hearing in two weeks. May the Goddess grant that in the meantime nobody else decides to show up and ask if they can have them." A bell rang at the school fronting the playing field. "That's my next appointment. I'll be in touch."

The final clangs of the school bell were lost in the screams of children and the tramping of small running feet. A horde of children emerged from the entryway. They spread out to fill the field of vision in all directions, but the main body made straight for our bench. Several grabbed Sue by the cloak. A pair seized each sleeve. Even while they made sure of their prize, they danced her away toward the church. With no arm free, Sue turned her head back and smiled goodbye. She said something, but I lost it in the din of small voices singing out her name.

If Sue had ever been angry with me, she was over it. It seemed strange she'd said nothing about my other client, didn't so much as ask me a question. Had Mike just made the whole thing up? That didn't seem like him.

53 Paranoia

The young Nazis who attacked Gödel could have had any of a number of reasons. Kurt and Adele were walking on a quiet street near the university. The hoodlums seized Kurt, struck him and knocked off his glasses. Adele was the better street fighter. Blows from her umbrella drove the youngsters off.

Nazi youth gangs were a regular feature of Vienna life by then. Sometimes they singled out people who they thought looked Jewish or intellectual. Sometimes Nazism was simply their excuse for attacking people at random.

Gödel might have been targeted. He was not outwardly anti-Nazi, but Gödel did nothing to support the Nazis. Letters in the archives show that the Nazis were aware of Gödel's choice of friends and none too happy about it. Far too many Jews and liberals.

In March 1938 German troops had marched in and made Austria part of Germany. Gödel spent the next academic year in the United States. Back in Austria things grew worse. His friends in the U.S. warned him that it was a mistake to go to back to Austria in June 1939, but Gödel ignored them. Gödel was bizarrely unconcerned for a man with a secret that could put him in a concentration camp. Back in Vienna, he even bought a house.

Gödel finally realized the dangers he faced sometime during November. Early in the month he had moved into his new house, but by the end of November he was trying to get out of Germany as fast as he could. Perhaps it was because of the young thugs. If so, they did him a favor, because he was acting none too soon. World War II had started, the Atlantic was a war zone, and Gödel was about to be drafted into the German Army.

○ ○ ○ ○ ○

Fear is not irrational. Real dangers are out there. They strike paranoids as well as healthy people. Healthy people recognize danger and take precautions. Then they stop thinking about it, smell the roses, and get on with life. Paranoids follow the logic of fear until it is a danger of its own.

Food poisoning was Gödel's main fear, but there was a long list of others. At different times, Gödel worried about death plots by foreign mathematicians, poison gases from refrigerators and ventilation systems, and the police coming to arrest him. Adele became used to dealing with these, but the weeks when Kurt was telling everyone that she had given all their money away were exasperating even for her.

At bottom, none of these fears are irrational. Spouses squander each other's money every day. No professional mathematician has killed another that I know of, but Schlick, the leader of the Vienna Circle, was shot dead on the steps of a university building by a former student. Death does pour into the air from unsuspected sources in buildings, and ventilation systems have taken a steady toll over the years. In Hitler's Vienna the police were bound to come for Gödel eventually, something he should have realized sooner.

Food poisoning is unpleasant and it can kill you. But when your stomach tells you that you are starving, you have to stop thinking and eat, or you will die. Gödel ignored his stomach and followed his logic.

Mystics spoke of the limits of logic before Gödel. Gödel ended the debate for all time with a proof that the mystics were right, a proof so strong that even skeptics are forced to accept it. To create a proof that coercive, Gödel created in himself the greatest logical mind of centuries. Then it persecuted him and killed him.

It always seemed so sad to me. But perhaps Gödel was thinking of himself when he said that we cannot judge our happiness from this reality alone. The personality we see here is only a small part of what we really are. The life it leads is the raw material from which, in our real, fuller existence, we are learning to be happy. Gödel presents no proof for this, but I want to believe.

54 Tightrope

At his draft physical, Gödel kept a secret from the doctors. If they knew about his sanatorium stays, they would have exempted him from military service. But Gödel was wise to keep quiet. The Nazis called people like Gödel "mental defectives". By the end of war, the Nazis had forcibly sterilized hundreds of thousands of "mental defectives". Hundreds of thousands more had been sent to concentration camps, where they died.

During the 1930s, as the Nazi influence in Austria grew, Gödel's reticence and shyness turned into depression and paranoia. By 1935 these problems were serious enough to force him to resign his post as visiting scholar at the IAS and return to friends and relatives in Vienna.

Gödel never spoke of his feelings about the Nazis. He had a strong need to accept authority. But Gödel was not a Nazi and he didn't try to act like one. And he had to notice what the Nazis were doing to his friends from the Vienna Circle, who as teachers were also authority figures for him. One by one they were being driven out of the country.

Moritz Schlick, Gödel's friend and mentor, didn't leave fast enough. He was killed in June 1936. Hans Nelböck, the student who shot him, may have acted alone and out of personal motives, but the Nazis applauded the killing. When they took over in Austria, Nelböck was released from prison with a full pardon.

Not long after Schlick's murder, Gödel became obsessed with fears of food poisoning. He entered a sanatorium and probably would have died there if it were not for Adele. When fear prevented Gödel from eating, she acted as his taster. He trusted her and would eat. She fed him a spoonful at a time until he gained thirty-five pounds.

Gödel's family objected to Adele. She was six years older and her profession was a matter of suspicion. Even today, we don't really know how she earned her living. She said she was a dancer, but she was never in any of Vienna's ballet companies.

Gödel's family had a legitimate concern. At the time, German society

160

did not regard marriage as a completely personal choice. A socially unacceptable marriage could destroy a man's career. But the family saw that Kurt functioned well when he was with Adele, and literally could not live without her. In 1938, they attended her wedding to Kurt.

They'd decided well. Gödel's paranoia did not leave him, but marriage made it less dangerous. His sanitarium visits ended and he resumed his work.

○ ○ ○ ○ ○

Marriage to Adele stabilized Gödel's life, but it remained a tightrope act. While spectacular feats went on high above, a net of hospitals and sanitariums waited below. Tightrope acts are riveting. There's a reason for that and it doesn't say good things about us. If there's a fall, we don't want to miss it.

Many worried that Gödel's mental problems would creep into his work, that one day he'd start submitting gibberish for publication. It never happened. In fact, Gödel's record is nearly perfect.

This is not common in mathematics. Far from it. Mathematics is difficult and it doesn't get easier at the professional level. The best mathematicians make mistakes almost routinely. Long proofs tend to be dismissed out of hand. If a proof is long enough, the reasoning goes, there has to be a mistake in it somewhere.

At the mathematical journals, referees are the first line of defense. They read the papers before they're published. In 1970 Kurt Gödel submitted a paper on the structure of infinity. Kurt knew the field better than anyone alive, and his work was known for flawless execution. But the rule says every paper must be refereed, so one was assigned.

The referee found himself in a difficult position. He could not make sense of the paper. Usually, if the referee can't understand a paper, it's rejected, or at least sent back for clarification. But this was Kurt Gödel, the expert who confounded the other experts. If it was Gödel's word against the referee's, the paper was going to be published.

The editor was a friend of Gödel's and got in touch. It turned out that Gödel had submitted the paper while under medication. Gödel, his mind clearer, said the paper was "no good" and withdrew it. Gödel was a perfectionist. The phrase "no good" is harsh. The paper contained enough material of interest to be published after Gödel's death.

Gödel never made another mistake. The error of 1970 is the one piece of evidence from his professional work to show that Gödel had a human intelligence, fallible like our own.

55 Escape

Outside of his work, Gödel's human fallibility was all too evident. The timing of his decision to leave Hitler's Europe was about as bad as it could get. The draft physical had found him "fit for garrison duty." The authorities' dislike of him meant he had no academic post, and with no job, he was very likely to be drafted. With the war on, the Germans seemed unlikely to allow someone of draft age to leave. Gödel's secret mental problems made him unlikely to be able to deal with military service. Once these problems came out, the Nazis would deal with him as a "mental defective".

Assuming Gödel figured his way out of this bind, the United States was a safe haven. The U.S. was not yet in the war and the IAS would be happy to give Gödel a job. But there was the problem of how to get to Princeton. The Atlantic was closed to Germans. The only way out was through Russia. Hitler and Stalin, after years of bitter propaganda against each other, had stunned their own people and the world by signing an alliance. This tense alliance would end in a few months with a surprise attack by the Germans on Russia, but for now a German with desperation and the necessary papers could try to cross Russia.

From Princeton, the IAS went all out to pull strings on behalf of Gödel. Neither the Nazis or the Soviets wanted to irritate influential forces in the powerful and neutral United States. With the IAS's help, Gödel got a German certificate of leave and Russian, Lithuanian and Latvian visas. The Gödels left Germany on January 16, 1940.

They crossed Lithuania and Latvia headed for Moscow and the Trans-Siberian Railway. Almost no one else escaped Germany by crossing the eleven time zones of Russia. In theory, valid Russian and German papers made the Gödels safe from the authorities. In reality, they were going through remote areas of Siberia where the commissars must have had difficulty getting used to the idea of the Germans as allies. In a few months Germany and Russia would be in the most brutal conflict ever waged between two nations. Adele later told a friend they traveled mainly at night, in constant fear of being stopped and sent back.

162

56 Tuesday After was Also Bad, Part 3

PG

My guess was that they tried to deliver the certified mail again today, I'd missed it at home, and it wasn't back at the post office yet. But the return trip took me right by the post office. I might as well try.

They had it. The letter was the one that the woman from the California Bureau of Security and Investigative Services had promised. The complaint that I was an unlicensed PI. I'd forgotten. I had thirty days to respond. There was a fine of a grand. I had better not forget it again.

57 Physics Class is not the Problem

The Gödels' journey across Russia ended at the Pacific port of Vladivostok. From Russia they traveled to Japan. They arrived in Yokohama on February 2, 1940. Their boat to San Francisco had sailed the day before. They booked the next one.

In Japan also, the Gödels were racing against time. Japan had been at war in China for a long time, but was not yet at war with Russia or the United States. If the Gödels had been caught there when war began, it's not clear what the Japanese would have done with them. Certainly not let them travel on to the United States.

The *President Cleveland* arrived in Yokohama on February 20 and took them to Honolulu, then San Francisco. The boat was American, but almost all Gödel's fellow passengers were Chinese. The Gödels landed in San Francisco on March 4. They had traveled three quarters of the way around the world, twenty-four thousand miles, all of it through countries on the verge of the most destructive war in their history. Now they faced one last hurdle.

A question on the immigration form asked, "Were you ever in a mental institution?" A "yes" meant making the whole journey in reverse, risking arrest and internment all over again, and wondering the whole time if arrest and internment wasn't preferable to what awaited Kurt in Germany.

Gödel was given to telling the truth at inconvenient times, but the answer on the form is "no". He may have recognized the value of being economical with the truth, or someone may have answered for him. Kurt and Adele went on to Princeton by train.

Gödel left no account of his 1940 journey. When a colleague asked about his experiences in Hitler's Europe, Kurt confided that the coffee in Vienna was wretched. After the war, Adele went back to Europe several times. Kurt never returned.

○ ○ ○ ○ ○

There's no science versus God problem. Evil is another story. God and evil in the same world together don't seem to fit. Where did it come from? Was it something God didn't create? Doesn't he care? Or does he just not know? Maybe God deliberately created the evil. Maybe God took a vacation and his replacement screwed up while he was gone. They're not very satisfying explanations.

If evil were totally eliminated in the world, for most of us that would take care of the problem. For Gödel's God Proof, it wasn't going to be that easy.

Remember, we'd learned that if God is even possible, he must exist. The idea was that God is not a "maybe yes, maybe no" kind of thing. He's either part of all possible arrangements of the world, or He's just nothing. God has to be more than just a lucky break. If it's even possible that God does not exist, then he doesn't. That's a killer.

If evil is not compatible with God, and it's hard to see how it is, then it's not enough to eliminate evil. If evil is even possible, then there's a possible world without God. And that's a proof that God does not exist.

And why should anyone ever suffer? Why should there even be a possibility someone might suffer?

If you talk to people who don't believe in God, or who doubt, not many lost their faith in Physics class. It's the evil in the world. One day they'd just seen too much evil in the world. And for them, from that day on, every glance they took at the world they lived in was one more piece of evidence against God.

58 Tuesday After was Also Bad, Part 4

PG

From the bottom of my stairwell, I looked out to sea. No Armenta. It was cold even for January. When I reached the landing, I found my door open a crack. I pushed it open softly.

Locks were never Lorraine's thing. She was sitting in one of my rocking chairs, almost glowing with happiness. I'd never seen her so beautiful.

"Wherever you went to, it agreed with you," I said. "God, you had me worried."

"I've been thinking a lot about you," she said.

I started to hope that everything with Lorraine and I was going back to where it once had been. "I've missed you," I said.

"I needed the change."

"Oka will be very pleased."

"Oh," she said. "You can't tell him you saw me. I mean, please don't. It would ruin everything."

I forced myself to sit down in the other rocker and gave it time to settle. "The police think you were murdered," I said.

"I know," she said calmly. "That's OK."

"It's nothing like OK. They think I murdered you."

"Nobody's arrested you yet. You've had to answer some questions." Lorraine and I were not going back to where we once had been. Not right away.

"I need to tell the police I've seen you," I said. "I can't give them a runaround."

"You never had a problem with that before."

I rocked back. "I'm old and slow now," I said. "I don't want the police thinking I'm a murderer. I don't want our friends wondering whether I strangled you, stabbed you, or beat you to death with a rock. Maybe it's innocent until proved guilty in court, but if you decide a guy might be the

166

moody type who kills his girlfriends you don't invite him by like you used to. Especially if you remember her as the nice sort."

"There's no reason to suspect you."

"The police don't agree. Somebody called here after your plane landed. I was here, but didn't hear the calls. The police are sure I'm a liar."

"That was me," she said. "I called you three times. Why didn't you answer? I didn't even get an answering machine."

"I had the line disconnected."

Lorraine looked at me hard.

"I was doing stuff with the DSL modem," I lied. "Anyway, the police are convinced I'm holding out on them. Now you want me to hold out on them for real. It's a problem. A big problem. I could wind up in serious trouble."

Lorraine sighed. "I didn't mean for this to become such a mess."

"Why didn't you tell me you planned to disappear?"

"I did tell you."

"You did?" I said. "When?"

"On the phone."

"Lorraine, please. That's not something I'd forget. You've got to take this seriously. A lot of people have been very worried. And I probably haven't allowed myself to realize what the whole mess has been doing to me."

"This visit should fix things."

"Your moving here will fix things."

"Stop it, Josh, please." She started to cry.

I said nothing.

Lorraine gathered herself together. "Oh God, how this went wrong," she said. "You really don't know then? You didn't understand what I told you in October?" She was lovely smiling through the tears.

"I guess not. Did you tell me you were going to get on an airplane and never get off?"

"I hadn't planned that part out yet. I just told you I wanted to leave."

"Right. Leave Heavensent."

"No. No." Lorraine laughed. She got up and turned away, dabbing at tears with the back of her sleeve. Behind her the lights of Lover's Point, Seaside and Sand City sparkled through the window.

"You remember on my birthday I talked about Marpa."

"Yes. Your ex of a thousand years ago."

"Be funny if you like. Do you remember my saying I've learned something new about the Yoga of Forceful Projection?"

"Is that the one called the Yoga of No Effort?" I was going to listen this time.

She spoke in the slow, determined way that you speak to a dear child who doesn't get it, but who is going to, you are just sure he will. "I said you could use it for entering the Action, remember? And that way you fix both difficulties, the one with entering the Action, and the one with the Yoga of Forceful Projection."

"Yes. OK." I remembered her talking that kind of gobbledygook. And her point?

"So that's what I'm going to do," she said the way you say things when you are forced to say what you had hoped was obvious. "Enter the Action."

59 Entering The Action

The Nyang Valley, Tibet, March 17, 1063 AD

Only two weeks into Marpa's journey, Atisha's news was bad. Naropa had entered the Action. It didn't sink in at first. Marpa hadn't spoken Sanskrit in years. He assumed "entering the Action" was basically the sort of scam Atisha and the Tibetans had been pulling on Nalanda University for the past ten years. Marpa wondered why Atisha made "entering the Action" sound so involved. The scam on Nalanda may have been a thing of beauty, but complicated it was not.

Nalanda University prized Atisha. Marpa had met him there, and while he was there the Tibetans had talked Atisha into visiting them. This threw the students at Nalanda into an uproar. They were prepared to get rough in order to keep Atisha. But forcing someone to teach you non-violence doesn't make a lot of sense. Atisha promised to return in three years and the students backed down.

Three years later, Atisha's health was not as good, and he didn't think he could take the journey back. He'd also come to like Tibet. He felt needed. So the Tibetans sent the message back to Nalanda that the great Atisha was dead. Soon it would be a scam no more. Atisha was now almost eighty and very weak.

But as Atisha continued to talk about "entering the Action", Marpa felt more and more lost. They spoke Sanskrit because Atisha had never learned to speak Tibetan well. Atisha enjoyed Marpa's visit. Usually he had to speak through his small group of translators.

"Since you won't see Naropa," Atisha said, "stay with me for a while. You can translate for your old teacher."

"Master, I promised Naropa I would return. I've raised a lot of gold for the journey. I will visit Naropa discreetly so nobody will know that he isn't really dead."

"Oh," said Atisha, realizing that Marpa did not understand. "Naropa is not hiding. He is nowhere to be found. There is no secret. Naropa has entered the Action."

Marpa looked bewildered.

"Perhaps I should explain about entering the Action," Atisha said. "Our bodies are just an appearance. What we see as our body is only a small part of the reality of our selves. Our view of even this small part is clouded by our delusions and distorted by our misdeeds."

Atisha shivered and pulled at a blanket without effect. Marpa got up and rearranged Atisha's coverings. Atisha was working toward something, and Marpa let him speak. "We and those around us are very focused on the body. When we die, we prolong its appearance beyond its time. This causes the body to remain behind as a corpse, even though the real self no longer has any use for it. A great teacher can just let the appearance of his body go, and his wisdom is contagious. Some will think they see the teacher's body ascend. But whether it ascends or not, no corpse is left behind."

Marpa was still confused. "But you say Naropa has not died."

"Some highly realized teachers do not wait to die before they let the body go. They may have reached such a level of consciousness that they cannot keep a physical presence. Their physical existence dissolves into pure activity. We call that 'entering the Action'. Someone who has entered the Action may seem to disappear. He can reappear for a time, even in several places at once. Most of the time he will not be found anywhere."

"So I have hardly started my journey to Naropa and it is over? And I will never get the special yoga Naropa prophesied."

"Naropa promised you a special teaching?"

"Yes. That is why I am making a journey to India at my age. My family is sure that bandits, disease, the weather, or just a false step on an icy ledge will kill me. Many younger men have died on the journey. In fact, they hid my provisions to stop me from going." Marpa gave his old teacher a description of his departure. He left out some of the less inspirational details.

Atisha laughed. "Your Tibetan pilgrims were all tough, but you were always the toughest. What is this special yoga?"

"It's the Yoga of No Effort," said Marpa.

Atisha's right hand tightened on the chair. He said nothing. Marpa broke the silence. "Do you know this yoga?"

"Are we talking of the Yoga of Forceful Projection? The one that allows you to project your consciousness into another body, either human or animal?"

"Yes, teacher," said Marpa. "The texts Naropa gave me say that in this way you can avoid the bardos of Death, and choose a rebirth directly."

"And avoid facing your karma in the bardos." Atisha's face was frozen.

"Teacher, is there a problem?"

Atisha took some time to answer. "Please do not take anything I say as a criticism of Naropa, who is far more accomplished than this old man. But I do not see the need for the Yoga of No Effort. When did Naropa promise it to you?"

"He gave me a coded song on my last trip. I didn't pay it much attention until last month, when a dream revealed its meaning. But now I guess I'll never receive Naropa's last yoga."

"Your will is powerful and your karmic connection is strong. You will see Naropa when you are ready for what he wants to teach you. Though I wonder if this Yoga of No Effort is something anybody is ever ready for."

"What do you mean?" Marpa asked.

"Ask yourself why it is, that you can't tell me the real reason you want this teaching?"

Marpa shifted under Atisha's gentle glance. Marpa's doggedness was his greatest strength as a student, and his greatest obstacle.

Atisha leaned back. "You're aware, of course, that this will be the last time you see me. Your return journey will be years from now, and I think I will be in the bardos of death in a few months."

"Teacher . . ."

"Let me go on," Atisha said. "The bardos are not something to avoid. Facing our karma is the only way we learn. It just seems to me that this Yoga of No Effort, where you simply pick a suitable body and pop into it, is also a Yoga of No Reward. Worse, it could fall into the wrong hands, and cause harm. Karma is not a trap. Karma is the way we learn to get out of the trap. Even Buddha would never have sought enlightenment, if he had not observed the sufferings caused by karma. But I said I would not second guess Naropa, and now I've done it."

"I have the utmost confidence in you and your teacher. I admit I wondered what Naropa was doing when he picked an angry young Tibetan as one of his main pupils. But he saw beyond your lack of self-control to your determination and your devotion to understanding yourself. Once again, Naropa has made me wonder. But I must try to believe that he sees something I do not."

60 The First Asking

PG, Tuesday

You cannot reason people out of insanity. It took me a lot of heartache to learn that and a part of me never has.

"Are you telling me that for the past three weeks," I asked Lorraine, "you have not existed in time and space?"

"That's a funny way to put it," she said.

"It's a funny thing to do."

"Josh, you read all these things, too. What's the point if you don't believe a word of them."

"They are metaphors for our spiritual experience. They are to help us cope with the material world, not escape it."

"Is life is about coping? What a horrible thing to think. What an awful thing to believe. Why bother just for that? The world of time and space is the escape. I don't need or want an escape from God any more. Let me go, Josh, let me go."

I walked over to Lorraine and put my arms around her waist. "No," she said and knocked my arms apart.

I grabbed her right wrist and turned her until her right side faced me. She was not willing, but could not win a wrestling match. If it came to that, I was glad to talk to the police if she was.

Lorraine winced when I touched the bandage below her ribs. I released her wrist and stepped back. "It must be tender. Is it a nasty cut? Get that recently?"

"I need you to let me go. Will you?" She wasn't going to answer my questions. I didn't need her to.

"Women do what they like. For better or worse, that is the law."

Lorraine smiled and waited. At least her insanity was the patient kind.

"Yes," I said, "I will let you go if you wish. Wherever it is that you're going. But I have to tell the police I've seen you."

"Can you wait?"

"Wait?"

"They won't do anything in the next two weeks. By then I'll have taken care of things."

The police would think I was lying unless I produced a live Lorraine. Lorraine was not facing charges for anything and I couldn't arrest her even if she was. The trespass at the Spencer House was a misdemeanor. A real kidnap is not a good way to beat the rap on an nonexistent murder.

My choice was simple. Give her two weeks. Or answer police questions about a story that sounded even hokier than my first one.

"I can't promise anything," I said. "If they put the screws to me, I'll have to rat you out."

"And if they don't?"

"Then you got two weeks. But please don't stretch this out."

"Thank you," she said. "I should have taken more time to explain."

She grabbed me and hugged me, firmly, but favoring her left. Then she stepped back and looked at me.

"You are the toughest thing for me to let go of." Tears were back in her eyes.

Then she moved to the door and was around it and gone.

"Wait!" I hear nothing on the stairs. I ran out and looked down. It was astonishing she could be out of the stairwell that fast, impossible she had gone far. I ran down and out to the curb. Nothing in any direction.

There was only one direction in which she could have disappeared so quickly. I ran to the walkway alongside the building. Nothing. The walkway only led one place, Mermaid Lane. I ran back there and looked its length. Empty.

Where had she gone? The light was fading. There were dark recesses all along the crowded, narrow alley. I walked a block in each direction looking around cars and trash cans. I saw nothing, which left only two possibilities. Ignoring what the neighbors might think, I flattened myself to the pavement so I could see under the cars.

She'd have looked foolish hiding under a parked car. But she wasn't hiding and she didn't look foolish — I did. Foolish was just the right way to look when contemplating the one possibility that remained. Lorraine had dissolved into thin air.

However she'd done it, she was gone. I went back upstairs. My section of coast is now pricey real estate, but it was not always so. Early settlers rejected Pacific Grove as foggy, cold and dark. The first large community here was summer only. Even today, there are a lot fewer people here in the winter. Usually I prefer the quiet, but tonight it was gloomy.

○　○　○　○　○

Taking this talk of entering the Action seriously for a moment, I didn't think combining it with the Yoga of No Effort was likely to solve the problems of either one. The annoyance about entering the Action has always been that popping into and out of the Action is uncontrolled. You don't do it, it happens to you. It's a sign of high spiritual attainment, but sometimes damned inconvenient.

The Yoga of No Effort is a very controlled thing. You take your consciousness, pick a target, aim, and shoot. And it's just plain bad news. Since the messy death of Young Teacher back in the eleventh century nobody else has dared to touch it.

That's assuming these yogas ever existed. I'm more inclined to take the Tibetan scriptures at face value than most. Scientists say that nobody in a lab has ever entered the Action, or projected his consciousness, and that nobody ever will. They're right on the first two and putting themselves way out on a limb with the third.

It's a limb they've had sawed off. Westerners said that yogis who claimed to control their heartbeat were talking nonsense. That talk ended around 1939, when Krishnamacharya seems to have stopped his ticker cold for over two minutes while a team of French doctors monitored him. I say "seems" because while nobody disputes this incident, I can't find a journal publication for it either.

No matter. In 1970, Swami Rama let Elmer and Alyce Greene wire him up at the Menninger Institute. The Swami then stopped pumping blood for sixteen seconds. There is a publication on that and you can look at the EKG for yourself if you like.

Ditto with body temperature. Western science said that nobody could raise their own before some yogis chosen by the Dalai Lama let Herbert Benson hook them up to instruments. The journal article on that came out in 1982.

The record is pretty clear. Western science has bad luck when it comes to telling yogis what they can and cannot do. And yogis only make lab demonstrations when it serves their purposes. If someone knew the Yoga of Forceful Projection, why would he want to prove it in a lab? No reason I can think of.

Do I believe in these yogas? Not really. Am I sure? No. Some people can be proved wrong, make a quick fix to their theory, then turn around and announce with total assurance that they once again have certain knowledge. I'm not one of them.

61 The Bandit Kingdom

India, 1064 AD

After leaving Atisha in the Nyang Valley, Marpa traveled two hundred lawless miles west to Khala Chela Pass. He climbed to its fifteen thousand foot summit, then descended toward India. Nalanda University was four hundred miles beyond.

Tibetans did not go straight there. They had learned not to, the hard way. Almost no germs live in the cold, thin air of Tibet, so that Tibetans arriving directly in the lowlands had no immunities. Whole expeditions had perished within weeks of arrival on the hot plains.

On his first visit, Marpa had spent three years in Katmandu, which was half way down and temperate. This time Marpa was acclimatized from two previous journeys and in a hurry. He stayed only a few months. An old teacher and friend, Paindapa, agreed to join him. A year after Marpa had left the Lhotrak, Marpa and his companion reached Nalanda University.

Marpa and Paindapa had stayed healthy. But no one at Nalanda could tell them where to find Naropa. Marpa and Paindapa began to travel around, asking whoever they met if they'd seen Naropa. In most places they had heard of the mahasiddha Naropa and his miraculous disappearance. A few pretended to know where he might be, just to be friendly. This sent the pilgrims off in random directions, and saved them the trouble of deciding where to look.

A few months of wandering brought Marpa and Paindapa to an inn in some remote foothills east of Nalanda. Their hosts were enthusiastic. The mahasiddha Naropa had passed through, they told the travelers. He was headed east. Marpa and Paindapa made little of this. Everyone who misdirected them was enthusiastic. As a Tibetan, Marpa appreciated optimism.

But Marpa soon wondered if more than optimism was at work. Barely two hours from the inn, the pilgrims walked straight into officers of King Dakoiti. These stopped the pair, and invited them to an audience with the king in his palace. The two were made to understand it would be very unwise to insult the king by refusing this honor.

King Dakoiti had started as a bandit lord. In India, this was not unusual.

Marpa and Paindapa had been assured at the inn that King Dakoiti's bandit days were long behind him. But to Marpa, it now looked like a set up. Marpa was carrying a lot of gold for Naropa. They hadn't told them that at the inn, of course, but everyone knew pilgrims often carried gold. Marpa had a bad feeling when Dakoiti's officers separated him from Paindapa, the luggage, and the gold.

The audience hall showed that the old bandit chief had done well for himself. It dripped gold leaf and crystal. But his court also showed a lot of sophistication for this corner of India. Dakoiti's guard, while more than adequate, had the dignity of a king's retinue, not the swagger of a bandit's men.

And you couldn't miss the Lady Devata, Dakoiti's queen. Very young, she had a beauty which promised to last like a stone carving. She'd dressed the other women of the court in a new style. It was the first time Marpa had seen Indian women wearing upper coverings in a formal setting. Only Devata bared her breasts. Two of the women, apparently Greek, looked at home in their blouses. The shoulders of the others were restless. They had to make a conscious effort to keep their arms at their sides.

The blouses and skirts were so sheer, it did not seem to Marpa to make much difference whether they wore them or not. It had taken him a while to get used to Indian courts. The higher her rank and the more formal the setting, the less an Indian woman wore. Some courts would give audience to a newly arrived Tibetan just to enjoy his openmouthed amazement at the dozens of women wearing only diaphanous skirts and jewelry. "The barbarians of Tibet do not know what women look like" was the saying.

A woman's real clothing at court was her jewelry. Devata's was all gold. On her head was a diadem and large earrings. From her triple necklace, a fourth strand dropped between her breasts, divided over her hips and rejoined at her back. Her arms sported narrow bangles and thick armlets. A belt of three strands held Devata's skirt. All that gold must have been heavy, but she didn't seem to mind.

As the king questioned Marpa, Devata kept the silence of one accustomed to being heard when she chose to speak. When she took over the questioning, Marpa thought he recognized the accents of the Pala court. It was clear that she knew far more about Buddhism than anyone else in Dakoiti's court. Marpa guessed that this beauty had not been raised among bandits, and did not care to be considered a bandit's wife.

Satisfied, Devata turned to her husband the king. "This Tibetan is truly a great scholar and yogi. And I've heard of his teacher. He was one of the four gatekeepers at the university in Nalanda, but resigned to advance himself even further. Men like these are wish-fulfilling jewels."

Marpa warmed to the beautiful queen's praise. "Noble lord and lady, I have vowed that I will search for my teacher. You and all beings will benefit if I have your gracious permission to pass through your kingdom on my way east."

"You say he has entered the Action?" Queen Devata asked.

"I am assured in Nalanda and Phullahari, by those who knew him, that he has."

"And so he could appear anywhere."

"Wherever the karmic connection is right, devout lady."

"He could appear here, could he not, as easily as on some leech-infested trail?"

Marpa had no answer to this. Devata continued, "We need a high priest. An accomplished yogi in our court would greatly benefit our subjects."

The King looked thoughtful. "It would make our court the boast of these hills."

"Indeed, my generous and loving Lord. And of more than these hills. In the court of my father in Gauda they will speak with envy of such a high priest."

Marpa's hunch had been right. The queen was from the great Pala court. A princess, no less. He began to speak, but the discreet touch of a spear point in his back reminded him that this would be out of protocol. When the king and queen spoke with each other, the rest of the court was to listen.

"My husband and my lord, I feel we should have this holy man for our court. Highness, I beg this of you."

"Beautiful queen, my concern for this kingdom would force me to grant your request if my love for you did not. Guards! Escort our new high priest to his rooms!"

62 Much Love, Cilla

In the morning, I wanted to go back to the Marpa book. But I had a paying client and I needed to force myself to think about something besides Lorraine. I took out the Gödel notes.

The year of Gödel's one mistake, 1970, was the same year Gödel first showed his God Proof to Dana Scott. This wasn't coincidence. Gödel was very sick in 1970 and they were both things he wanted to get off his desk in case he died.

Was the God Proof another mistake? The timing is no reason to think so. Gödel's "no good" infinity paper of 1970 was something he'd thrown together hastily at that time, and he withdrew it as soon as he was well. Gödel had worked on the God Proof for decades, and had probably put it in the form he showed Dana Scott long before 1970. He never renounced it. In any case, the Lost Notebooks were from 1945 and 1946. There's no chance Gödel's 1970 illness affected them.

Gödel had addressed challenge after challenge, and settled them with the kind of proofs which force people to change their minds. He had answered questions about the future of freedom, the need for intuition, the roles of reason and faith, the possibility of time travel. These were questions everyone assumed could never be settled before Gödel ended the debate with coercive proofs.

Had Gödel answered the question of God's existence? He thought so. His record was almost unblemished. He'd recanted his only known mistake within weeks of making it. The God Proof he'd stuck to for decades.

Armenta's rock was covered by the tide, and would be until early afternoon. Around ten I checked email. I saw a message with "the godel books" as its subject line. I cringed at the misspelling. Please, folks, it's *Gödel* if you have an umlaut and *Goedel* if you don't.

There was no sender. I thought it had to be from Sue and sat down to read it. The signature stopped me cold: "Cilla".

○ ○ ○ ○ ○

Josh, hi!

I know the notebooks have come to me for a reason. These books have a special role to play. And you are called to help in this wonderful enterprise, which will bring our planet a new awareness.

I have been receiving profuse guidance ever since these notebooks came near me. They are spiritual transmitters which never stop. I've hardly been allowed to sleep.

They are not books you read and analyze. They speak. They tell me things. I have much already and will soon have it all.

You too have your role. These books want to extend their message out to all the wretched. You have a role in making sure the technical details are right, so that even the most deluded skeptic cannot miss the message in stupid quibbles.

Circumstances prevent me from getting email replies. Run the attached program and leave your answer in a file named BLESS on the Desktop.

Don't let yourself down on this. Your role is a wonderful one. Let it happen and you will transform your life and the world.

Much love, Cilla

○ ○ ○ ○ ○

Priscilla had not offered me any money. Maybe she expected me to betray clients for free.

Court order or no court order, it didn't sound like the notebooks were coming right back to us. Priscilla made no mention of her CTS buddies. I didn't know how much to make of that. Priscilla was what you could call a self-starter.

Nothing identified the email as Priscilla's except the name at the bottom. The headers were the defaults that come with new accounts. But I felt it had to be genuine. An imposter would go to the trouble of faking the headers, while Priscilla might be too much in a hurry. Anyway, who would want to fake being Priscilla?

I expected BLESS to be a trojan horse, a malicious program she was trying to trick me into running. A few minutes of research on the Internet confirmed it. Priscilla had picked up the Agatha Trojan from the Internet, renamed it BLESS, and sent it my way. Once I ran BLESS, Priscilla could read anything she wanted on my computer, run programs, delete files, whatever.

I wanted to fall into her trap. Since she had the notebooks, it was best to play her along. But I couldn't do that without talking to Mike first and I didn't want to call him from my phone. Priscilla intended to hack my computer and to defy a court order. Tapping telephones is very illegal but surprisingly easy. I printed two copies of her email and headed for Monterey.

63 Devata's Offer

Eastern India, 1064 AD

Looking through the high priest's rooms, Marpa was pleasantly surprised. He half expected a jail cell. The compound included a functional bedroom, an impressive study and even a small hall with stone tables and an altar. The view from the bedroom and study swept over the low hills to the jungle below. A well kept garden connected the rooms. It was almost enough to make Marpa forget the guard at the door.

The study had a library, apparently that of his predecessor. The collection was large, but heavily weighted toward black magic. Marpa did note some of his favorite texts, like the *Hevajra Tantra*. Many black magicians used these. But perhaps his predecessor had been thinking of becoming a Buddhist. It would certainly have been a good move to please the queen. Marpa wondered what had become of the fellow. Why were his books still here? Had he no disciples or heirs?

Servants brought Marpa a sumptuous dinner that night. Afterwards, he watched the sunset from the garden. He thought of Queen Devata's words. Wasn't she right? Naropa could appear here as easily as anywhere. They needed the word of Buddha as desperately here as anywhere in the world of humans. Marpa went to sleep thinking well of the queen's offer.

○ ○ ○ ○ ○

Marpa had not just searched for Naropa in India. He had also looked in the Dream Bardo.

The Dream Bardo is one of the three bardos of the living. Bardos are usually spoken of as after-death experiences, but they're more than that. "Bardo" means "suspended in between." It's any state where you're neither here or there. In a state like that, you're confused and afraid.

Our everyday, waking life is the Waking Bardo. The Waking Bardo is as much a bardo as any after-death experience. You're in unreliable territory, on shifting ground.

Naropa taught Marpa methods to find ease and stability in the Waking Bardo. He did the same for the Dream Bardo, teaching Marpa to dream consciously, and to direct his dreams. But Marpa's efforts to find Naropa in the Dream Bardo were as ineffective as those in the Waking Bardo, until that night in the high priest's bedroom.

Marpa dreamed he was sitting in his garden, facing the low stone wall that ran along one side of it. The wall was wide, and smooth enough to walk on, if you didn't mind the sheer cliff on the far side. Earlier in the day Marpa had no problem hopping on top for a look down. In much of Tibet a far more dangerous precipice is the main road into town.

But Naropa was not Tibetan, and looked out of place on the precarious wall. He trotted along it nonetheless, alighted in front of Marpa, and smiled hello. Naropa seldom spoke. Most lessons from the mahasiddha were totally silent. He simply sat and radiated a calm, powerful joy. New students of the mahasiddha, expecting to hear secret teachings, often felt disappointed. Senior students had a suggestion for those who wanted to leave: try to achieve that same deep joy on your own. Most of those who tried, stayed.

Naropa pointed left. A richly jeweled woman in voluminous Tibetan robes glided the wall. Pearls studded her cascading raven hair. Her coal-black face was so lovely it hurt to meet her jet eyes. Marpa recognized the goddess Wisdom Form.

Rippling her four arms for balance, Wisdom Form stepped down. She greeted Naropa with a kiss. Naropa turned to Marpa and pointed back along the wall. A woman dressed as a ladies' maid approached. Her only jewelry was the beaded belt that secured her skirt. Her blouse was a simple, square cloth with a neck hole, tied in back. Marpa drew a breath when he realized this was Queen Devata.

Naropa extended a hand to the queen to help her down from the wall. He whispered in her ear. Devata looked impishly at Marpa. Naropa stepped aside. Devata met the goddess's eyes, then met Marpa's again and put a hand to her mouth to hide a laugh. She stepped over to the goddess to whisper. Whatever the queen said made Wisdom Form laugh. The goddess fanned out her arms.

Devata stepped behind the goddess. She reached around, between the upper and lower pairs of arms, undid the jeweled clasp topmost on the goddess's cape, and let it fall to the dirt. A small vee opened in the rich silk robe and a luminous sliver of throat was exposed.

Wisdom Form held steady. When the second clasp dropped, the goddess's skin glowed like an ember. With the third, the robe parted. Whatever was behind it was as bright as a torch. Marpa had averted his eyes by the time he heard the fourth clasp fall. The goddess shone like the disk of the sun.

Shading his eyes, Marpa caught glimpses of the queen piling the goddess's clothes on her shoulder. The jewelry Devata dropped to the dirt.

Queen Devata stripped the goddess quickly, then stepped back. Devata offered the goddess's clothes to Naropa, who put them on a bench and picked through. Devata returned to crawl at the goddess's feet. Marpa couldn't watch Devata. The light from Wisdom Form was too intense.

Naropa found the goddess's cape and pulled it out of the pile. He rolled the other silks onto the cape, and pulled the cape's corners together to make a bundle. Naropa swung it, at first tentatively, then faster. Once he was spinning as hard as he could, he swept out three full circles and let the bundle go, high over the canyon.

Naropa stumbled back. The cape unfolded like a huge bird. The rich garments spilled out and danced in the strong updrafts.

Devata rose up. The goddess's jewelry filled her hands and overflowed onto her wrists. She walked over to Naropa. Naropa chuckled, grabbed a jasper armlet and hefted it at one of the garments. He missed. The jewel crashed into the vegetation.

Devata laughed and slid the jewels onto the bench. The two took turns throwing gems at the goddess's clothes. The updrafts were tricky, but twice Naropa hit silk. Each time Devata squealed with laughter and vowed revenge.

The queen took aim at a floating undergarment. A silver anklet with moonstones and a mean spin scored dead center. The hard thrown jewel wrapped the wispy fabric around it, and spiraled into the ravine twirling its new silk tail.

Devata bounced up and down and whooped triumph. Naropa caught her in mid-jump, leaned back and twirled her by the forearms. Devata shrieked with joy. Her ankles lifted up and away. Her blouse and skirt pulled outward.

The two ended up in the dirt, queen on top, laughing and gasping. Naropa pulled her up to his face. He tilted her head toward Marpa and whispered in her ear. With another impish smile, Devata rolled off Naropa. Still prone, she twisted to face Marpa, then reared up on her hands. Her skirt was torn and the loose blouse bared her left breast.

Devata flexed, put her weight on her feet, and came upright. She took a step toward Marpa, then caught his gaze and followed it back to her half undone blouse. She put her hand behind her back, finished the job and whipped the blouse to the ground.

She fingered the clasp of her belt and looked at Marpa. The belt slid down her leg. Her eyes went back to him as her finger moved to where the pleats in front of her skirt tucked into her waist string.

Devata undid a pleat. She read his face as her answer for the next three pleats. With the last pleat between her thumb and forefinger, she lifted her head again. A second later, Devata dropped the ruined skirt behind her. She now wore only a drawstring underskirt.

Devata stepped forward, but stopped short when her eyes lost Marpa's. His were on her drawstring knot. This took longer. Devata could not comply and keep her hair in place. She lifted her arms to the back of her head. She was breathtaking. Marpa would have been happy if she took her time. But the slave whose half-slip Devata wore never let her hair down with less ceremony.

The queen's fingers returned to her waist. With the skirt no longer tucked into it, her drawstring was already a little loose. Devata undid its knot and pulled the half-slip over her head. When she lifted it over her eyes, Marpa was staring into them. She smiled and held her slip out. He took it and tossed it aside.

"You no longer seek Naropa?" she asked. Marpa looked around. Naropa was gone.

"If you want me, come." Devata gestured. Marpa stepped forward. Devata backed toward the goddess. The light hurt Marpa's eyes. He put up his arm to protect them and tried to follow.

Devata stepped between Marpa and the goddess. The light dimmed. Marpa looked up. Curves flowed in Devata's silhouette as she turned. She walked behind the goddess. Again the light was too much. Marpa turned away, fell to the ground and covered his face.

After a second, the light wavered, then softened. Marpa looked up. The goddess was draped in the remnants of Devata's clothes. She flickered with a final adjustment of the torn skirt, then looked at Marpa and spoke softly.

"If you had looked directly at me, you would have seen the truth naked. Seeing reality as it truly is, you would have gone forever beyond fear or anxiety. You would be one with the Self which never dies. You would have no need of the mahasiddha Naropa. But your gaze did not hold steady on the truth. Desire controlled what you saw. If where you look is controlled by desire, you can never find the teacher. Naropa has headed east." Then she turned to follow the others.

○ ○ ○ ○ ○

The next day Marpa told his guard that he needed to relay a message to the king. Marpa did not speak the dialect of this section of India, but his request had the intended effect. He was visited by the chief vizier of the court.

The chief vizier was cool as he told Marpa that Paindapa had been escorted out of the kingdom. He was chilly when he told Marpa that his gold was in a safe place and would stay there. He was icy as he told Marpa that he did not care to discuss what that place was. But he melted and trembled when Marpa said he could not accept the position of chief priest.

The vizier begged Marpa not to force him to take that message to the royal couple. Marpa insisted. On the way out, the vizier stumbled into one of the peacocks in the garden. When the queen entered a few minutes later, the poor bird had barely recovered enough to stagger aside before being trampled.

"You needn't speak," she said. "My vizier told me of your insult to me and my dear, generous king. So much he wants to do for his subjects. And to be refused by an insolent, snub-nosed barbarian beggar! No real teacher would turn his back on the needs here. You are simply another parasite who begs in the name of the Buddha. You and the human realm are both better off if you are sent quickly to burn off your sins in the Hell of Unceasing Pain.

"It's a shame we sent your partner in beggary out of the kingdom. If he'd been allowed to stay, he could be executed with you in the morning. Your gold can at least be used to help us bring a real Buddhist siddha to this kingdom."

The queen turned and stormed out. The peacocks were all behind plants or off in safe corners. Marpa thought and did nothing for a long time.

64 The Double Game

Highway 68 runs along the spine of the Monterey Peninsula, with ocean views in three directions. It's not the most direct route to Monterey. Near its crest, there's a fieldstone wall with a brass plaque announcing the entrance to a subdivision. I turned into it and twisted along quiet roads past expensive hillside homes until I spotted a hundred-foot stretch that was straight, flat and wide-shouldered. I circled back to it and pulled over. After counting down three minutes on my watch, I did a U-turn, circled the other way, pulled over and counted three more minutes. Then I descended into Monterey.

That should have burned any car tail. The high speeds and screeching tires you see in the movies are counterproductive. The slower and easier you go the more obvious your tail looks. Not to mention slow and easy is less likely to get you police attention.

In Monterey, I didn't go straight to Mike's office. I wanted to repeat on foot what I'd done in the car. Mike is seven blocks from the Fisherman's Wharf complex. I parked halfway between and walked to the Wharf's Convention Center. This has two main hotels, on opposite sides of busy Del Monte street. A glassed-in pedestrian crossover connects the second floors of the hotels and lets conventioneers and tourists go back and forth without braving the traffic.

It was perfect for my purposes. It's long. There's no place to hide. If my tail didn't stick close, I could just continue into one of the hotels and be long gone. I crossed five times. I was alone. If someone was watching me at Mike's it wouldn't be because I led them there.

Not that my antics would have burned a law-enforcement-quality team tail. That's three skilled ops, absolute minimum. With multiple trained ops, when I pulled my stunts, one op would just go on, and another member of the team would pick me up. But that kind of tail costs serious money, more than I hoped the CTS was willing to spend.

I called from a pay phone. Mike was out. Veronica put me through to Zoe.

"It's Josh Bryant. I'm working with Mike on matters relating to Sue Shrift and her notebooks."

"Yes. I remember you, of course. Mike's in court."

"I think there's a complication about the notebooks. Do you know if they were handed over to Judge Gaunilo?"

"I assume so. I haven't checked. Why?"

"I've heard from the CTS. I think they plan to defy the court order."

"What did they say?"

"I can show you. It's in an email and I can bring it."

"Good. Can you do that today?"

"I'm here in town. I'll be there in a few minutes."

On the phone, Zoe had been friendly but unconcerned. When I arrived at Mike's office, she was agitated.

"I talked to the Clerk of Court and one of Gaunilo's own clerks. They didn't get the notebooks. It turns out they called here and left a message for Mike, which I didn't know when you called. I don't dare call the CTS lawyer on my own. Mike would want to handle that. I did call Sue, though. She asked you to wait here for her."

"Good. I'd like very much to talk to her about all this."

"Would you like some coffee?"

"I know where to find it, thanks. When will Mike be in?"

"This afternoon. I'll leave him a message, but I doubt he can do anything until then."

"I do have an idea. I think a lawyer from Princeton showed up at the hearing. If you call him and alert him to what's going on, he'll probably appreciate it. He'll probably also contact the CTS to ask them what's going on."

Zoe's eyes sparkled. "And I bet I could get him to return the courtesy and pass on to us what the CTS told him. Good idea. I don't know the man's name, but I can look it up. He's probably back in New Jersey by now."

I gave Zoe a copy of Priscilla's email and asked her to run a copy off for Sue. Zoe set aside a conference room and I removed to it with coffee and magazines. In the unlikely event Mike's legal practice should falter, I think he'd make a killing running a magazine stand.

Sue arrived an hour later. Zoe and I briefed her, then sat silent while she read Priscilla's letter.

Sue looked uneasy. "You are not going to take her offer, are you?"

"Under no circumstance. You hired me first. I'd hate working for Priscilla, so it's not even a temptation." Not to mention Priscilla had not offered me a dime. Money means so little to Sue, she sometimes forgets the role it plays for the rest of us.

With Sue nervous on the loyalty issue, I did not want to start talking about the double game I was planning. I'd wait for Mike to help explain why we should play Priscilla along.

Sue twitched a little and pursed her lips. I waited for her to follow up about Priscilla's letter, but instead she pulled a cellphone from her blazer. She studied the unit, sighed, poked it with a finger and cradled it to her ear.

"What's the matter?" She said into the phone.

The voice from the cellphone struck a shrill, soft, moaning note and held it. I could not make out any words, but it sounded like a dial tone begging for its life.

Sue caught a brief waver. "Calm down," she soothed into it.

I signaled to Zoe that we should leave the room. Sue waved a negative. Switching the phone to her left hand and ear, she got up and looked out the door. She pointed to Mike's office. Zoe nodded. Sue entered Mike's office and shut the door.

An atmosphere of fear left the room with the cellphone. Zoe and I caught each other inhaling with relief and exchanged smiles. She was the first to feel the need to fill the silence. "I could only do so much to free up Mike's schedule. He has this one o'clock that I don't think . . ."

Veronica leaned in. "Sorry to interrupt. It's Kingman Quincy. I thought you might want to take it."

To me, Zoe said, "This is the Princeton lawyer." She was already getting up. "Yes, thank you, Veronica." Then, to me again, "Sorry."

"No, talk to him. I am dying to know his story."

Zoe was already around the doorjamb and the last part of my speech was to the air. I turned to the magazines. I read the article on B17s in World War II, then reread the article on the Schuar. I had time to go back and study some of the pictures before Zoe returned.

"Mr. Quincy had a lot to say," she said, resuming her chair. "He talked to the District Court and had several calls with the CTS attorney. The District Court hasn't gotten the notebooks or anything else from the CTS. Bill Wallace is the CTS attorney. He claimed to be surprised, which Quincy thinks may be genuine. If the CTS decided not to comply with the court order, they might well not inform their attorney."

"What about the cash?"

"That was to come here and we have not seen that either."

"You say 'if' the CTS decided to defy the court. Is there any doubt left?"

"In the law we are trained not to draw conclusions until necessary. When we go into court Gaunilo will want our evidence, not our conclusions. We train ourselves to doubt even the obvious, so that our minds are constantly taking in new evidence. There is no such thing as too much evidence."

"How could the CTS be in compliance, but the court not have the notebooks?"

"Right," said Zoe. "Wallace called Quincy back and said that the people to whom they had entrusted the notebooks are no longer acting on CTS instructions. Wallace said the CTS itself was complying fully."

I groaned. Zoe smiled and continued.

"Quincy did not let them get away with that. He asked if the notebooks had been reported stolen. Wallace didn't know. Quincy assumed that meant they had not been. He told Wallace that he believed the CTS was already in contempt for letting the notebooks be stolen without immediately reporting that to the police and the court. Wallace said he'd call back. When he did, he told Quincy the crime had been reported to the police. He didn't say when."

"Is the CTS stalling?"

"Quincy tells me he thinks at this point they are very afraid of contempt proceedings. If Gaunilo finds it necessary, he can put people in jail until they cooperate. The CTS may have been stalling before, but Quincy thinks that now they are falling all over themselves to comply. In their place I certainly would, because Gaunilo could put people in jail, I mean, like, today."

"Do they say who has the notebooks? They must know where they were last seen."

"The report is that they were last known to be in the possession of a Carrie Beedis at an address in Soledad, which is very interesting."

"Carrie was one of the people on the raid. It's not Priscilla?"

"Who?"

"Cilla. Priscilla Wolf. She's the one who sent the email I showed you. Wasn't that what was interesting?"

"Now that you point it out, that is interesting, but I was thinking of them being in Soledad. Sue lives there."

"Oh," I said. "Oh. That is interesting. There's nothing there except lettuce fields and the prison. If it's coincidence, it's quite a coincidence. I take it Mike will ask for contempt charges."

"We don't really call them charges." Zoe went on to explain some of the ins and outs of contempt proceedings. I was well prepared for those questions on the Bar Exam by the time an exhausted Sue dropped into the chair nearest the door with an announcement.

"That was Carrie."

"Carrie Beedis?" Zoe asked.

"Yes," Sue said. "We've been talking to each other now and then."

Here I had been, thinking that Sue might not be able to deal with the idea of playing Priscilla along. That Mike and I were going to need to ease her into the idea. All this time, she'd been playing double with Carrie, and me without a clue.

"Can I get you something?" Zoe said. "Coffee?"

"Just water," Sue said. "I could really use a half shot of gin, but I don't expect you've got that."

"Mike has a bottle of bourbon. Is that OK?"

65 The Sword of Devata

Devata's kingdom, 1064 AD

When Marpa began paying attention to his surroundings again, the sun was low in the sky. On the far side of the canyon, a couple embraced in the yews. The man leaned the woman back. She went out of sight among the vines. Then he did.

Marpa thought of Ocean back in Tibet. He was going to die as a sacrifice to the pretensions of a spoiled young bandit queen. All Ocean might ever learn was that he had been executed. The news would take months to reach her. Or it might never reach her. Ocean would wake up every day for the rest of her life wondering if this was the day he would return.

"How hard I'd be on a student who went to pieces like this!" Marpa told himself. "Ordinary people face death with courage all the time. Even degenerate men. The bandits who chased me on the Ganges, greedy for gold and the blood of pilgrims, staked their own lives without a second thought."

Marpa remembered the last night's dream, how passions and delusions denied him the goddess. "What would I assign a student who went to pieces like this?" he asked himself.

He knew the answer. Follow the breath. He assigned that to every new student. They wanted to go straight to advanced practices, sorcery or sex or both. Marpa told them they could do advanced practices when they were advanced students. Marpa had a way to spot advanced students. Advanced students realized that following the breath was an advanced practice. Beginning students did not.

Marpa found his breath and felt his terror. He tried to hold onto the breath and the terror, but the terror soon became thoughts. Fears for tomorrow, regrets for what he had done. Marpa's attention was swept away from his breath. Marpa collected himself, took himself back to the breath and the terror. Then the thoughts came and he lost the breath again. Patiently, Marpa kept taking himself back to the breath.

Marpa knew that the breath would lead him to the secret of power: the present. Fear and regret block energy. You can't fear for the present. It

191

just is. Fear is always of the future. You can't regret the present. Regret is always about what might have been.

Marpa told himself what he told his students. The terror wasn't real. The terror was a trick of the ego, to keep you from being aware of the breath, of the present. The terror is a gift. The stronger the terror the greater the gift. It's tells you you are close to power. Power to deal with life. Power to deal with the bardos of death, when it comes to that.

After an hour, Marpa decided to stretch his legs. He found the entrance to his compound heavily guarded. Going back through his anteroom, Marpa noticed a fish on a side table. He hadn't eaten since the queen's visit. It had a white belly, fantastically ribbed dark green fins, and sparkling, iridescent scales on back. Marpa didn't remember any fish from the meal last night. The service had been attentive. Marpa thought everything must have been cleared. He certainly thought he would have remembered such a remarkable fish.

Marpa wolfed it down. He was hungry. Fish had never tasted better. The taste was as complex as the coloration, like a hundred different foods all at once. And it was just the thing for his meditation. Marpa's thoughts steadied. He reflected it was a fortunate thing that the fish had been left behind, because even now he felt a little hungry.

An hour later, a much calmer Marpa decided to stretch his legs again. He strolled around his compound. Reentering his anteroom, he spotted another white bellied fish on the side table opposite the first one. This second fish had also escaped his notice. This was really strange, but Marpa wanted to resume meditation, not speculate about fish. Of this second fish, Marpa ate half and left half.

Marpa realized he could sleep. In fact he was very tired. It seemed a good idea to rest for what awaited with the light. The bed of the high priest was inviting and Marpa dozed off in seconds.

○ ○ ○ ○ ○

A light thump on the bedclothes awakened Marpa. The room was very dark. Something small hit the stone floor next to the bed. Marpa assumed a rat, until he heard a giggle from the door. He saw a woman raise her arm. Another thump on the covers. Marpa sat up. He checked that he was in the Waking Bardo. He was. She was not a dream.

Another plunk on the floor. It was a pebble. More giggles. The woman left the doorway. Marpa followed into the garden.

"Do you know what a woman is?" Marpa recognized Devata's voice. Jewelry clinked in the moonless night, but no clothing showed.

Marpa drew close, and wrinkled his nose. An odor like the white-bellied fish. Devata smirked. "Wives in Tibet, consorts in India, women on the way back and forth. And still you are such a fool."

Devata let his hands slide along her. Indeed she wore neither cotton or silk. Marpa decided he didn't care about the smell.

Her left palm pressed his chest. She leaned into him. He closed his arms behind her. "So now I will show you what woman really is." She was warm under his fingers.

Something told Marpa not to bend his lips to hers. He argued against his intuition. Then he realized his artery pulsed against a very keen blade. He'd almost cut his own throat.

Devata let him step back, but her eyes warned him not to move quickly. The blade followed the artery. She held a small executioner's sword, short and hooked, with an unusual crystal handle. Marpa had once offended a Nepalese executioner by implying the cruel hook was there only for its intimidating appearance. Marpa had, for politeness sake, then to listen to a long explanation of its various alleged practical advantages, none of which he believed then or remembered now.

Hooked or not, this sword could do the job. Devata's grip had authority. Her eye suggested experience. Nude, she'd have no trouble washing off a lot of blood. The sword's size and custom handle suggested that it was made especially for her.

Devata studied Marpa's face. Before this night, Marpa had assumed that he would retain clarity of mind after death and recognize the lights in the Bardo of White Light. And even if he missed them and wound up dealing with his karma in the Bardo of Hyperreality, he felt sure he would correctly recognize at least one of the lights or deities there.

Most people, Marpa knew, didn't even realize they were dead. They were panicked, or at least bewildered, by the lights, noises and creatures of the death bardos, and they missed all the opportunities for enlightenment and quality rebirths. Marpa now saw that this could happen to him.

He struggled to remember the signs that you were in the death bardos. If you could not see the sun or moon, you were dead. But it was a moonless night. If you spoke to people and they took no notice, you were dead. But Devata was the only other person here, and she could ignore the living as easily as the dead.

No matter. There were other things to watch for. A loud noise, like a windstorm or an earthquake. The five clairvoyances. Inability to eat, drink, cast a shadow or leave a footprint. The ability to travel anywhere, except the place of his next rebirth. A change in skin color, appropriate to his karma.

The ability to see other spirits in the bardo. A feeling of motion, upward or downward, again depending on karma.

Devata's eyes flashed. Through the metal, Marpa felt her fingers tighten. But Devata pulled the sword back and turned it around. She added her left hand to the grip. "See what a woman is!" she said, then thrust herself and the sword together until the hilt met her sternum.

Marpa reeled from blood which never came. Trick blade? No magician in his right mind used a trick blade that sharp, but the queen was not a magician, much less one of the rare right-minded sort.

Devata pulled the sword out and dropped it. The metal was clean. No blood, no wound. Just a slit between her breasts.

The slit widened. It did not expand the way that ordinary things do. Ordinary things grow into space taken from other things. They are aggressive. They displace. They live by killing. Devata's heart unfolded its own space. New space. Nothing was forced aside. But so vast was Devata's heart that everything else soon seemed just a frame around it.

Marpa felt her hands on his shoulders. Devata's eyes caught his. With hands and eyes, she sat him down. Then she sat astride him. Her heart center touched his. From hers flowed a force like a typhoon, warm, soft at the edges, unstoppable. The wind hit Marpa's heart dead center, blew it open and poured in.

Aloft in the stream were gods. Goddesses. Real pasts. Imagined histories. Possible worlds. Impossible universes. Alternative futures. Futures that live only in remorse. Naropa's face. The Action.

Naropa's face sailed away, following the other images. Devata whispered, "Let go. Just let the images go by. Don't watch for them. Don't try to hold them." She kissed Marpa's ear. "It will help if you imagine we're having sex."

The heart currents had swept sex out of Marpa's mind. Devata's words brought it back with a vengeance. Marpa held back. "It will be OK," she assured and he fell like a man who slips on a Himalayan glacier and slides into a crevice whose bottom no man has ever seen.

The waking world that framed Devata's heart narrowed to a rim. Then it was nothing. Devata's heart was now the book, of which our world is just pages, torn from it and scattered. The pages spiraled into mandalas and danced. They swirled out of blackness and fell back in. Devata's heart remained the blackness, unchanged, untouched.

All of knowledge, Devata urged him to know her totally. Marpa's heart filled itself with Devata's outpouring, but it could absorb what she gave only in pieces. And in the changing pieces was born time, then death.

Within Devata's heart, Marpa saw Wisdom Form and heard her voice. "Only life comes out of me. But because you take just part of all I would give, you get limitation and death from it. They are not from me, but come when you do not take me totally, fully and immediately.

"You are attached to your limits. And so you create death. Death is the trick your limitations use to make you believe in them. A trick they invented to make them and their desires seem real. Time and death are the clothing you put on me.

"In your dream you did not look on me. You must be able to see the goddess to see any woman. You feared my nakedness. You saw me as a temptress and as your death. There is only one woman, and she is the goddess. The temptress is the goddess you fear. You feared me and made me your executioner.

"At every moment, the world is exactly what it should be to lead you to enlightenment. You have only to open yourself to it.

"Now I have something to ask," she said in a voice like the wind over the ocean. Marpa rejoiced. He could do something for this force of all forces? He had dissolved into her. What could she ask that Marpa would refuse?

"You must leave me," she said. Marpa heard her sentence him to life, the way he'd heard the death sentence that morning. Now Marpa knew why it had been so hard to get Naropa to leave the Action. It was like asking a fish to leave the sea.

"Remember your vow to serve my children in the Waking Bardo," she said. "Take what I have shown you. Go back to them, and bring them to me, so I may love them and you all the more. Be born to the world of change and death once more, for the love of me."

And then Marpa was lying on his back in the garden. The first rays of sun hit the tree tops. Birds tuned up. Shouts echoed off the canyon walls. The vision of Devata was gone.

66 Symposium

Sue nodded and Zoe popped out for the bourbon. I pondered this new side of Sue's personality. Would she pull out a revolver and start cleaning it? I'd have figured Sue for a small automatic, but Zoe's advice about avoiding conclusions in favor of evidence was starting to make lots of sense to me.

Zoe came in with the bottle and two glasses. "I'd join you, but I have enough to explain to Mike already." She set the bottle and glasses in front of me.

I felt awkward playing host, but any argument would just have made things less comfortable. I guessed at a half shot and offered the effort to Sue. "Perfect," she said.

I splashed an attempt at the same amount into the other glass and raised it. "Confusion to the enemy," I said. Sue smiled and emptied hers.

I took a pull at mine. Suspecting Zoe would be happy to get the bottle out of sight as soon as possible, I pushed it toward her.

Zoe pointed to Sue's glass. "Let me clean that."

"Thank you," Sue said as she handed it over.

I took the hint, finished mine off and surrendered my glass with Sue's. I don't enjoy drinking these days like I used to, but this had hit the spot. Zoe breezed away.

"Should we wait for her?" I asked.

Sue gave me a long, thoughtful look. "Do you know where Soledad Mission is?"

"Yeah."

"Could you be there tomorrow at ten?"

"Sure," I said warily.

"I need you to meet Carrie there."

"You want me to talk with her? What if I say the wrong thing? I might scare her off."

Sue smiled weakly. "I have confidence you're smart enough not to get pushy. But you're right, Carrie is terrified nearly beyond speech. Be careful. I want you to talk to her because she may tell you things she doesn't want to say to me. The Mission is near their safe house and they have only one car, which Cilla pretty much monopolizes. Carrie can walk to the Mission. She'll tell Cilla she has gone there to pray. Cilla will believe that."

"Help me out here. Priscilla reports to Carrie, no?"

Zoe returned. We updated her on my appointment with Carrie.

"Technically, yes," Sue answered, once I had repeated my question for Zoe's benefit. "But, as we discussed, Cilla tends to take over things. The CTS wanted Cilla on this detail because of her experience with me and her enthusiasm for the task. But they also were uneasy about trusting her."

"Fools, but not complete fools," Zoe said.

"Yes," Sue said. "So they put Carrie in command. Carrie was devoted to them and would not go off the deep end on her own. But the CTS didn't think it out. They like Carrie because she's docile. They should have realized it would not be long before Cilla reduced her to a figurehead. After all, that's what she did with me. The difference is that, once cornered, I realized I had to control my own name and work. Carrie just wants to avoid trouble."

I suspected that Sue bounced Priscilla long before Sue was anywhere near cornered. "How did you contact Carrie?" I asked.

"I don't know who contacted who. They staked out my home and one really cold night Carrie got stranded in the chaparral wearing almost nothing."

Zoe interrupted. "I have a feeling, once you get going on this, I'll forget all about lunch. Why don't we order in? Mike will buy."

67 Stakeout

Soledad, California, October, 2001

Priscilla learned of the Gödel notebooks back in 2000. After Sue bounced her, Priscilla took her talents and grievances to the Center for Total Surrender. It was Priscilla who convinced them that much of Sue's work came out of their books. In particular, that the notebooks were based on their ideas. And that they could claim their property under copyright.

This is silly under the copyright laws. But the CTS folks weren't lawyers. They feel their publications are necessary for a correct understanding of God. So either you have no understanding of what God is, or you are using their ideas. It made sense to them.

The CTS spent a lot on legal advice without anyone pointing out their mistake. If a lawyer tells you you've got no copyright, he makes almost nothing. If he encourages your claim, he can make a mint. The more dubious your claim, the more litigation and the more the lawyer makes.

The leadership of the CTS dispatched Priscilla and Carrie to Soledad to locate the notebooks and prepare the way for their seizure. The two women rented a safe house among the lettuce fields west of Soledad and within a few days began to watch Sue's house. Sue lives on the other side of town, several miles into the cattle country of the Gabilan mountains.

Sue already knew she was being watched when Priscilla picked a hill above Sue's home as a lookout. Don't ask me how. In a lot of detective stories, the PI badgers, berates, threatens, spies on and insults his paying clients until he has learned more embarrassing personal details about them than he pretends to care about. I've never understood what joy he gets from this behavior, much less how he stays in business. A business which needs customers who have nothing to hide won't last long. At least that's my experience.

Neither Priscilla or Carrie had a background in surveillance. Neither could legally conduct one. In California, you need a private investigator's license for that. For that matter, their lookout was on Sue's property. A PI license does not allow you to trespass.

Priscilla picked up a few surveillance skills quickly, and passed them on to Carrie as it suited her. They took turns doing watches. On a few days, each of them did a watch, but more often Priscilla substituted a car tail for hers.

Theirs was a low budget operation, but Priscilla would have bought the same car if she had five times the money. She spotted a 1980 California special Saint George police car on a lot and insisted on it. The lot was happy to oblige her. Saint George's are maintenance nightmares. Police departments had quickly dumped them. Production ended with a small 1981 run.

Nonetheless, Saint George's do have fans. They are tough. You can take all four wheels five feet off the ground and land without a bounce. And they look like police cars. Hollywood loved them. Hundreds were bought to be destroyed in films. In Hollywood, love is a difficult thing.

Priscilla's rescue from the Saint George class of 1980 was blue where the rust didn't show, and needed more body work than it was worth. Priscilla usually drove. She did all the car tails. She told Carrie that car tails were a skill that Carrie did not have.

Priscilla never actually rear-ended Sue, but it was easier to forget that you're towing a trailer than it was to miss one of Priscilla's car tails. Sue eventually had to talk to the police. They would have arrested Priscilla if Sue hadn't asked them not to.

Since Priscilla did all the car tailing, Carrie got surveillance and lots of it. Carrie took a while to get the hang of it. She did not bring any water at all on her first surveillance. By the time Priscilla picked her up, Carrie had early symptoms of dehydration. But Carrie was convinced that she was doing God's work, and accepted physical hardship. It was Sue who cracked first. That happened two weeks into the stakeout.

What did it was the first night watch. It was one of Priscilla's sudden brainstorms. She decided on it late one afternoon. They had to hurry to get Carrie to the lookout before nightfall.

Carrie quickly dropped a Gatorade, food bars and toilet paper into a plastic bag. She had on a short skirt and a sleeveless blouse. It was hot in the valley. Carrie grabbed tennis shoes on the way out the door. She put them on as they drove through town and left her mules in the car.

The sun had just set when they reached the trailhead for their lookout. Priscilla told Carrie it was important that the car not be there long, and was as good as her word. The car was already turning around when Carrie raised her hand to wave goodbye. Carrie didn't think Priscilla saw.

It occurred to Carrie that might be best. She was not sure if waving goodbye was something partners on surveillance did. Priscilla might not like it. Carrie felt sad that she was doing so poorly at relating to Priscilla, and resolved to do better as she disappeared into the bushes. If she didn't get going, she knew she'd finish the climb in the dark.

At bends in the trail, Carrie caught glimpses of the town of Soledad cooling in the fading sun. Down in the valley during the afternoon, her outfit had felt comfortable. Up in the hills in the twilight, the air was brisk.

The three hundred foot climb to the lookout took the chill off. Carrie settled herself on an ergonomic rock and pulled out binoculars. Dimming light made magnified vision poor and Carrie's bare arms soon shivered, so she put the binoculars away. The wind was rising. Carrie walked about, but that did not help much. She remembered her food bars and ate one. Five minutes later she was shivering again and ate another.

Half an hour later, her food was all gone, and Carrie sat on the rock, arms clasped around her bare legs. Carrie told herself she was being silly, that it was all in her mind. She looked about for other things to think of.

In her daylight watches, Carrie had come to like this place. The Gabilans were either restful or entertaining as her mood required. Every bush became a friend, and the changing light gave the landscape a new look every hour. The hills of the Gabilans floated in the background while Carrie's thoughts drifted.

As sunset approached, the Gabilans changed personality. The air smelled different. The hills no longer soothed. In the valley, the lights of the maximum security prison were bright. As the darkness deepened, Carrie looked toward the prison more and more.

There's an exact time when the night mammals start their rounds. It's just when the last daylight is gone, when you can't say it's twilight any more and have to call it night. Once that time comes, a different animal shakes the chaparral every few minutes. A dusky-footed woodrat was the first. He whisked through the brush as near Carrie as he could get and still be hidden, then sniffed the air. The terrified girl did not register as food or predator. The woodrat scurried on. He needed to find food before daylight made him visible to the hawks.

With every sound in the bushes, Carrie grew more afraid. She bent her head forward between numbing arms. The wind crooned. Carrie wanted to weep, but all that came out was a soft whimper. A light came on in Sue's house down in the hollow. Carrie didn't notice.

68 The Smell of Fish

Devata's kingdom, 1064 AD

Marpa leaned up. He tried to locate the shouts. It was well toward dawn. Where were his executioners? A morning execution should already be underway. The shouts did not sound right to be coming from the entrance to his compound, but finally that was his only guess. Marpa walked to the anteroom.

He couldn't enter it. The room was filled to overflow with white-bellied fish. Even sound could not penetrate the densely packed fish. In the echoes, Marpa heard the king exhorting the guards to clear a path. The king's words were good news. The guards were carrying out a rescue, not an execution. The appearance of the fish was seen as a miracle. Marpa's miracle.

The way fish were packed into the anteroom, they'd be a while. Marpa searched his rooms. The crystal sword was where it had dropped. No queen.

Marpa made two more leisurely searches for her. No sign except the sword. He settled down. He had a long wait. When a hole finally appeared at the top of the door, Marpa saw why. As fish were cleared, those to either side slid into the gap. It was like bailing water.

When the fish lowered to eye level, a guard spotted Marpa and yelled back in dialect. Soon Marpa could watch the guards work. They often lost footing in the slippery fish. And the stone floor, slick with oil, was even more dangerous. Several times men fell. One started to leave, cradling an arm.

By then, the queen had arrived. She'd somehow gotten to the other side of the fish, fixed her hair, and put on a skirt. Did she know of a hidden passage out of his compound? Was this a devious play for power in the bandit kingdom? Devata thanked the wounded man as he left, and urged the rescue on.

When the fish were shin high, the queen ordered the guards aside. She faced Marpa. Her face shone with tears. She waded forward and threw herself and her expensive silk into the slick mess, prostrate, palms up.

"Forgive me, Mahasiddha. Spare this queen. At least spare her sinless king and his innocent kingdom."

Marpa minced onto the treacherous floor, and extended his arms to the queen. "Rise," he said. "Rise, devout queen."

The queen grasped Marpa's hands tightly and levered herself up. Her breasts streaked his robe with oil. A smell of fish and musk, so familiar from hours before, assailed Marpa's nostrils. Marpa lifted the queen off her feet, and carried her to the king. The old bandit was still quite strong. He had no trouble taking her from Marpa's arms, and holding her in his own. She cried softly into his shoulder.

Everyone waited for Marpa to speak. He heard himself say, "Blessed majesties, your queen surely has accumulated great merit in her previous lives. Throughout India I have sought my guru, Naropa. Not a dream, not a vision, not a sight, not a word, until I came to your realm, noble Dakoiti.

"Night before last I had a dream, in which Naropa appeared to me alongside your gracious queen Devata. I did as I thought my dream instructed. I asked to follow my guru to the east. But I did not understand my dream. The true journey east must be within."

The queen continued to cry, and the king nearly joined her. Marpa laid it on thicker.

"My teacher and the goddesses found this most blessed queen a worthy way to purge this humble pilgrim of his delusions. Last night the Sky Dancers granted me a vision of the Action. Now I am ready to seek Naropa. All those who have witnessed this miracle of the fish will be spared rebirth in the lower realms for their next seven incarnations. All those who partake of these fish will be likewise blessed."

Some guards bent to scoop up fish. The king coughed and looked at the captain. The captain looked at the guards. Fish plopped to the floor. The king looked back to Marpa. Marpa bowed.

"Powerful, noble and devout Majesties, grant a humble pilgrim leave to cross your realms on his journey east."

Marpa was granted passage. His luggage was restored, his gold doubled, and gifts added besides. The king gave Marpa another gift for Naropa, doubling the gold once again, and detailed a guard to go with Marpa for as long as it took him to find Naropa. On his way out, Marpa promised Devata that he would find the kingdom a suitable high priest.

Marpa met Paindapa on the road east, at an inn just outside Dakoiti's lands. Paindapa had decided to make sure the news of his friend's fate reached Ocean of Awareness back in Tibet. Marpa had found Paindapa watching the road, waiting to ask the next traveler if he knew about Marpa, and if the execution had been carried out as scheduled.

Marpa wrote a letter recommending Paindapa for the job of high priest.

It took some talking to get Paindapa to carry it back to the king and queen. But the rich gifts convinced Paindapa that Dakoiti was sincere. Paindapa had to admit that the job needed doing.

A messenger from Dakoiti passed Paindapa on his way to the palace, and caught up with Marpa. The messenger brought Marpa the crystal sword. The queen, he said, had found the sword in the high priest's compound, where Marpa had forgotten it. Marpa carried it back to Tibet and often used it in ceremonies. He told his disciples that it was a special sword, one that severed attachments and cut through delusions.

Paindapa stayed on as high priest until his death many years later. At his cremation, Devata ranked second among the mourners. Foremost was her son, Bharatapala, born with nine auspicious signs late in the first year of Paindapa's priesthood, and now beloved ruler of a respected Buddhist kingdom.

Many days and miles to the east, Naropa appeared to Marpa. They greeted each other as old friends. Naropa, impressed with his student's determination, taught him the secret of the Yoga of No Effort, the yoga which enables the student to avoid his karma, bypass the bardos, and forcefully project himself into another body.

But Naropa added a condition. He demanded a solemn vow from a reluctant Marpa. In Tibet, to this day they speak in whispers of how Marpa broke his vow, of the terrible price he paid, and of the Yoga of Forceful Projection, forever lost.

69 How Bear Knob Got Its Name

Soledad, November, 2001

Before she had turned on the light, Sue had taken a nightscope out onto her deck. She was worried. Sue knew it was Carrie out there in the lookout. Sue was watching the lookout, because she'd been tipped off that the blue Saint George was on its way.

Sue had not asked people in town to watch for the Saint George. Her friends in Soledad were loyal, but not always discreet, and Sue did not want word to get back to Priscilla that she knew that Priscilla was in town. But with Sue's neighbors in the Gabilans, this caution was less necessary and probably useless. A new car making daily trips up and down Soledad Road was going to be noticed and asked about.

When I was a child and heard a car coming, my playmates and I would run out to watch it. From the sound, we could tell how fast it was coming, and how fast we needed to run. If it was new or otherwise interesting, we'd stand on the road and watch it until it was out of sight. If we thought it was of such interest that our parents might hear us out on the topic, we'd proceed straight to them as a unit.

The road where I grew up was paved, traffic picked up, and our games grew more interesting than passing cars. Every year, fewer roads are left in the U.S. where a passing car is a source of excitement. Soledad Road is still one of them.

Sue told one neighbor that she'd be obliged to hear of the movements of a blue Saint George, and the others soon heard. Sue's story, that it was a trespass issue over which she preferred not to trouble the police, was repeated with more respect than belief. Most on Sue's road were ranchers, and hardly a one did not have a former employee, ex-spouse, current relative or would-be lover about whom they might ask their neighbors, but without caring to offer any information in return. By the time Carrie arrived at the lookout, Sue had three calls warning her.

Not for the first time since the CTS team had arrived, Sue bent her head to ask God to guide her. She lifted it back up almost immediately. Her inner guide had been very short with her. "What purpose," it had asked Sue, "do you feel will be served by letting Carrie die in the chaparral?"

Sue cast about for a bag, two flashlights, and a blanket, then headed out. She got just beyond the house and realized she needed a warmer jacket. Sue hated to go back, as that same cold told her how much Carrie must be suffering. When Sue started again, she had a larger bag.

On top of the hill, Carrie had begun thinking about death. She was living her life for God and would die doing His work as she had always hoped. It was just that dying this way seemed kind of stupid.

Carrie thought back to what the CTS had taught her. Ask for your deepest, inmost desire. You will get what you seek. Carrie searched for her inmost wish. The cold was now painful and her fears so overwhelming that she could not think as hard as she felt she should. A pretty hymn kept running through her mind. Carrie tried to soul search with the music as background, but it didn't work.

"Is this going to be it?" she wondered. In the moment of death she was unable to practice presence of mind. She was going to die as one of the unaware. In *The Days of Zurvan*, it said that dying unaware meant a rebirth that was no better than her current one. Carrie actually did not resent her birth or dislike her life, but the CTS had taught her that advanced spiritual people strove for better rebirths. Carrie wanted very much to be a spiritual person and an advanced one as well, if she had the choice.

Carrie listened to the hymn playing in her head. She did not know what kind of hymn it was. In the CTS, they did not sing. Some of the words sounded OK. Carrie decided she'd use the next line of the hymn as her wish. She hoped it didn't sound silly, but like a real wish.

It did, and Carrie felt easier. It sounded nice, in fact, although Carrie was not totally sure what the wish really wished for. But she closed her eyes and wished it with all her might.

"May I see thee in thy glory."

Something resounded in the thicket. Carrie dismissed this as a temptation or distraction and fought to bring her attention back to her wish. "May I see thee in thy glory."

The bushes shook again, and this time it was nearer and louder. Carrie lifted her head. "Maybe this is my wish," she thought. "Instead of a stupid death shivering on a rock, a big animal will kill me like I was in a lion's den in Babylon."

The bushes in front of Carrie crashed open. Sue emerged and showed her face to Carrie with the flashlight. Then Sue turned the beam on Carrie.

"You poor thing," Sue said. Sue put the flashlight on the ground and it started to roll. She blocked it with her foot and dropped the bag, mouth into the light.

Carrie sat, not moving or speaking. If she had any thoughts, she does not remember them. Sue says Carrie was smiling.

"Dear love. Look at this wind!" Sue said. She pulled the unresisting Carrie to her feet and helped her into a spare coat, a scarf, and two mismatched mittens. Sue pressed a flashlight on Carrie. Carrie took it, but her coat fell open. Carrie tried to do the buttons of the coat while holding the flashlight. Sue took the flashlight back so Carrie could work the buttons with two hands.

"Come," Sue said, presenting Carrie with the flashlight for the second time. "Can you walk?" Carrie looked willing, but did not move. Sue grabbed an arm and used it to aim Carrie into the same dark gap in the bushes from which Sue had appeared.

○ ○ ○ ○ ○

Once they were off the summit, the wind lost bite and Carrie's walk steadied. By the time they reached the house, Sue no longer had to slow her pace for Carrie.

Carrie recovered speech even faster. They started talking as if they had met while looking at the same display in a store window. Indeed, after some remarks about the weather, they talked about shopping in the Soledad area, the clothing stores there and some stores in Southern California they both knew. Sue had Carrie build a fire while she finished dinner. She decided Carrie would want something hearty, brought out her soup stock, and threw in chicken until it was more stew than soup. She had already planned bread, salad, and teriyaki vegetables. Finally, Sue had been presented with some very tempting fudge brownies and was grateful for the chance to inflict them on a younger metabolism.

In front of the fire after dinner, the first real pause in the conversation gave Carrie a chance to think. She remembered her anguish on the hill and it occurred to her to ask Sue about it.

"How do we know what to wish?" Carrie realized the question might sound strange out of context and rephrased it. "I mean not just wish, you know, but our inmost wish."

"We should only have one wish. 'Let God's will be done.'"

"Oh." Carrie was surprised, but the answer made a lot of sense to her. "That's in the Bible," Carrie added, thinking aloud.

Sue said, "If that's hard to wish, then you say 'Not my will, God, but your will.' "

Carrie noticed Sue often answered questions Carrie was just about to ask. That was nice, but sometimes left her at a loss for words. Her eyes fell on a colorfully painted leather circle hanging on the wall. She'd wanted to ask about it all evening. "What is that? It's nice."

"The drum, you mean? It's part of my shaman's equipment. The swirling design symbolizes the journey into the world of spirit."

"What is it equipment for?"

Sue went to the wall and took down the drum and its wooden clapper. "I use it in ceremonies and for my own meditations."

"Are you really a shaman?"

"Yes. Many of my tribe live in Soledad, which is in our lands. I lead ceremonies, and I am registered with the state as someone to do the proper observances when Indian graves need to be moved."

"The State of California? I thought your tribe was a myth." Carrie had heard this from Priscilla, but once she said it, she regretted it and added, "I mean some people say that."

Sue gave no sign of being offended. "I know many say so. I am actually registered as a 'most likely descendant' under another tribe, which is fine, since there has been so much intermarriage. There have not been any pure-blooded Pranashta for a long time. When Indian remains are found in Pranashta territories, the county knows to call a Pranashta 'most likely descendant', even if we don't have official recognition as a separate tribe.

"Tribe is a matter of the heart. My father was a Pranashta shaman and the son and grandson of one. I had a shaman's drum before I could walk. A DNA test will never change that."

"Can you show me?" Carrie asked. "About the drum I mean."

Sue struck the drum and out came a sound like a voice from deep in the earth. Carrie marveled that anything made of skin, wood and leather could sound so far beyond human scale. "Play some more," she pleaded.

Sue played and Carrie floated with the rhythm. When Sue stopped, it was like someone flipping the switch that turns the gravity back on. Carrie wanted to express dismay, but Sue spoke first.

"I have recorded some of our ceremonies." Sue was fumbling among a pile of CD's. She cupped one between her hands and fed it to a black box. Some pecks at a few buttons forced the electronics to obey, and hidden speakers took up the drumming.

The recordings lacked the power of live drumming, but interested Carrie.

Sometimes there was chanting or a flute. Usually there were other drums. Some of the passages were just drums, two, three, or more.

"Oh, I'd love to be able to do that," Carrie sighed.

"I have another drum," Sue said. Carrie didn't reply. She had only been thinking aloud. She didn't really believe that she could be a part of such wonderful sounds.

Sue got another, smaller drum with its clapper from a closet. Carrie hardly dared touch it, much less hit it with the clapper. Sue coaxed, banging her clapper on the oak coffee table to give Carrie her beat. Carrie was still shy. When Sue joined in, Carrie softened her beat, then lost it. Carrie stopped.

"I feel like I'm ruining it," she confessed. "Yours is so earthy and powerful."

"They are both earthy. My drum is chthonic, from deep in the earth, the underworld. Yours is telluric, rooted here at the surface, in the fruitful ground, Mother Earth. It is not possible to ruin it, because shaman music is a ceremony, not a performance."

Carrie looked doubtful. Sue elaborated. "In a performance you've practiced before doing it to get it right. We do not practice for ceremonies because our music is always a journey. It is taking us somewhere. If you are already there, you don't need the journey."

"I shouldn't have stopped," Carrie said.

"In our ceremonies, often one of us stops and restarts, like on any journey."

"Oh. Thank you. I mean, that helped."

Sue tapped out Carrie's beat on the coffee table again and Carrie took it up with more confidence. Carrie found herself drawn in much more now that she was part of making the sound. Sue showed her several different rhythms before suggesting, "We should also have the celestial. Wait here."

Carrie waited. When Sue returned, it was with a double drum. To Carrie's great delight, Sue handed it to her.

"This side is another telluric drum, like you've been using. The other," Sue said, pointing to the smaller drum, "is celestial, of heaven and the sky. You will play both."

Sue showed Carrie how to arrange herself behind the drum. Sue spent some time banging on the coffee table to give Carrie rhythms for each side of the drum, and to be sure she could do both at once. But Carrie, who felt bewildered about much in life, found the art of the double drum a matter of common sense. She couldn't wait for Sue to take up her drum so they could start in earnest.

Carrie was not disappointed. The effort of keeping both arms in motion forced her heart to beat its own strong rhythm. Her racing blood transmitted the heartbeat through her entire body. She felt her drums resonate just below her heart and at the top of her head. Sue's drum she felt at the bottom of her spine.

Carrie learned to follow her heartbeat and the drumbeats. She adjusted her drumming when one of the four beats was too strong. Several times Sue slowed them to a stop, letting Carrie rest her untrained arms while speaking to her of the lore of the drum.

It was after one such soft landing that Sue pointed Carrie to a stunning truth. "Isn't it getting about time for Cilla?"

"Oh my God, what time is it?"

"Just after three."

"I hope she's not early."

"She won't be," Sue prophesied.

They put the drums away. Carrie gathered up her things. "I left my bag and Gatorade up there."

"I'll take care of it when the sun comes up. There are mountain lions up there at night."

"Mountain lions?"

"And bears. In fact, they call it Bear Knob." The lookout actually had no name, though bears did often visit it. Sue believes strongly in the shamanic tradition, which requires her to look out for others and allows her to stretch the long bow now and then. "When Cilla drops you off, just come down here. You can sleep on the deck or in the barn if I'm not in."

Carrie doubted Priscilla would like this, but for once Priscilla was not the most intimidating factor. Priscilla was not likely to kill her and eat her. Carrie wanted to meet Priscilla dressed as she came, but Sue insisted she take something. They found a very beat-up horse blanket in the barn and Carrie also took a flashlight and a large garbage bag.

With the headlights, Priscilla would be visible quite some distance down the road. Carrie could discard the bag behind a rock. In the unlikely event Priscilla looked around, the bag was something that might have fallen from a truck. Sue would retrieve it the next day.

Sue tried to convince Carrie to keep the blanket and tell Priscilla she'd found it, or if pressed, that, yes, OK, she had stolen it from the barn. But while Carrie feared Priscilla less than bears and mountain lions, she still feared her more than a chill. The specter of large predators did enable Sue to convince Carrie to walk back to the trailhead along the road, avoiding the newly named Bear Knob.

○　○　○　○　○

Sue rapidly became the closest friend Carrie could remember. Carrie was a natural at the drumming, and Sue taught her other things. Carrie found that Sue had read *The Days of Zurvan* and had much to say that helped her understand it. Sue also had very good suggestions about how to get along with Priscilla.

Carrie did worry about Priscilla. Carrie was certainly watching Sue. And Sue never asked questions that Carrie felt uneasy answering, like about Priscilla's movements. But Carrie doubted Priscilla would approve. Carrie left out of her reports the stuff that Priscilla would not understand. Sometimes that was a lot of stuff. Carrie did not like the idea of living a lie, but it seemed a happy lie for everybody.

Priscilla was excited to report such long and detailed surveillances back to the CTS. She was amazed at all the stuff Carrie was able to observe, especially as she had always thought Carrie a bit dim. Priscilla decided that she had trained Carrie well.

Carrie and Sue soon settled into a routine. If there was a change in plans, Carrie called ahead. Carrie was one of the handful of people who had Sue's cellphone number. I didn't get it until that lunch at Mike's. Sue would have given Carrie a key, but neither could think how to do that in a way that was safe from Priscilla. Much more than a key, Carrie wanted to attend one of Sue's ceremonies. But this was not possible until we got Priscilla out of the way.

70 The Honeypot

We had a lot to tell Mike when he returned. Once he got all the news, I requested my honeypot top the agenda.

"Yeah," Mike agreed. "We want to play Priscilla along. So what is it you need from us?"

"Priscilla is attempting to hack my machine, get access to all my files. I want to give her access to a fake machine full of what looks to her like juicy stuff. It's called a honeypot, after the things bears get stuck in."

Mike wrinkled his forehead. "Can you be more specific? The reference to Winnie the Pooh is only so useful."

"I have some old files that look like my client stuff but are mine or non-proprietary. There's a whole bunch of stuff from an old client that went out of business, and two-thirds of a book on device drivers I started and never finished. I'd like to get stuff from you that will convince Priscilla she's hit pay dirt, but which you don't mind letting her see. Because she will see it and try to think of ways to use it."

"Zoe, we've got some moot cases, don't we? I don't think Priscilla will know the difference."

"Sure. I can get those." Zoe said. "What of the stuff about the Durant settlement?"

"Perfect," Mike said. "A lot of storm and fury in the discovery process, then the guy goes to Rio and it just ends. Priscilla could spend hours on it and not have a clue."

I didn't either, but it sounded great.

"What about drafts of my books?" Sue suggested. "Cilla won't be able to publish them."

"No, we can prevent her," Mike said.

I didn't like the idea. "Well, I wouldn't. She might put them on the Internet."

"If she does you can get them removed, right?" Sue had directed the question at Mike, but I jumped in.

"Yes. But others will get copies and then you gotta chase them. You'll spend a fortune and never quite get the cork back in the bottle."

Mike helped me out. "He's right. Most of the folks we'll be chasing will not think they were doing anything wrong and will take it off the Internet as soon as they see my letter, but meanwhile their friends will have gotten copies and so on. There's no realistic way of getting everyone out there to delete their copy and the problem never goes away."

"I have just the thing," Sue announced. "My Pranashta tutorial."

Zoe looked perplexed. "I thought we were going back to the publisher on that one."

"Ereshkigal take the publisher! They'll do it, but they won't promote it, it'll lose money, they'll deduct that from my other royalties and for years I'll have to listen to what martyrs they've made of themselves."

"Yes," Zoe said. "So that's the business. They see themselves as doing us a favor, and maybe they are. Their terms will be the best you'll get. You'll forgive me, Sue, but it's pretty dense stuff, and the academic presses will not touch it, so it's hard to find it a home."

"I say," Sue announced, "that if Cilla wants to publish my tutorial, we let her."

Mike had seen where this was going and was already nodding his head. "Nice," he said.

I thought so, too. "I think that's my honeypot," I said. "And I've got another angle on locating the notebooks. But I need help."

"What's that?" Mike said.

"I think Priscilla or Carrie may be connected to an outfit called the Bhadrachakra. Can you get that checked out?"

"Who ..." Mike began. He stopped. He was looking at Sue. She'd gone stiff.

I answered Mike's question as if I didn't notice. "The Bhadrachakra is a kind of Buddhist think tank, founded by a guy named Bhadra. Pretty respectable these days, but their name came up."

"Came up how?" Mike asked, one eye still on Sue.

I got a little creative to hide the Heavensent business. "The notebook's shorthand is long obsolete. In looking it up, I've learned that folks from the Bhadrachakra are doing the same thing. It could be coincidence, but that sure seems unlikely."

Sue unfroze. "Mike," she said quickly, "I have a feeling this is important. I want this followed up."

"OK," Mike said. Then to me, "Get me their address." Mike and I had the same feeling: Sue wanted to change the subject.

It was time to break up anyway. Mike needed to make calls. Zoe had to collect honey. The honeypot had to be built quickly or Priscilla would get suspicious. I wanted to have it up before I went to Soledad in the morning. It looked likely that all of our opposition would be lying low except for Priscilla and Carrie. This meant a phone tap was unlikely, so they could conference me in to a meeting if useful.

Sue stopped me in Mike's lobby. "Veronica says we can still use the conference room. Can you spare ten minutes?"

"Sure," I said. I figured she had something to tell me about the Bhadra-chakra. Instead Sue wanted to know what I'd learned about the proof. Once I gave my report I asked Sue if the stuff about Carl Hempel had turned out useful.

"Absolutely," Sue said. "Thank you."

"I'm glad. Yeah, the real problem for God is not science, it's the existence of evil."

"Oh," Sue waved me off. "I have that taken care of." I tried to stay deadpan. Sue's cellphone rang. "I need to take this," she said. She started toward the door.

"No, I'll go," I said. "I've got to get started on the honeypot. Want the door shut?"

Sue nodded yes. She waved as I left.

Solved the problem of evil. Uh huh. Mike's bourbon must have quite a kick.

71 Trap and Trace

Even if Sue had the problem of evil licked, it might be too late for Armenta. She was not on her rock when I got back to the office. It had been a week. Killer whales will eat harbor seals. And sometimes, like the rest of us, seals just get sick and die. There was nothing I could do. I had a honeypot to bring up.

I have two computers. I can crash and burn one while reading email, keeping my books and getting out reports with the other. Fortunately my crash dummy PC was almost clean. I downloaded some logging software for the honeypot and backed it up. I hoped that Priscilla had configured her trojan so that only she had access to hack me, rather than just opening me up and leaving me at the mercy of every punk on the Internet. But I could rebuild quickly if need be.

Zoe had offered to drive by with the honeypot files on CD. She did, alas, with her boyfriend. An affable fellow, he told me how grateful he was that I'd given Zoe the excuse to duck out of the office early. Yeah, guy, any time.

Ever so alone again, I read in the CD and double-clicked the Aunt Agatha icon. The trojan ran so quickly I thought something was wrong, but I checked around and Agatha was at work. As easy as being the guest of honor at the unveiling of a new guillotine.

I could now lean back and draft my answer to Priscilla. I asked for one-third of the royalties. There wouldn't be any royalties and I couldn't trust Priscilla anyway. But if I didn't ask for anything Priscilla would get suspicious.

I put this pack of lies on the honeypot in a file named BLESS, as Priscilla had asked, and settled into studying her email. Every email contains the record of its journey in its headers. Usually your mail software hides these from you.

For good reason. They're long and usually not interesting even to a serious email geek. If you ever want to look them up, I'm talking about the Received headers. Reading the Received headers is the email equivalent of an autopsy. It's not everyone's idea of fun. It takes training

214

to do. But if you suspect foul play, it yields fascinating details you get no other way.

Every machine the mail passes through, so long as that machine plays by the rules, adds one and only one `Received` header. This tells all: Time. Date. What software handled the mail. Name of the current machine in the chain. How the previous machine identified itself.

Of course a bad guy does not necessarily play by the rules. A machine in the chain can lie about who it is. It can fake the whole chain of `Received` headers up to that point. The art is to spot the point at which the lies end and truth begins. That's the 'scene of the crime'.

The story was simple. No trickery with headers. Priscilla was using an account at a local ISP. She was probably dialing up on a phone line, the way most people do.

I called Mike. He was on the phone but called me back, starting right in with his own news. "Our client is driving me nuts here."

"She's gotta be upset about what might happen to the notebooks."

"It's not that. It's the Carrie thing. She does not want Carrie put in jail."

"How's that a problem? I mean if you don't ask for jail, no jail, right?"

"It's not that easy. Contempt is an offense against the court. That means I gotta get up there and convince Gaunilo that the judicial system, and with it the Republic, is gonna fall unless he goes after these characters hammer and tongs. It's hard to combine that message with 'please, no slammer time for these gentle flowers.' "

"You'll do it, Mike, I have faith."

"Exactly what our client was just telling me. You called me. Was it to give me this kind of bullshit, or did you have a serious purpose?"

"It was mainly to extol your virtues, Mike, but I did have something else on my mind. How is recovering the notebooks going?"

"Not well. The CTS did report them stolen, but they didn't ask for a high priority with the County Sheriff, so it didn't get one. They did cough up the names of the two girls and their address, but apparently Sue is ahead of everybody there."

"Between you and Sue, you should be able to get the County Sheriff out there."

"Exactly what I suggested and exactly how I got into this whole mess with Sue about Carrie. Sue believes all that's at the safe house now is Carrie, so she wants the Sheriff to hold off. Aren't you seeing the dizzy little bitch tomorrow?"

"I have that high honor and distinct privilege. Careful how you talk about your client's favorite people," I warned playfully.

After Mike's response, which I won't repeat, I asked, "Any clue where Priscilla is?"

"None. Sue says she left the safe house yesterday, taking their car, the notebooks, the cash, the works. Carrie's at the house with her clothes and that's about it."

"I think I know how to find Priscilla."

"Jesus, not you too."

"How's that?"

"Sue tells me she can sense where Priscilla is. That's just ducky, but we're not going to get a search warrant based on that."

"I think I can do better. Priscilla is using dial-up to a local ISP to stay in touch with me. All we do is trace the calls."

"A wiretap warrant is hard to get. It could take a while."

"A trap and trace is a lot easier. You only need a law enforcement officer to certify that its results might be useful in a ongoing investigation. The court is not allowed to refuse a properly certified request. Trap and trace will tell us where she is calling from and that's all we need."

"It'll probably be the U.S. Marshals Service that Gaunilo asks to investigate. Can they handle this?"

"I think so. The technicians at the phone company actually do most of the work, and they get a lot of these."

"Have you called the ISP or the phone company?"

"Neither one. The phone company won't be interested until we have the authorization from the court. And if the ISP hears this first from us they may just delete the account."

"There's an attitude."

"The ISP will think it's the percentage move for everyone. It fixes the problem and almost every victim eventually decides it is too much trouble to prosecute, so any extra time and trouble the ISP puts in winds up being for nothing."

"Makes sense," Mike conceded. "When you see Carrie tomorrow be sure to ask about the cash."

"Carrie? Should she have it?"

"I don't know. We didn't get it. The CTS says they never got it, and now it's stolen by Carrie and Priscilla. I'm telling them that's bullshit. You don't start looking for the money after the deadline in the court order. I've told them that if I don't have a certified check in my hand at the hearing tomorrow, I'll ask Gaunilo to put the entire CTS leadership in jail. Once they're all locked up, we can decide who it's useful to keep on ice until they cough up the money, and who is not worth the trouble."

"Is Gaunilo really going to put all those actresses and millionaires in jail?" I asked. "Think of the press. Gaunilo sounds kind of cautious for that."

"I'll ask him to do exactly that, but Gaunilo will probably start by demanding they show up in his courtroom to explain to him in person why they should not go to jail. That should do the trick. If it doesn't, and they simply defy the court, Gaunilo will have laid the groundwork and shouldn't have trouble with the press."

"Not that judges ever read the newspapers."

"Heaven forfend," Mike said. "Anyway, as backup, if you can find anything that leads to any of that cash, it'll help."

Mike and I spent some time getting exact wording for Gaunilo. While we talked, my honeypot had an intruder. It was Priscilla, and I was able to give Mike an up to the minute report. The U.S. Marshals would need more details, but I'd talk to them tomorrow.

I set up my screen display to track Priscilla's progress through my computer, relaxed into a rocking chair, put on some music, and watched. Priscilla dropped offline at six thirty in the evening. I got up to burn my logs onto a CD. Sue called while I was setting it up. I answered her wearing headphones and typed while we talked.

"Sorry about that," I told Sue, as I moused the last steps. "But I think we need to get Priscilla's trail onto a CD before she comes back on. She might decide to erase my hard disks."

"No. Good idea. It's not a bad time to talk?"

"It's fine. What's up?"

"I wanted to talk to you about Carrie tomorrow. I don't think she can stay at the safe house and she probably won't want to. She can stay with me."

"Great. You want me to tell her?"

"Try to learn all you can about the notebooks first." Sue briefed me in detail on her progress with the Sheriff, then concluded, "Best of luck for tomorrow."

"Thanks."

I hung up and watched my monitor for a while. When I turned out the lights for an early bedtime, the screen bathed my office in a glow whose color and intensity changed with every new alarm of Priscilla.

72 Marpa's Promise

The Lhotrak Valley, 1067 AD

Ocean of Awareness never found out who had sent the drunken archer. She asked everyone, but no one claimed to know. Certainly nobody wanted to be connected with Ocean's tragedy. But perhaps, as some said, the old archer in white, bad tempered and fond of chang, was a spirit who arose from karma, and disappeared once it had come about.

The chang the archer drank was real enough. He downed the strong barley beer almost as fast as Ocean could fill bowls and carry them to the table. Even by Tibetan standards, this was heavy drinking. But Ocean was not going to give her guest any excuse to accuse her of lack of hospitality. She had to refuse his very flattering request on behalf of the Lhotrak fair, and wanted to do nothing else that might be taken as an insult.

The archer asked that Marpa or one of his sons honor the fair, two days off, by agreeing to preside over it. He expected that a yes answer was a mere formality. And he would have been right in ordinary circumstances. Marpa, or at least Young Teacher, his eldest son, would be expected to accept.

But the archer did not even get to see Marpa or Young Teacher. They were in the first year of a three year, three month and three day seclusion, and they were going to stay in seclusion. Ocean could not even tell the archer why.

During Marpa's stay with Naropa in India, Naropa had found out that Marpa planned to pass the leadership of his order to his oldest son, along with the family farm. And that he intended to use the Yoga of No Effort to make sure his son inherited.

In India, spiritual leaders did not inherit the job from their father. Naropa insisted to Marpa that spiritual insight was not like a pig, a cow, or a good plot of land. Marpa told Naropa that things were different in Tibet. In India, teachers didn't run farms. He had to. They usually did not marry. Marpa had a family and was expected to provide for it. Indian Buddhists did not eat meat or drink chang. You couldn't survive a Tibetan winter without doing both. Rules which applied in sweltering plains of India didn't work in the treeless mountains of Tibet.

Naropa had a very bad feeling, but Marpa was adamant. Naropa was forced to compromise. Tibet, after all, was very different, and he could not in the end enforce rules on a former student a year's difficult journey away. Naropa imposed two strict conditions on Marpa. First, he and his sons must go into seclusion the moment Marpa returned and stay there for three years, three months and three days.

Second, the Yoga of No Effort was simply too tempting in the hands of a man so attached to his own flesh and blood. Naropa now was very sorry he had passed it on to anyone, and especially to Marpa. Naropa insisted that Marpa promise that the Yoga of No Effort would die with him. Above all, and on penalty of the worst possible consequences, Marpa must never, ever pass it on to his sons.

On his knees, Marpa promised. But Marpa had hardly said hello back in the Lhotrak Valley before he began drilling Young Teacher in the forbidden technique.

Marpa had not told Ocean about the Yoga of No Effort, or his double-cross. But Ocean knew that the retreat was something to take seriously. Her recurring dream told her.

In the dream, Young Teacher breaks his seclusion. He is finely mounted, riding behind four men on foot. It is after noon. They seem to be returning from some sort of gathering and very excited about it. They've clearly been drinking chang. Most of the talk is about Young Teacher. How well he led the gathering. How fine his speech was. Especially, how well he expounded Buddhist teachings.

The loud men frighten a nest of young partridges. The birds take flight. The horse rears. Young Teacher is thrown. The horse runs off. Young Teacher stays down. The dream ends with blood, blood everywhere.

All Ocean told the archer was that neither Marpa or any of his sons would attend the festival, she could not tell him why, and he could not speak directly to any of them. She knew he could not be happy with this answer. He wasn't. Finally, he told Ocean he could not bear to carry such a shabby answer back to town, and that he intended to leave the Lhotrak entirely, taking a back route. He marched off toward a side road, never to be heard of again. Ocean was surprised he could stand, what with all that chang.

The archer had not spoken softly. By the end of the conversation he'd fairly shouted. Everyone in the castle heard him, but Ocean gave that little thought until the day of the fair.

That morning, Ocean was taking breakfast up to Marpa a little ahead of schedule. Young Teacher almost walked into her on the staircase. He was dressed in best clothes. Shamefaced, he darted down past her.

"Where are you going?" she said.

"The fair. I can see from my window, everyone is heading there, from toddlers to people old enough to know this will be their last one. Mother, let me go!"

"Have you asked your father?"

"I've asked you, and that will be enough."

Ocean thought fast. If she begged him not to go she'd soon be talking to air. "Make me some promises. Not to sit at the place of honor. Not to accept gifts as the guest of honor. Not to give the dedication speech. Don't give a sermon. Don't drink beer. Don't stay past noon."

Young Teacher looked relieved. He hadn't exactly gotten permission to go, but almost. "Certainly, mother, I promise."

"And one more thing! Don't ride horses!"

"Certainly," he shouted back, already on his way.

73 The Plain of Solitude

Soledad, Thursday, January 17

My drive to Soledad Mission went well. I followed the old highway of the King of Spain, El Camino Real, and for the first time made no wrong turns. Three modern roads follow the former El Camino Real, but each soon bends east into Highway 101, which is faster and where most everybody wants to go. To follow the colonial road, at each of those three bends in the road, you have to turn right onto a road with a different name. These turns look no different from lots of other right turns which take you off to dead ends deep in the hills. But I caught all the good ones and none of the bad ones, just like a local. Except the locals probably use Highway 101. It's faster.

Before the town and the prison, Soledad was a Franciscan mission. Missions were, of necessity, more than churches. Each was a large ranch, capable of self-defense and lengthy self-sufficiency. In the old Spanish colony, the missions were most of the economy. They fed not just themselves but the soldiers in forts like Monterey.

Soledad was the least independent of all the missions. More than survival was probably never even hoped for. The first Spaniards, men of wide experience in such things, thought this stretch of sand where two parched rivers meet was one of the most desolate places they had ever seen. Soledad Mission's primary purpose was to serve as a way station on El Camino Real.

More of a trail than a highway, El Camino Real connected the missions and therefore the colony. Spanish California had no inns and few towns, so if the distance between missions exceeded a day's journey, that meant a campout. This was always uncomfortable, and could be risky if the natives were hostile.

I made it there early. To kill time, I walked around the restored portions of the mission, one side of the quadrangle with a chapel. The original church has yet to be rebuilt. It's not even a ruin, just a restored floor with three graves marked.

There's a mystery about the graves. Two are of prominent people, as you'd expect for someone buried in the floor of the church. One is the

Spanish governor, Arrillaga, who came here to die in the care of his friend, Father Ibañez. Father Ibañez is the second grave.

The third grave is a woman's. She's buried right in the front of the church, so she obviously was important. But we know nothing of her. The church historian Engelhardt published long extracts from the burial register in 1929. He's got a lot to say about Arrillaga and Ibañez. Of the woman, not a word. Since then the burial records have disappeared.

While Soledad Mission was active, droughts, wild animals and earthquakes took turns at it. The climate was horrid, freezing and wet in the winter, hot and windy in the summer. Many of the friars became sick, from arthritis, rheumatism or just plain dreariness. There was a lot of turnover.

Worse than all of these were the floods. The two rivers, dry most of the year, often overflowed when they ran. The flood of 1824 destroyed the church. Reconstruction was not complete in time for the second flood in 1828. In 1830, a trader passing through found Soledad to be "the gloomiest, bleakest and most abject-looking spot in all California." The third flood in 1832 found very little to destroy. At least Soledad was spared Indian attacks. Raiding Indians wanted fatter pickings.

I walked back toward the parking lot and saw Carrie coming around the chapel. I expected Carrie to be glad to see me. Even so, when she ran up and flung her arms around me, she nearly knocked me on my rear end. "You're here," she said, drenching my solar plexus with her tears. "I'm so glad you're here." It had been some time since a woman had held me tightly. I am not sure Carrie realized how much strength she had gained from the drumming.

"It's alright," I said. I put my arms around her and waited for her to tire. It took a while. "I like to look at the statue whenever I'm here," I suggested, while the circulation resumed in my sides.

Carrie leaned back to look up at me. "The statue?"

"Yes. The statue of Mary clothed in black. Have you seen it?"

"No. I've never been here before."

Once Carrie released me, I started toward the entrance. She was not with me. I looked back to find her waiting for assurance that it was OK to come along.

When my wave had brought her alongside, I asked, "What's going on with Priscilla?"

"I don't know. She didn't say anything. All her stuff is gone. I haven't seen her in two days."

"Did she always have the notebooks?"

"I never saw them after we got back from the raid. Cilla put them somewhere safe."

"So you don't know?"

Carrie's eyes slewed.

"I mean when she left to look at them, was she gone long, did she have to go to an airport?"

"I don't think she flew anywhere. She'd have the car for hours, though."

"No idea where she went?"

Carrie nodded no. "But I did save your books."

"My books?" Preoccupied with the Gödel notebooks, I had totally forgotten about my copies of Sue's novels.

"The books your friend gave you. Sue told me to save them." Carrie looked off into the distance. "Cilla was about to throw them away. Sue said they were important to you."

It would have been easy for Carrie to figure out that my copies of Sue's novels were gifts. Lorraine had inscribed all of them and in a couple of the books her inscription ran on for pages, to the point where it amounted to a handwritten preface. I wondered why Sue was so sure that the books were important to me. It may have been Sue's pride of authorship coming out. Sue usually acted indifferent to how others treated her work, but I didn't see how she could become as successful as she had without having more feeling for her creations than she usually let on.

Carrie and I had reached the door to the chapel. I don't like to talk in church. I certainly don't feel good about it as a venue for leaning on someone in a business matter. Break their arm outside the church door is my belief. I mean, where are we without a code to live by?

The statue of the Virgin in black was in front, behind the altar. I pointed to it.

"That's Sue's lady." Carrie said when we got outside. "She's got one in her house in a special room. It's Siawata."

"Siawata from Sue's books?"

"I think so. She says she offers to it, but has never really told me about it. I always thought the black lady looked gloomy. Sue cries in front of it a lot."

"Oh."

"Yes. About her daughter I think."

"Her daughter?"

"She never told you? Her daughter died September 11 in one of the airplanes." I didn't say anything. Carrie answered my look. "A friend of

Sue's died and Sue adopted her daughter. Sue wanted her to have a normal life, so she was a secret. Most people didn't know."

The courtyard was deserted. Beyond it, fields dotted with lettuce shimmered in the sun all the way to the treeless hills. A lone tractor moved, too distant to be heard. Where the courtyard met the plowed earth, there was a large barbeque pit. I pointed to a bench next to it. "Is here OK?"

Carrie sat, looking too solemn for her frilly floral top with open shoulders. She slid next to me on the bench, thigh to thigh. "Are they going to arrest me?"

"I don't know. They might."

Carrie started to cry and grabbed my arm. "Will I go to jail?"

"It's possible. It's possible."

She turned and put her arms around me. "Don't let them do it. I don't want to go to jail."

I held her. I wanted to lose myself in the embrace, but I worried a priest might pop out at any moment and insist that we get married, immediately and at a side altar.

"Sue and I can't help unless you tell us everything you can about the notebooks," I said. "I don't think Sue wants you to go to jail. You are completely sure you don't know where they are?"

Carrie nodded her tear-stained face yes.

"It's really OK if you lied before, but it's important now for you and everybody. You have to tell me whatever you know that might help us find them."

"I think I have. I don't know very much, do I?"

I untangled myself from Carrie and looked at her. Should I ask her about the Bhadrachakra? Carrie started to look scared. "Would you like to stay with Sue?" I said.

"Yes. That house gives me the creeps now. And I don't have any money. Cilla took it all."

"Hang on," I said. I cellphoned Sue.

The call was short. "Sue's in town. She'll be along soon," I said. "Priscilla must have found another place to stay. Any idea where?"

Carrie shook her head.

"I guess if Priscilla kept all that money, she left herself a lot of choices. If you stick near Sue, you are as safe from arrest as you're going to get."

Sue's arrival was announced by the roar of an old half ton pickup. The two women ignored me and went into a lengthy greeting more easily rendered in musical notation than words. Once the overture to their conversation faded,

Sue took its first spoken passage. "I've brought a pickup from the ranch. We should give Mr. Sanchez back his place. Do you have much furniture?"

Carrie shook her head.

"Well, I've got rope in the pickup and if there's a lot of stuff we can hire some men nearby. Look, love, we've got to go to the Sheriff's Office first."

Carrie began to cry softly.

"Don't do that," Sue soothed. "You're wanted for questioning about the notebooks. They won't arrest you. You'll have to answer some questions and perhaps sign a statement. So don't cry. We're going to have to clean you up before you get there. They're going to think I beat you up."

Carrie smiled.

"OK," Sue said. "This is important. If what you've told Josh and me is true, that you've not been hiding the notebooks, we're fine. But if not, you should get your own lawyer before you talk to the Sheriff. If you lie to them, it's a crime and you could spend months in jail."

"I don't want a lawyer," Carrie said. Her tone suggested she thought the right to the advice of an attorney was much like the right to a last cigarette before being shot.

"Fine, then." Sue turned to me. "Would you like to come with us? I want to look in at the graves." I found it hard to meet Sue's eyes. I wanted to say something about her daughter, but not with Carrie there.

"I'd love to. I was looking at them when Carrie arrived."

"So you know who's buried there," Sue said. She turned to Carrie, "Josh told you this is Siawata's grave."

Carrie looked confused.

"I didn't tell her that, because I didn't know it," I said.

Sue led the way. "This is the place in the Plain of Solitude where Siawata had her statue. *Soledad* is Spanish for 'solitude'. Tradition has it that Siawata asked to be buried here, and since then so have many of our tribe."

We were at the grave. Sue looked across the lettuce fields back to the hills. "The unknown woman in the unmarked grave was a shaman," she said. "The friars used the fact this was a sacred spot to help draw our people to the church. For the same reason, they sometimes buried our shamans in their churches."

"Which they wouldn't emphasize in the histories," I said.

Sue looked down at the shaman's grave. "Yes. It's not the sort of thing the Fathers would mention in the church records. Just as they wouldn't say that they chose the statue of Our Lady of Solitude because our people would worship her as Siawata."

"So the statue here really is Siawata," said Carrie.

"It's one," Sue said. "The original is in Monterey. The statue here is a replica, but this is Siawata's home church. And it's my favorite. Only here are the stations complete, because they circle to and from Siawata at the altar. In the other churches the circle is broken."

I remembered Sue's black hood and cloak when she'd met me at the Presidio Chapel. When I spotted her, she'd been sitting right under the statue of the Virgin in black.

Sue hugged Carrie. "Let's say goodbye to Mr. Bryant. He came a long way to talk to you and has a lot to do for me back in Pacific Grove."

Carrie kissed me goodbye. I hugged Sue. The women climbed into the half ton. Its engine roared the way an large internal combustion engine roars when it knows any roar could be its last. The pickup lurched out of the parking lot, raising tendrils of dust. They hung in the dry air for a long time after the truck was gone.

74 The Bardos of Death

The Lhotrak Valley, 1067 AD

Great Magician and several other students of Marpa's soon caught up with Young Teacher. Ocean had rounded them up as an escort. They were a rollicking group. The unexpected leave to attend the fair went over big.

Arrival at the fair did nothing to dampen their spirits. Even with its master of ceremonies a no-show, the Lhotrak fair was going to be lively. A lot of fairgoers had limited contacts with people. This annual celebration was always a special day for them. The fairgoers had given up on having a proper guest of honor, so Young Teacher was received like a miraculous appearance by Buddha himself.

In the overcrowded fair, no one else would take the guest of honor's seats at the head of the gathering, and all the others were taken. Once Young Teacher took the first seat, the customary gifts were pressed on him. To reject them meant dishing out a long series of insults to generous and kind neighbors and friends. And having taken the first seat and the gifts, there was no escaping giving a dedication speech. Young Teacher turned out to have a talent for ad lib oratory, and delivered a dedication speech whose equal Lhotrak fairgoers had never heard.

Afterwards, fairgoers surrounded him. Many had brought their homebrew chang and Young Teacher sipped at each. All the while people praised him and asked his opinions. Young Teacher referred questions to Great Magician, who handled them very ably. But when Great Magician was asked what the six bardos were, he came up with seven. Victorious Sheep, a young farmer, caught this. Young Teacher felt it necessary to come to the rescue.

"There are three bardos of the living and three of the dead. The three living bardos are the Waking Bardo, the Dream Bardo and the Meditation Bardo. The three bardos of death are the Bardo of the White Light, the Bardo of Hyperreality, and the Bardo of Entering the Womb.

"You'll sometimes hear of people speak of 'the bardo' as if there were just one. They usually mean the Bardo of Hyperreality, because this is the main place for the working out of karma. It's there, after going through the white light, but before we commit to a human rebirth, that we face lights, noises, gods and demons, and react according to the fears and desires we have not managed to eliminate. Fears and desires, until we learn to control them, control us."

Victorious Sheep beamed, "I admit not even my teachers in Lhasa ever put it so clearly. But I do have a further question."

"I will be glad to answer as best I can," said Young Teacher.

"My teachers in Lhasa insisted that the Bardo of the White Light is one of the bardos of life. Your father teaches White Light meditation to people very much among the living. We enter it in sleep. And those who come near death but return without dying, do so from the White Light bardo. But you have listed it as a death bardo."

This was the point which had tripped up Great Magician. He'd tried to list it both as a bardo of life and a bardo of death, and wound up with one bardo too many. Great Magician looked at Young Teacher.

Young Teacher nodded. "The enlightened can move from any bardo to any other, so the Bardo of White Light is not special in that sense. In fact, we glimpse all the other bardos in the Waking Bardo. It is true most souls returning from death to life do so from the Bardo of White Light, because it is the first bardo of death. But most entering the Bardo of White Light die. So we call it a death bardo."

Cheers went up, but Young Teacher wanted to say more. Great Magician waved the crowd to silence.

"Let us remember that the bardos are all classifications of delusions. They are signposts erected in a cloud, objects seen in a mirror, wisps of smoke. They are the path between two places glimpsed in unrelated dreams. We list the bardos only to help you see the bardos as unreal.

"If I were in Lhasa, I would teach the way they teach in Lhasa. Like all our teachings the bardos are a tool. The best tool is the one you can use best, and that is not the same for every person.

"In the most important sense, all the bardos are bardos of life. This fair is taking place in the Waking Bardo. This Waking Bardo, the here and now, is the best opportunity to work with energy and karma. The lights and noises of the Bardo of Hyperreality appear in the Waking Bardo as the ordinary distractions, conflicts, and routines of this life. They are all here in this fair. Don't wait to die to work on yourselves. This is your best chance, right now."

This time the cheers rang out unchecked. Some in the crowd tried to hoist Young Teacher onto their shoulders, but the disciples managed to persuade the crowd that this was not appropriate. Victorious Sheep's rank didn't require such nice attention to protocol, and he was carried aloft as if he'd won the debate.

Great Magician pointed. Bobbing above the crowd beside Victorious Sheep was the head of a magnificent horse. The man leading it toward them was hidden in the crowd, but Young Teacher recognized White Shouldered Raven, his uncle's and probably the valley's finest horse, arrayed in its best trappings.

Angling up to see, Young Teacher staggered a bit. "All those sips have added up. Maybe there should be a Bardo of Chang."

Great Magician laughed. "Someone who gives as good a sermon as you do is entitled to invent a seventh Bardo." He realized what he'd said and lost his smile.

Young Teacher kept his. "It's OK. That was a sermon, by anyone's standard. And it's already past noon. At least the horse won't insist I sample his home brew, or ask me a question about the bardos. Was that all the promises? Was there another?"

"Here, ride!" It was Diamond Tiger, the uncle. He was leading the horse himself. That really was no surprise. The uncle had hired the best ostler he could get, but hated to let anyone else touch his horses. People joked that Diamond Tiger's ostler had the easiest job in Tibet.

"I promised my mother I would not ride today," said Young Teacher.

"Ocean is my kid sister, and cannot have meant you couldn't accept my gift."

"Gift?"

"I hadn't intended to come this year, but when I heard someone from my sister's family would preside, I wanted to be here with a special gift!"

White Shouldered Raven was much spoken of back at Marpa's castle. Young Teacher looked forward to seeing his father's face when White Shouldered Raven trotted onto his farm.

"We could just lead the horse off," said Great Magician.

Young Teacher saw his uncle's face cloud and gently punched Great Magician on the shoulder. "Great Magician is devoted to my parents and would sooner have three incarnations in the Hungry Hell than disobey my mother," Young Teacher said to his uncle. "The son-disciples often put me to shame with their devotion.

"But my mother meant hopping onto strange horses, races, stunts, that sort of thing. Surely she'd not want me to refuse her brother's gift! And if she were here she'd insist I ride around the fair three times to show everyone.

"It befits a relative of your standing to make the finest gift of all. Everyone who sees White Shouldered Raven from now on will speak of my luck in owning him, and my uncle's heart, as big as the Northern Plain."

Young Teacher looked around. He bent his head toward Diamond Tiger and pulled Great Magician in to hear. "Anyway, uncle, circling the fair with this horse will be a good way to make our exit. The way things are going, I'm not sure I'll ever be allowed to leave, and what with all the chang going around there's sure to be a fight. This horse will allow me to make a smooth, quick exit. You've come to my rescue and my mother will thank you."

Diamond Tiger laughed, tossed Young Teacher the reins, bowed and walked into the crowd. Young Teacher took Great Magician aside. "On the third circuit, I'll wave goodbye and head right up the road. Have the other students already on the road ahead of me."

And so it was done. Young Teacher showed the horse off beautifully, and on each circuit saluted his uncle. After the third salute, he waved to the crowd, reined White Shouldered Raven around, and galloped off.

Had Ocean watched, none of this would have alarmed her. The fairgrounds and the town did not match her dream. Neither did the road, before it narrowed into a ravine for the climb back up to the castle.

And now if Ocean of Awareness had watched, she'd have seen her dream unfold. The narrow trail along the rapids. Great Magician leading the horse. Young Teacher impatient at being led like a child. Great Magician giving him the reins. The loud voices as Great Magician joins the others, walking ahead.

In the bushes, six nervous young partridges. The mother partridge trying to calm them. The hooves of the powerful horse hammering the rocks. Mother partridge, now also terrified. The noise as they take sudden flight, sharp and loud like the start of a rock slide.

White Shouldered Raven rears. Young Teacher falls. Blood. Blood everywhere.

Great Magician caught the horse. He handed the reins to another student and ran back. Young Teacher's skull was broken in many places.

"Young master!" Great Magician said. "Can you be alive!" Young Teacher's head was a pair of eyes in a matted ball of blood.

"It's OK," said Young Teacher. "When consciousness went out of my body I ejected it back in. I can keep doing that."

"How? You'd need the Yoga of Forceful Projection," said Great Magician.

"Yes, the Yoga of No Effort." Young Teacher spat to clear the blood from his mouth. "Father taught me."

75 The Game Begins

The tide was just below Armenta's rock when I returned, but she wasn't on it. I sat down at the computer and picked up the phone to call Mike. Priscilla's first email came when I was still on the phone, giving Mike some language to help put her in the slammer.

Priscilla: "What language are these things in?"

Me: "German."

Then a long pause.

Priscilla: "You're lying."

Not yet, I was tempted to say, give me a chance. I explained about the Gabelsberger shorthand, even pointed her to a web page with a sample.

Priscilla: "Show me how to read them."

Attached to the email was a photo of a line from one of the notebooks. Priscilla wanted me to take her through the notebooks, squiggle by squiggle. Thank God I had found the Gabelsberger book. Though I suppose I could have made it all up and she wouldn't have known the difference.

As soon as Mike hung up, the Marshals Service called. Priscilla and I searched for God while the Marshals and I looked for Priscilla. The Marshals were perplexed the first time I asked them to hold while I finished typing an email to our fugitive, but they wound up quite amused.

The call with the Marshals took an hour. Mike called again around four. Gaunilo had scheduled another hearing for Tuesday, Mike told me. To ensure her appearance, Gaunilo issued a warrant for Priscilla's arrest. It was official. Priscilla was a wanted woman.

Mike told me that the CTS had delivered a cashier's check for the $20K made out to Sue. Their executive committee would not be holding its next meeting in jail. A warrant had also been issued for Carrie. I told Mike that Carrie was staying at Sue's ranch. He said he'd call Sue and left me to Priscilla.

Priscilla had more stamina for Gabelsberger than I thought. We were picking up pace. To me, it felt like being handed the pieces of a jigsaw puzzle one by one and having to describe the picture as you went along. At one point I suggested that we take a less random approach, but Priscilla told me she was being guided. I took it as a warning.

The photos bounced back and forth between the two notebooks. Priscilla blocked out those lines she didn't want me to see with pieces of paper, but it was always easy to tell which notebook was in the photo. The lost philosophy notebook had a spiral binding. The binding on the theology notebook was sewn. If a picture from the philosophy notebook had an equation in it, I could even tell roughly where it came from, because my lists of equations were copied in order. The theology notebook only had four equations and none of them made it into any of the shots.

Dark arrived without Armenta appearing. Priscilla gave out about seven PM. Our last word for the day was *Farbe*: "color". So far, I'd really only learned one thing from the lines Priscilla was showing me. A lot of them mentioned monads.

Mike's last call was at half past seven. He'd informed Gaunilo's office that Sue would be personally responsible for Carrie's appearance Wednesday and asked that the warrant be recalled. Gaunilo did not act before leaving for the day. In theory the Marshals Service could have driven down to Soledad in the dark and gotten out to Sue's ranch to arrest Carrie around midnight. They decided that they had better things to do.

76 Monads

Three hundred years before Einstein and Gödel were friends in Princeton, their favorite philosophers were friends. Leibniz and Spinoza only met once, but they kept up a lively correspondence. Lively and secret.

Leibniz was a high-ranking courtier to the house of Hanover. He had a lot to lose by knowing Spinoza. Spinoza united the religions of Europe. Catholics, Protestants and his own Jewish community all agreed that he was an atheist and should be executed along with an assortment of his supporters. He was not a safe choice as a friend.

Spinoza was Einstein's favorite philosopher. Leibniz was Gödel's. And those monads I was finding in the notebooks had everything to do with what Einstein, Gödel and Leibniz thought about God and why Spinoza was such a dangerous person to know.

Einstein once said the hardest thing to understand about the world is that we are able to understand it. He was not being flippant. The problem is that there has to be only one reality, if reality means anything. But we have two completely different sources of information about reality. We have ideas in our minds, and we have what our senses tell us about the physical world. They match up, which is something that those of us who are not Einstein sometimes take for granted. Why?

Math is a mental construct, but it describes the physical world. In fact, we can use math not only to describe the physical world, but even to predict it. Why? Sheet music and printed pages are just marks on paper, but play the notes or read the words and worlds appear in our minds. Why?

Spinoza explained it this way: There's one reality because there is only one thing in the universe. That thing is God, or Nature. Spinoza said God and Nature are exactly the same thing. Spinoza's Nature-God has an infinite number of what he called attributes. One of the attributes is Thought and it is the world of ideas. A second attribute is Extension and it is the physical world. Strangely, Spinoza never says what the other attributes are.

Whatever Spinoza did with the rest of Nature-God's attributes, he goes to town with Thought and Extension. The mental world and the physical world match up because they are both attributes of God. That's why math works. Divine Will and Natural Law are the same thing, because God is Nature. The God which is Nature arranged everything in advance so that ideas in the mind and physical reality are always in sync.

Einstein took Spinoza very seriously. This was why Einstein said that God did not play dice. Spinoza's God had set firm ground rules. In fact, He was the ground rules. If He changed them, He stopped being what He was. God was not going to turn Himself into a slot machine.

A lot of people can't warm up to the God of Einstein and Spinoza, and some of these are pretty high rollers, intellectually. Gödel told Hao Wang that he thought Einstein's uncaring God was impersonal because It was "less than a person" and I'm sure Gödel gave Einstein an earful on the topic.

Spinozism has its attractions. For Einstein, Spinoza amounted to a religion. Spinoza handles the problem of the mental and physical worlds quite nicely and his logic is very solid.

But there are a lot of things that Spinoza doesn't explain. Randomness and alternative possibilities don't happen in Spinoza's reality. If we see them, Spinoza says it's because we're deluded. Free will does exist, but it's not something most of us would recognize as such. Freedom, says Spinoza, is just realizing everything is inevitable and deciding you are going to be happy about it if it kills you. As for any sense we have of free choice or responsibility for our actions, that's just more delusion.

Leibniz was optimistic and ambitious. Given any kind of choice, he'd try to have things both ways. He definitely liked Spinoza's way of centering reality in God and of explaining how reality can appear in various forms. He didn't like that Spinoza took away things we clearly sense are out there: randomness, alternate possibilities and real choices. For all he'd left of free will, Spinoza might as well have called that a delusion too.

Leibniz fretted over another issue. An influential courtier in the German Principality of Hanover, Leibniz was also a philosopher, mathematician and scientist. He was busy. Being burned at the stake as a Spinozist did not fit into his schedule. Not to mention it would embarrass his generous patrons in the House of Hanover.

Monads were Leibniz's way out. Monadology was an idea from one of the few women philosophers of that time, Lady Anne Conway. Leibniz replaced Spinoza's single God-Nature-Substance with zillions beyond zillions of little self-contained, eternal monads. Each monad is a self-contained substance with a spark of divinity. Each has its own point of view, and its own likes and dislikes.

All the monads are free, but God is the central monad. He coordinates the others. Our souls are monads. Animals have soul-like monads. Monads make up our bodies. Every last rock or speck of dust is a monad. Monads fill all of space.

What Rube Goldberg did to the mousetrap in the twentieth century, Leibniz did to Spinoza in the eighteenth. It was pretty bizarre and people said so. Leibniz's monadology did pull off one feat. Anyone who wanted to burn Leibniz for atheism first needed to figure out exactly what Leibniz was trying to say. This left Leibniz to die of natural causes at a ripe old age, still pulling in a tidy income from the Hanovers, by then the new British Royal Family.

Strange as it is, monadology has its charms if you're in the frame of mind for them. It keeps Spinoza's solid explanation of why the physical world makes sense to the mind, and of why mental constructs like mathematics work in the physical world. And with the monads there's also room for randomness, freedom, alternative possibilities and all the choice even an overreacher like Leibniz could want.

But monadology just seemed too weird to describe reality. Until they discovered quantum mechanics. Suddenly physical reality started to look very odd and the problem with monadology was whether it can manage to be weird enough.

Gödel was the all-time pro at finding theories weird enough to be real. We know from Hao Wang and others that he spent years studying monadology, which in itself was a mystery. All Gödel's other lines of work, including many he spent much less time on, had left traces in at least his unpublished writings. Nothing Gödel left in Princeton has so much as a line about monadology.

The emails from Priscilla told me one thing. Where Gödel's monadology work had gone.

77 Case 2008 Closed

PG, Friday, January 18

In the morning, Armenta's rock was underwater. Judge Gaunilo withdrew Carrie's arrest warrant. The Marshals Service had learned everything they needed from me the day before. Priscilla began to slow up. Things had calmed down enough for me to call Oka Ohoma and close out the Heavensent gig.

Mike hadn't pressured me about Heavensent since Tuesday. On the other hand, the way we'd left things, he'd consider it a betrayal for me even to talk to them. And as for Oka, he'd hired me to help find Lorraine, and I was going to withhold from him that I'd seen her. That was pretty clearly a betrayal. So my conversation with Oka would double-cross everyone I was working with except Priscilla. Her, I was already playing false.

But I had to call. Honor demanded it.

"My good friend," Oka greeted me. "How are things?"

"Good. I just wanted to tidy up our contract. Should I close it out?"

"What were the final hours and expenses?"

I gave Oka the numbers.

"Wonderful," he said. "And thank you for all your help."

"How's the chicken business?"

Oka talked about Sallisaw and the family. I was just about to say goodbye when he asked, "Don't you care about the DNA test? We got the results."

Oh, God, I thought. I've blown it. I've given away that I know she's alive. "Yes, of course. I do."

"Our spy was not Lorraine. The DNA from Lorraine's hairbrush doesn't match. They will also check the criminal databases. I'll call you if they find anything."

"Thanks," I said, hoping I sounded normal. It made no sense. What had Lorraine's wound in the side been?

"And Mrs. O'Brien says hello," Oka said. "You remember, the lady at the door in your old apartment house."

"Indeed, I do. How is she?"

"Much happier now that we got her money back."

"You got her money back? You mean from that IPO? How'd you do that?"

"Actually I only got her sixty cents on the dollar. I knew of the people who did the Vaportouch IPO and there were irregularities."

"As with a lot of them."

"But I am speaking of irregular irregularities. I don't want to go into details. But I told them if they didn't help her out, I'd share all those details with her attorney."

"Good for you. I assume she still thinks I'm dirt."

"My friend, your association with me has given you a reflected brilliance in her eyes."

"Glad to hear it. Good work. Take care."

"And you too, my friend."

I didn't know how to take the news about the DNA. Was someone else using Lorraine's hairbrush? Maybe the lab had screwed up. I wished I could have asked more, but I had given Oka far too much to go on already. The clever Mr. Oka would ask himself what it was that made me so sure that the lab results were wrong.

Oka might have lied in order to test me. In which case, I'd lucked out. There was nothing to do but assume the best, get back to business, and pray the next knock on the door was not the police.

78 Game With the Gods

PG, Friday

That second day with Priscilla, some of the pieces she was throwing at me began to take their places. Richard Feynman, the great physicist, once described his field of study as a game of chess played among the Gods. It's a strange way for Feynman to put it. I don't think Feynman believed in any Gods. But certainly it matches an intuition most of us have — that not just physics, but all of reality is a game we play with a higher force.

Spinoza and Leibniz had derived God's existence from a few quick preliminary principles, then built the rest of their systems with God at the foundation. In Spinoza's day, even the most skeptical believed there had to be some kind of creator. There seemed to be no other way things like the brain and the eye could have come about.

Darwin had come along, of course, and made a very convincing case that time and the slow accumulation of random events might have produced eyes, brains and the rest of us. So Gödel had to start with the only thing people still do accept on faith — everyday reality.

Everyday reality is complicated, complicated enough that a few people try to make that a God proof all by itself. Sights, sounds, smells, tastes and touchings; numbers, space and time; fate, choice, and natural law; bodies, souls and minds, all have to fit together in one common reality. Gödel's inventory of the run-of-the-mill ran to quite a few pages. In this section Gödel used some "comprehension principles", so it turned out that of the dozens of equations I'd initially thought were comprehension principles, twenty or so really were.

Something has to hold everyday reality together, and you can call that God. Some people do. But this makes God into a kind of cosmic duct tape. Gödel was having none of it.

For Gödel, the dance of the monads is the magic behind everyday reality. To show this, he'd developed a lot of new math, tackled head on just about every issue in philosophy, and developed completely new treatments of physics and biology. And that was just what was in the parts of the notebooks I'd seen.

Today thousands of academics spend full time on research in areas that Gödel opened up, and the results of that research provide work for millions. The notebooks opened up at least a dozen more new fields. Never mind any God Proof, these notebooks were important.

The monad ballet was just the setup. Gödel was taking the God Argument in a totally new direction. The week before, I'd seen the game theory pattern in the equations. I traced it to an article Gödel published in 1958, glanced at it, and dismissed any connection as absurd.

That 1958 article was Gödel's last major published work. It may be his most difficult and mysterious, which for Gödel is saying something. It contains rules for turning the steps in a logical deduction into the moves of a game. It's the instructions for a Truth Game.

The Truth Game is Gödel's way out of the limits he himself had discovered in the Freedom Proof and the Doubt Proof. In Ancient Greece, Socrates had urged his students to know themselves. Across 2300 years, Gödel answered: "not likely."

Remember, Gödel's Doubt Proof tells us we can't even know if our thinking is coherent. If we think we're coherent, we are certainly not coherent. With a start like that, you can't expect to get far in terms of self-knowledge, and you don't. A host of other results followed from Gödel's and today we know that just about every question that involves knowledge of our own state of mind is unanswerable.

But the Freedom Proof has a very small loophole and that is the Truth Game. We can't know we're coherent, but another person can. The truth about ourselves can emerge from moves and countermoves in a game. In games, computers can be checked for viruses, and brains can be shown to be thinking consistently.

Gödel's 1958 article never actually mentions games. But if you look at it with game theory in mind, the resemblance is pretty obvious. We can be certain that Gödel knew about game theory — the first book on it was written by his two close friends Oskar Morgenstern and Johnny von Neumann while they were all in Princeton.

A game, in the sense game theory means it, can be many things we don't usually think of as games — anything with moves and players. Any learning process is a game. Evolution is a game where winning is surviving.

Since humans can learn in game situations, do the Doubt Proof and the Freedom Proof really apply to us? We're not really fixed systems, so why should the limits of fixed systems apply to us? Actually, this is a question about computers, too. Currently computers don't really learn or evolve, but there's no reason they can't. It's just that right now we're not good at programming computers to learn.

We can certainly learn over time that our earlier selves were consistent. But "earlier" is the crucial word. After having learned that our earlier self is consistent, we still don't know and can't know that our new, more learned self is consistent. Which means we really can't be sure we've learned anything about our earlier self.

Learning does not get around the Freedom Proof or the Doubt Proof. All the limits of self-knowledge stay in force, and every new self or system comes with a new set of liar sentences, another long list of things that can't be known. Each newly evolved system still can't know that it's coherent, and still can't check itself for mistakes. And since the new system has to suspect that it might be incoherent, it has to be in doubt about everything it's learned. The Truth Game is not a way around the Freedom Proof. There's no such thing. The Truth Game is a closer and more careful definition of the limits imposed by the Freedom Proof.

Can't the process of evolution itself be made into a system? Can't we have a self-evolving system, one that evolves as part of what it is? Wouldn't that get around the Freedom Proof?

The answer is that it can't happen in reality, and even if it did, it still wouldn't work. We might be able to evolve forever, but we will not actually reach forever. We can count toward infinity, but we can never get to infinity. There's no end to learning. We can evolve, but we can't become the whole process of evolution all at once. Not in the real world.

Even if we could reach infinity, it wouldn't help. When we get to infinity, mathematicians have discovered, it turns out to be the first of a very large and complicated series of infinities. Mathematicians have yet to finish exploring these levels of infinities. For a very simple reason — it's impossible. The Freedom Proof forbids it. Each infinity creates another one so vast that it couldn't be imagined without the previous one.

Through all of these layers of infinity, the Freedom Proof and the Doubt Proof stay in force. This makes sense, because of what freedom and doubt are. We learn and evolve because we are free. The limits of systems are what drive us to become better and better. And when we stop doubting, we stop learning and we stop evolving.

Gödel's Proofs, baffling as they are, are as solid and as stable as truth can get. They remain true in worlds we wouldn't recognize. And once the shock is past, we see their truth when we look inside ourselves.

79 End Game

I'd hoped the trap and trace would find Priscilla before the weekend, but matching the right phone line to the right account took time. The Marshals Service, the ISP and the phone company are all twenty-four-by-seven operations, but once five PM Friday rolled around I knew that as a practical matter the three would not put their heads together until Monday.

Priscilla and I kept going well beyond that. I was getting excited. I thought I saw where Gödel was heading.

Gödel's notebook focused on one particular Truth Game. In this game, one player was always a reasoning monad, seeking to discover the truth. Human beings are reasoning monads along with, according to Leibniz, at least some of the animals. From what Wang tells us, Gödel may have cast the net even wider. But even if not every reasoning monad is a human being, every human being is a reasoning monad.

Now came another of Gödel's surprise twists. The key to the proof lay in who the reasoning monads play the Truth Game against. It's not each other. Our opponent in the Truth Game is God.

Why is God against our finding the truth? The reasoning here was tricky and fascinating. God is not lying to us, Gödel said. That is impossible, because this Truth Game is creating Truth as it proceeds. God is trying to make the universe be as coherent and harmonious as possible.

As harmonious as possible? Isn't everything possible to God? No. There is a serious limit to the amount of harmony and beauty that God can put into our human world. Gödel took the idea of this limit from Leibniz, but he gave it his own special twist. Gödel said the limit was set by thc Freedom Proof.

It's not that God is subject to the Freedom Proof or the Doubt Proof. According to Gödel, He's not. But we have to be, or else we are not free. So our truth game with God turns into something like Feynman had described. Feynman's Gods, every time physicists think they have the rules of the game figured out, throw in a new wrinkle. They let people like Feynman make

241

progress, but if the Feynmans of the world learn too much, physics will stop being the joy and challenge that it is. The Gods don't let that happen.

Gödel's God has to be very careful about how he lets our universe unfold. If the world becomes totally controllable and comprehensible, we'll be God. God does not object to that. In fact, according to Gödel, that is our destiny. But it is also the end of us as free human beings. And human freedom is an essential part of the beauty of God's universe.

Think of us as God's children. If you love children, you wish them everything, including wisdom. But once children are wise, they are no longer children. If everyone was wise, this would be a universe without children. And for God, that would be an universe far less beautiful than the one She has.

o o o o o

The tide exposed Armenta's rock in mid-afternoon, but it stayed bereft. I looked forward to a long weekend and more finds from the notebooks. I didn't realize that Priscilla was getting antsy.

80 Ratlos

Armenta's rock was above tide when the sun came up, and empty. Priscilla didn't come online until almost ten.

I was eager to get started. Yesterday, Gödel's Player-God had seemed strange, too incomprehensible even to be wrong. Today the idea was sinking in.

In fact, the Player-God idea worked uncannily well. From a "hard facts", observation-oriented, materialist point of view, how do we know other minds exist? We can't read other minds, so we don't have direct evidence. We conclude other people have minds because we see them making moves to achieve outcomes. When we see drivers on the road we conclude they have minds which have decided they have places they need to be. Show us someone who is playing to win, and we see a mind making choices.

A game, I realized, is not a strange way to prove the existence of another mind. Not at all. It's the usual way of doing it. Know the moves God makes in the Game of Truth and we know God as well as we ever really know anyone.

I was getting more fluent with the text and was eager to see more, but Priscilla was slowing down. The end came around noon. I'd just translated the word *ratlos*, German for "baffled". That may have been what did it.

"We're taking another approach," Priscilla said in her email.

Me: "Sure." I was determined to be agreeable right up to the point she began work on a striped suntan.

Priscilla: "Show me how the books prove things. Prove I'm The Revelator."

I had no idea what she was talking about. I emailed back some nonsense.

P: "We need to find out if the notebooks are genuine."

I assured her they were certainly Gödel's notebooks.

P: "No. I mean genuinely divine. A genuine revelation. If they prove God's existence and God is truth, they should show I'm The Revelator."

I asked her what a "revelator" is.

P: "I am The Revelator. I am the one chosen to reveal these notebooks. The current situation shows this beyond doubt. How do the notebooks show that?"

I thanked The Revelator for her insight and promised to get her answer that afternoon. That gave me a few hours. Sitting quietly for a moment made me realize how tired I was. I made coffee, went out on my balcony and wondered how to play this madwoman along.

81 Does Ultimate Reality Exist?

PG, Saturday

Bluffing Priscilla was a possibility. But I expected a cross-examination. Priscilla might see through a lie. It didn't seem worth the risk.

I was just getting used to the God of Game Theory at that point, so I wasn't about to try to explain Him to Priscilla. Anyway, Gödel's short 1970 version of the God Proof was familiar and it contained enough to answer her question. Stick to it, and I would be comfortable with anything Priscilla threw back at me. So I thought.

I reread the email to Priscilla several times. The proof, I told her, was of a God which is Ultimate Reality. God's church is everywhere and nowhere. He favors no denomination. He does not favor one of His creations against another. I didn't say so directly, but I left it pretty clear that while Priscilla could see herself as a Revelator if she wanted to, she was no more Revelator than anyone else.

"Does Ultimate Reality exist?" That was Anselm's Proof in four words. Certainly, if there is an Ultimately Real, that pretty much has to be God. Whether you like Him or not. How much sense does it make to say there is an Ultimate Reality, and there is a God, but they're two different things?

But a lot of people have a desperate need to say exactly that. Ultimate Reality doesn't fit their agenda. And woe to God if He gets in the way.

82 Revelator

I hadn't been able to get out and walk since the trip to Soledad. As I watched the sparkling waves hit the rocks, I worked hard at telling myself how at peace I felt. I stayed out on the trail for fifteen minutes, keeping Armenta's rock in sight. The weather was why I wasn't enjoying the walk, I told myself. It was cold. There were gusts. I found myself almost running back. The answer had come.

Priscilla: "Is that really what the notebooks say? I'll have to destroy them. Much love, Cilla."

The message was a few minutes old. I typed a reply quickly, then stopped. It wasn't good. I revised, then started over, then stopped again. After fifteen minutes, I deleted everything I'd written and sent her a one word message.

Me: "Why?"

P: "They'll deceive people. It's for the best."

Me: "Deceive people how?"

P: "Isn't it obvious? The notebooks have been guided to me. That's a fact. But they don't validate that. They're deceiving people. It's best to burn them."

A quarter century of consulting experience has taught me how to crawl. "I think I've read them wrong," I emailed. I added copious thanks and gratitude to her for shining light into my benightedness. Yes, I went so far as to say that this indicated to me that she was indeed the Revelator. I won't share my exact words. They make my stomach sick to this day.

"You haven't burned them, have you?" I asked. I knew that I was giving away my desperation, but I needed to know.

P: "I'm keeping my options open for now. So there is a proof that I'm the Revelator?"

Yes, I said. I was sure of it.

She wanted to know how it went.

I threw some general bullshit at her. Priscilla wanted more, of course.

I told her that having made a fool of myself with my error, I wanted overnight to get the details down and check it. Was that OK? Please, please, please.

P: "I'd like to see it. Tomorrow morning, then. Much love, Cilla."

83 The Coin

Priscilla's threat to burn the notebooks was no bluff. If she thought they blocked her ambitions, she would not take ransom. Her lifestyle was spartan. Priscilla was not finicky about how she came by money, but money to her was only a means to power.

Greed gets a bad name. When people aren't motivated by greed they lose touch. A greedy person may be a bad one, but you can deal with her. When someone without greed goes off the deep end, there's trouble. If greed is not a virtue, it's as close as a lot of people get.

I had a desperate new insight into Gödel's God, his player of the game that guards our freedom from absolute truth. I was no longer sure that what I'd told Priscilla about Gödel's Proof was true. If God plays a game as Guardian of the Truth against each of us separately, is he really the same to each of us?

The German philosopher Schopenhauer, according to Joseph Campbell, speaks of a design in the life of each of us. Looking back, he says, we can see a purpose in our life, a purpose which is unique to us. Somehow, Schopenhauer says, a force arranges that others are agents of the purpose in our lives, and we are agents in the purpose of their lives.

I'm perplexed that Schopenhauer would say this. He's said to have been an atheist. But Schopenhauer's purpose of life seemed to be what Gödel's Game of Truth was about. The Player-God can have a special intention for each of us. He might even choose one of us to be The Revelator.

Right now my goal was to avoid my own special destiny as one of History's Prize Idiots, the one whose big mouth got Gödel's God Notebooks destroyed. The Player-God was a complicated story. Priscilla is not a person who likes complexity.

It was dark now. I'd promised the answer for the morning. Should I start to write up the Player-God answer, or keep searching? My rational decisions had backfired. I pulled out a coin. Heads, I start writing. This way at least I could blame it on the coin.

I never flipped it. I looked at the coin and the answer came to me. Priscilla was the kind of girl who might love a good modal collapse.

84 Modal Collapse

PG, Saturday

Some people say things don't happen by chance. Anything that is true, has to be true. When everything that happens has to happen, that's called a modal collapse. In a modal collapse, there's no such thing as chance, or probability, or possibility.

Some people thought Gödel's God Proof relied on a modal collapse. Gödel made God a sure thing, they said, because Gödel made everything a sure thing.

That would be a problem. A modal collapse simplifies the world too much. Every day you do a lot of things and make a lot of decisions that depend on possibilities. You buy insurance and lottery tickets. You shop in several stores because a different store might have a better deal.

You even pay hard money for possibilities. If you think a car is more reliable, you'll pay more for it. Reliability is nothing but a better possibility that bad things won't happen.

In daily life, almost nothing is totally for sure. Daily life is modal. If Gödel's God caused a modal collapse, what that meant as a practical matter was that Gödel's God didn't exist.

○ ○ ○ ○ ○

Logicians call different possible situations, "possible worlds". We can just call them "worlds" as long as it's clear we're not talking about other planets, but just different ways things might happen.

Unless Gödel's God exists in every possible world, He does not exist in any of them. You can't say God only exists if it rains. You can't say God does not exist if New York wins the World Series. I couldn't say there was no God if Armenta was dead. God is a sure thing, or nothing. So far, so good.

But one of the things that is true about God, said the critics, is that if He exists, He exists together with us. And if God is a sure thing, since one of the truths about God is that He exists together with us, we are all sure things as well and all of us exist in every possible world.

250

∞

That was a modal collapse. If I was alive, or Armenta was alive, it was because we had to be, because our coexisting with God is something that is true about God. Because there was nothing random, or modal, or possible about God, there was nothing random, or modal, or possible about us. Every waggle of Armenta's flipper, every mite on every last seagull was foreordained. And while in a way that's a comforting outlook, it bears no resemblance to the reality we live in. It sounded bad for Gödel's God.

From the notebooks, I could see where the critics had gotten it wrong. They confused being a sure thing in one possible world with being a sure thing in all possible worlds.

Yes, Armenta and God existed together in one possible world. Yes, God existed in all of them. Yes, what was true of God had to be true everywhere. But all that was true about God and Armenta was that in one possible world they existed together. Being with God in one possible world didn't leverage you into any of the others. Gödel had never said that it did.

All Gödel had said was that Armenta had to exist when and where she existed. Which is not exactly big news. And which was not going to bring Armenta to life if she was dead.

○ ○ ○ ○ ○

How did this help me with Priscilla? The obvious role of chance in our lives would rule out a modal collapse for most people, but my guess was that Priscilla was not one of them. My guess was that, if a modal collapse turned Priscilla into The Revelator, she'd be all for it.

Priscilla, I said in the email, the facts prove you are the Revelator. Gödel's God exists, I told her, as the notebooks would establish. All the things about Gödel's God were sure things. No woulds, shoulds, coulds, ifs, ands or buts. Gödel's God and Priscilla the Revelator coexist. Therefore Priscilla the Revelator exists, a sure thing, of necessity and in all possible worlds. No ifs, buts, woulds, shoulds, coulds or quibbles.

I said I was sure we'd find much more in the notebooks about her. I thanked her. I slept.

85 The Second Asking

There was no email from Priscilla when I woke up in the morning, and no Armenta. I felt calm. It might have been exhaustion.

I heard a commotion at Lover's Point. I went out onto the balcony and leaned out to look. A footrace was getting underway. It looked like it was coming my way.

I leaned back in, sat down, and waited. Indeed, a few minutes later Ocean View Boulevard under my balcony was filled with runners. Fresh from the starting line and tightly bunched, the pack soon disappeared around Armenta's Point.

Races which start at Lover's Point often double back to finish there as well. The spectators below me seemed to be holding their ground, so I expected to see today's runners back in an hour or so for the final stretch to the finish. I went inside to check my email.

Priscilla had replied just before the starting gun. The modal collapse argument went over well. "It has possibilities," she said, without intending the irony. "There may be hope. I'll be in touch tomorrow."

Gödel's God, the Player in the Game of Truth, certainly appealed to me. It was a beautiful poem, a powerful key to understanding, a moving story. But was it a proof?

Gödel had inventoried the commonsense world. Then he'd invoked the basic assumption that we live in a single reality. The world may show us many faces, but there has to be a single truth behind all of them. Gödel's writings in his lifetime hinted that Absolute Truth was best described in a game. In that game, we are one player, and a Guardian of Truth is the other. From the world we see, we can draw conclusions about how this Guardian plays Her half of the game, and from that we know who She is.

This could work. I'd seen only fragments. Gödel tended to really nail things down. I expected to find missing details in the parts of the notebooks Priscilla was keeping from me. Soon, maybe Monday, she would be on ice, and the notebooks would be back in my hands. I also had a feeling that I was missing not just details, but something obvious.

Ω

I took Dowman's translation of Ocean's autobiography onto the balcony, waiting for the racers to return. I was too tired to read, but glancing at the pages made me content. Armenta's rock was empty. I looked at Loma Prieta. I watched race spectators straggle and officials hustle on the closed street. And I saw something unusual on Bouchard Beach.

A pinniped had half scaled the beach's thirty foot bluff. "Pinniped" is a marine biologist's word. It covers both seals and sea lions. It means "finny feet", but has the advantage that you can say it without small children laughing. This is probably important to marine biologists.

I'd long wondered just how much rock climbing finny footed critters can do. This seemed a good chance to find out. I put the book down, left my apartment and crossed the deserted racecourse to the parking lot for the beach. Bouchard Beach is down a steep bluff, but there's a stone staircase between two aloe veras, cactus-like plants the size of pickup trucks. I went down the stairs and crossed the sand to within twenty feet of the pinniped.

It was a sea lion. He was a little large to be a harbor seal, but the real giveaways were his color and his small ear flap. Excelsior, I decided to name this Edmund Hillary of pinnipeds. Excelsior was a solid gray. Harbor seals are dappled and their ear is just a hole.

Excelsior was in an unusual place for a sea lion. It's harbor seals that tend to be seen alone, and who are more tolerant of human company. But even harbor seals don't come ashore on beaches people use a lot, like Bouchard's. They usually stick to the rocks offshore.

Sea lions have forelimbs which are good for climbing. Excelsior's perch may have been unattainable for a harbor seal. He had parked his five hundred pounds on a rock shaped and angled like the hip of a steeply pitched roof.

It was the probably the best spot to watch the race if you happened to be a sea lion. The rock slanted Excelsior nose up into a 180 degree view. My proximity didn't distract him. Excelsior's nostrils were flared, sucking in the endorphin-laced air. He wouldn't have noticed if I had slapped him on the rump.

When I was a kid a two-by-four fell from a roof and hit me in the head. The impact immediately deadened the pain and the initial feeling was almost pleasant. The soft voice, inches behind my ear, felt like that. "Hello," it said.

I turned. "Lorraine."

She radiated into the cold air through a sheer white cotton dress. I heard her the way a fighter hears himself being counted out. "Love," she said. "I need to ask you three times."

Above us, a commotion. The advance guard. Police, spectators, race

253

officials. Winners were on their way. The winds blew into the bluff, were caught, and swirled Lorraine's dress around. Her voice sounded far away. "I asked you to let me go and you said yes once. Say it now this second time."

The sounds up on the bluff were loud. The men's leaders. A blast of wind flattened the cotton onto her belly. Soft muscles in white, like a marble statue about to warm into life. She spoke again. "After this asking, this will be only one more. Say you will let me go."

More commotion from above. Lorraine's dress blew to the side and caught the curve below a breast. I counted ribs. More noise above. The women's leaders. My glance swayed down her hips to a leg like a pillar in a temple. Had she spoken?

She pulled me forward by the jacket. "Let me go," I heard. "Say you will let me go." I put my hands on her wrists, automatically fighting the grip. With the touch of skin, meaning connected to words.

Lorraine's voice stayed soft. "Say you will let me go."

"I will let you go." I repeated it like a phrase from a foreign language. One which I would need. Maybe for a trip soon.

"Thank you." Still gripping my jacket, she stepped on a rock, pulled herself to my face, and kissed me. Then she let go and dropped back onto the sand. The wind blew her dress tight against her. She turned. The dress swirled. A gust caught it and whipped it against her. She ran to the staircase.

"No," I said. I followed. With every step, I sank into sand above my ankles. How had she crossed so quickly? She seemed to float. I reached the staircase. Lorraine was not in sight.

I ran up the steps and came out between the aloes. The parking lot was empty. I had a wide view beyond it. The winners were in. Runners-up trickled by. Spectators wandered. No Lorraine. Had she gained that much time in the sand?

I went back down to the beach. Excelsior was leaving. He'd gotten his final blast of hormones. Staggered with bliss by that last killer cocktail of testosterone and endorphin, he skidded to the sand, reeled ecstatically toward the water, and plunged headlong into an ocean that he saw today the way he'd never seen it before.

The swift, the fast, and the beautiful had finished. Excelsior was gone. Those who ran in the lead in their better days, those happy to finish at all, those of us who wondered when it was that the race left us behind, we did not exist for Excelsior. He did not wait on the results for the middle of the pack, the runners whose feet now pattered above me. Excelsior did not care what would become of the man standing alone on the beach.

86 The Yoga of No Effort

The Lhotrak Valley, 1067 AD

"We'll make a stretcher," Great Magician said.

"No, put me on the horse," insisted Young Teacher.

"You'll die. Young master, forgive me, your wound is terrible."

"The Yoga of No Effort is powerful. I can keep projecting my consciousness back into my body every time I die. The horse will be faster. Uncle Golek can lead the horse, and the others can hold me. You run ahead and tell them at the farm."

After helping the others bind Young Teacher's head, put him on the horse, and tie him to it, Great Magician ran to the farm with the unspeakable news. Students were immediately sent to scour the valley for a fresh, intact body.

All that could be found was an old woman who died of the goiter, and a pigeon. A hawk had chased the pigeon into a temple. A shepherd was worshiping there. The pigeon landed in front of him. The hawk flew on, but the pigeon was dead. Its heart had stopped from fear.

Marpa and Ocean did not think the immaculate pigeon body miracle enough. They begged Young Teacher to eject his consciousness into one of them.

"No," Young Teacher said, "this is not right. It does not make sense for a son to come back in the body of his parent. It would not accomplish anything, and I can never repay what I owe you as it is."

Marpa, Ocean, and the disciples wanted to continue the search for a good body, but Young Teacher asked them to stop. "I can keep ejecting myself into this body forever, but it is just pain with no purpose. I'd rather face my karma in the bardos. They say the Yoga of No Effort is enlightenment in one lifetime. It is not enlightenment. It is a ghoulish flitting from body to body."

Young Teacher had them prop him up. "The Yoga of No Effort is nothing but eternal misery. Facing our karma in the Bardo of Hyperreality, and learning from the rebirths we are not wise enough to avoid, is the road to enlightenment. Please, father, gather the disciples, so I may say good bye." Ocean began to weep.

When the disciples were gathered, Young Teacher told them, "Nothing good will ever come of the Yoga of No Effort. But if I do not demonstrate it now, many will say my father is a liar. So I will eject my consciousness into the pigeon. It was delivered here by karma. I will take a human body across the mountains in India, then never use the Yoga of No Effort again. When that body dies, I will enter the bardo and face whatever karma I have accumulated in the three bodies."

They brought the pigeon and laid it on the pillow next to Young Teacher. He asked Marpa to come near and whispered, "I beg you never to teach or use the Yoga of No Effort again. Let it be as Naropa said. Let it die with us."

Young Teacher's face clenched, then paled. The feathers on the pigeon ruffled. Young Teacher exhaled his last breath. The bird opened his eyes. It staggered to its feet and stretched one wing, then the other. Ocean wept.

The pigeon seemed to bow to Marpa. It made the same movement toward Ocean. It began to walk around them. Once it started to circle the parents a second time, nobody doubted that it was performing the three circumambulations of the traditional leave-taking ceremony. Ocean cried so hard it seemed she must die from the effort. When the pigeon had finished walking around Marpa and Ocean for the third time, it flew out the window and up the valley.

Marpa ran after it and yelled out the window. "My son, there must be a cremation." A moment later, the pigeon was back, perched on the sill.

Marpa asked Ocean to take the pigeon to the top story, but she only sobbed. They left her as she was. Two senior disciples took the bird up and fed it, while the others prepared for the cremation.

Nobody wanted delay. It only required that a hearth be built, and the body laid on it. Marpa led the offering and lit the fire. There was no time to invite people, but word of Young Teacher's accident had spread and a small crowd gathered. They made way for Great Magician to roll out a path of silk to the hearth. The pigeon alighted at the far end and started to walk its length. The crowd murmured when Great Magician bowed to the bird. Many were still uncomprehending as the bird turned to walk around the fire. They took a few moments to step back and let the pigeon by.

All eyes were on the bird's first two circumambulations, but few saw the end of its third. Halfway through, Ocean ran out of the castle. She headed toward the fire. Two neighbors caught her. Family and son-disciples surrounded Ocean, begging her not to throw herself in. When she seemed calm enough, two disciples supported and guarded her in a circuit around the fire.

The pigeon stood quietly while Ocean walked. When she finished, the bird again took wing up the valley.

Marpa took Great Magician aside as the crowd dispersed. "Prepare the shrine room for Young Teacher." Answering Great Magician's look, he said, "Young Teacher was always too impatient. He'll need food, directions, and rest to make it over the mountains." Great Magician did as he was told. Sure enough, the pigeon returned that evening, exhausted.

The next morning a smaller crowd witnessed the pigeon's final leave-taking. Ocean attended, to please Marpa. For her, the last of Young Teacher had burned the day before. The bird meant nothing to her. She sat next to Marpa and stared absently as it once again walked around them three times. This time the bird also bowed to them three times. Then it flew away for good.

Three days later, in the middle of a funeral in India, a pigeon alighted on the corpse of a young Brahmin boy. The boy sat up, and the bird fell off him, dead. The grateful parents noticed that their son, restored, was much more gentle, devout, kind, and loving than he had been. He became a great teacher named Pigeon.

Marpa never again taught or used the Yoga of No Effort. As he grew old, his greatest regret was that he had lied to Naropa. In his eighty-eighth year, he told his disciples that Naropa, Ocean, and Devata had appeared to him in a dream. They were together in the Blessed Realm of the Sky Dancers. Naropa asked Marpa to be his attendant there, and in that way burn off his karma. That night he died quietly in his sleep.

Marpa left his farm to the other sons, none of whom became teachers. Great Magician became his spiritual successor. Propertyless, and content to be so, he traveled Tibet preaching and composing songs. Milarepa, as he is better known, became Tibet's greatest poet and its best loved saint.

One of Milarepa's students traveled to India to study with Pigeon. But Pigeon never taught anyone the Yoga of No Effort, and at his death he cheerfully faced his karma in the bardo. For although appearances in the bardos can be terrifying, they are products of our own mind, and we are always free to change our mind.

87 Raid in the Retreat

PG, Monday, January 21

There was no Armenta the next morning, but the trap and trace came together. By ten thirty we had an address and were writing up the search warrant. It's complicated for law enforcement to get a warrant to search the home of a suspected criminal. A private party that wants to barge into your home on a copyright raid has it a lot easier. Most of the work was for Mike and the Marshals Service. Mike relayed a few questions to me. He had already guessed the answers.

There was big news at noon. At the request of the CTS, the Appeals Court agreed to look at the notebook case. The Appeals Court would be a better source of copyright law, but on the whole this was bad. With Gaunilo, things were going our way. The Appeals Court was a crap shoot.

Gaunilo issued the search warrant at about two. They didn't tell me the address. The U.S. Marshals Service didn't want me to run right over and fix things myself.

Dark fell with no sign of Armenta. At seven, Deputy Wang came to pick me up in a Marshals van. Sue was with him. I had heard nothing from Priscilla all day. Whatever she was up to, it kept her busy.

Priscilla's safe house wasn't far. Wang drove a mile east along the coast, then turned into Pacific Grove's Retreat. Three blocks up the hill, he parked. Wang told us that the stakeout was a couple of blocks over. Sue and I were to stay in the van and out of sight until someone came for us.

They call Pacific Grove's oldest neighborhood the Retreat because it started as a Methodist summer camp. Eventually, all the tent sites were converted into building lots. The dense ranks of detached homes on absurdly tiny lots, just thirty feet by sixty feet, make the Retreat either cozy or cramped, depending on your attitude. The City is eager to preserve the feel of the old retreat, but I'd be just as happy to forget that Pacific Grove was once an overcrowded campground.

The van was full of surveillance equipment, which Wang had turned off. We had a one-way mirror that was parked into a wall. There was a toilet. Wang had left that operable.

"Mike told me you were busy, so I didn't call." Sue leaned back into her seat. We seemed likely to be there a while.

I stretched myself across a bench seat. "Thanks for that. The first days were pretty intense. Maybe I should have thought to call you during the weekend. I was pretty worn out, though."

"What did you find out about the notebooks?"

"Priscilla sent me photographs, dozens of them. But I could only see one or two lines in each. She'd block out the others with sheets of paper. The girl is seriously weird."

Sue debriefed me on the past few days. She had many more questions than I could answer, but seemed pleased with what I did know. After, I said something I had wanted to. "Carrie told me about your daughter. I'm sorry."

"Thank you. I kept it a secret so she wouldn't have to grow up with being a celebrity child, and I'm glad I did, but now that she is gone, I have nobody to share it with. Even in Soledad, most people don't know. Losing a child is worse than dying yourself. It's like losing not just life, but your connection to life."

"It must be hard."

Sue turned to face the wall of equipment. An LED was blinking a feeble yellow. "I've learned from it. It was Celeste's death that showed me there was no evil."

That was a little much for me, but I didn't say so. "Celeste was your daughter?" I asked.

"Yes." Sue waited. She knew I had a question.

"Sue, how can you say there's no evil?"

"Do you believe you're a soul?"

"I'm not sure."

"Not sure," she said. "So you think you might just be a piece of warm meat?"

The van began to feel confining. "I suppose I do. I don't want to, but I do."

"I believe. Help Thou my unbelief." Sue was quoting St. Paul. "Something in you must feel that there has to be more?"

"Yes, I guess so."

"And isn't even that vague feeling something more than a piece of warm meat would have?"

"I don't know. I don't know."

"Don't believe in evil, Josh. Refuse to."

Sue had lost me. "What's that have to do with the soul?"

"As long as you believe in evil, you don't believe in the soul. Every evil you think of is something that involves the body. Nothing hurts the soul. If the soul is what's important, there's no evil."

"I have to believe what I see."

"No, you don't. You see things in dreams and know they're not real. You see your reflection in the mirror, and know it's not real."

"But I know I live in the material world."

"And that's the most important thing?"

I didn't answer.

"The soul is either the most important thing," Sue said. "Or it doesn't exist."

"So what is this world where we're boxed together in this stupid van?"

Sue smiled. "Gödel's game with God is not new. The Hindus teach that life is lila, a game played with forces beyond our understanding. In my tribe, we have many stories of Coyote and the games he plays with us. In Japanese, the most refined and cultured way of speaking is called 'play language'. Instead of saying, 'I'm going to Kyoto,' you say, 'I will play at going to Kyoto.' In play language, everything is spoken of with enthusiasm and joy.

"When you play a game, you play it hard because that's the fun. But you know it's just a game. This van and this life are a game the soul plays. The game is not important, but we must play it with all our heart. And all our soul."

The yellow LED turned solid. I couldn't think of anything to say.

Sue gazed into the one-way window. "We have to realize that those we love are always with us. We can either believe it or live in hell. This seems harsh, but it's like your Anselm proof. Hell is the way it is because of what hell means. Believing in death is how hell is defined.

"We express ourselves in games. Our soul expresses itself in life. Celeste is no longer in my game. But moves in a game are not evil or good." Sue wiped at a corner of her eye. "I'm sorry. Game or not, I miss Celeste."

I waited. Sue's eyes shone all the brighter for their moistness. "I think because of my grief I might have overdone it with the notebooks," she said. "I have a bad feeling about tonight."

"You planned years ago for the notebooks to come out now, didn't you?"

"Yes, but the way I've done it. The hopes I've had. Things are not going right. I get the feeling it's all a message."

A car pulled up. Somebody unlocked our door. Deputy Wang poked his head in. "Can either of you identify Priscilla Wolf?" he asked.

"I can," I said. I turned to Sue, "And you know her quite well, don't you?"

"Yes, Deputy," Sue said. "I can identify her."

Deputy Wang got in and drove us three blocks to a dimly lit parking lot with diagonal stripes. The other Marshals had parked askew them. So did Wang. A massive mausoleum and two large churches loomed at the far corner. This was their parking lot.

We got out of the car. A small house was dug into the slope between the mausoleum and one of the churches. In front of the house, an alley sloped to the sea. Wang headed toward the alley and Sue and I followed. Wang took the two steps down to the house's patio and Sue followed him. The patio was small and I waited above in the alley. The Bay was just three blocks away. I turned my face into the salt breeze and saw the lights of Moss Landing on the other side of the water.

Wang tapped on the right side of a frosted glass double door, opened it and stepped inside. "All ready for the tourists?"

After a second, a voice answered, "Yeah. Bring 'em."

Wang went in, leaving the door open for Sue. I stepped down into the patio. It was at the same level as the basement of the church and the mausoleum. Dark walls towered in all directions. I followed Sue inside.

I shaded my eyes against the change of light. A Marshal walked up to Sue and identified himself as Deputy Fisher. He pointed to a woman, handcuffed and leaning back against the wall.

It was Lorraine.

88 The Dice Play God

Gödel's Truth Games made sense to Sue. You only had to see the game to see past the evil.

To God, all the games are real. As games. There's no good or evil in a game. Her creatures went out to the games, played hard, then came home to Her. Our individuality, our variety, is a delight to God. We are Her way of seeing the world.

For Priscilla, the game was real, a battle of good and evil. God had to take sides. God would not play dice with good and evil. Good and evil have to be sure things, not matters of chance.

For Sue and for Gödel, there is no modal collapse. God is in the possibilities. And that means He is everywhere. When we try to locate a subatomic particle, God changes its momentum. Try to measure momentum precisely, and God moves the particle. One way or another, God ain't gonna let us know where that particle is going. I don't know where people who believe in "hard facts" think they'll find them. Not in matter or energy.

Sue tells me that life's uncertainties are not misfortunes. They are God showing up in our game. God does not play dice. He is the dice.

89 The Third Asking

PG, Monday

Lorraine looked like the female lead in a sixties spy movie. Tight black pants. Black boots. A sleeveless shell top, also black. With her wrists cuffed back, her upper arms were emphasized. Lorraine was well-muscled. It was a good look on her. I kept my mouth shut.

Marshal Fisher summarized. "Won't give her name, but does deny being Priscilla Wolf. No ID. No explanation for being here."

Sue will know this is not Priscilla and that may be enough, I told myself. Let Sue speak first.

Sue stayed silent. Marshal Fisher swept a weary look around the clean, sparsely furnished room. "Come on, folks. Yes or no."

"It's my sister," Sue blurted out. "She's Lorraine Garten. Apologize to the officers, Lorraine."

I noticed my jaw drop and snapped it back so quickly I nearly bit my tongue. Fortunately the cops weren't looking at me.

How did Sue know Lorraine's first name? Had they met? That was possible. And what was with the Garten moniker? It rang a bell, but I didn't remember why. I wondered if it was another of Lorraine's circus names. The sister act seemed like a risk. I hoped Sue knew what the hell she was doing. If I was keeping my mouth shut before, I sure would now.

"I have apologized," said Lorraine.

"So why didn't you tell them who you were?"

"It's not their business. I'm sure not Priscilla and that's all they need to know."

"You should be answering their questions, not deciding whether they are appropriate." Sue turned to the officers. "I'll take responsibility for her."

"Not so fast," Deputy Fisher said. "Mata Hari here is going to be brought to PG lockup and booked in the morning on burglary. I understand your feelings for your sister, but her being your family is not exactly an extenuating circumstance. Not to mention she has blown our stakeout."

"But Deputy, she's not here to steal. It's just a mistake."

"It's a mistake which blew my stakeout, and depending on how much you know about why she's here, you're an accessory."

"I knew she was looking for Priscilla is all. All we're talking about is bad timing."

Deputy Fisher believed he was talking about considerably more, and said so. I exchanged a glance with Lorraine. Could all this be bringing her to her senses? Hope hurt as much as fear.

Sweet-talking law enforcement is not one of my skills. I left Sue to deal with Deputy Fisher and sought an easier conversation with Deputy Wang in the kitchen.

The briefcase Sue had brought me two weeks earlier was open and empty on a circular table. Deputy Wang didn't give me a chance to ask about it. He dragged me over to a counter and pointed to a pile with one of Lorraine's jackets on the top.

"Sister's story would smell fishy to a guy who worked on the Municipal Wharf. See this jacket. Mata Hari says it's not hers, must be Priscilla's. Look at her." Wang waggled a finger at Lorraine's nervous figure. "In this temperature wearing only that top, I think she'd be cold. This here jacket matches her outfit perfectly. I bet it's her size."

I shrugged my shoulder. "So she panicked and lied about the jacket. I mean, it's not right, but people you catch on raids must lie to you all the time."

"Here's the deal." Wang lifted an evidence bag. Inside was a very nice set of lockpicks. "These were in the jacket. Burglary tools." I looked over at Lorraine. She didn't look back.

"Now get a load of this," Wang lifted the jacket. Under it was a three foot antenna with a black box on one end.

"What is it?"

"It's a radio tracking receiver. You can use it to locate something if you plant a transmitter in it."

"What was she tracking?"

"The briefcase. It's got a matching transmitter inside. You didn't know that?"

"No." My surprise showed. For once that was good.

Wang moved on. "What about your friend Sue?"

I made eye contact. "You mean, did she know about the briefcase? She's a client. I don't know what she knows."

"Saying I should ask her?"

"Saying I don't tell you how to do your job and I don't run my clients' lives, they run mine." Hoping this went over, I pointed at the briefcase. "What happened to the notebooks?"

"Missing. Along with about half the cash. We put the rest into evidence bags, rather than leave it lying around."

"Look, thanks. And I'm sorry about the complications. I hadn't a clue."

"OK. Wanna bring Agent 98 her jacket?"

I forced a laugh and went back into the living space to find Sue. Lorraine, still cuffed, had accepted a chair. She looked worried. Well she might. The conversation between Sue and Deputy Fisher had reached a point where each welcomed an interruption. Sue and I walked out into the parking lot.

"How's it going with springing Lorraine?"

Sue shook her head.

"I have an idea," I said. "But I think it's best you try it. When I talk with law enforcement, bad things happen. It needs to be presented right, so their backs don't get up."

"I'm at a loss, so let's hear your idea."

"OK. They don't have a case for burglary. Lack of authorization is an essential element. The idea is you can't burgle a place if you are allowed to be there. If they can't show lack of authorization, the judge grants summary dismissal. It doesn't even go to the jury."

Sue looked skeptical, but she didn't stop me.

"Well, technically, Priscilla might have authorized Lorraine to be there. To establish burglary, they have to produce Priscilla to say she didn't."

"OK." Sue perked up a bit.

"Anyway, burglary is usually prosecuted based on victim complaint. Who's the victim? Priscilla? She's not going to show up at a police station to complain. Why give a shit before Priscilla does? Just because they're pissed off at Lorraine?"

Sue looked pensive. "It might work. I certainly can't think of anything else."

We went back in. Sue went to work on Deputy Fisher again. I thought the best thing for me to do was keep Lorraine company. I pulled up a chair.

"Got time to talk? Need to run off somewhere?"

"Very funny," Lorraine pouted.

"Your sister, I think, can get us all out of here soon."

"Half-sister," corrected Lorraine. This flummoxed me. I figured the sister act of Sue's for another shamanic stretch, and not a particularly happy one. Lorraine would know better than to try to improve on a dumb story. You repeat your story all night, no matter how stupid it sounds.

Deputies were within earshot, but I couldn't help myself. "Half-sister?" I said quietly.

Lorraine was not reticent. "Yeah. We had the same mother."

I looked around to see if any deputies had caught that. They looked busy with other things. "I thought you had no relatives you knew about," I said.

"That was true until October. Sue called me. It was wild. Like, this famous person calls me out of the blue. I thought I'd won a contest I'd forgotten I entered or something. Then she says we're sisters. My mom was Katrina Garten, her mom."

It hit me. "Oh my God. Katrina Garten from the Einstein letters. You're her daughter, just like Sue. How'd you wind up out for adoption but not Sue?"

"Sue was also a foster child."

"She was?"

Lorraine nodded. "Sue in her publicity just says her foster parents are her parents. They were wonderful people, and they raised her with respect for her traditions and everything."

"I thought they kept sisters together when they were put up for adoption?"

"Sis was right. You should have been told all this. I guess we got quality time together for it now." Lorraine leaned back as best the cuffs allowed and sighed. "When Sue was nine, her mother told her to expect a baby sister. Mom's husband, Sue's father, was off in Texas. They fought and he'd often go away for months."

"Who was your father?"

"We don't know who he was or if we should try to find out. Anyway, next thing Sue remembers, she asks Mom about me and Mom just loses it. She tells Sue never to mention me again." Lorraine teared up.

I went into the bathroom, got a box of tissues, and dabbed at her face. "Had Sue seen you?" I asked. "Did your Mom bring you home?"

Lorraine started to sob.

"I'm sorry," I said.

"No," Lorraine choked out. "You need to know this. I should have told you."

After some moments Lorraine resumed, still crying softly. "Sue doesn't remember if she ever saw me, whether Mom ever brought me home, if Mom went somewhere to have me, nothing. Sue was terrified. Joseph drank and was violent. If he heard about me, there's no telling what he might have done." Lorraine blinked to clear her eyes. "Imagine a nine-year-old with a secret that might get her Mom killed.

"Sue repressed it all. All we know is that Joseph Shrift, Sue's dad, came back and by then I was in a foster home and never mentioned again. Joseph still drank. He died when his car fell off a mountain road. Mom died in 1967 of cancer. Once she got really weak, she had to give Sue up, but she was able to find her a wonderful foster home."

"Sue must have been thinking you were dead." My tissues were almost all gone. There was a towel in the bathroom if I needed it.

"Sue didn't think anything," Lorraine said. Her tears had stopped. "She was so frightened that she totally buried every memory of me. On her deathbed, Mom told Sue about me. Sue had no idea what Mom was talking about. Sue figured the medicine had made Mom delusional."

"What made Sue change her mind?"

"There were the notebooks. Sue started thinking about them and that got her remembering things Mom had told her. The stuff about me began to come back, but Sue was not sure what to do."

"Well, she can look you up, right?"

"Lots of people think the adoption secrecy laws have changed to make it easy, but actually not. And they look for both sides to say they want to be put in touch and of course I'd done nothing."

I remembered what Lorraine's attitude had been toward whoever it was that had dropped her into the foster homes. It had made lots of sense to me at the time. "So what happened?" I asked.

"You know about Sue's daughter?"

I nodded.

"Of course that was quite a blow, and it jolted back all Sue's memories about me. She decided she had to find me whatever it took." Lorraine looked around for Marshals, but they had given us a wide berth since she started to cry. She continued softly, "Rules don't always have to be a problem if you have Sue's name." Another look around. "And her money."

I saw a stray tear on her face and wiped at it. "Look," I said. "I should have stayed in Silicon Valley with you. I'm sorry."

"It's alright. It's worked out."

"The hell it's worked out. I'm sorry."

"It looks like I'm going to jail."

"No, you're not." I tried to speak with an optimism I did not feel.

"God I hope not."

"A few more minutes and you can go. Don't worry."

"Now listen," Lorraine said. "This is important. You must not follow me."

I gave the handcuffs a glance. "Are you leaving?"

"That was the third asking. The first two times you chased me. This last time you must not."

I was slow to get it. Then I realized the question about going to jail had been a trick to get me to speak the right words.

"So the words are just some formula, they don't even have to mean anything?"

"You don't have to understand, just respect what I want. I have something I want to do."

And it does not include me, I wanted to say. But I kept silent. Why should she include me? She'd been abandoned by everyone all her life. Even her sister had just forgotten her for forty years.

"I'd better get a wet cloth for your face," I said.

Just as I was getting up, two deputies came over, lifted Lorraine out of her chair and uncuffed her. Behind the two were Deputy Fisher and Sue.

"I want you tourists out of here. We gotta close up," Deputy Fisher snarled. "And you," he said to Lorraine, "I never want to see again. Here's your jacket so you don't freeze and die, like it wouldn't be a blessing." He waved the lockpick set. "These I'll keep. Souvenirs of a wonderful evening."

90 The Mother of All Tuesdays, Part 1

PG, January 22

Like Lot's family fleeing the wrath of God, we climbed silently through the parking lot. We did not turn around until we were behind a church and out of sight.

Lorraine hugged her sister. "Thanks, Sue. I was so frightened."

"So was I. But thank Josh," she said.

"Did that authorization business really work?" I'd acted confident, but I'd have hated to have my freedom hanging on it.

"It didn't do much more than get Deputy Fisher listening. It was whatever you did to make her cry. I could see it in his face. As soon as he saw Lorraine in handcuffs and crying, he couldn't stand it. It suddenly became a lot easier to convince him that putting her in jail wasn't worth the trouble."

"I was telling him about Mom," Lorraine said.

"And about time you did. I just don't understand you. Why all the hurry and the mumbo-jumbo?"

"This mumbo-jumbo is what you taught me."

"This mess is not what I teach. In these last weeks, you've hardly listened to me. I am worried sick about where this is going. Why haven't you been in touch?"

"Look. It was just bad luck. How was I to know Josh would locate Priscilla?"

"What's done is done. I want a sister more than I want the notebooks."

"Please, Sue. Not again. It's time for me to enter the Action."

"There is a time for leaving the world. It has not come for me and it has not come for you. I want you here. Josh wants you here."

"You both can survive without me. You've been good at it."

"Sis," Sue said. "Please."

"And first I have to do everything I can to save the notebooks Kurtele left us. With what happened tonight, they'll be in danger. Priscilla will be desperate."

"Let the Marshals do their work. Let's forget it."

"The Marshals won't find them now. I know where Priscilla will go."

"Just tell the Marshals."

"They won't listen. Not now."

"Lorraine, please. I'm begging you."

Lorraine hugged Sue. "Everything is alright. Josh has said the third yes."

I'd been about as involved in this as the lamppost, but Sue turned to me now. "Did you?"

I shrugged and grimaced.

"He spoke the words," Lorraine said.

"You used another trick," Sue accused.

"Trick or magic or miracle, in the spirit they are all the same."

"Except if we are fooling ourselves. We can deceive others into the truth, but not if we lose sight of it ourselves."

"Stop, Sue. We have already spoken of this and you know it is settled." Lorraine turned to me. "Josh, my love, thank you. Good bye."

Lorraine backed away two steps, then turned and walked down toward the ocean. I looked to Sue.

Sue was looking down the street. "No," she cried. "Come back. This is wrong."

Lorraine would not change for me, but if both Sue and I begged, she might. I ran after her. Lorraine heard, looked back and ran. I knew she could not outrun me on the street. She'd relent. She'd have to.

Lorraine crossed Central Avenue. When I reached it, of all the stupid luck, a car parked up the street started pulling out. I had to hold up at the curb.

Then Lorraine stopped and turned. My heart soared. She'd listen. She was waving. She was excited. She pointed toward the car.

I turned to see when the loud lumbering crate would get past. It was not keeping its lane. I remember it coming up on the curb after me. If I knew more about cars I'd have recognized the distinctive grill of a 1980 Saint George.

91 Josh Bryant, Victim of the Year

PG, Tuesday

Pacific Grove is not a violent place. My attempted murder had a clear shot at PG crime of the year. It was especially newsworthy because Priscilla was technically a PG resident. An actual murder might edge me out, but many years PG doesn't have one, and usually victim or murderer is from out of town. Often both are. If Priscilla had killed me, the sky was the limit. She could have laid claim to Pacific Grove's crime of the decade.

Sue recognized the car and described it to police. It was found, its broken windshield smeared with my blood, just over the city line in Monterey. A serious manhunt was now on for Priscilla.

I had a bruised tibia, several broken ribs, a mild concussion, and other bruising and cuts. I remember only a few things from the hours after the Saint George hit me. I was in the ER. Carrie was there. The police tried to talk to me, but I don't think they got anything coherent. Carrie loaded me into an SUV and took me home. Somehow she got me up the staircase and into bed. I remember trying to say gracious hostly things about make yourself comfortable, thank you so much for everything you've done, and so forth. I fell asleep, probably in mid-sentence.

92 Reflections on Priscilla

Evil never goes away. According to Gödel and Sue, it can't, not without taking God with it.

Sue tells me that I should see Priscilla and myself as just souls. Then I'd gain perspective on the attempt by Priscilla's body to turn my body into pothole filler. I would have compassion for Priscilla's confusion. I would regard it as a minor matter whether I ended up home in bed or as one of PG's street repairs.

There's a strange sense to it. Eliminating evil seems to mean eliminating possibility. And in the notebooks, Gödel was showing that God comes to us in the possibilities.

I remember the Freedom Theorem: No totalitarian system is self-sufficient. Creative individuals are always needed, even by systems that hate individual creativity. But malicious creativity is as possible as the good kind. You can never get rid of bugs and viruses, and because of that you are free.

I also think of a big house with a warm fireplace, a nice, wide mantle, and Priscilla's head mounted above it.

93 The Mother of All Tuesdays, Part 2

PG

I could have used more sleep. It was not yet eight when the alarms began. Judging from the racket, every police, ambulance or fire vehicle in Pacific Grove was in front of my apartment. This turned out to be true and then some, for vehicles from many jurisdictions got involved.

That much activity would ordinarily have gotten me straight to the balcony, but I was a bit shy of one hundred percent. Every time I moved, it hurt. I located the crutch I'd acquired in recent hours and maneuvered out into the kitchen. There was a big note on the counter under my keys.

Josh –

Sorry not to be here. If I don't go to the hearing they put me in jail. Be back soon I hope.

Love, Carrie

All Carrie's punctuation and some of her letters had smiley faces. I got the hang of my new crutch as I advanced. In the living room I found two new arrivals. A small paisley overnight bag was tucked into a corner. Next to it a green sleeping bag was rolled up.

Under my balcony, Ocean View Boulevard was a snarl of people, cars, and trucks. Those people not dodging an oncoming vehicle were looking out to sea. The Coast Guard cutter was out, but most eyes were on a lone fishing boat very close inshore. Cursing the pain in my leg, I went back in for my binoculars.

The crew of the cutter was also very interested in the fishing boat, a purse seiner named the Collie. A woman was running around on the deck. She reminded me of Priscilla. I fought the idea back. Priscilla on the brain, I told myself. I looked again. It did look like Priscilla.

My door shook. With all heavy vehicles on the street below, I didn't think much of it until I heard what sounded like footsteps descending the staircase. I lowered my binoculars and saw Lorraine leaving the entryway.

I called after her. She turned, smiled and waved. She had on a wind-breaker, a wrap skirt and weird rubbery black leggings. Her hair was done up in a bun. She turned again and continued to the parking lot above Bouchard Beach.

When I turned to put the binoculars on a chair, the sting in my leg reminded me that my odds in a street chase had dropped greatly in the last twenty-four hours. I tried to remember what the doctors had said. Stay off my feet for a least a month, I think it was. Well, they didn't say which month.

I opened my door. On the landing there was a floppy disk. It had a label: Read Me - L. I leaned forward to pick it up. The pain brought tears. I couldn't reach it.

I tried sitting down next to the floppy instead. That hurt, but I could do it. I grabbed the disk and gingerly pushed myself back up with the crutch. A bookcase was right next to the door. The floppy went on top.

Overnight the staircase had become a well designed torture device. My descent was one full minute of misery. But it ended. I was on the street.

At ground level, Ocean View Boulevard was louder and messier than it had looked from the balcony. Lorraine was in the parking lot, intent on the offshore action. She was not a rubberneck. She'd only come out to watch if she had business. This morning, business meant Priscilla.

In front of me, vehicles were trying to get into the action or escape it. All of them ignored traffic rules. Lorraine had danced across, between lanes and along curbs.

My injuries forced me to take the long way. I started across to the walking path. An ambulance with a wailing siren was forced to stop and wait for me and my new crutch. I felt its tailwind on my heel.

Once I reached the path, Lorraine was half a football field away. She'd stood still for several minutes. Only this gave me any chance. Two minutes of wincing brought me into the parking lot. First down and goal to go.

That's when the first rifle shot rang out. All the birds within a mile took off at once. Everyone hit the dirt but me. Falling down and getting up again would have hurt too much. I decided to take my chances getting shot.

A cameraman from a local station was taking a crowd shot when he heard the rifle. He ducked behind a car. The camera angle careened, then settled. I was right in the middle of the frame, standing upright amid a prone, scrambling, screaming crowd. My crutch was on my other side, out of the shot.

I saw the frantic crawl for cover later, on TV. My attention was on Lorraine. She had bolted straight between the aloes guarding the staircase down to the beach. Lower on the staircase, she came back into view. Skirt and windbreaker were gone. She had stripped to a wetsuit. That's what the black leggings were.

Lorraine bent to remove her boots at the foot of the stairs. At the second rifle shot, she lifted her head. The crowd around me in the parking lot panicked. It's a miracle that no one was injured. On the video, I look like something out of the days when an officer stood tall in the face of rifle fire, setting a fine example to his men and providing good material for his obituary.

Boots off, Lorraine walked across the sand into the water. She looked sturdy in the wetsuit. Lorraine picked her way through the rocks. When the water reached her narrow waist, she dove forward and swam toward the Collie.

Priscilla had emptied her first clip. The cameraman huddled behind the car. He had no intention of leaving cover. I was all he could see without lifting his head, something he thought would be very foolish. I looked exciting enough. For all you can tell from the video, bullets were whizzing around my ear. I was useless. I felt stupid. I looked like a pillar of strength.

Lorraine had to swim through a kelp bed to get to the Collie. She spent enough time in the tangle for Priscilla to empty another clip. As Lorraine emerged, Priscilla loaded a third.

Off camera, the Coast Guard and police were showing real courage. Priscilla was firing in the general direction of the cutter. The Coast Guard had plenty of firepower on board. A gun battle would have ended fast. But they backed their boat away. They did break out guns and ammo in case it came to that. On shore, the police displayed the same restraint.

Amid all the firing, only the experienced seamen noticed the first wisp of smoke from the hold. I didn't.

Priscilla had been raised by an uncle who owned a purse seiner. Though she'd never been a crew member on the books, she knew her way around a fishing boat. In her current corner as a fugitive, she fell back on what she knew as a kid.

She had taken the notebooks to the Monterey Municipal Wharf and hijacked the Collie. Once at sea, she figured she could come to an arrangement with the authorities. Priscilla took two measures to prevent them from forcing issues before she got her best deal. The rifle was one.

Measure number two was a threat to burn the boat. Priscilla put a welding torch in the hold. So she could make good on the threat quickly, she left the flame on. That's not a good idea.

Priscilla's knowledge of the workings of a purse seiner was never complete. Ten years absence from the fishing fleet had not improved it. Getting out of harbor, she had scraped hull three times, twice against other boats. That brought Priscilla to the attention of the Coast Guard even before she called to start the deal-making.

As the cutter backed off, Priscilla started up to the bridge. Lorraine bobbed up near the stern. Priscilla saw Lorraine climbing in and went back to meet her. Priscilla carried her rifle, but kept it pointed in the air. Lorraine sat on the railing and they appeared to talk calmly. What either had to be calm about escapes me.

Ignoring Priscilla's worries, which I am inclined to do, the list of problems was long. Lorraine was confronting an attempted murderer unarmed. She was seriously interfering with law enforcement for the second time in twenty-four hours. She was blowing my lies to Oka Ohoma. She was revealing my failure to keep my promise to the police. She was also risking immediate death from burning, drowning, smoke inhalation, and explosion.

For the smoke from the hold was now evident to the dimmest landlubber. Lorraine was pointing to it. Priscilla was shrugging her shoulders.

The first lick of flame up the side got the two women into motion. A purse seiner is so called because it deploys a net, or seine, around fish. Then it hauls the seine in like a purse. A smaller craft, called a seine skiff, is used to put the net out or "set" it. The seine skiff is high sided, well built, and has its own engine. In case of trouble, it's the lifeboat of choice.

Priscilla dropped the rifle and made a dash for the bridge. She returned with a bag. The two women released the skiff and were soon aboard it. I relaxed enough to remember how much pain I was in. I soon forgot.

The bow of the Collie was invisible in the smoke. The skiff did not get underway. Priscilla later told police they could not start the engine. We never found out why. The skiff was later recovered and the engine ran fine.

A hot fire sucks in a lot of air. Indrafts kept the skiff thumping against the hull of its doomed mother ship. On board the cutter, they did not know how much fuel the Collie carried. Bravely, they decided to go in for the rescue.

But Lorraine acted first. She pulled herself back on board the Collie. With a cloth over her face she headed into the smoke, toward the bridge.

Nobody saw Lorraine after that. She must have reached the bridge. Control resumed at the helm and the Collie pulled away from the skiff. It headed straight toward Armenta's rock.

How long Lorraine stayed at the helm, I don't know. The billow of smoke grew until it completely hid the Collie. The black cloud chugged slowly toward the rock, reached it, then engulfed it. Splintering. The black cloud stood still. The splintering continued. The Collie was grinding itself to pieces on the rock.

After a minute, the engine stalled. No more splintering. The fire burned quietly. People on shore took a breath. It was a silence that could have been mistaken for peace. I looked for a swimmer.

The Coast Guard was picking Priscilla and her bag up from the skiff. Fire engines on shore tried to throw water out to the Collie. Before they did much, the fire found the fuel tank.

The Collie exploded. Flames shot high over the rock. Debris rained. My ears hurt. Black smoke thickened, moved toward me. The flames dimmed to a backlight.

In the video, the smoke comes in from the right. At first you think it's just shadows. Not until the first wisps reach me, do you realize it's smoke. The cloud grows dense. For a while my white jacket shines through. It's the last thing you can make out before the screen goes completely black.

I never move.

94 Letter from Lorraine

PG, Tuesday

I wanted to stay but there was no sense in it. I was coughing up soot. My balcony was a better vantage point. It might let me see over the black cloud.

Climbing the stairs was less painful than descending. It still hurt plenty. I sat down on the floor just inside the threshold and rested. Then I remembered the floppy.

I hurt everywhere. I hated the extra steps necessary to close the balcony door to keep the smoke out. I sat at the computer. The floppy contained one file.

○ ○ ○ ○ ○

Josh –

Nearly seeing you die tonight has made me realize how hard it must be for you, because you think you are losing me. You are not losing me, but I know that's what you think and that won't change quickly.

I talked with Sue. She's been saying I've been too hasty with you, and now I realize she's right. I cannot now change when I enter the Action, but I want to do more for you than I have. Sue has lent me her laptop and I can write you this. Sue says it will help and I think so, too.

I want to warn you today of all days, let go and let what is behind the appearance reveal itself. Please do this. If it is hard, remind yourself that appearances are bringing you nothing but pain.

Before I met you, I often felt dissatisfied with my life. After I met you I came to realize how stupid and unhappy my life had been. I lived for the power I could exert over men. I didn't know why I was so able to captivate men with my body, what drew them on so powerfully. But I loved the power. Men do the silliest things.

∞

You felt different. I could experience my power, not just use it. And once I felt the power myself, using it for control, which I'd done so much, seemed so petty and stupid. I owe this to you.

Then came my promotion and your departure. I had something new to face. I thought we were doing the right thing, but I felt so lost.

Why does happiness depend on physical things? Why did a short separation bring me to pieces? Isn't that dependence, and not happiness? Real happiness can't be a matter of who and what is where. I refuse to believe it. And I decided then and there that, from then on, I would accept only real happiness. Nothing else.

I looked, and read more and more. Then Sue called. I couldn't believe it. And she made a lot of what I had been reading come together. I've found what I want.

You were more to me than life. My love, it turned out that you were nearly more to me than God. Please be happy with me about what I am doing.

God will find you, too. You won't be able to escape God. But you are strong. Strong enough to create time, and within time delay. Don't be strong, be weak and everything will happen for you.

– L

o o o o o

Even sitting down hurt. I didn't give the letter more than one reading that day. Whatever Lorraine had planned, it looked like it had gone very wrong. The police, once again, would want to talk to me. This time I'd need a lawyer.

95 Josh Bryant, Crime Fighter

PG, Tuesday

Carrie was sitting on the bed beside me when I woke up.

"You're awake. I've made soup."

"Oh. Thank you. What time is it?"

"It's seven. I had a hard time getting here, but I've been back since three."

"I haven't heard any news. Did they recover the notebooks?"

"Yes, it's amazing, they weren't even wet a drop. And I don't have to go to jail!"

"Wonderful." It would have been nice if I had asked Carrie about her hearing first, but she didn't seem bothered.

"Sue wants us to meet her at San Carlos Basilica tomorrow afternoon. Is that OK?"

"It's great. It'll be nice to get out of here."

"She said to bring your notes about the Gödel books. She told me you'd know what that meant."

"I do." I looked over to the shelf where I'd put them. Next to them were my keys, just as I'd left them last night. I looked at Carrie. "How'd you get in?"

"Lorraine let me in."

"Lorraine? Lorraine is alive?"

"Sue picked her up at Lover's Point. They dropped me here."

"Lorraine's not hurt?"

Carrie had to tell me several times that Lorraine, though very tired, was more than well enough to climb the stairs and pick the lock on my door. By the third telling Carrie looked nervous. "Lorraine is really nice," she said.

I dropped back into the pillows. "Yes," I said. "Yes. Lorraine is really nice." Making an effort, I squeezed her hand. Carrie smiled.

I drew in a deep breath. "So," I said. "Tell me how the hearing went."

Five minutes into her story, Carrie noticed the clock. "Oh! I've got to get the TV." She darted out of the room. I tried not to let the thumping sounds from the front room bother me. Modern TV's are durable. After a minute, Carrie appeared at the door.

Aha, I thought. Another Jeopardy addict. Anyway, nice of her to drag the TV in to share.

But it was the news Carrie wanted me to see. "You're on TV! You've got to see it." I pointed her to the TV jack and an outlet. She piled up pillows against the wall that I use as a headboard, and we leaned back.

This was the first time I'd seen the footage taken by the cameraman from behind his truck. There sure was a lot of me in it. There'd been a good deal of action all around. I was disappointed to see so little of it.

They had been more than disappointed at the station. One of the big stories of the year and the camera truck comes back with next to nothing. The cameraman and the producer got into a shouting match. The producer had a lot to say about journalism and courage. He listed journalists dead in the field, pausing to point out as deeply personal losses some of the fallen whom he had almost met. The cameraman spoke with less eloquence, but much force, about low wages and managements on the far side of the hill from the action.

The anchorwoman closed her door against the shouting. She pondered what she had heard about my tracking of Priscilla, and Priscilla's attempt to kill me early that morning. She put down a few notes, opened her door, told the producer to switch to decaf, and dragged an editor off to an video suite.

The voice-over she did was more felt than heard, like the music in a well-scored film. She spoke of an intrepid investigator. Computer wizard. Skilled crime fighter. Dedicated. Single-minded. Ignorant of the meaning of the word "fear". Carrie thought it was stirring stuff. I enjoyed its effect on her.

96 2078

I wasn't able to drive for several weeks. Carrie took me to the Basilica. Sue met us outside, in her black cape.

Once she had gotten me out of the SUV and put me safely on my crutch, Carrie ran ahead to hug Sue. The two had time for a minute or two of warm greetings while I caught up.

When I did, Sue said to Carrie, "Love, could you get me a latte on Alvarado Street? I need to speak alone with Mr. Bryant."

I wanted one, too. Carrie kissed Sue goodbye and leaned to do the same to me. A mismanuever with my crutch made her first try a miss. She connected with the second, and skipped away.

"Carrie says she saw Lorraine last afternoon," I said.

"Yes, and I've seen her since and may again from time to time. You won't see her again. It's pointless to look. You won't, will you?"

"I understand. No. I won't. I'm glad she's alive."

"Oh, God, so am I," Sue said. "I don't know how I could have borne it. This was not the right time for the notebooks."

"They're OK, I hear."

"Yes. Look, Josh, I've done something with them and I hope you won't be upset."

"Sue, if you want to burn the damn things, it's OK with me." I thought I might have been too outspoken, but Sue looked relieved.

"I've asked the Firestone Library to keep them until 2078, under seal," she said. "You're alright with that?"

"I'm just fine with it."

"I'd already been thinking of this before the raid on Cilla. I should have told you that night in the Marshals' van. But I wasn't sure and this morning Cilla has forced my hand."

"I thought Priscilla was safely on ice."

Sue chuckled. "She's on ice, but I don't think there is a safe place for Cilla."

"I know I'm probing, but I can't help myself. Can I ask what Priscilla did?"

"You have to promise never to tell a soul." I nodded and Sue continued. "The notebooks were in charge of someone at a bank. I know him, and knew his father for years. Cilla started an affair with the son. He's got a wife and a small child. Cilla had pictures."

"The inside man at the bank is how she knew that you'd taken the notebooks out?"

"Yes," Sue said. "And I knew that she would be told. I learned what was going on. I prefer not to say how." Sue met my eye.

I shrugged. "It's not important. You would want to keep tabs on her and you did."

"Yes. Lorraine and I were working on the notebooks. We knew the CTS would act as soon as we had the notebooks out. What we didn't know was what they would do. Lorraine told me you were the perfect person to have look at them, and bless her, she was so right. You've been a Godsend."

"I'm glad you're pleased." At the time, Sue had been less sure of me. That was why the briefcase with the tracking device. "Still, Priscilla's in jail. Can't we just get the pictures? If not for the notebooks, then for the sake of the jerk at the bank . . . "

"And his child," Sue said.

"Right. So why not deep six the pics?"

"We will, but that's why I had to make a deal on the notebooks. If she's charged with stealing them, she was going to raise a defense that made the pictures exculpatory evidence."

"Like what?" I asked.

"She could claim the man at the bank was the ringleader, for example, and that he seduced her. To get the pictures in as evidence, all she has to do is show that it's a defense that might convince one of the jurors. That's not hard."

"So what's the deal?"

"I drop the charges for stealing the notebooks, and give them up to Princeton," Sue said. "They join the rest of Gödel's effects there, but they'll have special treatment. They go under seal until 2078."

"Why did she want them put under seal?"

"She wants us to work from our memory of them." Sue smiled. "Especially you. She says that with the text in front of you, you quibble."

I smirked. "So Priscilla didn't find what she wanted in the actual text. Now she can say what she likes about them and nobody can tell her she's wrong. She's seen them, so she'll claim to be an expert."

"I'm just as happy."

"How's that?"

"I need to finish up with *Hypatia's Quest*," Sue said. "And I want to spend more time with the Pecunia Institute. The notebooks have done for me what they are going to do. I think the fact I had them all these years was why I've always had God first in mind, and that's meant everything. There are people who can do things with these notebooks, but I'm not one of them. They'll have to wait for 2078."

I felt a little disappointment.

While I thought, Sue was gathering words. "Josh," she started.

"Yes."

"Part of the deal . . ."

I had my notes out before she finished the sentence. "You want these?"

"Cilla insisted that all notes be included. Everything."

"It's OK, Sue. Really. It's just fine."

"You're being very reasonable about this," Sue said.

"You're the client," I said. "They're your books. The notes are your property."

"Josh, could you also give me the Gabelsberger book?"

"Sure. How did you know about it?"

Sue blushed. "You told me, didn't you? I mean you must have."

"I don't remember." I looked away, to the old church, and thought. "It's Lorraine's. The right thing is for you to have it."

"I promised it to the IAS in Princeton. They want it very badly." Sue let a breath out slowly. "It seems their copy is missing." I met her eyes. "It disappeared from the Firestone Library."

"I'll make sure it gets to you right away."

"Thank you, Josh. Thank you."

"No thanks are needed. If I can ask, why 2078?"

"You suggested the date to me," Sue said.

"I did?"

"When you talked about Anselm. It'll be the thousandth anniversary of Anselm's proof. The millenary. I don't think either of us will have to worry about it by then."

I smiled. "They may delight Carrie in her old age. I have no problem with this, but it is a surprise, so I'll have to get back to the office to calculate what I owe you on the retainer."

"Are you quitting? We still have a deal, I hope," Sue said.

"How is that?"

"My publisher wants a book on the proof. You know a lot about it, even without the notebooks or your notes. You, Carrie and I will be the authors. That's three of the four people who've seen them."

"All except Priscilla," I said. "Are we sure we can take care of the CTS claim?"

"We have settled with the CTS. They are in on the project. Carrie will be their representative."

I must have made a face. "Carrie is confused and lonely," Sue said. "For anyone to look down on her for that is wrong. For you to do so is foolish."

97 The Bad Way

PG, January 24 to February 13

It was quite a few days before I could move much. I had plenty of time to think about Kurt Gödel and his God Proof. I think it's pretty clear why Gödel hid it until 1970. Gödel, in coming up with his revolutionary results, insisted on proving them beyond doubt using uncontroversial methods. When he couldn't do this, he didn't publish. He said as much to Hao Wang.

This is why, outside the notebooks, we don't have any work from Gödel on Leibniz or monadology. This is why he gave the God notebooks to Eva Garten to keep for a better time.

When it comes to God proofs, the prejudices of the time are less stiff than in Gödel's day, but not much. Most mentions of Gödel's God Proof are brief and when they're not matter-of-fact, they're derisive. Proving God's existence is not taken as evidence of insanity for Anselm, Spinoza, or Leibniz, but it is for Gödel.

What's more mysterious is the 1970 proof. Why, when he thought he was dying, did Gödel put out a version of the proof very different from the one in the notebooks, and very different from the philosophy he described to Hao Wang? Wang's books don't help us here. He admits he wasn't interested. So I'm left to speculate.

Gödel knew the world was not ready for the proof in the God notebooks. Game theory was very new. Even in his purely logical work, when Gödel used game theory, he kept it veiled. As for the other things, monads, higher beings, a new theory of biology, Sue has decided the world still isn't ready, and I can't argue with her.

The 1970 proof was a compromise. It's against the spirit of our time, but it uses methods accepted in the past. Gödel made a significant improvement in these. He showed exactly what is necessary to make the Anselm proof work. He stated these requirements as assumptions in the 1970 proof. Then he pointed out in "Philosophy Notebook Fourteen", one of the notebooks that he left in Princeton, that doing so was "the bad way." Gödel may have thought that would be enough for a future logician, working in a time which encouraged this kind of investigation, to find the same answer that he had found, the one he had put in the notebooks he gave to Eva Garten.

With this, I thought I had all of the story I or anyone was going to have until 2078. When the last piece came to me, it was a surprise.

98 Josh Bryant, PI

PG, February 13

The messy end Priscilla brought to case 2007 got a lot of attention. Sue's publisher was very eager to do the book deal, and Sue arranged an attractive one for all three of us.

The deal took a few days to put together. Did you know the right to sell a book in French, the right to sell a book in France and the right to publish a book in France are three different things? We took these details seriously. The French think we Americans are all fools, and will find our story very affirming. It's important that it get out to them.

Sue's book deal gives us movie rights, which Mike is dickering over. Sue has become good friends with the two A-list actresses in the CTS and they are excited about the project. It would be the first time they've worked together. The idea already has the actresses' agents working together. They tell their clients that projects with this kind of limited appeal are how actresses fall out of the A-list.

I can't see Armenta's rock these days. It's inside what's left of the Collie. The wreck attracts a bad crowd. They drive up, gesture at it, take pictures. Sometimes they even get out of the car, but more often they gun the motor to make up for the time they lost slowing down to take the picture. Thank God it's not Lorraine's gravesite. As it is, I pray for the winter storms to take the Collie away.

Carrie is watching for Armenta. Sue tells Carrie that Armenta foresaw the wreck of the Collie, and decided to get in some traveling. I know there's good evidence that animals can foresee natural disasters. Tsunamis and volcanoes can kill thousands of people and not catch a single wild animal. Maybe it's a vibration that animals can feel, and someday humans will build an instrument to detect it too. What vibration told Armenta weeks ahead of time to watch out for pirated purse seiners, I can't imagine. Anyway, I would be glad to see her.

Even if Armenta made it out of the way in time, some marine life did not. A lot of oil spilled. A good deal more burned into the acrid soot which still smudges rocks and buildings along this coast. This, defiance of a court

288

order, piracy, attempted murder, illegal discharge of an unregistered weapon, arson, and theft mean that Priscilla should be gone for quite some time.

With the proof that I did not murder Lorraine, my lies and broken promises were forgotten by most. Oka Ohoma called me. I hadn't dared call him. He talked about Sallisaw and the chicken ranch for an hour. Heavensent's interest in Lorraine ended when it became clear she left her job willingly. They paid my bill without a murmur.

In fact, Oka did me a big favor. He got me out of the PI license bind. The news footage extolling my crime fighting ability is being widely shown. There's going to be a rock video. The station owns the footage so there's nothing I can do about that. Nobody wanted to make me a poster child for California's arbitrary way of granting PI licenses.

Oka Ohoma offered to certify my work at Heavensent as relevant experience for a PI. This isn't terribly regular. But paid informants are said to have had their time spent ratting on their fellow criminals certified as relevant investigative experience, so I doubt anybody's conscience suffered.

Of course, I could have fought it out against the licensing law over the principle of the thing. That rock video may not stay long on the charts, though. They might simply outwait my fifteen minutes of fame and nail me but good.

Gil would approve if they did. Gil was the guy on the raid with Oka Ohoma who wouldn't let me have the Gabelsberger book, and who spotted the spy. He was actually a San Jose police detective, there to catch me in incriminating actions and statements. In the stuff Oka had me copy out and sign was a Miranda warning. Gil was very disappointed when he heard Lorraine was still alive, so I am told.

I don't know who the Spencer House Spy was and may never know. Lorraine's reappearance meant the spy was no longer wanted for questioning about her murder. They tell me Priscilla had some sort of wound in her side when arrested. I can't find anything else out about that. If there was an autopsy report, I could look it up, but unfortunately Priscilla is alive.

People who've toured the Spencer House recently tell me the guides now talk about the spy. They say it is the ghost of Indra Spencer. Puzzled by all the activity around her once quiet rural home, she's returned.

Priscilla did put Sue's Pranashta tutorial online, billing it as a secret, stolen text. After the Collie explosion, the news media mirrored it. Sue waited until it had been copied many times to announce that it was free to all, public domain. Even this didn't slow its circulation. Her publisher was besieged with requests for the more handy printed copies, and Sue expects an initial printing of fifty thousand.

99 Case 2007 Closed

PG, Thursday, February 14, 2002

The morning is mine. I now move around enough to do paperwork. Carrie spent last night at Sue's ranch, but she will be back for Valentine's Day. She has stopped spending the night in a sleeping bag in the living room. With all my bruises and breaks, I worried she might be disappointed, but she seems happy. I hope she stays so.

There's a lot to catch up on. Part of it is closing cases 2007 and 2008. I have a routine for this. My case books are bound, lined and have numbered pages. I've been told such records if properly kept are admissible in court as evidence, though I've managed to stay out of court, and it may all be superstition on my part.

Case 2008, the gig with Oka, fills most of one page. There's room to print "Case closed" so that it spans three lines, and to put a box around it. That ends the page. The casebook goes back on the shelf, awaiting its next case.

In the book for case 2007, two thirds of a page is left. I'm about to write "Case closed", but I stop. I had thought I was missing another piece of the argument, something obvious. I was. I was making the problem too hard.

Yes, you can put an argument together from the Truth Game that the player who was the Guardian of Truth is God. People have had worse concepts of God. Gödel might make that pretty solid.

But the Truth Game doesn't have to prove God exists. It doesn't have to be a definition of God, or explain everything about Her. The 1970 proof has already established that if God is consistent, She exists. All the Truth Game has to do is show that God can be part of our world without creating a contradiction.

You might compare it with the design of a new airplane. They build a model and test it. They don't have to prove that the model is the airplane. They can't and it's not. All they have to do is show that the model of the airplane does model the airplane, and that the model flies.

The Player-God is a model of one of our most difficult intuitions, our sense that God acts directly in the life of each of us. Spinoza would say that this is a delusion. Spinoza says that God acts through natural laws, laws which don't care about individual persons.

But the Player-God knows and cares about each of us. And She fits into a world governed by natural laws. The model flies.

I write in the book.

1078: If possible, then real.
1970: If consistent, then possible.
2078: Consistent.
Case closed.

100 Armenta's Rock

PG, February 14

Carrie is back before one PM. I haven't quite finished, but I have time to put things away for tomorrow, because I have twelve red roses waiting for her. I didn't get a vase with them. A major part of the enjoyment is the initial fuss over finding water and a container.

Carrie outdoes previous records. Apparently nobody ever bought her roses before. She determines that nothing in my cabinets will do, and goes house to house in the neighborhood. I gain a solid half hour for my paperwork.

Carrie comes back with a vase she's borrowed from one of the multimillion dollar palaces which line this stretch of bluff. I don't know plastic from crystal. The vase Carrie borrowed may be worth more than everything else in my apartment combined.

From Soledad, Carrie brings back a new chapter by Sue and a chapter of mine which Sue rewrote. Sue is mystified how things are so clear when I explain them to her, and so opaque when I write them down. The trouble is, while her rewrites are clear, they don't say what I said.

Sue says she might send Carrie back again with a tape recorder and a list of questions for me. Maybe Sue means it as a threat, but the thought of more time with Carrie is pleasant.

Carrie always brings back some food from Sue's ranch. There is vegetarian lasagna, enough for a week. A fruit salad. A jug of spiced cider. A dessert which Carrie refuses to disclose.

Couples are out on the walking path. Debris from the wreck litters the beach below them. A few houses along Ocean View Boulevard have yet to wash off the smoke. The couples gaze past the wreck of the Collie to the sweeping view of the Bay. On the other side, behind Loma Prieta, Lorraine's apartment is empty. I don't know what they did with the furniture. Two strangers will move in soon.

The spiced cider is just the thing to drink hot out on the balcony. I'm from New England and refuse to admit it's cold unless water freezes, but

Carrie is a California girl. Once we're seated she feels a chill and wants blankets. I am nearest the door, so I go in for them.

Carrie's shout gives me quite a scare. I drop the blankets and rush to the balcony. I don't know what I imagine. I'm nervous these days.

Carrie is leaning over the railing and pointing. "Look! Armenta!"

I look at Carrie and let relief flow through my veins. She grabs my arm and turns me around to face the wreck. I see the same charred wood and the same twisted metal.

"No." She grasps me tighter. "There. The porthole."

I didn't care about the porthole. I try to wrap Carrie in my arms. But Carrie is serious. I look and see the same old porthole, with the same old blackened edges.

Then a motion.

Carrie shakes my arm. "It's Armenta. She's alive."

A nose pokes out, then a face. Armenta slides through the porthole and plops onto a board. She looks at us and snorts. Then she settles in.

God may not exist, but She never goes away.

Acknowledgments

I could not have written this book without help. Gayle McCay told me to leave out the boring parts. Jody Holzworth pointed out that it needed a romance and a happy ending. Kim Hall and Kelly Potter made sure I read the right things. Printing the first copy of this manuscript when my own printer failed me was just one of the many ways in which Bob and Susan Reikes helped and encouraged me. Michelle Irwin's hospitality never stinted. Nicole Blatt made my research in Pacific Grove much easier, more than making up for the way she skunked me at word games. Ellen Pastore, Jean Chapin, Denise McAbee and the rest of the capable staff of the Pacific Grove Library made my research possible. I also owe thanks to David and Nancy Lehenky, Chris Livanos, Bill Foley and Mitch Tilner.

I owe a special debt to two long-established writers who took time away from their own projects to help a newcomer. A gentle but shrewd critique by M.G. Lord (*Forever Barbie*, *Astro Turf*) of an early draft helped me reshape this book. Charles Mann (*1491*, *Second Creation*) read a later draft and provided very acute feedback on how to polish it.

About My Sources

Kurt and Adele Gödel, Johnny von Neumann, Oskar Morgenstern and of course Albert Einstein are historic figures. As a general rule I have treated them as history rather than as characters in historical fiction. Everything I say about them is either supported by evidence or is speculation by my narrator, identified as such. I made two exceptions to this rule.

The most important was Eva Garten. I know that Gödel and Einstein were together on May 13, 1947, but Eva Garten is fictional, so she was not with them. All the events involving Eva and her descendents are fiction.

The other exception is Gödel's citizenship hearing. This happened more or less as described, but the only primary source, Morgenstern's diary entry, is delphic. Even the most careful biographers don't stick to it. This story has migrated from history into legend and I followed it.

When it comes to the Tibetan saints, Marpa, Ocean of Awareness, Great Magician (aka Milarepa), Naropa, Atisha and Lotus Born; and the Western saint, Anselm of Canterbury, we are clearly in the realm of legends told by the pious. I believe all of these people actually lived, but the accounts we have of them were not written as history and cannot be read as history. I did not attempt to retell their stories as history, and felt free to elaborate when it made a better yarn. The original legends are deep and rich and for the most part I stayed with them.

The mathematics is genuine and carefully researched. I developed enough skill at it to spot the typos and other minor errors even the professionals sometimes make and had the very great pleasure of participating in a very small way in the expansion of knowledge in modal logic. Melvin Fitting, Jordan Howard Sobel and Edward Zalta all have been kind in acknowledging my help.

Since this is a novel, I felt there were certain liberties I had to take, though I worry that scholars idle enough to glance at my efforts may not be happy with me. I've given new names to Gödel's proofs. The God Proof is usually called Gödel's Ontological Proof. In textbooks, the Freedom Proof and the Doubt Proof are usually called Gödel's First and Second Incompleteness Theorems, respectively. The term "incompleteness" is a mistranslation which became established in the literature. Rather than inflict names on my reader that are difficult, wrong, or both, I chose to use names that suggest the meanings, even where these are controversial.

I, of course, do not know what Gödel said in his missing notebooks. To learn what he might have said, I've used Gödel's surviving notes. I've drawn on the work of professionals and others who have studied Gödel's work. And I've added a lot of speculation. I believe I have restricted myself to the possible, but I may have wandered from the probable.

About the Author

Jeffrey Kegler is a published mathematician and former Lecturer at the Yale Medical School who lives in Northern California. He has spent most of his life in the software business, and for many years maintained a solo practice not unlike Josh's in the novel. In 2000 he hit it lucky in the stock market and decided to take time off to write this novel. It was harder than he thought. Jeffrey is the author or coauthor of numerous technical publications. This is his first novel.

Made in the USA
Lexington, KY
13 December 2010